P9-DIE-644

DON'T
FENCE
ME IN

DON'T FENCE ME IN

Author: Charlene Abundis
Cover Design by Charlene Abundis
Artist: Norman Johnson

Published and distributed by
Two Angels Publishing Company

2026 Cliff Drive, Suite 200
Santa Barbara, CA   93109

Copyright @ 1997 by Charlene Abundis
    ALL RIGHTS RESERVED
No part of this book may be reproduced or used in any manner
whatsoever without written permission from the Publisher
ISBN 0-9656058-0-9

To the memory of my precious sister Annie, as well as to all those who are searching for meaning in their lives and feel lost.

To my family and friends (some who have passed on to spirit) who have been my greatest teachers in life, and who have filled my soul with love and memories. Thank you!

A special thank you to Reverend Foard. I learned so much from him in the short year that I knew him. We talked almost every day during that year and, together, he and I selected poems from his published book of poems, Inspiration, to use in this book. Also to Lois Cook and Iris Boroughs, for their love, constant enthusiasm, and encouragement. To Judy Johnson and Margie Yahyavi for their suggestions and their loving, patient and listening hearts.

But most of all, I thank God who created me, heals me, is within me, is my silent partner in life, and who patiently waited to be recognized by me.

ONE

THE GOOD EARTH

I'm looking up, up to the tops of the trees
So majestic and secure in their girth,
And chant with the breeze their hymn of delight,
"I'm a part of this beautiful earth."

I sing with all nature the mad song of love,
And tremble and sway with the green
While the beautiful earth caresses my feet.
This hearth, oh, my beautiful queen!

When the long dirge has come to its close,
And the stars of the night light her dome,
This beautiful earth unfoldeth her arms,
And welcome this husk to her home.

This beautiful earth, so fragrant and clean,
Gives substance and life unto all,
And always so near to prove her great love
Will rescue in time of your fall.

                    Reverend Edmund L. Foard

Ghandi wrote: "Our prayers for others ought never to be, God give them light Thou hast given to me, but give them light and truth they need for their highest development."

This book is about how not to be fenced in by anyone, and to help you learn to tune into and use your God given power within that will guide and help you in all decisions that you will have to make in life. It will help you to realize that you are a free person and can be in charge of your own destiny.

It also exposes how organized religions and our politicians have fenced us in for hundreds of years with all of the rhetoric and propaganda that they have thrown at us, which have caused most of the problems that we have in the world today. It is now time for all people to take their heads out of the sand, speak out, and say "no more" in order to clean up the mess we have helped create in the world and allowed to happen by being passive and allowing others to control us and speak for us. It's time for all people to take their power back now!

As a teenager I was guided by my feelings. If something felt right to me, I would do it. If it didn't feel right to me, I felt warned, and I didn't do it. Years later, when I started my search to find God, I realized that my feelings were the same as intuition, an inner knowing or that little voice within you.

It's all God! Without realizing it, I had already found God as a teenager and was being guided. I just didn't know it. When I finally realized that in my early forties, a light within me went on, and I then knew that I was in charge of my life. Betty Bethards, who wrote Dream Symbols for Self-Understanding, writes in her book that we are all the writer, director, and producer of our own life.

It is my hope as you read this book, which includes the experiences that I have had on my journey, that you will also find God's power within you if you are not already aware of it. You will then realize that He gives us all free choice in making our own decisions in life and that you can ask for and receive anything you want in your life as long as it is positive and feels right to you. I hope that you will realize that you

2

are the writer, director and producer of your life; and you then will never be fenced in by anyone or anything because you will be in charge of all that happens to you. I also hope that this book will open your eyes to the facade that people in organized religion and politics have put on for years.

The following article was published in the Santa Barbara News-Press on December 31, 1994.

SANTA BARBARA NEWS-PRESS/FRIDAY, DECEMBER 31, 1994

VOICE FROM SANTA BARBARA/CHARLENE ABUNDIS

Feed Catholic spiritual hunger

After reading in the news media that the Roman Catholic bishops now acknowledge church bias, they once again change some rules and say that woman leaders can be altar servers, theologians, chief financial officers and college presidents - but they still cannot be ordained as priests. The Pope and the bishops just don't get it - changing the rules will not stop people from leaving because people are spiritually hungry, searching for answers, answers they are not getting from the Catholic Church.

The Catholic Church encourages passivity and that encourages helplessness, and who needs that? Many Catholics have left the church and have started the New American Catholic Religion, which does not accept the teachings of the Roman Catholic Church. Their priests can marry, and divorced Catholics can remarry, and the use of artificial contraception is accepted.

The Roman Catholic Church is all about control, fear and guilt. I know because 54 years ago I was baptized a Catholic. It was not until I was 42 years old that I found freedom and realized that I have the power within me and that God is all good, that everything is possible in Him, and that He encircles everything in the world, that He, not religion, governs.

I am not out to bash the Catholic or any other religion. I am just going to share my experience of being a Catholic, and how it kept me in bondage for years due to having no other beliefs, and because of it I got married in the Catholic Church, baptized my children Catholic, put them in private Catholic school. It was not until I started to have a recurring dream that I was in the library reading books about God that I found answers. I felt the dream was giving me a message, so I went to the library and took out an armful of books about God. I went many times and got more and more books. It didn't take me long to start feeling like I was whole, that I am in charge and had the power within me, not religion.

When I was about to enter second grade the local Catholic school, which had a church connected to it, told my parents that their children would be able to attend without having to pay tuition because we were Catholic and poor. My parents attended another Catholic Church, but children that attended the school had to also attend the church connected to it.

It was not long after we entered the school that the priest came by to meet the whole family one evening. His visits became weekly, and we felt so special that he had taken such an interest in our family. The following year my sister who was 8 and I, who was 7, made our first holy communion. That meant that we had to go weekly to confession and confess our sins. The nuns told us that a sin was lying, cheating, stealing, unkind, swearing, etc. My sister and I discussed what a sin was and felt the only thing we did sometimes was lie but we felt we needed to tell the priest more, so each week we went to confession and told the priest lies so that we would be able to go to communion on Sunday. The nuns sat in the front rows of the church and if you did not go to communion they would stop you before leaving the church and ask why.

By the end of the first year of making our communion, the priest that came to our house weekly was also the one who heard our confession and after a confession he asked both my sister and I to go and wait for him in the rectory until he was through hearing confessions. When we both realized he gave us the same message, we didn't know what we had done, but we went to wait for the priest. He came in to the rectory and was very kind and talked with us a few minutes before giving us some cookies and candy. We were so excited, we ran all the way home. We were poor, so this was a special treat for us.

After several repeats of the above incidents, he then hit on both of us at the same time. I immediately got a sick feeling in my stomach and ran out the rectory door with my sister following. That same evening the priest came by the house to visit and I wanted to throw up. I had told no one, nor did my sister. We felt this was all our fault. After

4

that I refused to go to confession and waited out on the church steps for my sister to come out. I hated that priest. I always went to communion Sunday so that I would not get in trouble with the nuns. So you can imagine the guilt I was carrying with me at such a young age. I was sinning, afraid to tell anyone for fear of getting in trouble.

Due to a disagreement with the school, my parents took us out and put us in public school. We had to walk home each day for lunch because we never had money to buy it at school. One day a blizzard started while we were in school. The teacher said that those of us who had no lunch should go down to the cafeteria for a free one. I was so excited. I was given a tray with a Sloppy Joe on it, chips and milk. As I walked over to sit next to my sister who was eating, I got a sick feeling in my stomach. It was Friday and I couldn't eat meat on Friday - it was a sin. I was hungry so I ate. By the time I got back to the classroom, I was crying. The teacher asked me to step out into the hall. She asked me what was wrong and I told her I had just sinned because it was Friday and I ate meat. She put her arm around me and said, "Honey, God understands. Don't worry about it."

I felt better as I went back into the classroom, but I knew that I would have to go to confession the next day and tell the priest I had sinned. By the time I got to the church I again had the sick feeling in my stomach. I told the priest that I had eaten meat and why. He said, "Well you should have had better control." I was 9 years old. He knew how poor our family was, and if we had any breakfast we were lucky.

He gave me 10 Hail Marys and 10 Our Fathers to say. I now realized that eating meat on Friday was a bigger sin than swearing, lying, cheating, because when I told him those lies, I was only given four of each to say. I left the church crying.

It wasn't long after that experience that I overheard my parents talking. My mother was crying and said, "I can't have the operation. The priest said I would be excommunicated from the church because it was a mortal sin." My dad said, "You have seven kids to look after. You're gonna have the operation." It was a hysterectomy, and she had it, and we were all so grateful that she was not excommunicated.

I was around 16 when the church changed a rule that it was OK to eat meat on Fridays. I didn't know if I wanted to laugh or cry.

When I was about 19, my oldest sister got engaged to marry a divorced man with a child. My father was furious and the priest said she could not marry him. If she did, he would have to excommunicate her.

I remember her crying a lot over this but she was in love, so she decided to get married by a justice of the peace, and another sister who also was older was going to stand up for her. One Friday evening I came home at midnight and heard my sister crying. She said that the sister was told by the priest that he would have to excommunicate her if she stood up for her.

I felt anger well up through my whole body and I said, "I will stand up for you."

When my dad found out, he was furious. He told me that the priest wanted to see me. I went, and less than five minutes later I stood up and said, "Father, you can do what ever you want with this church, it doesn't work for me, and I am standing up for my sister." I walked out of the rectory feeling great. It wasn't until years later that I realized that great feeling was my spirit soaring. It was a first for me.

Several years later I moved to California and all the guilt came flooding back.

When my daughter was preparing to make her first communion, she told me that she would not go to confession because she had no sins to tell. I said, "Honey you have to, otherwise you might have to leave the school, because you are Catholic and you can't make your communion without going to confession." I told her to just go to the confession and tell the priest what she told me. After I picked her up she said, "I told the priest that the only reason I was here is that I had to go to confession for my communion, but I had no sins to tell, and if I didn't make my communion I would have to leave the school." His response to her was wonderful! He told her to just be happy and say a prayer.

Back to the age of 42. Everything I was learning I shared with the sister who was afraid to stand up for my oldest sister. Over the next 10 years we found so many answers together, and we realized that being spiritual didn't mean you had to have a religion or be religious. I've found that the secret of power to do anything is within yourself.

This sister unexpectedly passed to spirit in June of this year. She was only 57 years old. My youngest sister phoned me and asked if I would be flying home for the funeral and I said yes. She then asked if I would like to read anything at the service. I said yes, that I would like to share that my sister passed to her new life knowing that we live on and tell how she found her peace within.

When my sister picked me up at the airport, she said that the priest from the same church I walked out of 34 years earlier wanted to meet with me before the service because he wanted to approve what I was going to read.

Five members of my family went with me to meet the priest. The meeting lasted more than an hour, and we were oceans apart. I said, "Father, this is my sister's funeral and her service and as a family member I should be allowed to read what I know is true about her. The church teachings did not help her, and they do more harm than good and you give the people no answers."

He said, "I can lead and guide them."

"No," I said. "You work very hard at taking their power instead of helping them to empower themselves."

When I first started my search, I wrote down two quotes that I have with me today: "The light within teaches us that we must be our own savior" and "No more cunning plot was ever devised against the intelligence, the freedom and the happiness of mankind than Catholicism."

Life is meant to be enjoyed, happy, sharing and loving. Love is the great power in the world. No one can experience the above if they are living in fear and guilt.

There is a Buddhist saying: "Do not blindly believe what others say, not even the Buddha." See for yourself what brings contentment, clarity, and peace. That is the path to follow.

There is priceless wisdom to be found in books, and it's free. I know! I thank God daily for my library dream; not only did my research set me free, but it gave me another tool to use on my path. Dreams!

Over the years I have had many letters published in the editorial section of the Santa Barbara News-Press. From time to time they shorten or delete a paragraph or a word or two, but for the most part, the letters are published as I wrote them.

The article you just read was not published in its entirety. The following thoughts were left out: (1) How I was always amazed when a certain person or book would come into my life, and I found more answers. (2) How a very special medium had come into my life and blew my socks off. I will share more on these thoughts in later chapters.

I did not expect to get the response that I did from writing the article "Feed Catholic Spiritual Hunger." I received a total of 54 phone calls. Fifty were ladies and four men. I also was a guest on a local radio talk show.

The following is a sample of the calls I received: One man said he was a doctor, and that he agreed with my article completely. I asked him if he was Catholic, and he said, "No, I am a very happy Lutheran, and we pretty much feel as you do." When I asked him why he called, he said that he wanted to tell me it was a good article, and that he could relate to it because he had worked for years in a Catholic hospital.

Another caller, a 31 year old lady, said that she was a fallen-away Catholic and that in reading my article she cried. Her emotions were still high as she started to cry again. I felt her pain, and I cried with her without even yet hearing any of her story. She said she was raised in a very strict Catholic family, and it never felt right to her. She said that even today, in spite of having left the church years ago, that she still walked around with guilty feelings. She also said that part of the reason she was so emotional was because I wrote her story, and that she now felt a new beginning and could start with new strength.

One lady called and said, "We need to make this world a better place. We need to talk about our problems from the grass roots and leave religion out of it because it is the cause of most of society's problems."

Another caller, a lady, said, "I left the church. I wish I hadn't waited so long to do that. I share all your feelings and resent any religion because it is all about control."

One friend called, and she said, "I never knew all that about you, Charlene. My mother always said it doesn't matter what church you belong to. You make your own heaven and hell right here on earth."

An 87 year old lady said, "I relate completely to your article. But I do have one question. How did you find your power within?" That question at her age impressed me very much. She was still searching for answers and her power within at 87! What a lady. More on her later.

Another elderly lady said that she loved me, that I should be very proud to have written such an honest story, and that I had planted a seed to help many others. She asked me to speak at a senior citizen group she belonged to.

I found myself crying with three other ladies who also said, "You have written my story."

One lady that called really piqued my interest. She said that she was 63 years old, and here is her story as she told it to me: she said she had wasted more than half of her life playing the part, that each and every Sunday she and her husband would attend mass at a Catholic Church. She wore her best clothes and furs. She said, "We always dressed to the nines. We were pillars in our community. My husband was usually up on the altar reading from the scriptures and everyone thought that we were such a lucky couple to have money and prestige in the community." She then got emotional. It took her a few seconds to get her composure back, then she continued. "I was so empty inside, angry, and desperately unhappy. People envied me. No one knew how I felt."

I asked her if she had always felt empty and unhappy or if that just came later in her life.

She responded, "No, in the beginning (I assume of her marriage) I didn't feel that way. I had wanted children and had several miscarriages, so my husband and I decided to adopt a beautiful baby boy when he was just a few months old. He was the light of our life, and we were very happy. At the age of 18, my son was killed in an auto accident." She paused with more emotions before she could continue. "I didn't want to live after that. My husband and I felt such anguishing pain. Our hearts ached, and we turned to our religion for answers, feeling it would comfort us. When it didn't, it was then that I realized this vast emptiness within. I had not found God in my religion. All those years of going to church and going through all the motions, and I now questioned, Where's God? He certainly was not a part of my life up to that point, and never had been, and I only now realized that truth.

"That is when I became very angry with God and the church for not being able to give us any answers and help us with our pain. I was looking for some answers; I needed to know more. My anger increased within me, and I resented

God for taking away our son. I resented the church and other people, and it was not their fault. I was angry with my husband when he said that we would have to continue on in the church, but I kept those angry feelings inside.

"Six years later my husband died, and I almost had a nervous breakdown. I left the church, and in spite of friends telling me not to sell my home, I sold it and moved out to California. It was here in Santa Barbara that I slowly started to feel whole again."

I asked her if she would like to join me and a few other ladies that also called and wanted to meet and share more thoughts.

She said, "No, I have found God in nature. I walk the beach when I am here in Santa Barbara, and I now find God in all of nature, and He now talks to me. He is my salvation."

I desperately wanted to have more conversation with this lady, so I pushed a little more and asked her if just the two of us could meet and talk. I told her how I felt about nature and how it fills my cup whenever I am low on energy. She responded that she was leaving shortly to go back East for a few months and that she would keep my number. I asked her if I might have her number and she said, very kindly, "My dear, I would prefer not to give it out. I am unlisted, but perhaps I will call you sometime after I return to Santa Barbara. I just wanted to let you know that it was an excellent article and to thank you."

I said, "I do hope you will call me when you return. I would love to meet you."

The reason her phone call piqued my interest so much is that I have always felt a oneness with nature. After I got married, my mother told me a story about me when I was around three years old. She said the family and other relatives had joined together at a lakeside for a picnic and to spend the day. She said that I had wandered off without anyone noticing, and they looked for me for several hours. When they found me, an older man was walking towards her carrying me. She said she was so happy to have found me that she took me from the man and forgot to thank him. She asked me where I was going, and I told her to visit the trees.

She said a minute had only gone by when she turned to thank the man, but he was gone. She said that she looked in all directions, but he was nowhere in sight. She said, "We were standing in an open field, and in all directions there were trees. There is no way he could have walked back into the woods so fast, and that has always puzzled me." She asked me if I remember being lost.

I said, "I remember a man carrying me and my feet hurting."

She said, "You had cuts on your feet and between your toes that were bleeding. You walked off without any shoes on."

By the time I started high school, whenever I would read or hear a quote that impressed me or lifted my spirits, I made a point to write it down so I could save it. From time to time I would take the box I saved them in and sit outside on the grass and read them. I have never stopped collecting quotes. Today I have several thick files that I still read when I want to lift my spirits.

Throughout the book you will read some of those quotes. If I have the author's name I will include it. I never thought that I would ever be writing a book; therefore, I was careless at times and didn't write the authors responsible for the quotes.

As a teenager the one place that I could go to that made me feel alive and happy as well as peaceful was nature! It always lifted my spirits as it wrapped its arms around me. I know now without a doubt that nature was my salvation before I found God within me. It is peaceful, pure, beautiful, simple; not complicated like life was for me. When I'm surrounded by nature I feel total peace and always have loving, happy thoughts. It raises my emotions of love. I know that nature loves me as much as I love it.

The following quotes about nature are my favorites and I hope that they will lift your spirits as they do mine.

1) "Speak to the earth and it shall teach you."
2) "Nature never did betray the heart that loved her."

3) "One touch of nature makes the whole world kin."
4) "All nature whispers the beautiful message of God which is love."
5) This quote came from the book of The Life of Jesus: "Nature obeys all who believe and pray, for faith can do everything."

Richard Jefferies wrote, "If you wish your children to think deep thoughts, to know the holiest emotions, take them to the woods and hills, and give them the freedom of the meadows; the hills purify those who walk upon them."

Robert Louis Stevenson wrote, "Though we should be grateful for good houses, there is no house like God's out of doors." I love that quote because nature fills my soul. Elbert Hubbard wrote, "That our souls are like our body that needs nourishment. We nourish our souls by reaching out to others in the spirit of love, by the glorious beauty of nature that is all around us, by the arts and music." That quote reminds me of the song, "The best things in life are free." Nourishing the soul is simple and costs nothing. It is free!

Many of the callers asked the same question that the 87 year old lady caller asked. How did I find my power within? An easy question to answer: from my experiences of life. But most of the credit must go to the dozens and dozens of wonderful authors who wrote the many books and quotes that I read which inspired me and filled my soul with knowledge that translated into wisdom for me. A quote by Channing explains it well: "God be thanked for books; they are the voice of the distant and the dead, and make us heirs of the spiritual life of past ages."

The only credit that I can take is that in reading the books, whatever felt right to me I accepted and applied to my life. I knew that God was guiding me. I felt His presence with every book that I read. There is an old saying that when the student is ready the teacher appears. When I started my search, God was my teacher. He just kept me going by putting more and more in front of me to help me, and He still does today. He will give you the experiences that you need on your path to help you grow and find the answers you are seeking. He knew I was seeking truth.

Will Durant wrote, "Knowledge is the eye of desire and can become the pilot of the soul." Horace Mann wrote, "Keep one thing forever in view, the truth; and if you do this, though it may seem to lead you away from the opinions of men, it will assuredly conduct you to the throne of God."

When that dear 87 year old lady asked me how I found my power within, it boggled my mind. At her age I would have expected that she would have found it just from living so long. It actually made me feel sad because she was so sweet. She said that she had followed the Catholic religion for too many years, and when she finally left, she decided not to get tied to any other religion. Organized religions of today with their hierarchy, control, and teachings are to blame for taking that dear lady's power away as well as the power of many other people.

As you read the first part of this book, please keep in mind that some of it I wrote at the age of 44. It was only for myself. I had already started my search to find God and what life is all about because of the dream that sent me to the library. But I still had some anger and resentment towards my parents for not giving me what I needed as a child in order to feel secure and to be able to relate to life when I was younger. I felt that if I put my thoughts in writing, it would be very healing for me.

I also did not expect to find what I did in my search, and should you decide to start your own search, I hope that you will find what I did, and that is SIMPLICITY! For me it is the answer to all things in life. "Simplicity of all things, is the hardest to be copied." This is one of my favorite quotes.

TWO

PREACHERS OF GLOOM

There's a lot of chicken little
On every platform in the land.
It's good to scare the little folks
For all their nerves can stand.

The stronger Souls resist the threat,
And shore up their fragile wall.
For common sense does not allow
That tomorrow's sky should fall.

But nothing stops the preachers
In their work of spreading fear.
Hysteria breeds fanatics,
And their day of doom is near.

True logic works against them
With its wisdom by design,
For reason's pure and holy light
Proves logic is divine.

A thousand years of gloom has failed
To bring their judgment day.
The sky is not about to fall.
God put it there to stay.

Reverend Edmund L. Foard

By the time I turned 42, I felt a deep emptiness within me, and I could not figure out the reason I felt that way. I was happily married, had two beautiful children, a home, and what most would say, "The American Dream." Because I could not figure out the cause, I didn't know how to fix it. I had daily thoughts that plagued my mind as I tried to figure out why life now felt empty to me.

I thought if I went back to work on a part-time basis it would help, but every time I looked in the paper for job openings, I would get sick stomach feelings. The same feelings I had while I was growing up. I didn't understand it back then, and I didn't understand it now.

In our fifth year of marriage, our daughter Catana was born and 2 years later our son Armando. Up until the time Catana was born, I worked as a secretary in an office; also my husband and I set up a small business. We agreed that when children came along, I would stay home with them and do the bookkeeping for the business in the home. It was very important to both of us to always be there for our children at every turn, and we didn't want to miss anything.

I didn't know how to deal with the emptiness that I now felt within me. It made absolutely no sense to me. It was as if I woke up one day and the lights went out. No joy, no gaiety, nothing mattered to me. I kept on with the family routine like a robot thinking that I was going crazy. I told no one, not even my husband, and we shared everything. I was not unhappy with my family.

Several months before the empty feeling, I started to have the recurring dream of being in the library reading books about God. But now with the empty feelings I was having it three to four times a week. I decided that the dream must be giving me a message, so I followed through with the dream and went to the library and checked out some books.

Once I started reading the books, it didn't take long for that emptiness to start filling up. I realized that I had God within me. Having been raised in the Catholic religion, I never believed, or was told, that I had God in me. I was taught about the pearly gates of heaven up in the sky somewhere, where I would meet St. Peter and then God with all the white clouds. Of course, I had to worry about the fires of hell that all sinners burned in as well.

I liked the idea of the pearly gates, St. Peter, the white clouds, and God. But I hated the idea of burning in the fires of hell. As children we were brainwashed to believe that we were sinners, and I lived with so much fear because I didn't want to burn in hell. I can only imagine that millions of other children also felt as I did, and some still do today, and that thought makes me angry. I had no choice. I had to walk the same path my parents did until I was old enough to be in charge of my own life.

The first conscious thing that bothered me about my religion was when the church said it was okay to eat meat on Friday; they said it no longer was a sin. Do you know that I went through hell as a child knowing if I ate meat on Friday, even if it was an accident, that I had sinned and had to go to confession in order to save my soul? In the article, "Feed Catholic Spiritual Hunger," I explained about the experience I had while in grade school.

When I was around nine years old, I was attending a public school, and if you were of the Catholic Religion, you were allowed to leave school an hour early one afternoon a week in order to attend Catholic studies. I really didn't want to go, but I wanted to get out of class.

It was December. The church that I went to for lessons was connected to a small private school. Our religion class had practiced for several weeks in order to put on a small Christmas program for the children that attended the private school.

On the day we were to present our talents, two other girls and myself decided that we would change the words of the song we were supposed to sing, "We Three Kings of Orient Are." We all agreed it would be fun and a neat idea. Well, when our turn came to sing, we sang, "We three Kings of Orient are, trying to smoke a rubber cigar. The cigar was loaded and we exploded following yonder star." We then sang the rest of the song with the proper words.

I cannot tell you how angry the nuns and the priest in the room got. We were nine and ten years old, and we thought they would enjoy the humor in our change of words, and to this day I still cannot believe their anger. They verbally punished us in front of the class and gave each of us a note to take home to our parents. I had to go to Saturday morning lessons for a month. I also received a bad grade which, as I remember, affected my report card. I never gave the note to my parents. I did attend the Saturday classes because we had freedom to leave the house and play outside without any supervision or anyone checking on us. I would go on a Saturday morning and do my hour and go back home. No one in my family ever knew.

When I moved to California in my early twenties, I still considered myself Catholic, but not a practicing Catholic. I had no other beliefs. Since my religion did not work for me, I did not pursue any other.

THREE

AWAKE

Awake, little child, now
There's excitement afield!
Delirium is rampant,
And it's magic revealed.

Awake, for tis morning,
and the bright light of day
May not be lasting.
Don't waste it on play.

And now it is evening,
And life's daylight a drain,
No time for lamenting,
Or do over again.

All you missed on the journey,
Farewell and forget.
No return this late hour.
The sun soon will set.

So live best this moment.
Beg hard for the break.
The chance to serve others
These few hours awake.

Reverend Edmund L. Foard

It is not my intent to make my mother or father look uncaring or unloving in this book. I know that they had a lot of love in them and that they did love me in their own way.

My dad drew many people around him all the time, not only from his side of the family, but my mother's side as well; and he had many friends. Looking in from the outside, everyone thought that we had a lot of love in our home and family; and we did, but I felt it was always directed towards other people.

I did not feel it. I don't ever recall sitting on my dad's lap or my dad putting his arms around me, giving me a compliment, or an encouraging word; my mother, somewhat, but my dad, no. I know that my dad's childhood was not the best. He lost his mother at an early age, and perhaps he had passed on to me exactly what he received as a child.

It wasn't until I had my own children that it became obvious to me that as a child I needed so much more than I received from my parents. My children were encouraged in all they did and allowed to express themselves freely and share their feelings. As a child I kept all of my feelings to myself and that habit stayed with me into my adult life, and I know that stopped me from growing in many ways.

Growing up, I always knew something was missing in my life. I always knew it, but I didn't know what it was. I often thought there was something wrong with me because I felt different when I was around most people because I was unable to connect with them and with all that was going on around me. I always thought other people had the answers to life that I didn't have.

I now believe that everything that happens to us is for a reason, and feeling and experiencing what I did growing up has helped me to give our children everything I never had. I am not talking about material things. I am talking about open communication, love, emotional support, being there for them, and always putting them ahead of friends and tuning into their needs. It helped me to be a parent at a level I knew was important.

When I was very young, there were two people that I did experience love from that made me feel special, my precious Aunt Lena and precious Uncle Walt. They were very bright lights in my life and even though they both passed back in the 60's, I always thank God for having them there for me. Unfortunately, they would come and go; and I remember wishing they would always stay with us. I loved them more than I loved my parents. Their love for me and my brothers and sisters was unconditional, and it wasn't until I moved away and they both passed to spirit that I realized it.

As I got older and into my early teens, I also felt special love from my precious sister Annie, and my precious Uncle David. Annie had it very difficult because of my father. If she would have written her story, you might have cried through the whole book. She had it tough. In spite of her being only four years older than I was, I could always turn to her. She would stand up for me to my dad even though she knew the end result would not be pleasant for her.

Not only was she there for me, I know she gave a lot of her time and energy to others. She was a very giving and loving person. When I got into high school, she started to confide in me about her problems; and believe me, she had many. But in spite of them, she remained positive. I do have pleasant memories because of her, and I know that we were both thankful that we had each other.

My very special Uncle David, my dad's brother, I don't think he even knew what an impact he had on my life growing up. I also loved Uncle David more than I loved my father. I would be so excited whenever he would come to the house. He shared his love with me as well as with my brothers and sisters, but I needed so much that I may have blown what he gave me out of proportion. When I got into high school, I asked my Uncle David if I could work at his Lebanese night club, "The Cedars," on weekends, and he said yes. He often complimented me on my work there and gave me words of encouragement. He was also tough, but I didn't care. He recognized me for me. He made me feel as if I had something to offer, that I was special.

Today my Aunt Lena, Uncle Walt, sister Annie, and Uncle David are all in spirit. With all the love they so freely gave while they were here, not only to me but to many others, I know that they are in a very special place and happy. I thank them for their love and for being there for me and giving me some of the most precious memories of my childhood and teenage years.

As a child I did not know what end was up. I remember at the age of 4 or 5 lying in bed night after night crying my eyes out, hoping that my mom and dad would not die, and that I would die before them. That lasted for several years. I knew that I felt different than most other kids, maybe it was because we were poor. At the time I was not able to figure anything out. I now know that in spite of whatever anyone thought of me, I was a very lonely, insecure child, and according to my parents, a non-stop talker. I laughed at everything whether it was funny or not. I was always the last to sit down to eat and the first one to finish.

I know that I did the above for attention. Whenever I would laugh, my mother would say, "She is so silly," and she would always tell people that I was the fastest eater in the world. I was desperate for attention at a very early age. My mother said that as a baby I cried all the time.

I grew up in a family of seven children: five girls and two boys. I was the fifth to come along, and the oldest then was almost six, so you can see how close we were. By that time, my mother had to be worn out. My mother would always get upset with the priest because he would make fun of us kids being "steps" whenever he would come over.

My dad was not much help for my mother back then. He always did his own thing. He loved to hunt and fish with his brothers, and any free time he had he used for himself and his own activities; so you can see why my mother had a long row to hoe. With seven kids and being poor, it was not easy for her.

My dad was good at telling stories, and he would often gather all of us kids together and use our names in the stories he would tell us. He had a great imagination. He was also very talented and could play by ear any musical instrument. I enjoyed it most when he would play the concertina and the mouth organ.

As all of us kids got older, because of his love for fishing, he would often take us. We would also go for rides during the summer while he would listen to the baseball game on the radio, and before going back home, we would always stop for a root beer and a Coney Island (a hot dog).

When we would ask, "Dad, are we going to stop for a root beer?" he would say, "I don't know."

But we always knew we would stop and we also knew he would get us a Coney Island, too.

The stories, the fishing trips, the rides ending up with root beer and Coney Islands, those were happy memories for me.

But what I needed was his approval and attention just for me. I was always trying to do the right thing to get his attention and his approval. I wanted him to tell me he loved me, and I know my sister Annie felt the same way.

Whenever my dad would tell me to do something I quickly did it for two reasons. One is that he ruled our home life. Two is that I feared his temper would rise, and he would verbally abuse me. I had also hoped that by responding quickly he might respond to me with some praise or a kind word like he did to other family members and friends that came to the house.

I remember times when our immediate family would all be together, and my dad always gave attention to my oldest and youngest sisters as well as my two brothers. I often thought, "Why doesn't he give me or my sisters, Annie and Barbara, the same attention?" I feel great emotion as I write this because the feelings I had back then I can feel now. It was very obvious to me, then and now, that he favored the others. I could never understand why.

I was a good actress all through my childhood and into my adult life. No one would have ever suspected or thought that I was insecure and felt alone. I worked very hard at putting on a good show and pretending that I was happy.

Parents who are not aware that each child is sensitive in his/her own way, that each child is different, that each child in a family deserves and needs equal love, even though one might stand out or be brighter than the others, do great harm to their children because children can't figure anything out when they are so young. When the parents don't treat all the children with equal love and attention, you can be sure the children that are lacking are very much aware of it, and it hurts. All children deserve unconditional love.

FOUR

I'M LOOKING

Where did you hide me,
Ye Gods of all time?
Why have you taken
That which is mine?

I have spent time just looking,
Searching both land and sea.
A lot of time wasted
Just looking for me.

Not knowing why
I just want to be whole.
I want my one being
A complete living Soul.

Half man, and half infant,
Half woman, half child,
Half saint, and half devil,
Half pure, half defiled.

Oh! Where do I search now,
For I'm riddled with doubt?
Imprisoned, a sad Soul,
Inside looking out.

The paths I've exhausted,
Brought darkness and din,
But something keeps showing
A Soul looking in.

So maybe I'll follow,
And look deep in me.
It's the last place I'd think of,
But it may be the key.

Ah! Won't I be proud
To find me at last,
And let the world see me
In my own chosen cast.

So I'll look to the inside,
And guided by prayer
To help me, to find me,
I just gotta be there.

Reverend Edmund L. Foard

The first six verses written
on a train between Chicago
and Marina, Indiana: the
last three verses came much later.

1941.

In the Spring of 1949 I was nine years old. Each day as I would leave school to walk home, I would see this big truck parked, and kids were lined up in order to climb on the back. It looked like they were having so much fun that I decided, after a few days, to go up to the truck driver and ask him where he was taking the kids. He said to work on a truck farm. He asked me how old I was, and I said nine. He said, "When you turn ten years old, get permission from your parents so you can work." Well, I cannot tell you how much I wanted to get on that truck and be a part of all that fun.

For about a week or so I watched each day as the kids got on, but I knew that I would not be ten until October; so I decided to go up and tell the truck driver that I had just had a birthday and was now ten. When I walked up to the truck, it was not the same driver, but I told him that the other guy told me I could work for them when I turned ten. I told him I just had a birthday and asked if it was okay to start. He said, "Yes, but you better bring a pair of slacks to work in."

I said, "Okay. I will be here tomorrow."

I went home and told my mother I was going to work after school on a truck farm, and she said okay. She never checked it out that I know of. I now think, "My God, anything could have happened to me." The following day I wore slacks to school, and after school got on the truck.

When we arrived at the farm, the other truck driver, who I found out was Mr. Johnson, the owner of the farm, came over to me and said, "I thought I told you that you had to be ten."

I said, "I know. I just had my birthday, and the other driver told me it was okay." I know he didn't believe me, but he let me stay.

They put me in a field of radishes and showed me how to bunch them together and to sort out the bad ones from the good ones and to take out the weeds. They said, "You get 35 cents a bushel, and there are 32 piles to a bushel, 4 bunches to a pile."

I started to bunch, and when it was time to stop, I didn't even have one fourth of a bushel. Some of the other kids around me had two and three bushels. Well, I was smart enough to know that I would have to work faster so that I could make more money.

The following day I decided to work very fast, and I was not sorting the bad radishes from the good ones or taking out the weeds. I was just pulling and putting a rubber band around each bunch; I was going so fast and I was so excited. I had a couple of bushels on the ground when a supervisor came along and started to check out my bunches and told me I had to go back over all of them. I was so hurt I almost started to cry. I also was embarrassed when the other kids had to help me because it was dusk, and I could not get it done by myself.

Mr. Johnson told me to sit in the front cab of the truck on the way home; he said he wanted to talk to me. I got a sick stomach feeling because I knew he was going to tell me I could not come back. He told me that I no longer could work for him and gave me what I had earned for the two days.

I started to cry and said, "Oh, Mr. Johnson, I am sorry. Please, please give me another chance. I promise I will do better. I just wanted to be fast like the other kids." I begged him all the way home.

When he dropped me off at school, he said, "Okay, just one more chance." It was dark. I jumped out of the cab of the truck and ran all the way home. I was so happy.

I worked on the farm until I was almost 15. We worked in the spring, summer, and fall. I had Saturdays off.

When I was in the tenth grade, I came home from school one day with plans of going to work on the farm, but my Mom said that a lady had called from a local cafe and wanted me to come to work that same day. I got so excited. I had filled out an application for the job the summer before. Again I lied about my age and said I was 15 when I was only 14. I waited until the farm truck came, and I ran out and told Mr. Johnson that I no longer would be working on the farm, that I got another job as a waitress. I was happy about the new job, but when I told him, I almost started to cry because our families had become good friends, and I knew I would miss the farm. He said, "Well, Charlene, we are going to miss you. If your new job does not work out, come back and work for us."

FIVE

YOUR TRACKS

Today is changing all the days
Of tomorrows yet to come.
Its shock and hurt is not yet known,
For we're left here cold and numb.

You'll never know the full impact
Of your living here on earth,
And now, without a guiding light,
There's want in home and hearth.

Where'er you go, we know 'tis good.
And trust that love will lead.
That gentle Soul will show the way,
And attend your every need.

Leave something here to lift and heal
Against our trying day.
So leave some tracks upon the sand,
And we'll follow in your way.

                    Reverend Edmund L. Foard

All through school I did very little work during class. I would just sit at my desk pretending I was listening when the teacher was talking and absorb absolutely nothing at all. When it was time to take a test I would die inside. I always cheated, and then I would be lucky to get a D.

Growing up my dad had always told me that I was nothing but a "goddamn dummy." When you are told that over and over again you believe it. I know I did. I never tried in school at all; I always felt like a dummy. Believe me, I was not copping out, I honestly felt like a dummy, so I went through school without ever trying because I thought it wouldn't do any good anyway. I was always very polite and pleasant to the teachers, hoping that they would give me a higher grade, and they always did. They gave me D's; I didn't deserve a D and I knew it. I should have gotten F's. I knew my dad would be furious when he saw my report card, but I did not care. I was happy I didn't get F's.

I started a diary in the 10th grade, and years later when I read it, I did not have much written in it, but I did write something that I would like to share with you: "Why is life so mixed up? I feel no one loves me and no one cares. My days start out bad and seem to get worse. The feeling of no one needing me is sad. Where do I turn? I wonder if it would not be better to be a bird or a horse. They look so free and happy. Why does life exist? What is it all about, all the uneasiness with other people? Why can't people have love and compassion towards each other? It would be so nice. No one understands me, and I feel no one is there. All I want to feel is love and understanding. Where is it? Where is the kindness and guidance? Why do others have to point out my flaws when I already know them? It hurts so much, if they only knew. Where is God? Why doesn't He help me?"

It wasn't until years later that I realized that I did have the love from my Aunt Lena, Uncle Walt, my sister Annie and Uncle Dave. They were there for me, but at the time I didn't realize it. I felt very alone.

I recall one math teacher in the 10th grade, Miss Carleton. She was about 60 years old, small, petite, and very stern looking. Most of the kids called her a bitch. She had never married. She told us that she had dedicated her life to teaching. In spite of what the other kids said about her, I did not agree. I felt she really cared and was there for us. She must have perceived my lack of self-confidence within me because one day she asked me to come and see her after school. When I told her that I could not, that I had to go to work, she then said, "Well, then you come tomorrow to my room during the lunch period and bring your lunch with you."

I was scared to death. What had I done? I immediately felt shaky and sick to my stomach. I didn't ask her what it was about. I was almost sure it had to do with my not doing well in class, and I just knew she was going to tell me that I would have to leave retail training. I went to a vocational high school, and if you did not do well in math in that field, you would have to choose another field. My stomach felt so sick; I cannot tell you how sick.

I chose retail training because I thought it would be the easiest thing to take. I knew I was not smart and what would happen to me if I took something else. I had no answers and no one to talk to because I was always acting. No one knew how I really felt.

I went to work that day after school. I worked from 4 p.m. to 8 p.m. during the week and from 8 a.m. to 2 p.m. on Saturdays. Anyway, that night at work, I don't know how I got through it. I was a good waitress. My boss liked me. It was a small restaurant, eight to ten bar stools and five or six booths. I worked it by myself and I always felt good. None of my customers or even my boss knew how insecure I felt. I made good tips, but that night I did not take a dinner break. I was too nauseated. With no one to talk to and keeping everything to myself, I did not want anyone to think badly of me.

I got through with my work that night and went home. I never did homework all through school because my parents never asked me if I had any, and I thought it wouldn't do any good anyway. I left for school the next morning with the sick stomach feelings. I got through the morning, took my lunch at lunch time, and I went to Miss Carleton's classroom. She was not there. I have never felt so nervous and scared in my life. As I sat waiting for her to

31

come into the room, I felt that my whole world was going to fall out from under me. About ten minutes later she came into the classroom. She told me to pull up a chair as she sat at her desk. She apologized for being late, and I felt a warmness from her that I had not felt before.

I pulled the chair up to her desk and she got right to the point as she always did. She said, "Charlene, I don't understand why you do so well in the class and not on your tests."

I thought to myself, "I do well in class?" I was shaky and almost to the verge of tears. I know she felt it. I asked, "Do I do well in class?"

She said, "Yes, but not on your tests."

I had never thought about it before. I just did what I was told, and she did have a way of taking the class step by step and explaining things, and that worked for me, without my realizing it. I never put any importance on what I did in class because I always felt the grades came from all the tests, and I knew I never did well in tests. In fact, to this day, if I have to take a test, I get that same sick feeling. My mind still panics at the word.

I told her I didn't know, that I wasn't very smart, and when it was time to take any test, I would get sick to my stomach and not do well.

She said, "But if you can do it in class you should be able to apply the same learning."

I said, "I don't know."

She said, "Well, you come back here tomorrow during lunch, and I will give you the last test to take over again. Let's see how you do."

I thought, "Oh, God," and I started to cry.

She asked, "What is the matter, Charlene?"

I said, "I am not very smart and tests make me sick to my stomach."

She said, "That's the second time you told me that. Look, Charlene, I won't grade it. Let's just see if we can work this out."

I said, "Okay." I thanked her and I left the room. I threw my lunch in the trash. I felt too sick to eat it.

Again I got through the night at work, and when I left the next morning for school, I still had the sick stomach feelings. I went to her room during lunch. This time she was waiting for me. I was shaking so bad inside. I had to take a test and I was the only student in the room. God, I wanted to die! I took the test and I knew I did terrible. The next day during class, I found out how bad I did. She again told me to come and see her the following day during lunch. I thought, "Oh my God, why doesn't she just leave me alone." I knew she was trying to help me, but I had gone through two days with sick stomach feelings and keeping it all to myself. Now she wanted to see me again.

The next day she said, "Charlene, you did not do well on the test, but let's go over each problem to see what it is you don't understand."

I pulled a chair to her desk. She again took me step by step, and I clearly understood all the problems, and she knew I did.

She said she would like to talk to my parents. I again wanted to die inside and started to cry. "Oh, no," I thought, "What is my dad going to say to me?"

She asked me what was wrong as she put her arm around my shoulder. I felt myself sobbing. I couldn't even talk. As I write this I am crying; the feeling was horrible.

Here was a teacher trying to help me, and I just wanted to be left alone. She asked me some questions about my home life. I got myself together and answered the best I could. I do not recall many of the questions or even my answers. I only remember that when I told her I was not very smart, she said, "You keep saying that. Now who said you are not smart?"

I said, "Well, I have always gotten D's, and my dad said I am a dummy. My older sister has all the brains."

I asked her to please not contact my parents. I did not want to get into trouble. I don't even know if I would have. It was just the way I felt, and I was afraid it might have opened a can of worms that I didn't want opened because I did not understand why any of this had to happen, and I felt drained.

Well, at the end of my sophomore year I was getting A's in math. She did not contact my parents. She worked with me during class and showed me how to apply what I learned in class when I took a test. On occasions she would ask me to come into her room at lunch to boost me and tell me how proud she was of me. I guess it was the start of my realizing that I was not a dummy. I had so much love and respect for her because she believed in me.

I remember the last day of school I went in to see Miss Carleton, making sure no one saw me because I didn't want anyone to think I was "kissing up" to a teacher. I went into her room and she was not there. I walked across the hall to the office, and she was standing at a bulletin board reading.

I went up to her and said, "Miss Carleton, I just want to thank you," and gave her a big hug. She had tears in her eyes, and I left quickly because I did too. I didn't want her to see me crying again.

I still did not do that well in other classes. I continued to get D's and some low C's, but for the first time in my life someone had faith in me, and it made me feel very special. I loved her for that.

GOD UNDERSTANDS

On the path of experience where reality lives,
And awakens the traveler to all that life gives,
And through all the struggle, the good and the bad,
No God says to thee, 'THOU ART TRULY A CAD."

Fear not, should ye stumble or stray in the cause
For answers are written in immutable laws.
As ye close in on wisdom, with a taste for the win,
No God says to thee, 'THOU ART LIVING A SIN."

Look up, little Angel, and know thou art wise
In searching the shadows for all it belies
With standard held high, and know all is well.
For no God shall fault thee or commit thee to hell.

And when at the closing, the long journey o'er,
The want of the chase can haunt thee no more.
Then time, the great master, tames the restless
and wild.
There a God says to thee, 'THOU ARE WORTHY MY
CHILD."

Ye pressed forth in the search; ye win, or ye lose.
I know not thy path. I walked not in thy shoes,
But still all the good shines forth in its might.
Then a God says of thee, "A TRUE CHILD OF
LIGHT."

Reverend Edmund L. Foard

My mother was never one to verbally abuse me like my dad did, but she never disputed what he would say to me. It did not mean that she agreed with him. She didn't have the time to give us individual attention or have the energy to stand up to my dad. I now realize she lived her life the way my dad wanted her to. He was the boss and she knew it. She was very submissive towards my dad.

In later years, when she would speak her mind from time to time to my dad, it would cause an argument and my stomach would knot up, and it made things more stressful for me at home. I hated arguments or fights; I always wanted everything to go smoothly.

I remember one of many times. My two brothers were fighting in the kitchen. My dad got involved, and someone went through the kitchen window just as I was walking out the door crying.

Living with so many people in one house, we had our share of fights, and I couldn't handle it. I would always go down to the church, which was a few blocks away, and try to pray. As I sat there trying to pray, I wondered to whom I was praying. If there was a God, I didn't know how to find him. I never got anything out of going to religious studies. The church services and sermons were in Lebanese, and I didn't understand but a few words of what the priest said. Most of the people that attended the church services, in my opinion, were only there for show and to dress to the hilt.

In fact, I realized at the age of 18 that I also was doing the same thing, dressing to impress other people. I found myself shopping for shoes, hats, purses, gloves, and jewelry all to match a dress.

I felt there were a few people in church on Sundays that were there for God. They sat in the first three or four pews of the church, and all of them were elderly. I often wondered how they found God, and I wanted to know what God's rules were. Many times I had the urge to go up and ask them. I wanted to know what they were experiencing and feeling. I never followed through, but I had a deep nagging in me way back then to find God.

I wrote about my sister Rose's wedding in the article in the first part of the book, "Feed Catholic's Spiritual Hunger." The following gives more of a detailed picture.

My sister Rose got engaged to a man who was divorced and had a child. Of course, the Catholic religion did not approve of marrying outside of the church, let alone marrying a divorced man. I don't know what emotions she was feeling deep within herself, but I can tell you what I experienced and felt during that time. When she told me that my sister Annie could not stand up for her because the priest at the church and my dad were really making her feel guilty and telling her she might be excommunicated from the church if she did, I felt angry.

I said, "Rose, that is terrible. What are you going to do?"

She said, "I asked a girl at work today if she would stand up for me, and she said yes."

I responded, "With four sisters you are not going to have someone at work. I will stand up for you."

"What about dad and the church?" she asked.

"What about them?" I replied. "I love you as a sister, and when there is love, compassion follows, so I will do it. I don't care what anyone says. God understands." It surprised me to have said, "God understands." It just came out.

When the priest found out, he contacted my dad, and my dad told me that I had to go and see the priest, that he wanted to talk to me. My dad was furious with me because I was going against him and the church. I got those sick stomach feelings again, but I went to see the priest. I decided that I would be strong and not let him put a guilt trip on me. I think that this is the first time that I knew I would stand up for something that I felt was very wrong, and I was very scared.

The priest told me that if I stood up for my sister Rose, I also would be excommunicated from the church, and that my sister Annie was wise not to stand up for her and also that my sister Rose was wrong in marrying outside of her religion.

I told him, in part, "I am sorry father. She is my sister and I love her, and if there is a God, He knows what I am feeling in my heart. You can do whatever you want with this church; if you want to excommunicate me from the church, go ahead. It doesn't work for me anyway."

I turned around and walked out of the rectory, and I cannot tell you how happy I felt. I did not wait around for him to try and put a guilt-trip on me. I only knew what I felt in my heart, and I knew what my sister was going through.

When I got back home, my dad called me many names. My mother, bless her heart, did not say a word, but I could tell that she was with me 100 percent.

My brother Johnny also felt as I did, and we both stood up for Rose. She got married by the Justice of the Peace, and no one came to the service, only the four of us were there. My mother, in spite of my dad's obnoxious behavior, went ahead and made all the arrangements for an open house. My dad also felt that my sister was not marrying someone good enough for her; besides, he wanted all of his kids to marry someone Lebanese.

When we arrived at the house from the Justice of the Peace, my dad was upstairs, and he would not come down for the open house. He was concerned what his friends and family would say, and he was ashamed that his daughter went against the church and his wishes, and he did not think that any of his Lebanese friends would come. My mother went upstairs. I don't know what she said to him, but he eventually came down. At the end of the day, my dad felt better because all of our Lebanese friends came, and they stayed into the night hours. We had a packed house all day long.

SEVEN

A DARK DAY

The sky is cast over with a dampness and chill.
The air all around me is heavy and still.
My garment of woolen around me infold,
But nothing can shut out the bit of this cold.

Why can't I make sunshine, at least in the mind,
And melt every cloud that my despair can find?
So I charge for the shelter, the warmth it can give,
For the elements are plotting against me to live.

There's a shadow of pall sweeping over my frame,
And adding to gloom, there's a few drops of rain.
Has the mantle of darkness shut out the light,
And given my thoughts unto failure and blight?

What's wrong with my world as I query and wait
For an answer to lift and to alter my fate?
Then there comes a sweet song from up in the gray.
My old mockingbird thinks it's a BEAUTIFUL day.

Reverend Edmund L. Foard

I had a friend, Pat, who had moved to Santa Barbara, California, and she wanted me to join her. She was living there with her aunt, and said I would like Santa Barbara. I knew I was not happy living at home with all the fighting. Family life did not mean much to me. It's not that I did not love my sisters and brothers. We all went our own way, and at times we did things together, but I felt no close unity except with my sister Annie. I was going with a man who was 10 years older than I, and he told me that he loved me, that he would put me on a pedestal, give me minks, anything I wanted, but that his mother would always be first in his life. I thought, "My God, if I can't be first, forget it." I had enough sense to realize it would not work out.

I had one aunt who told me I was crazy to let him go because he was Lebanese and "loaded." She said I would be foolish to leave Minneapolis, Minnesota, and move so far away from him. Even though I thought I was in love, I started to make plans to move, and once again my dad was furious. I remember one night when some relatives were at our house. They had all come to the conclusion that I wanted to be a loose woman, that was why I was moving to California.

One uncle said, "Why do you have to be so different than all your brothers and sisters? They all live at home."

Only two had moved out, my brother Charley and my sister Rose, because they got married; but five of us were still at home. I didn't try to defend myself or explain what I felt. In my mind, I thought, "Why are you all trying to put a guilt trip on me now? This has nothing to do with my welfare; it is all about control."

I kept my thoughts to myself because we were raised to respect our elders, and it was also the time when children were seen but not heard, and I knew better than to speak out against what they were telling me.

Several weeks before I was to leave for California by bus, I overheard my mother and father talking in the kitchen. My mother wanted to give me a surprise going-away party, just for the aunts and uncles and a few friends. But my dad was angry and said no. My mother gave the party anyway. I didn't want a party because I knew how

40

they all felt, but I didn't say anything because I wasn't supposed to know about it.

Years later I found out that it was my dear sister Annie who pressured my mother to give the party. Annie would always speak out if she felt something was not fair or right.

My family knew how to give a grand party and add joy in order to have a good time. The word around was that if you wanted to have the time of your life, get invited to my family's and relatives' parties. They were the best and had a flair to them that even I haven't experienced since. People wanted desperately to be invited, and many were, and they never failed to show up. My relatives loved making outsiders happy, and other people always thought we had one great, big, happy, loving family.

There were times when I was working at my Uncle Dave's nightclub, and all of the family were down in the basement in the party room, dancing, and Lebanese music was playing, and the people who were upstairs in the dining room eating dinner, strangers, wanted to know what was going on downstairs with all the gaiety, laughter, and music. They would go down to check it out and end up staying at the party with the family. Some people would leave their full wine bottles and almost full dinners to go down; and my dad, uncles, and aunts opened their arms to them. I often would go downstairs and ask them to come back upstairs to finish their dinners because we had customers waiting for the tables. They would say, "Clear the table. We don't care. Just give us the bill." They had a ball!

That same scene happened over and over again, and I felt that I must be lucky that so many people loved our family parties; and that made me feel special. I have many good memories of the parties, but I needed so much more, and I knew that I would not find it in Minneapolis.

When it was time for my party all the aunts and uncles came. It was obvious to me that none of them wanted to be there. It was like a funeral, and that bothered me for years. I remember how anxious they made me feel, and I wanted the party to end, and it only made me glad that I was leaving. As far as I was concerned they could all shove it.

Hopefully, by moving to California, even if it would only be for a few months, I might find some answers to help fill the void that I had within.

I bought my bus ticket and was scheduled to leave on a Sunday around three or four in the afternoon. I heard my parents talking the week before I was to leave that they would be going fishing the same weekend that I was leaving. They loved to fish, and they often planned the trips in advance. I felt a lump in my throat when I heard them making the plans. Surely they would be back before I was to leave. I knew how my dad felt about my leaving, but I couldn't believe they would not want to see me off and say good-bye on the actual day.

That morning, when the day arrived to leave, I asked my sister Annie if she thought that they would be back in time to say good-bye.

She said, "Oh, sure, honey, I'm sure they will be back."

But as I continued to pack items in my suitcase, I knew they would not be back before I left. My sister knew it, too.

Since we were very close, she always came to me to help her understand her problems, and I always had her to listen to my troubles. I sensed her sadness for me, and she knew that I was hurting. Annie could usually come up with something to fix a problem for me or take the pain away or make it less. This time there was nothing that she could do for me, and I knew it bothered her very much.

We were both very sensitive, and always living with so much chaos around us was as difficult for her as it was for me. The difference between us is that when the chaos would start I had to leave the room or house to get away, and she would always put herself right in the middle and try to help solve it, and it only made things worse for her and the situation. She always got into trouble trying to protect others.

Annie and some friends took me to the bus depot. I honestly don't remember who was there. I once again was knotted up inside with my "famous" sick stomach.

She had said so many loving words to me to try and ease the pain she knew I felt inside, but it only made me feel worse. When I got on the bus, I was crying, and I am sure she was too. I couldn't even look back at her to wave good-bye. I sat very tense in the seat, anxious for the bus to leave, and I really could not believe that my parents had not come back early to say good-bye.

I knew then I would never come back home to live with them. I felt they didn't love me after all; otherwise, they would have come home to see me off. Many thoughts came to my mind, waiting for the bus to leave. I felt so alone. I asked myself the question, "Are you doing this just for attention?" Not knowing what the road ahead of me would be like, I was scared to death. I was really searching hard for some answers, but inside I felt nothing but total chaos. An elderly man sat in the seat next to me, and I turned my head towards the small window of the bus so that he would not see me crying. The bus finally started to move, and I only hoped that my precious sister understood why I couldn't look back at her, as tears were running down my face.

I had left Minneapolis with only $35, so I was watching my money carefully. Whenever the bus stopped for us to eat, I would buy a small carton of milk and a candy bar. A young, hippie-type guy who sat about four rows ahead of me in the aisle seat opposite the side I was sitting on kept looking back at me. He scared me, and I was afraid that if I started to talk to anyone it might give him the idea that he could talk to me. I knew of no other way to protect myself, so I stayed away from all of the passengers whenever the bus stopped for us to eat.

Three days later the bus broke down in Victorville, California. The bus driver told us another bus would arrive in a few hours to pick us up. Most of the people that got off the bus had walked over to a small cafe that was open in order to get something to eat. I decided to also walk over and order something inexpensive. I stood in line with the rest of the passengers at the cafe. The seating was limited. The gentleman in front of me was talking to a lady, saying that we had no choice but to wait because this was a one-horse town with everything else closed up.

I eventually was seated in a small booth with an older lady who was almost through eating. I had hoped she would stay there with me, but she got up shortly after and left so someone else could sit down. The hippie guy came over and sat in her place. It upset me so much that I thought my insides fell out. I knew that he had pushed his way up to sit with me because he was near the end of the line and I was standing in the middle of the line. The waitress came over and handed each of us a menu. I was so knotted and scared inside, trying to deal with all the other feelings I had, and now this. He asked, "Can I buy you a hamburger?" I don't know how I managed, but I said, "No, thank you." I know that he was aware that I didn't eat much at the various stops.

The waitress came back, and I ordered a hamburger and milk. I should have got up and left the booth, but I was afraid of what he would think, and I felt the waitress would expect me to order something. I had hoped that he sensed my coldness and would get up and leave, but he didn't, and he ordered food.

He made small conversation, but I was not encouraging any of it. He told me that he had called some friends from Los Angeles, and they were coming down to pick him up. If I wanted, they could also give me a ride. I told him that I was meeting my family in Los Angeles and had no way of contacting them because they didn't live there, so I would just wait for the bus. I didn't want him to know that I was going to Santa Barbara.

When the waitress put my hamburger in front of me, I ate it very fast. Still shaking inside, I asked the waitress for my check, and when she handed it to me, he grabbed it, but I pulled it back from him, and nervously said, "Thank you. I'll pay for my own hamburger."

I got out of the booth, paid the cashier, and went back to the bus depot. A bus arrived a few hours later, but since it already had some people on it, about ten of us were not able to get on. I wanted to get on that bus so badly but, always wanting to do the right thing, I allowed others to go before me, and I was left behind.

We were told again that another bus was on its way to get us. The hippie was still waiting for his friends to come. It was now dark, and I just knew something terrible was going to happen to me. A while later his friends showed up in an older-type station wagon and he got in. He must have said something to them because I felt them all looking at me. I turned around and said, "God let them leave, please, please do not have him come over and ask me again. What if they force me into the car?" Terrible thoughts were going through my mind. I quickly walked over to be nearer the rest of the people that were also left behind.

After a few minutes the car finally drove off. I was so relieved. I stayed near the small group of people who were laughing and having a good time. The bus arrived around nine or so and it was empty. We all got on and went to the back of the bus. We sang songs; some told jokes, and everyone was so kind. It was a fun group that I enjoyed being a part of. I realized my sick feelings were gone.

When we arrived in Los Angeles, I had to find the right bus to get on in order to get to Santa Barbara. The bus depot was large and packed with people, and I had to wait an hour before my bus would leave. The sick feelings were back. When I finally arrived in Santa Barbara, it was around three or four in the morning. My friend Pat, her Aunt Eve, and Joe, a friend of hers, were waiting for me.

When we arrived at Eve's house, I was shown where I would be temporarily sleeping. I closed my eyes and thanked God for getting me there, and also for a bed that looked so comfortable. I was exhausted. It was August, 1964. The first day of the Santa Barbara Fiesta, a yearly event that continues for five days.

I slept until the afternoon, and when I woke up, no one was home as they had gone to work. I went into the kitchen to get something to drink. There was a note from Eve which said there was food prepared in the refrigerator, also some lamb chops that I should cook. There was also lots of love in the note! I cried. I had never felt such kindness from someone I hardly knew.

I ate, then I decided to go for a walk. I was awed by the beautiful nature around me. There were orange trees with oranges on them in the front yards of the homes in her area. Everything was so green and there were flowers everywhere. I felt this must be paradise. I was not sure if I should pick an orange off of a neighbor's tree, but I couldn't resist it. I grabbed one and continued on with my walk. My sick feelings were gone.

When I got back to the house, I started to unpack my suitcase. They had even emptied a few drawers of a dresser for me to put my clothes.

I then heard someone come in the front door. It was Eve. She said, "You must get dressed, honey. We have a party to go to." I was included in all of their plans, and Pat made sure I didn't miss any of the Fiesta activities which were being held around town. Eve and Joe were kinder than I could have ever imagined. It was obvious that Eve loved her niece, Pat, very much and that was one of the reasons that she and Joe were so kind to me.

I remember how safe I felt once I arrived in Santa Barbara and I thought to myself, "There must be a God." I left Minneapolis with so little money and everything, in spite of my deep concern, worked out. Eve, Joe, and Pat all came from the heart, expecting absolutely nothing in return. It made an impression that has never left me.

A few weeks later Pat and I found our own apartment. Eve loaned me money for the first month's rent. I was happy to be out of Eve's home. I was so grateful for all the kindness that she and Joe gave me, but it was hard for me to accept it because I wasn't used to it.

I found a job as a bookkeeper, and once again I lied. I told the man that interviewed me that I knew how to use a bookkeeping machine. I was put on a two week trial and I was unable to learn how to run that complicated machine. The girl who was training me became very frustrated after a week. I told her I had lied only because I was so desperate for a job. She was very nice and worked even harder to help me understand how to use the machine, but I still had no self-confidence. I was called into the manager's office for my two week review. I knew that would be my last day. I felt badly that I had lied, so I came right out and told him what I did and why. He actually said that he understood and then left the room. He came back with a check for two weeks of pay. I didn't have a penny left of my $35 and that money sure came in handy.

I decided to look for a waitress job. I knew if I could get into a good restaurant I could make good tips. I applied at the best restaurant in town. Eve knew the owner and she put in a good word for me. They hired me! Two weeks later I realized that I was not making good tips then discovered why. Another waitress, who had started a few weeks before I did, told me she was quitting because the hostess was giving all the good tippers to the older waitresses that worked there. I quit with her.

Pat told me that she was being transferred to another department at her work and said that I should apply for the job she would be leaving. I applied and was hired in their statistics department. Once again I knew that it was because Pat was a good worker and well liked, and THAT was the beginning of my finding my first real niche in life. I was happy! I even sent love to my parents in the letters that I wrote to them. I finally felt joy inside, and I knew that my life was now on an uphill climb.

Several months after taking the job, my brother John made plans to get married. I was very excited because he was marrying one of my best friends, Joanne, and she wanted me to come home and be in the wedding.

I didn't think I would be able to get any time off, but I went in and asked for one week and explained why. When my boss said yes, and told me that they would also give me an early paid vacation, I almost did a dance. This was confirmation that they were pleased with my work.

Shortly after I returned from the wedding, my boss asked if I would like to set up a small office for one of their subsidiaries. I said, "Yes!" I was ecstatic because that was more confirmation that they were pleased with my work, and it gave me a self-confidence that I have never lost.

I knew without a doubt that the uphill climb I was now on would take me down a good road in life.

EIGHT

LIFE IS GREAT

Thou art a part of a beautiful plan
Coming down from the Infinite mind.
Meticulous care hath been taken of thee
That the law might be gracious and kind.

So long as life holds thee, a child of esteem,
And cradles thee close to her breast,
There is nothing to fear or nothing to dread
As ye come to this haven of rest.

And then with a walk on some far away strand,
And behold the great beauties aglow
Sweet thoughts will be lifting the burdens away
As the blessings of healing doth flow.

Then, with all hurts in their rightful place,
Let their hatred and rancor depart,
And facing the light and looking with love
Life's the greatest, wherever thou art.

Reverend Edmund L. Foard

I met Mel (my husband) several months after I arrived in Santa Barbara, and we dated on and off for two years. During one of the off periods I read that he, along with 30 other teachers, had been chosen throughout the United States and would be spending a summer in Spain on a scholarship. He was a Spanish teacher.

My sick stomach feelings came back. I knew how I felt about Mel, but I didn't think the feelings were mutual because he never phoned and told me about the scholarship.

A month later I decided I would leave Santa Barbara and I gave two months' notice at my work. I phoned my mother and asked her if she would like to fly out to California and then go with me to Mexico for a short trip before I returned back to Minneapolis. I no longer felt that deep resentment towards her and my dad for not coming back from their fishing trip to say good-bye. I told her I would not be moving back home, that I would get my own apartment. She didn't seem very happy when I told her that. She said that I should not plan too far ahead, and that she was happy I was coming home.

In order to pay all the expenses of the trip for my mother and me, I took a part-time evening job for two months. I had taken conversational Spanish a few years earlier and decided to take a quick brush-up course before going on the trip. My friend, Sherrie, decided to join me as she wanted to learn Spanish, too.

The first night that classes started, we were shocked to see that Mel was the teacher.

Sherrie was unable to go the following week so I ended up going alone. I arrived a half-hour early because I wanted to make sure I sat in the back of the room. Mel arrived a few minutes later. He walked back to where I was and said hi.

I said, "I understand you were in Spain over the summer. Did you enjoy the trip?"

He said, "Oh, yes, I took many pictures that I had made into slides. I must show them to you sometime."

We became engaged a few months later, and then married the following June, 1967.

In our first year of marriage, Mel was aware that I was being pulled in many directions by my friends. I always put everyone else's concerns ahead of mine. Mel said I should not allow people to continuously pull at me all the time. I knew he was right. I started to put myself first, and for the first time in my life I knew that I didn't have to respond to everyone that wanted my time or energy. I loved my new freedom.

Mel was Catholic, but he didn't feel the need to go to mass on Sunday. I decided that if he didn't feel it was necessary, then I would stay home, too. But the guilt never left me, and instead of going to church by myself, I tried to get him to go with me by telling him how guilty I felt.

He said, "I don't feel the need to go. If you want to go, that's fine with me."

I thought, "Why should I feel guilty if he doesn't?" I didn't go for several months, but the guilt feelings got so bad that I decided to go one Sunday.

I remember very clearly how I felt that day sitting in the church. NOTHING! I felt absolutely nothing. I walked out of the church knowing I would not attend another mass because of guilt feelings. I still had a nagging feeling within me, but that was my wanting to know about God and how I could find Him. I had no answers to help me, so I just let go of it and decided to concentrate on my happiness with Mel. I decided that I would have to live with my guilt feelings whenever they popped up.

In our fourth year of marriage, Mel and I spent our summer vacation in Minneapolis with my mom, dad, and family. My mom and dad now had a small home on a lake. My sister and her family lived around the lake from them. My brother and his family also lived near by, and they owned the night club across the road from my parents' house. My whole family managed to be there during our stay, and we had a grand summer of fun.

Two weeks after we returned to Santa Barbara my dad had a major heart attack. The doctors didn't think he would pull through. I made arrangements to fly back and spend time with my mother at the lake and to help her through this as did other family members, and my dad pulled through.

Two weeks later, my sister Annie was driving me back to Minneapolis to catch my plane, and we stopped at the hospital to visit my dad and say good-bye. He had just come out of intensive care. I told him, "When you get out of here, why don't you and mom come to Santa Barbara? You can fly out, and that way it will not be a lot of driving."

My parents had visited us once before in Santa Barbara. They drove out with some friends. My dad was scared to death of flying. In fact, he was afraid of dying as well. Those were the two fears he often expressed.

When he responded, "We might just do that," I was surprised because he said on his last trip, "You will never get me in an airplane. If we come again we will drive."

It was September when I returned to Santa Barbara. My parents flew out after the holidays that year and spent six weeks with us. When we arrived at the Los Angeles Airport to pick them up, I was anxious to tell them that I thought I was pregnant and that I would be going to the doctor that week to find out for sure. My dad and mom were excited for me, but my dad showed it so much more, and he immediately started to tease me. Several days later I realized that my dad was a changed man, and I actually enjoyed having him around.

In fact, I noticed that my mother was much calmer than I had ever seen her. My dad had a more loving nature towards her and life. It was amazing. Here was a man I knew well, but he was now very different. He had changed a lot. One night when we were visiting, I asked him about his heart attack. He said that the doctors told him he had stopped breathing for at least five minutes. They had worked so hard trying to get him breathing again by pressing on his chest that they broke all of his ribs.

He told me that he was out of his body, going through a tunnel, and when he got to the end of the tunnel, it was a beautiful, bright light. Then he reached a Man he thought was God; and that the Man told him it was not his time yet, that he had to go back to earth for one more year and make amends with his family. He said the Man told him he would return at the end of a year.

Well, I had read and heard of other stories like that, so I was not surprised to hear him tell me what he did. I asked him how he felt while he was out of the body and going through the tunnel. He said, "Very peaceful. I didn't want to come back. I no longer am afraid to die. I wasn't afraid to fly out here either."

My dad was a total delight to be with on this visit. When I came home from the doctor, he was so anxious to know if I was pregnant or not. I told him the doctor said I would know in a few days. When I got the news that I was, he was ecstatic.

We had such a good time while my parents were here that I hated to see them leave, and I wished my dad had been like that when I was growing up. He made me promise that I would send on the pictures of the baby as soon as possible. I was expecting sometime in September, and I promised him I would.

Catana was born on September 20, 1972. My dad phoned me weekly for five or six weeks asking if I had sent the pictures of her yet. I felt so bad each time he called; I told him that Mel had taken pictures from the day she was born, and I explained that we just had our hands full because Catana was so colicky. We finally had the films developed, and the next time dad called and asked about the pictures, he was happy they were finally in the mail. When he received them, he phoned and thanked us and said that she was beautiful. He passed one week after he received the pictures.

I now know that my dad held on until he saw the pictures of Catana, then he went on to his next life. That is why he phoned me weekly. He said he would leave us in one year. He passed one year and two months after his heart attack and his out of body experience.

My mother came out the following year with her friend Helen, to visit. We called Helen "aunt" as a sign of respect. Mom seemed happier than I had ever seen her. I felt sure it was because she had no one but herself to look after and to answer to.

After Mom's visit with us she returned to Minneapolis. She then had her breast removed for cancer. She recovered and continued to visit us over the years with her friend Helen.

Armando was born two years after dad passed. Mel and I were very happy. I still did not go to church, and whenever the guilt would hit me I managed to set it aside.

NINE

ARISE

The veil is rent asunder.
The might of ages yield
Forcing wide the door of reason.
And life's handy-work revealed.

In the all of all created,
Not one surpass the Soul.
It had witnessed life's beginning,
And have watched the ages roll.

The wonder and the beauty
Fill full thine eager eyes,
And changes doubt to knowledge
That the Soul shall surely rise.

Rise up, ye loved of Nature,
Above all pain and strife.
Step forth and claim they kingdom.
Thou indestructible of life.

For Mr. Jackson
Tucson, Arizona

Reverend Edmund L. Foard

Mel and I decided to put the children in a private, Catholic school. It was, I know, because of my guilt feelings. I had hoped that they might get from a religious school that was connected to a church what I had not.

I guess I was asking for a miracle because they were living with two parents who never went to church on Sunday. When Catana was in the fourth grade, she asked me why we did not go to church on Sunday.

I said, "Honey, you don't have to go to church to be a good person. Mom and dad have you and Armando in a religious school because we feel at this time it is the best for you. If you want to start going to church on Sunday, we will take you and Armando, and we will all go together."

They wanted no part of church. I realized they were very young and were following our pattern. I remember talking to Mel about it, and the decision was that if they pushed it, that meant that they really wanted to go, and we would then take them.

I was almost 42 at the time and had been having the recurring dream of being in the library reading books about God. I followed through with the dreams as I explained in the article in the first part of the book, "Feed Catholic Spiritual Hunger," and I realized that I had the God power within me! It was not religion. That is when my guilt feelings left me.

A neighbor girl had invited Catana and Armando to go to her church and Sunday School with her. They again asked why we didn't go to church since their friend did.

I told them that their friend and her family went to church because it felt right to them. It did not feel right for dad and me. I then sat them down and went into a lecture as to how I felt and why I felt like I did, and the reason we are here on earth, and what we had to do. I can share what I told them almost word for word because afterwards I was shocked. The answer I gave them, I had never seriously thought about. It just came out. So I immediately typed it to save it.

I told them it was not necessary to go to church. What was necessary was to go through life being kind to others, loving, caring, and sharing: to reach out to others whenever we could, to have compassion for all. That not everyone has a plate overflowing like they did, and that we should help others to fill up their plates. I told them, before judging others to put yourselves in the other person's place, to always be honest. Many people go to church thinking that because they do, all the wrongs they do during the week will be forgiven by God.

I said that our family had a lot of love and that we must share it with others. That it is in giving that we receive, and many times we receive back what we give in the heart with good feelings. I also told them that time will always be here. Our lives are short. That no matter what you do in life, give it your best.

At that time, I did not know where all those words came from. I could not believe what was coming out of my mouth. When I re-read what I typed, I realized that what I had told them is the way we were living our lives each day. I must share with you that when I got through telling my children what I did, they both said that I would make a good preacher, and we had a good laugh.

It was at this time that we also decided to take the children out of Catholic school and put them into a public school. We had good reason for taking them out, but the research that I was doing to help me find God helped us to make that decision without thinking twice about it. It was the best decision we ever made. They were now free to think for themselves and not have a religion thrown at them as it was at me. Once out of Catholic school, they no longer asked about going to church. They, on many occasions, said how happy they were to be in the public school system and out of the private school and not have to go through all the religious rituals that were forced upon them.

In spite of the happiness I had with my family and no more guilt feelings, I started to feel resentment towards my parents for not being there for me when I was growing up, the way Mel and I were for our children. I was comparing what I received from my parents to what we were giving our children.

When we planned to have a family, we both said that we would be there in every way for our children. Those were words. We had no idea what was involved in being good parents. We both thought we could have a family and still do the many things we wanted to accomplish in life. That was not to be because as soon as Catana came along, we realized we couldn't be good parents and still do all the things that we wanted to do. We ended the business we started because the stress of keeping it going and being there for the children was impossible. Ending the business was a good decision for us, and we have never had any regrets. We both now know that there is no harder job in the world than raising children if you want to do it right. We made our children the top priority of our lives and left absolutely no stone unturned in raising them. We threw nothing to the wind, and God did put some pretty high mountains in front of us to climb. We climbed every one of them feeling that, if we did not get to the top to see what was waiting for us on the other side, we might be on the losing end of life, and on the other side we always found the answers we were looking for.

I recall that when I was around 14 years old, I would often go upstairs into my brother John's room to read because it was such a cheerful room, and he always kept it neat. One day I fell asleep as I lay across his bed reading. When I woke up, I was facing a window that looked out to the top of the trees in our backyard.

I felt so depressed seeing those trees that I wanted to cry. I got up and left that room immediately, and I never went back in there to read again. Trees have often given me a depressed feeling, and I love nature, so it always puzzled me as to why. I always had questions in my mind, about "Who am I? Why am I here? What is this life all about?" Today I know that when I got a depressed feeling from looking at a tree, it was because they reminded me of life. They live for many years, and I was looking for answers to life and a reason for living.

Years later when I shared my feelings about the trees with my sister Annie, she said she often felt as I did, wondering why she was here. She said it wasn't caused by trees, just living life made her feel like that.

I, also, for years had the same dream over and over again, beginning when I was a teenager. Back then, I would have it at least once a week, and as I got older, more often. By the time I was 38 years old, I was having it 3 to 4 times a week. It bothered me so much. I tried to figure out why it kept repeating itself. At times I dreaded going to bed at night because if I had the dream, it would cause me such anxiety in the morning, and I hated having to deal with the emotions it stirred within me.

In the dream I was always in school, running up and down the halls frantically trying to find my room. The school bell would ring, and I would feel so lost; then I would be running by classes, looking in and seeing all the kids in their seats, and I felt totally and completely overcome with fear of being lost. I would wake up with the dream fresh in my mind, and I thought I would go crazy with the feelings I had in the dream. I came to the conclusion that I was having the dreams over and over because I never did well in school.

The reason I shared the tree and the dream story with you is that once I found God and my power within, trees no longer depressed me and the dreams stopped. I was totally lost because I didn't know how to find God. Once I did find Him, life had meaning for me. That is without a doubt in my mind the reason for trees depressing me and being lost in school in my dreams.

I continued to read book after book. I read every free minute that I had. I also started to meditate. I felt myself becoming patient with other people and life in general. I found a peace within that even surprised me. My family and friends also noticed a change in me.

Before I started to meditate, I would plan my day, and then run around in a tizzy, hurrying to get one thing done in order to get to the next thing I wanted to do. I would leave the house to do errands, and I would only be halfway through with the errands, and my busy mind would be back home already planning the next chore there. I hated being like that, but I couldn't stop it. But now that was behind me, I found myself slowing down and enjoying each thing I was doing. When I got in the car to do errands, I would actually enjoy the view along the way. Life no longer was passing me by.

TEN

YOU LIVE

No distance is, no space between,
No chasms to be spanned.
For all there is, is all there is,
In the heart of summer land.

It's nice to know that love transcends
Through all the hurts we share.
For bonds as these will last always
Sustained in silent prayer.

We lock you dear within our hearts,
The sweetest Soul of all
Enfolded deep within the deep
'Til the stars of night shall fall.

You are forever life, you gave
Unending love so dear.
You gave to all, the all you had,
So you are forever here.

                    Reverend Edmund L. Foard

When I turned 46, my mom was having another bout with cancer. My sisters did not think that she would live through the holidays, so we took the children out of school and went back for a two week period in order to spend Thanksgiving and some special time with her. I knew mom would be happy to have all of her children around her during the Thanksgiving holiday.

She had gone through hell before we got there, and the only thing that kept her going was all the love she was receiving from my sisters and brothers, relatives and friends. She knew she was loved, and they encouraged her in every way.

Mom was tired while we were there, and I know she did not feel like exerting herself or having a lot of company around, but she showed joy in having the family all together at the same time. We spent as much time as possible with her.

My sister Rose, with whom we stayed, had a home on the lake, so the kids were able to ice fish and ice skate. We all enjoyed the beautiful scenes of wintertime in the country during our visit.

The day before we were to leave to come back to Santa Barbara, I convinced my mom to let Mel and me take her to one of her favorite places for lunch. I had so much that I wanted to tell her, but she had no energy and after eating only a small part of her lunch, we took her back home. I knew then that I would have to call her from Santa Barbara in order to tell her all that I held in my heart. It was important to me that she knew how I felt about many things.

The next day as we stopped by her house to spend some more time with her before we left to catch our plane, I realized that this would be the last time I would see her. As I sat across from her in the living room, I was trying to absorb so much of her. My heart felt heavy. She no longer was feeling any emotions, and that did make it a little easier for me. When I hugged her good-bye, I felt such a sadness, but I managed not to cry. I went back to the words she told Mel and me at lunch, "I am tired and have no more fight left in me."

I know that Mel, Catana, and Armando had their own sad thoughts, and when they hugged her, she was so mechanical, and very distant. When I later shared that thought with Mel on the plane, he said, "Honey, how else could she be. She was already closed down." I knew he was right.

While we were in Minneapolis, I had a problem with my equilibrium and ears, which caused me to be dizzy on and off for days. I felt it was caused by the stress of knowing that I would not be there to help the family take care of mom. She would be staying at home until she passed. Also it was not easy for me to accept that the next trip we made back to Minneapolis she would not be there.

We arrived in Santa Barbara late Saturday evening; I phoned my mother the next day. I told her all the things that were on my mind, and I asked her to listen very carefully to what I was telling her because it was important to me that she knew exactly how I felt. I told her that all the family had a discussion and we all loved her so much, and that she needed to know that.

I told her that I knew her life had not been easy for her because of such a large family and daddy. I tried to tell her all the things that I felt she needed to hear. I said, "I don't know what anyone else might have told you, mom, but since you will soon be passing to your next life, I didn't want you to leave without knowing how I felt, and how much I love you."

I asked her to check on a baby that we had lost, Talya Ann, when she got to the other side, also that Catana and Armando wanted her to check on our cat, Cottonbell, that we had to put to sleep because of leukemia. I told her to give daddy and all the family in spirit our love.

And she said, "Honey, I will do all that."

It was easy for me to ask her to check on the baby we lost, and the cat, and to give our love to dad because of my dad's experience, and also from all that I had read in my search. After life here, I knew there was more and knowing that made it easy for me.

I also told her I loved dad, but didn't feel he was there for me like she was. I said, "Mom, I don't want to hurt your feelings by telling you that, but I want you to know my true feelings."

She said, "Honey, I understand." She thanked me for calling, and as I hung up the phone after saying good-bye, I felt good because she now knew how I felt, and I had a good cry.

My mom passed on February 26, 1987. I phoned her every night until she passed. In one of our conversations I told her that I was thinking about accepting a job that I wanted very much, but that I knew she would soon be passing and I would probably pass it up because I might not be able to take time off to come home for the funeral. She told me to take the job, that the family being together for Thanksgiving had given her plenty of joy. My mom passed several days before I was to start working.

I worked one day, and quit! I realized soon after I sat at my desk and the boss came in with some directions for me that he was a very negative and controlling person; and I learned from another lady in the office that I was replacing someone who had left for that very reason. I had been around the block a few times now in life and in no way was I going to let a job that was connected to any type of negativity or control add stress to my life.

I phoned the office the following morning and I told the lady that had hired me why I would not be coming back and she said, "I understand completely."

ELEVEN

LIGHTED CANDLE

I have lighted a candle
Against the dark night
For I worry of pitfalls
In the absence of light.

I lift up my taper
That its sheltering ray
Might push back the boundary
And mock the bright day.

O Soul of the beautiful
Teach me to see
The lesson I'm missing
As you planned it for me.

I shall let the hurts go,
And in the dusk heal the scars.
Now my candle is out,
And the sky's full of stars.

Reverend Edmund L. Foard

When my daughter Catana, was 13, she came home from school one day and said that some of the kids were talking about reincarnation. She asked me what I thought about it. I had read about reincarnation, but my goal was to find out about God, so I couldn't give her much of an opinion. I said having other lives was possible, and that the thought of reincarnation didn't bother me. She said, "Mom, I want to live on in spirit with the family I now have, and I don't want to come back into another family."

She had as many questions about reincarnation as I did, and I told her that we should just keep an open mind, and eventually we would find the answers that felt right to us. We both wondered that if there is reincarnation how could God allow the terrible abuse of young children that we hear about all the time in the news. That bothered both of us.

Several months later we had to put our cat Cottonbell to sleep. The day we put her to sleep was a hard one for all of us. We decided to bury her beneath a large, beautiful oak tree on our property, and the children went with Mel to bury her. That same evening I had just finished meditating in my bedroom when Catana came into my room looking very sad. We talked for a short while, and then she asked me if I believed that reincarnation also applied to animals. I told her I didn't know.

I received a phone call, and when I got through with the call, I noticed that Catana was out on the deck looking down at the oak tree. She was crying. I went out and put my arm around her shoulder and said, "Honey, I know it's hard. We all loved her so much." Catana was two years old when we lost a baby, Talya Ann. I said to Catana, "Tayla Ann will now look after Cottonbell for you and Armando."

She asked, "Mom, do you really believe that?"

I said, "Honey, I know from all my reading and Grandpa George's experience that we live on, and I don't for one minute doubt that we will all be together again, even with the other animals that we have had and have died, and now with Cottonbell. When you love as much as we loved Talya Ann and even Cottonbell, the strings are never broken.

Remember our souls live on, and animals are God's creatures. I am sure they live on."

We spent several hours on the deck that night. There was a warm, beautiful breeze, and the city looked like a jewel box. I knew that Catana's tears would last for several days, but I also knew that by telling her that Talya Ann would look after Cottonbell for her, she would eventually accept it.

When I went into the house, I went into Armando's room, and he was reading. I had earlier invited him to join us on the deck, but he said he would rather stay in his room. His way of handling the loss of Cottonbell was to keep busy and talk to no one. I asked him if he wanted to talk about Cottonbell, and his eyes filled with tears as he said, "I'll miss her."

I hugged him and said, "I know, honey, we all will." I asked him if he had any thoughts he would like to share, and we could talk about them.

He said, "No, mom, but I am glad we have some pictures of her."

I said, "Honey, we have some good pictures of her. I will get them out and see that you and Catana each have your own copies."

He said, "Mom, can I go back to my reading?"

I gave him a hug and said, "Okay, if you want to talk some more I'll be in the other room." I knew that Armando had many thoughts, but it was not his personality to openly share them, and he dealt with situations differently than Catana. As I walked out of his room, I thought to myself, I never realized that a person could love an animal as much as we all loved Cottonbell. And I knew that I would do more research on reincarnation because Catana wanted more answers. She is like me in that she never stops thinking about something until she has turned every stone over to satisfy her mind.

Armando and I went out to dinner the following Friday evening. Mel had left for a hunting trip and Catana was staying over at a friend's house. After dinner, Armando wanted to go to the book store to buy a few books. When we got to the book store, I told him I would be a few aisles over from him in the reincarnation section and that, after he selected his books, to come and get me.

As I turned to walk away, a very light, confused feeling came over me. I can't explain it any other way. When I finally got focused and the feeling left me, I stood there for a few moments with a feeling of now being lost in time. I turned my head to my left and I realized I had not walked to the reincarnation section as I was now facing a long row of dream books. I had passed the reincarnation section without even realizing that I had moved from where Armando was.

It took a few moments to clear my head, and as I looked at the dream books, I said to myself, "Oh, yeah, I've been wanting to read more about dreams." All of a sudden it was as if someone was guiding my hand and pulled out a book for me. I know this sounds strange, and I am only trying to explain the weird experience that I had. I looked at the dream book in my hand, and it was Betty Bethards' Dream Book Symbols for Self-Understanding.

I glanced through the book , and put it under my left arm as I checked out other books on dreams, but none of them interested me. I again looked at the book I was holding under my arm and decided to come back for it because I knew I only had enough money with me to pay for the two books Armando would be getting. But I was not able to put that book back on the shelf. It was such a strange feeling. I was looking through it when Armando came over and asked, "Mom, can I get three books instead of two?"

I said, "Honey, I only have enough money on me for two and I don't want to use a credit card." He left to put one book back, and I said, "Armando, that's okay. I'll charge it because I want to get this book too."

On the way home I thought about the strange feeling that I had in the store and also of passing the reincarnation section without knowing it. Little did I know what impact the dream book would have on my life.

TWELVE

THE RELIGION OF THE HEART

A quote from the Bible: "Be still and know that I am God" means that the Kingdom of God is within us. When Jesus walked the earth, He taught that God is Spirit and that He is in each one of us. He came to show us the way to God.

Jesus believed in religion, but said that religion was a way of living, and He taught that the religion of the heart, pure and kind, giving with compassion and charity for all, was the only religion to follow. He said that the Kingdom of God within us is the religion of the heart because it was without preachers, priests or rabbis. He wanted us to know that we had "Gold" within us - "God."

In this chapter, you will read more of the experiences that I have had that have helped me realize that I am in charge of my life's journey and no longer giving my power to anyone. Also in this chapter and the next chapter I explain why I feel it is important to take back our power from organized religion and our politicians who have fenced us in with all of their control and self-serving ways.

I hope that both chapters will open people's eyes, enabling them (1) to see the mess we have created in the world by giving our power away, and (2) to take the necessary steps to clean it up for the benefit of our children and future generations in order for all people to live as free people. If we don't take our power back now, our precious children will end up on the short end of life without ever realizing what happened and why, as we continue to slide downhill.

If what you read in both chapters, which you might find a little choppy as I try to get my point across, feels right to you, then I have touched a chord of truth within you that you can relate to. If it does not feel right to you, maybe you will get some benefit from it that will help you to find your own answers. The one point that I feel adamant about is that you must never give away your Divine power within you to anyone. It is for you to use to guide yourself along your journey in life.

Author, lecturer and Minister Eric Butterworth wrote back in the 1960's that man, for hundreds of years, has been on an eternal quest for truth and that the Divinity in man has been the best kept secret of the ages. He said that man has looked everywhere in vain for God, but he has failed to look within himself and that has been the greatest sin of mankind. The soul, he said, has been starved and kept in darkness and in spiritual ignorance.

Organized religions are responsible for starving the soul and keeping mankind in darkness and spiritual igno- rance. Thirty years after Mr. Butterworth wrote the above, people are finally waking up and walking away from organized religion. Mr. Butterworth wrote that God is not out there somewhere in space as many religions teach. God is the light within us, a living presence always with us. God, he wrote, is our answer to love, health, wisdom, peace, happiness and success, healing and guidance, and that all things are possible with God. He said that when Jesus spoke of Heaven, He was talking about the Divine in you.

If we tune into the God within us, He will guide us in all that we do; and His light and love, which is the same as intuition, will help us ride the high waves of life.

A quote: "You must never follow another person. If they are not in touch with God and his laws, but deal with worldly beliefs, they appear to be intelligent and wise but they are false leaders because the light they see is from the world and not from God." Many people blindly worship and have great admiration for priests, preachers, and rabbis because there is a common belief that they are accomplished, intelligent, and have the vision of truth. For years the simple in faith and heart have been easily converted because they accept what is thrown at them and do not question; therefore, their minds are kept in darkness.

The following three points were reported in the news media the latter part of 1996, and it has nothing to do with God or truth. It's just another way to control the people and keep them fenced in.

1. Cardinal John O'Connor, from St. Patrick's Cathedral in New York, told the church members that Adam and Eve may have been created in "some other form" than human and that is was possible that the first living creature was a "lower animal." Pope John Paul II agreed, saying that it is possible and that the theories of evolution are sound as long as the people accept that creation was God's work.

2. A church in Virginia passes out green play money after the services, and four people each Sunday can win $10 to $100 if the pastor's initials are on the back of the play money. The service lasts for two hours and only those who stay for the complete service can win.

3. In January, 1997, I read an article that 5,000 evangelical broadcasters, programmers, and vendors were assembling at a convention center in Anaheim, California, to study the internet as the next missionary frontier.

Preaching is a big business, and they pay a lot of money to be on TV, and now the Internet? Heaven does not consist of going to church and being preached to, as many believe. God is the fountain of life for everyone and He is within; and those who have faith, believe, acknowledge and worship God, and believe His laws of love, have the church within them. Heaven within is when we live God's laws of love and give charity and kindness to all people. The church and heaven are within man and not outside of him. God's light can only enter into our minds if we seek and desire truth, for truth is what attracts God's light. Knowledge is light; and knowledge, truth and wisdom of God is spiritual food for our soul. Man has free choice and will, and it is up to us to seek truth and knowledge so that we are not fenced in.

Elbert Hubbard, an American author, wrote, "Be yourself, and think for yourself, and while your conclusions may not be infallible, they will be nearer right than the conclusions forced upon you by those who have a personal interest in keeping you in ignorance."

I look at organized religion as huge financial institutions that have been very successful by presenting a package of salvation that has convinced many people to give them their power. It obviously has been successful because millions of people have followed them.

However, I believe the tide is finally turning and there is a spiritual awakening because people are finally tuning in. They are not only looking and searching for answers that organized religion cannot give them, but they are also looking for the answers as to why our society is so rampant with crime, drugs, and all the negativity we must deal with daily. People want answers!

A friend sent me the following quote, "Going to church does not put you in touch with God any more than going into a garage makes you an automobile." Religious super powers cannot lead us to heaven or to the bliss of happiness. Our destiny remains in the hands of God. You don't work your way through religion to God unless it is the religion of the heart that Jesus preached while He walked the earth. God is in each one of us, and He has given each of us our own power within to lead and guide ourself and to be our own savior.

He didn't put us on earth and say to give your power to someone else so that they can lead and guide you. He didn't say that your power is limited or that you need an agent or a middleman in order to communicate with him. The "Our Father" prayer has the words..."Thy Kingdom come, thy will be done on earth as it is in heaven." It doesn't say, "Thy Kingdom come, Thy will be done on earth as it is in heaven through organized religion." Faith in God is all you need for His power to work through you. Once people in the world realize that, and that God is within them, they no longer will look for God in organized religion because they will know that all they have to do is to look within themselves.

I have friends who are into organized religion, and we totally disagree with each other. I have asked them what religion means to them, and several friends have given me the same answer, "a bond between man and God." Then I asked, "If it is a bond between man and God why do you need an agent or a middleman to talk to or to be in touch with God, since that is what a priest, rabbi or a minister represents?" They were not able to answer my question.

It is obvious to me that some people find comfort in organized religion. Many I know follow a certain religion because their parents and grandparents did, and they feel that it is the way to God. To each his own, but why would anyone not want to use their own God given power within to lead and guide themselves? Giving your power away handicaps you. I have learned to use my invisible power within and I listen to that little voice (intuition) that guides me in all that I do. I have learned to trust it! It allows me to be a free spirit and to ride the high waves of life.

The news media had several reports in 1996 saying that recent research shows that people are walking away from organized religion. The pews of the churches are emptying because organized religion has failed to answer life's deeper questions for them. People are tired of hearing about the damnation of hell and the promise of salvation. They want simple answers.

Organized religion is well aware of what is happening, and they are now cooperating with each other and coming together to tell the world that all religions stand for the same message, that it no longer matters what religion you choose to belong to. To that, I say hogwash! I believe this is happening because they see very clearly the writing on the wall, and it is a desperate ploy to keep organized religion alive. They don't want to have people think for themselves or to lose control of them because that means they would then lose millions and millions of dollars every year.

The Catholic Archdiocese has paid millions of dollars to families whose children were sexually abused by priests, and God only knows how much more was spent in legal fees and getting help for the priests that abused our innocent children. Where do you think all the money that they paid out came from? From the parishioners! The Archdiocese has also been very skillful in keeping the abuse of children a secret for years. That is sick and criminal! Many of the children that have been abused are now pointing their finger at their abuser, and that is the reason they no longer can hide it.

What about the huge amounts of money that have been embezzled by some church clergy over the years, and I cannot fail to mention that the Los Angeles Archdiocese is currently spending 45 to 50 million or more to build a new cathedral.

On 5-24-96, the Los Angeles Times published an article, "Building a Bridge to the Heavens." In the article Jeff Dietrich, a Catholic worker in a soup kitchen on skid row, was quoted. He said, "The 45 million should go to social concerns first, and it is scandalous to build a new cathedral in the midst of the most impoverished area of downtown Los Angeles." I believe it is scandalous and a waste of money to build a cathedral anywhere when we have so many less fortunate people in the world who are in desperate need of a

72

helping hand. Monsignor Terry Fleming, who is the rector and archdiocese vice-chancellor of the old cathedral, St. Vibiana, said that, "Jeff Dietrich ignores the archdiocese's extensive good work at schools, hospitals, and charities. We educate people. We help the poor. We take care of all needs of society. We have a need, too, for a new cathedral."

Cardinal Mahony has told the news media that the cathedral should have something there that calls to his inner spirit. What he doesn't want is for people to walk by and say: "Gee that's an interesting building, I wonder why it is?" He also has decided to move to another area to build the cathedral due to the continuing legal fight with the preservationists, saying any more delay would shatter his dream of dedicating a new $50 million dollar cathedral in the year 2000.

Also, when he was asked about the protesters that want the money to be used for social concerns first, he said that he "would invite them to sing inside the new cathedral." It was reported in the news media that the comment was made in a joking manner. Joking or not, what a sad comment for him to make about the poor when many are without the basic necessities of life, a house to live in and food to eat. It is not a joke!

Robert Nathan wrote the novel The Bishop's Wife, and in 1947 Samuel Goldwyn made it into a movie which was nominated for five Academy Awards. It's a wonderful holiday movie that depicts the Christmas season, starring Cary Grant, who plays Dudley, the Angel; David Niven, who plays Henry, the Bishop; and Loretta Young, who plays Julia, the Bishop's wife. Henry is trying to raise millions of dollars from the wealthy people in the community and especially from Mrs. Hamilton, who has a very controlling nature about her and has status within the church and the community. However, Mrs. Hamilton has her own ideas about the cathedral, and Henry does not like her control.

After he meets with her in his home and she leaves, he goes into his office as he tries to sort his thoughts out and he asks God for some guidance. God sends Dudley to give him guidance because Henry has lost touch with the common people and those he loves as he deals with only the wealthy in order to get the cathedral built. Julia, as well as the characters in the movie, are charmed by Dudley, and this upsets Henry, but he is too busy with meetings trying to raise the money for the cathedral to do anything about it, and he feels that he is losing his family.

In the film, Dudley asks the Bishop why build a cathedral, reminding him that these are lean years for the world with so many people needing food and shelter. That one big roof (meaning the cathedral) could make many small roofs. I suggest that Cardinal Mahony and Monsignor Terry Fleming, as well as other clergy, rent the movie. It applies more today than it did in 1947, and it has a grand ending!

Cardinal Mahony and Monsignor Fleming's comments infer that they choose the cathedral over helping the poor. $50 million dollars could go a long way to help the less fortunate. Before the welfare reform was passed, Cardinal Mahony attacked the political parties in Washington because they were talking about reforming the welfare system and saying that many services would have to be cut. He said that they have lost touch with the most vulnerable and the poorest members of our society. He says the only reason he has spoken out and has become vocal is because of his great concern to help the poor. Cardinal Mahoney and Monsignor Fleming expose their insincerity as they talk out of both sides of their mouth. The welfare reform has now passed and they should put their money where their mouth is. God only knows that the poor are going to need a lot more help, especially children and the elderly.

It is also obvious that the extensive good works that Monsignor Fleming speaks of are not extensive enough. Monsignor Fleming and Cardinal Mahony's comments come across as immature and self-serving. They show that the Catholic religion is not sincere in making the poor a top priority. They throw out a lot of rhetoric hoping that the people will buy it and believe that they have their act together.

Perhaps Cardinal Mahony should take this current legal fight as a sign from God not to build this beautiful building just because he wants something to call to his inner spirit and because he doesn't want to shatter his dream to dedicate a new cathedral in the year 2000. It goes against everything Jesus preached while He walked the earth. Jesus felt the priesthood was corrupt and did nothing for the people. He preached the religion of the heart, pure and kind, giving with compassion, forgiveness, and charity for all. Other religions angered Him because they were a control of power over the people and did not come from the heart. He said the kingdom of God within us is the religion of the heart because it was without forms, temples (cathedrals) and without priests. He denounced the priests and the Pharisees. The luxury of power in any form upset Him very much.

Cardinal Mahony and Monsignor Fleming speak for the Catholic Church. They, and the Catholic Church, need to do some deep soul searching because they say one thing and then do another. They expose themselves and show that they do not come from the heart as they want the people to believe, but from desperation to keep their church doors open and fill the pews of the church as well as their egos. How stupid do they think people are?

It has to be obvious to all who follow the news that people are leaving the Catholic Religion in droves, and it is a great concern to the Catholic hierarchy. In their desperation, they have chosen to have the Pope work very hard, in spite of him not being that well, by sending him to countries where they never bothered to go before, and preach to all the poor people who are looking for a better life and are desperately searching for God's light and some answer to their poverty. What a sad and desperate picture the Catholic Religion presents to the world.

Hopefully the poor people will realize that they are not the top priority that the church claims they are and would like them to believe. Unfortunately, many will follow and be fenced in and controlled by the Catholic Church because they are so desperate for help that they will follow anyone that gives it to them, even if it fences them in. There is an old saying, "If you put a fence around people you get sheep." That's exactly what the church wants. Helping people by fencing them in with an agenda is not charity.

English author Leigh Hung wrote in the 1800's, "The same people who can deny others everything are famous for refusing themselves nothing." Not only does the Catholic hierarchy live well, but the hierarchy of most organized religions lives well. But they are not as visible in the poor countries like the Pope is, trying to convince the people that they are the religion to follow. The poor people have been kept in the dark for too long. They must free themselves from organized religion in order to become free people. Unless they realize that they have the power within to lead and guide themselves, they will never have a better life.

Ann Quinlan, a New York Times reporter, wrote an article in 1994. In it she reported that the American Catholic Bishops announced their new campaign against abortion, and she wrote that they are prepared to spend as much as 5 million dollars to convince the people that it is a mortal sin. Spending millions of dollars to tell people what is and isn't a sin is total control by the Catholic Religion. God has given each of us free choice and free will, and it is up to us to make our own decisions. He does not sit in judgement of us.

Ann Quinlan asked a question in her article that I also ask. "Can you imagine how many less fortunate families could be helped with all the money put into their campaign against abortion?" When I think of the millions paid out for the sexual abuse, the millions embezzled, and $50 million for the Cathedral, what a waste! It makes my blood boil!

The Pope travels all over the world promoting a religion that is controlling and closed-minded. I realize that he has no choice because it is his job; but for him to preach about helping the poor when people are aware of all the waste is sick. I personally believe that the Pope is a good and intelligent man who sees very clearly the mess the world is in today, and he chooses to ignore it.

No one can find their own worth without the self-knowledge that God is within them and that he will guide them every step of the way in life.

Reverend Foard, whom you will read more about in a few chapters, told me a story that I must share with you. He said he had met a Catholic nun through a mutual friend, and when she found out he was a Spiritualist and a medium, she was very vocal in telling him she didn't agree with what he was doing. He said that in spite of how she felt, from time to time he would end up in her company due to their mutual friend. He said, "I was very careful not to offend her by bringing up Spiritualism. However, every time we got together, she would be sure to let me know that what I was doing as a medium was wrong."

He said, "So, you can imagine how shocked I was when she came to me one evening when I was meditating. I had no idea that she had passed over, and she was very angry. She told me that she was not able to find God, that when she arrived in the spirit world, it was nothing at all as to what she expected it to be." Reverend Foard said, "The following day I phoned our mutual friend and asked her when she passed, and the friend said a few days earlier."

Catana had spent the afternoon wine tasting with a friend in the Santa Ynez valley. When she returned home she said, "Mom I have this great quote I know you'll love, it was in one of the places we stopped at: 'When it's over, I want to say all my life I was a bride married to amazement. I was the bridegroom taking the world into my arms. When it's over, I don't want to wonder if I had made my life particular or real. I don't want to find myself sighing and frightened and full of argument. I don't want to end up simply having visited this world.' "

Bishop Fabiran W. Bruskewitz of Lincoln, Nebraska, as of May 15, 1996, signed a decree that he was excommunicating Catholics in his diocese who refused to give up membership in the Hemlock Society, Masonic groups, abortion rights organizations, and groups of organized Catholics for a free choice. He made this decision because Catholics in the above groups are incompatible with the Catholic teachings. This is another prime example of control by organized religion to treat adults like little kids because they want to control their minds.

I think this is a good time for all those people that the bishop is excommunicating from the Catholic Religion to take responsibility for their spiritual growth and to tune into their own power within.

I recall when I was four or five years old, my mother sent me to the store which was a half-block away. The owner of the store was a distant cousin. I asked him for a loaf of bread and told him that my mother asked if he would please put it on credit. He said, "Go back home and tell your mother she has not paid her bill from last month yet." He gave me no bread to take home.

I remember feeling embarrassed at that young age when he told me that. When I arrived home and told my mother what he had said, she cried in front of me, and I felt her pain, and I cried with her. I have often thought about what happened that day, and as I got older I realized that with five kids, 10 years of age and under and so poor, she must have felt hopeless.

As far as I am concerned, back then, the priest never looked at our family and how poor we were. They just as much told us that we were powerless and that being poor was God's will, and if we did not give to the church on Sunday, things would not get better, maybe even worse. That is exactly how I felt back then, and I still feel that way today. We never received any help from the church.

I can well remember how poor we were; and even though finances got better in my early teens, I have a very clear vision of my mom and dad discussing how much money they should put in the church envelope on Sunday. I could never understand why we had to give money to the church when we didn't even have enough to buy a loaf of bread. We were the poor ones. They had the good life. As a young girl I thought it was very strange that the priest always had new cars, housekeepers, and cooks. I remember one time going with my parents to the rectory, and I was told to sit in the living room while they went into the office to talk to the priest. As I sat there, among the simple elegance, and saw how clean the place was, I was in awe of it all. Someone, perhaps the cook, was cooking in the kitchen. It smelled so good. But you know, it didn't feel right to me then, and I felt anger as I sat there.

Before my precious sister Annie passed to spirit, we would often have long phone conversations about life and growing up together, and she said that she also remembered how poor we were and never recalled the church helping us out either. I asked her if there was anything about the Catholic religion back then that made her angry today. She said, "Yes, I am angry that I did not stand up for sister Rose, because the priest told me I would be excommunicated from the church if I did." She also said, "Char, the Catholic Religion means nothing to me. The only reason I am involved in the church is because of all the family and friends." She said she enjoyed the camaraderie with others. I believe there is a very strong message in my sister's words.

People are walking away from organized religion not only because it is a mess, but because they feel lost and it does not fill the soul, and as I wrote a few pages back, give them the answers they are looking for. Look at all the people who have joined various cults throughout the years. Why? Because they are searching for answers, they want to connect with something that will give them meaning in their life and a purpose. People join cults because they are lost, and they don't know how to find God. We all know what sad stories have come out of many of the cults.

If organized religions for thousands of years have been the guiding light in our lives to keep us in touch with God, it obviously has failed, and that is the reason our society is plagued with so many problems today. Billy Graham, an Evangelist, who received a Congressional Medal from Congress in 1996 (which is the highest award that Congress gives) for his dedication for taking his message worldwide, said, "We are a society poised on the brink of self-destruction. We must commit our lives to God and to the moral and spiritual truths that have made this nation great. Crime and violence, drug abuse, racial and ethic tension, broken families and corruptions plague our society." I believe that Mr. Graham is sincere with his message, but I would hope that he would tune into his own words because they give a very strong message that organized religion has not, and does not work for the people. That is why we are on the brink of self-destruction. God did not intend for people to follow organized religion, as I have mentioned several times in this chapter, but to use their own God power within as guidance. However, people cannot commit themselves to God until they find Him. Mr. Graham was also on the Larry King Live show, and he told Mr. King that a good preacher that teaches the religion of the heart will bring all people together. He also told Mr. King that he had been to Russia several times and that they need real religion, genuine religion. I agree with Mr. Graham. He can help all people by telling them to tune into their own guidance (God) within and to follow the religion of the heart that Jesus taught while He walked the earth. That is the real religion, that is the genuine religion.

All organized religions, no matter what the creed, only need to teach the religion of the heart and to tell the people that they have their own inner God power that will lead and guide them. Churches should be a place where people can come together as a community in order to share, love, and to reach out to others with compassion in their time of need without any dogma or rituals. If the religion of the heart is taught, and people are told about their own inner power, then they will find their own answers, and will not be drawn to join a cult or organized religion.

Growing up in the Catholic Religion, I was taught that anyone that was not Catholic was living in sin and would go to hell, that only the Catholic church had a direct line to God that could save us and lead us to heaven. It didn't take long for me to realize as I got older what a bunch of hogwash that was. I had met so many wonderful people that were not Catholic, and I knew for sure that they would not be going to hell.

I was nine years old when my sister Darlene was born. I remember feeling anxious for my parents to baptize her because we were taught that if you were not baptized you could not get into heaven, and I wanted to make sure she got into heaven.

In the neighborhood where I grew up, we had two churches that were of another religion. Each day as I would walk by one or the other, on my way to or from school I would be scared to death to look in if the door was open for fear that I would be sinning. We were told that we were never to enter any church unless it was Catholic and that we should never attend a wedding in another church. And I just knew back then that all those people were not going to heaven. I felt sorry for them. How come they were so stupid not to know that.

I recall getting into an argument with a boy when I was seven or eight years old. He lived next door to a church that was not Catholic in our neighborhood, and one day when a group of us were all together, he said that he went to the church next door to his house.

I said, "I think you're going to go to hell then."

He got really mad at me and said, "You're the one that is going to go to hell because you're Catholic."

I said, "Only Catholics go to heaven."

He said, "Only sinners go to your church."

I became aware of the most disturbing thing about our conversation when I was around 14 years old. This boy's name was Wayne. He was so cute, and I liked him, and I knew if I had not told him I thought he was going to hell, he would still have been my friend. From the day I told him that he would be going to hell, we never got along, mainly because he chose not to be nice to me.

At that time other religions also preached that they had a copyright on God as well. As I got older and moved away and was able to be a free thinker, it amazed me how all the church administrations of all creeds had their own rules and regulations and were able to convince so many people that they were the religion that could save them. I couldn't believe that God had a different plan for each religion. Gipsy Smith wrote that on a boat coming from America a man said to him, "My church is The Church." He replied back, "Go fill your bathtub with salt water and say, 'This is the ocean.'"

I recall my parents talking to some friends when I was a teenager. The friends were visiting our home because my dad was not feeling well. My dad told them he needed to have surgery because his doctor (who was a family friend) misdiagnosed his condition. My dad had been taking a prescription drug for years for a problem he never had. When the real problem surfaced, after years of neglect, he needed to have surgery.

Since my father's condition had not improved over the years in spite of taking his medication faithfully, he should have sought a second opinion from another doctor. He chose not to. He innocently gave his power away because the Catholic religion that he was so devoted to never taught him about his inner power, or taught him to listen to his little voice within to guide him.

Another family friend, who was also our insurance man, came to the house every month for years in order to collect the insurance money from my parents. He convinced me when I was 17 that if I paid five dollars a month I would have a good insurance, a good investment that I would be able to cash in when I got older, and it would always be worth more than I paid into it. Even though I was working at the time, 38 years ago, five dollars a month was a lot of money to me. But I took out the insurance and faithfully paid into it for 11 years. After I got married, I decided to cash it in. It was almost worthless. I told the insurance people that surely there must have been a mistake and explained what I had been told 11 years earlier. There was no mistake, and my husband said that I had been taken for a ride. When I asked my mother about their insurance, she said that they also had been taken for a ride.

When we follow an organized religion, we also are being taken for a ride because they don't teach you the truth about your own power within. They don't teach you to listen to that little voice within that guides you. They take your power and tell you that they can lead and guide you. At my sister Annie's funeral, the priest that performed the service told me just that. He said, "I can lead and guide them," meaning the parishioners, and I said, "No father, you work very hard at taking their power away instead of helping them to empower themselves."

This priest was a pleasant man, but he was not without a large ego. I felt the same type of control from him that I chose to walk away from many years ago. For him not to allow me to read what I had chosen at my sister's funeral service only showed that he was a closed-minded person that lived in fear.

If he believed that the Catholic religion is the true religion that can lead and guide with all the answers, then he should have allowed me to read what I know is the truth about my sister Annie. His insecurity came through that day I sat in his office. I felt he feared a new seed of truth might be planted in the minds of the parishioners, and that they might open up new meadows to explore. I believe he preferred to keep them in a fog instead of allowing them to find new horizons.

After I explained to the priest how close Annie and I were, and why I wanted to read what I had planned at her service, I could not believe what he then said to me, "I knew your sister Annie." Of course he was telling me with that statement that he knew her better than I did.

I said, "Father, you only knew the kindness and love that my sister gave to everyone. Don't sit there in that chair and tell me you knew her better than I did. My sister and I have always been very close, even though I lived two thousand miles away, and this is not to upset any of my family that is sitting here in the room with me, but she couldn't share her deep feelings with them either. She told me everything." This priest knew Annie, at the most, two or three years.

The Televangelists with their religious programs on TV have ripped-off billions of dollars over the years from people all over the world who have been fenced in by following them. It is easy money for these rip-off artists to make, and what they represent is big business and has absolutely nothing to do with God.

If people would wake up and stop sending money to these Televangelists, they would then all fall to the wayside where they belong. Many embezzle millions from their followers, and they do it all in the name of God as they quote Bible scriptures that have been written and changed many times by man to impress the people that the Bible is God speaking. All this so that they can live a luxurious lifestyle.

Jim and Tammy Baker are just one example of living the high life style thanks to all the money that they embezzled from their followers. He was sent to prison and already he is out. He told the media that he plans to return someday to his ministry.

Jerry Falwell had no compassion for the situation the Bakers got themselves into. He took advantage of them, according to Tammy Baker. Then there is Jimmy Swaggart. Robert Tilton told his followers to send in personal prayer requests, and he was exposed on a television program as his office took the donations and threw the requests in the trash without even reading them. Larry Lea told his followers that he was almost wiped out after a suspicious fire so that his followers would send him money. It was reported that he had two other luxurious residences. Pat Robertson has been in the news media about the way his business empire raises money and spends it. There are others out there that are equally self-serving.

Prime Time with Diane Sawyer had a segment on April 17, 1996, on Reverend W.V. Grant. This was not the first time they had put him in the spotlight for fake healing and lies. Back in 1991 Prime Time also did a segment on him. But in this latest segment of Prime Time they took hidden cameras into the auditorium in order to film a week of his services. They reported that before each service Grant circulated among the friends and family of the sick, taking notes and interviewing them so that later he could call their names out of the audience and say that God had just revealed their names and illness to him in order to heal them. Later, when Prime Time questioned the people whom he lifted out of wheelchairs, every person said that all along they could walk. It goes on and on. At the services they filmed thousands of people lined up to give Grant money. It is reported that he takes in $6 to $10 million a year.

Former employees of Grant who did not want to be identified, according to Prime Time, told them that they saw Grant take large sums of money from the donations to use for himself, and that he pocketed hundreds of thousands of dollars. He bought expensive clothes and fancy new cars. He owned two homes, one being reported as a mansion worth a million dollars. Grant also convinced his followers to give him money, adding up to $350,000 dollars a month, telling them that it all goes to support 3,500 children and 64 orphanages in Haiti. He told his followers that not one penny went into his pocket; yet when Prime Time checked out his story, they found that he only gave two to four thousand dollars a month to just one orphanage which only had 17 children. According to an associate pastor with Grant's service, money was also sent to a lady at an orphanage whom Prime Time discovered had been dead for five years. The two doctors who are now involved in that same orphanage said they had never seen or ever met Grant, and they had not received one dime from him.

Grant also told Prime Time that due to their reporting he was financially devastated and had to sell all but one of his church properties in order to feed the poor children in Haiti. Prime Time discovered that was another lie. He actually had bought more property and now owned 19 different properties worth $11 million dollars.

It was also reported that Grant's mailings were similar to other Televangelists mailing lists; and in fact, they reported that the brochures in some cases were word for word. Grant told his followers that God told him to send "special Jesus wallets and cloths which had Jesus' face on it on to them." Prime Time reported that other Televangelists were sending out exactly the same gimmicks to their followers. Grant has pleaded guilty to tax fraud involving his ministry funds. The following article, "Evangelist Gets 16 Months in Prison," came out on 7-23-96.

<u>Texas 7-23-96</u>

Evangelist Gets 16 Months in Prison

A Texas televangelist who made a fortune from his weekly sermons was sentenced to 16 months in prison and fined $30,000 for tax evasion. Walter Grant Jr., the 50-year-old founder and pastor of the Church of Compassion near Dallas, previously pleaded guilty but tried to reverse his plea at the last minute. U.S. District Judge Joe Kendall refused to allow it. Prosecutors said Grant evaded taxes on more than $300,000.

Those who take advantage of other people will eventually be exposed and end up on the same losing end as those they take advantage of.

A quote by Mathew Henry, "That which is won ill, will never wear well, for there is a curse attends it which will waste it." And George Bancroft wrote, "So grasping is dishonesty, that it is no respecter of persons; it will cheat friends as well as foes; and were it possible, would cheat even God Himself."

I believe that the above quotes explain clearly what most Televangelists are all about. All it takes for those who follow these rip-off artists is for them to use common sense and open their eyes to see the facade that they put on. It is time for all people to take their power back and stop being fenced in by others who love to hear themselves preach, are self-serving, and could care less about the people that they preach to. Chesterfield wrote, "You must look into the people as well as at them."

You will not find true spirituality by going to church or following man-made religions. It comes from tuning into your God power within and living the religion of the heart.

THIRTEEN

THE QUESTION

We are turning stones and looking
For that we would unmask,
Or perhaps to find an answer
For a question never asked.

A restless stir within us
Yielding not to status quo
For nothing is so frightening
As the little that we know.

The urge to gather knowledge
Wherever it may be
Can lift the curse of darkness,
And make the servant free.

Then we hope to meet the challenge,
And work for might and main
Since the child can ask the question
That the old cannot explain.

Reverend Edmund L. Foard

Max O'Rell, a writer back in the late 1800's, wrote, "To be a chemist you must study chemistry; to be a lawyer or a physician you must study law or medicine; but to be a politician you need only to study your own interest."

The purpose of this chapter is to expose how politicians, with their lack of sincerity, have fenced us in for years, just like organized religion has. They say the right things in order to get the immediate vote. Their only concern is to get elected or re-elected.

They have easily been bought off by the lobbyist and they pass laws to help large organizations that eventually line their own pockets with money. They do not follow the same laws that apply to all people in our society. They make their own laws. They have given themselves huge pay raises when millions of Americans were out of work, barely able to make ends meet, and when many other Americans had taken pay cuts in their jobs in order to keep them or to help save the jobs of those whom they work with.

Politicians quickly become friends and they are good at protecting one another. They have failed us miserably over the years with their empty promises and self-serving agendas, and because of it, the common cause for the whole has been sacrificed. They are responsible for creating the corrupt political mess that we now have to deal with in Washington. Add to that, after 20 years in Congress, they can collect huge pensions at the taxpayer's expense.

A few years back, a politician lost the race for Governor of California. In one of her after-speeches, she said, "I guess we were in the wrong place at the wrong time with the wrong message." How in God's name can you be in the wrong place, at the wrong time, with the wrong message if you are sincere and believe in what your message is?

In the Spring of 1996, the Los Angeles Times reported that the current Governor of California had appointed more than two dozen workers from his failed 1996 presidential campaign to state jobs. Some of those that were given new state jobs had left their old state jobs to work on his campaign. Not only did they get their state jobs back, but because they left to work on his campaign, they received lump sums of money for leave time. When they were put back on the payroll with their new jobs, they received pay increases averaging 32%. The cost of this "you scratch my back, I'll scratch your back" syndrome will cost the California Taxpayers 1.3 million dollars a year according to the report, and that does not include the fringe benefits which adds another 25 to 28%.

June of 1996, the Los Angeles Times had another report saying that the Republicans, who took over the Assembly in 1994 from the Democrats in California, gave raises starting at 10% up to 47% to Republican workers. It adds up to $2.7 million a year in taxpayers dollars. Out of the GOP's 503 current Assembly staff members, 63% received pay increases and half of the hikes exceeded 25%. The report also said that jobs were given to the members' relatives and hired staffers who run campaign businesses on the side as well as filling key staff positions with former lobbyists.

The California people voted for Proposition 73 in 1988 to outlaw mass mailings by elected officials because they were tired of them using the taxpayer's money. Since 1988, legislators have found loopholes in the law and have spent 6 million dollars of the taxpayers' money mostly to advance their own careers.

In the November, 1996 election, Proposition 208 was also passed by the people of California to impose strict contribution limits on local and state politicians. The proposition didn't go into effect until January, 1997. Named below are some of the politicians who took advantage of the two months prior to the proposition going into effect: Governor Pete Wilson raised close to $500,000; Attorney General Dan Lungren raised more than $1 million; Controller Kathleen Connell raised more than $300,000; Assembly Speaker Cruz Bustamante raised more than $1 million; Democratic Lieutenant Governor Gray Davis, more than $200,000; Assembly Republican Curt Pringle, $250,000; State Treasurer Matt Fong, more than $100,000. The Los Angeles Times reported that a total of $12.5 million was raised by 120 legislators and 11 other officials between the November 5th election and January 1, 1997, usually a light period for fund raising. The arrogance of our politicians is disgusting! They know exactly what they are doing, ignoring the voice of the people and they just plainly don't care!

The 1996 Republican presidential candidates that dropped out of the race realizing that they didn't have a chance to win, said terrible things about each other before dropping out. Instead of dropping out and saying, "I cannot support the winning candidate," they sold their souls by now saying that he was the best choice for the next President of the United States. What a pathetic picture they present to the people. It boggles my mind that they can say such nasty things about their competition, and then, after they drop out, say he will make a good president! The average person would be ashamed or embarrassed to act like they do as they expose their insincerity. A quote, "Virtues are lost in self-interest as rivers are in the sea."

During the 1996 presidential race, an article in our local paper reported that a local GOP loyalist said that she had followed the Republican presidential candidate for more than 20 years; and if he was elected his wife would not be co-president, which has caused a lot of consternation. Of course, she was referring to Hillary Clinton for her role in the Clinton administration's health care reform.

I had never heard the word "consternation" before, so I looked it up in the dictionary. It defines "consternation" as, to terrify, sometimes paralyzing terror or horror; dismay, fear, panic.

It is this kind of crap that people are tired of. I hate to use that word "crap" but that is the only word that describes what the GOP loyalist said. You may or may not agree with the Clinton administration or what Hillary tried to do to bring health care reform to the American people, but the word "consternation" does not at all apply to Mrs. Clinton.

A Santa Barbara Assemblyman was also quoted in the article, and he said that Mrs. Clinton's enthusiasm and lack of experience got her into some real trouble, another asinine remark.

She didn't get into trouble; she shook up all the politicians and the medical establishment who wanted the status quo! They are the ones that yelled and complained about her. I took Mrs. Clinton's enthusiasm as intuition and a positive breath of fresh air. She is a very intelligent First Lady that I believe comes from the heart, and the Republicans are attacking her because of it.

It is a sad reality that some people will say anything just for the purpose of winning or trying to gain political power and to promote one another or themselves even if it is not the truth. It shows how very desperate they are for prestige and power. Emerson wrote, "Every violation of truth is a stab at the health of human society." And the Roman Philosopher, Seneca, said, "Where the speech is corrupted, the mind is also."

In 1995 a report came out that said 75% of the American people do not trust the politicians in Washington because they do not have the best interest of the American people at heart. The information on the prior pages gives a few examples of why! People are fed up with all the rhetoric that the politicians have thrown at them over the years. So it really should be no surprise to any of them that such a report has come out and that they no longer command any respect from the people. The media has reported that many members of the House of Representatives and the Senate have chosen not to run again for re-election. They're leaving Washington because they have been exposed, and all of their shenanigans are coming back to haunt them.

The American people deserve better, but we are not blameless. We have allowed the insincerity of our politicians and the government bureaucracy to go unchecked for decades without ever speaking out or getting involved. We elect them and then we set them free, never checking to see if they are actually doing or even trying to do all that they promised while campaigning. That is giving our power away, it's time to take it back.

The news media has its problems, but what would we do without them? They keep us well informed, and they deserve a lot of credit for all their digging and good reporting because it exposes all politicians in every state of the union, and keeps them under a microscope.

Elizabeth Dole took a year's leave of absence from The American Red Cross to help her husband run for the presidency. She said in an interview that people are surprised to learn that Americans give less than 2% of their income to charitable causes and if she became the first lady she would lead a campaign to increase charitable giving in the United States.

The following article came out in the <u>Los Angeles Times</u> in May of 1996; perhaps that is why the people give less than 2% of their income.

<u>NATIONWIDE 5-26-96</u>

United Way Leader Gets $292,500 Gift

The outgoing president of the United Way will receive a parting gift of $292,500, the equivalent of 18 month's pay, from the board members who say they appreciate her efforts to lift the charity out of the controversy created by her predecessor. Elaine L. Chao, 42, the wife of Sen. Mitch McConnell (R-Ky.), is receiving the cash from "between six and eight" board members, not from the charity, said member Paula Harper Bethea, one of those contributing. In 1992, when Chao took over, the charity was reeling from revelations about the free-spending habits of its ex-president, William Aramony, who was convicted of defrauding the charity of $1 million.

From Times Staff and Wire Reports

The article speaks for itself. However, I would like to know if these board members think that people are so stupid that they do not see through them. United Way is supposed to be the largest provider of health and human services in the country. If they are sincere board members and really came from the heart, they would have given that $292,500 for the common good of people that need it instead of to Elaine L. Chao. And she should have refused the money. This once again shows that the "good old boy network" that has been around for too damn many years is alive and well.

I started doing volunteer work at the Catholic Charities in Minneapolis when I was 18 years old. After I moved to Santa Barbara, I worked on and off in charity work up until the mid-eighties, then I dropped out. Six months after dropping out, I again started charity work and then I dropped out in 1994 for good. The following explains why.

Up until the mid-eighties when I dropped out, I had always been a volunteer worker. When I dropped out for good in 1994, I was the president of Anonymous Givers for Less Fortunate Children, a legal, non-profit group in our community.

What caused me to drop out in the mid-eighties and again in 1994 was that I never had a clear conscience in all the years I was involved. I saw very clearly what was going on around me and it went against my grain. I saw waste; I saw many people who got involved for their own advancement in life, whether it was to promote their ego or climb the social ladder, etc. It is not difficult to buy your way into society, all you have to do is get involved, and before you know it, you're on the same boat with many others just like you. It's disgusting. The insincerity makes you want to throw up; it is all the wrong reasons to get involved.

I honestly don't know why I stayed involved for so long before I dropped out the first time. I have always felt a need to help the less fortunate in our society and especially the children. In spite of what I saw, I simply chose not to digest it because I didn't know at the time how to change or fix what I was experiencing. I also convinced myself that I was helping to make a difference in other people's lives that needed a helping hand. One morning in the mid-eighties I woke up, and it was as if someone turned a light on for me, and I knew that I wanted out. I had had enough! I no longer could ignore my conscience, which was telling me that those who were to benefit were being short changed as well as the many people who blindly donated money without checking to see if their money was efficiently being used.

I had not planned to write about any of my volunteer experiences in this book; however, after Mrs. Dole's comments that the American people are surprised to learn that people give less than 2% of their income to charity and that the country is ripe for change in this area, I had to speak out. What I have experienced in my community is happening in every city across America, and that is why we are not reaching many in need. That is why we are not solving our homeless problems, in spite of the millions and millions of dollars that are donated every year to help the poor. We must change our course NOW because, if we don't, the problems will only continue to get worse during these already difficult times. I do agree with Mrs. Dole that the country is ripe for change, but not in the direction that she would like to take it. I am sure you will understand why I feel that way after you read the following experiences that I had as president of Anonymous Givers, between the Spring of 1992 to the fall of 1993. Let me assure you that what I am going to share with you is not unusual in our community. I could write a book just on my many years of experiences alone, but I chose the last two years before I dropped out because it will give you a very clear picture as to what goes on behind the scenes of charity work, and I do realize there are a few exceptions.

About six months after I dropped out of charity work in the mid-eighties, I was walking in Shoreline Park in Santa Barbara, and I passed a young mother with a small child, four or five years old, looking through a trash can. It bothered me, and that little voice within told me to walk back and ask if I could help. I turned around and approached her. She told me she was looking for something for them to eat. I looked at the little girl, who's face was looking up at me, and my heart fell! I asked her to please wait here, that I only lived 5 minutes away and would be back within 15 minutes with some food. I didn't have any money with me to give her. I left, and my heart was racing. I thought maybe I should have brought them home with me. I returned in less than 15 minutes, but she was gone! I drove all around the park area several times and the neighborhood, but I could not find them. I sat in my car and cried. All I could see was the face of that little girl looking up at me, and it stayed with me for the rest of the day. It never left my mind. That evening I knew that again I had to get involved, but this time I was going to do it my way! That same evening I began telephoning friends, and that is how Anonymous Givers for Less Fortunate Children got started.

There were eight women who made up our group of volunteers; no one received a salary. We contacted every social service and charity in this town by phone and/or letter. We explained our goals and asked them to please send us profiles of families with children who were trying to help themselves and who just needed a helping hand in order to stay in a home environment, and that we would pay rent and give them gift certificates for food. We received only two responses! One was from Catholic Charities, the other was from the Rescue Mission. They both asked for the money, and said that they would help the families. We said no. Eventually, four months later, Catholic Charities came through with profiles of families we could help. We never heard back from the second charity, and for that reason we decided that we would find families ourselves that needed a helping hand. When the word got around about what we were doing in the community, people from time to time contacted us and gave us names of families that they knew needed help.

We were very effective in our community during the years we had Anonymous Givers, helping many families with children by paying up to two months rent for each family. This ranged from three to seven hundred a month plus gift certificates for up to six hundred dollars that could only be used for food at a market near their home.

We began by raising money from garage sales, private parties, and dances. We had many wonderful people from the community that supported us by coming to our events and/or donating money and items to sell.

Because of work and busy family lives for all our volunteers it was done on a part-time basis. When we began receiving more profiles than we could help, we put on a public event at the Lobero Theater. We had wonderful people from our community that donated their talents to help us, and we worked hard for months. We felt that once more people in the community became aware of what we did, they would respond, and we would be able to help many more families. We had great disappointment, and did not attempt to do a public event again. The two area newspapers would not give us help in spite of our begging them to do a story on our group so that we could get some free publicity. That in itself spoke volumes to all of us. I could not believe it! Our group's only goal was to help the children! None of us had an agenda or an ego, unlike those I had experienced during my years of volunteer work. We were not after notoriety, and we told them that. It fell on deaf ears.

What our group did in this community was SO SIMPLE AND EFFECTIVE! By choice we did it without any noise or display and that, we were told later, when I pushed the issue, was the reason the local papers chose to ignore us. Telling me it was our own fault by staying in the background.

The Santa Barbara News-Press had an article on private giving a few years back. I responded with the following letter to the editor:

SANTA BARBARA NEWS-PRESS/THURSDAY, AUGUST 25, 1994

LETTERS TO THE EDITOR

Right acts of charity - for all the wrong reasons

I would like to respond to the editorial in the News-Press on private giving, being president of Anonymous Givers for Less Fortunate Children, a local non-profit group.

Two comments in the article caught my attention: It helps many causes, but less popular ones often lose out and people don't give money to causes, they give money to people.

It's a sad reality, but from my experience the above comments are true in our community. Before starting A.G. I did volunteer work here for more than 20 years, and I can tell you from my experience that I saw many people get involved for all the wrong reasons.

I saw social climbers, people with egos who had an agenda and who were great in promoting themselves; and those same people knew how to make enough noise in order to get others to follow them as well as our city government and news media. With such a following, it only inflated their egos more. We have a clique in this community that sticks together and fluffs each other's feathers and they are good at protecting one another.

Those type of people make up a good part of our tapestry here in Santa Barbara and they are partly responsible for the imbalance we have of not getting help to many who are truly in need.

Charity is love in action, and when a person gets involved for all the wrong reasons I do not consider that charity.

Charity means an act of goodwill that comes from the heart (not egos and agendas) to help those truly in need. In the theological sense it means supreme love of God, universal good will to all.

You can bet what is happening in this town is happening in every other town in California, and for that reason Michael Huffington's ad campaign to replace the welfare system with volunteerism and charitable giving will never work.

It would be wonderful if something so simple could be put into effect, but unfortunately we will always have cliques because some people love power and are self-serving.

I have shared my experience in this community hoping that it might raise the consciousness of those people in the community who give to people instead of causes.

Shakespeare wrote that the people are the city and each one of us can change the system. But in order to do that we must change our thought pattern because thoughts are reality, thoughts rule the world. Thought always finds its way into action.

Ralph Waldo Emerson said, "Man is what he thinks all day long." We must never give up hope - change is always possible.

Charlene Abundis
Santa Barbara

In the Spring of 1992, Anonymous Givers opened the AAE Rummage Center. We invited two other non-profit groups to join us. It was a great success, but the building we were in was put on the market to sell, and the insurance company canceled our policy saying they no longer could carry us at a reasonable rate. We had great difficulty in getting insurance to begin with that was affordable for us. We were also never able to get a lease on our place in spite of being told when we rented it that after a few months they would give us a lease. We ended up closing in the fall of 1993.

The first day the AAE Rummage Center was opened, a lady from another charity, the Council of Christmas Cheer, came in. She had immense anger in her voice and eyes and was very loud. She told me that what we were doing was more harmful to the community than good, that this community already had too many duplicated services for the less fortunate, and that the people who used them knew how to work the system and used all of them.

I told her that what our group did was totally different from what they did, which was giving free food and clothes to those that came into their charity. I said there is no charity in this town that does what we do. We pay rent and give gift certificates for food. She said many more things that made no sense to me. Before she left, she raised both of her hands to the ceiling, and looking up, she then brought them down, patted her chest 3 times, and said, "I want everything to come to me."

That year our local TV station held a marathon and raised about $200,000 for the Council of Christmas Cheer. In the past several years they had raised close to that same amount. In December, 1996, they raised over $300,000. The lady who came into our rummage center and verbally attacked our group was interviewed on TV during the '96 marathon. When asked what plans she had for 1997, she said that they are now going more into computer training and mentioned something about baby sitting. My question is how in God's name does training someone to use the computer help the less fortunate? Our local schools already have computer classes.

I believe the only reason she attacked us was because she saw us as competition. I can't understand that type of thinking. It is so sad. At that time I knew of no other group in Santa Barbara helping families stay in a home environment. With all the money that was donated to the Council of Christmas Cheer, they could have done wonders in the community instead of just handing out free food and clothes that they purchased with the money they received.

In the fall of 1992, I called the local Catholic Charities group asking for six profiles. Since they had given us profiles in the past, they knew exactly how we worked.

The lady in charge said she would get the profiles to me in two weeks. When I called to make arrangements to pick them up, she asked for another week, then another week, and another, and then several more days. This went on for several months, and she never returned my phone calls in spite of my being told each time that she had been given the message and that she would. I was busy running the AAE center. I waited a week after my last call to her then decided to try her one more time before I went to another charity.

I was told that she no longer worked there. When I inquired why not, I was told she left for a higher paying job. I then asked to speak to someone in charge, and a gentleman came on the phone. I explained why I was calling, etc., and he said, "Sorry, we are too busy."

I immediately turned around and called the local Shelter Services for Women. They happily gave us profiles, and we took care of the families. We also told them to send the families that we helped into our center for free clothes, etc., but only one family came.

Since it was the holiday season, we wrapped many new items of clothes and toys that had been donated to our center along with some food. We then donated it to the Shelter Services for them to pass out to the families.

Shortly after the holiday season, I received a call from a lady at the shelter asking if we would like to sponsor a room. This meant to give them money so they could buy new furniture so that when the families came in, everything would be new, nice, and clean. I told her no, that our goal was to pay rent and help with food. "However," I said, "You are welcome to come into our center. We have used furniture, and you may have free anything that you can use." No one showed up. Several months later I received another call from a lady at the shelter thanking us for coming aboard. I told her that we help other services in the community as well. She said that they were struggling, and that the United Way had just sent them a check for $35,000 so that they could meet their payroll.

A few days later, Barney Brantingham's column in the <u>Santa Barbara News Press</u> was titled "Doing Without. Job cuts hit United Way where it hurts most." In the article, he wrote that the leaders of the local United Way said that homeless families, frail seniors, premature babies, and at-risk teens would be hard hit if United Way did not meet its 1993-94 goal. The article said that they were $150,000 short, and the information that United Way gave to the reporter painted a very sad picture for the reader, in order to pull at their heart strings and gave exact numbers of those who would suffer: Fifty-three premature babies might not survive, 82 kids would be on the streets exposed to gangs and violence, 178 frail seniors would remain home bound without hot meals or caregivers, 492 people would not get help for depression, suicide or child abuse, 960 teens would not get counseling for their drug and alcohol abuse.

When they were asked how they were able to come up with exact numbers, their response was, "We can get very specific because the numbers are based on cost of area charities program and the number of people they serve."

With the sad picture the United Way painted in the article, I believe they have their priorities all mixed up. How many of the above people could have received help with the $35,000 that United Way gave to a charity so that they could meet their payroll? What is more important? And I could not help wondering if the people who gave to United Way would approve of giving money to pay salaries for a social service that buys new furniture, when they were offered good, used furniture. If they gave money for salaries to one organization, how would we know that they would not give to them again and to other organizations for that same reason.

In December of 1993, Anonymous Givers received profiles from another local charity, the Transition House. We were very impressed with their sincerity and efficiency. We chose 3 families and paid 2 months rent for each family as well as giving each family gift certificates in the amounts of $300, $500, and $600 for food. Our total cost was $4700.

If the $300,000 raised for the Council of Christmas Cheer in 1996 by our local TV station's marathon was applied to helping families like our group did, close to 180 families could have been helped to stay in a home environment and receive gift certificates for food for two months, and 360 families could be helped for one month, and THAT would have made a real impact on helping the poor in our community. Instead the money was used to buy food, clothes, etc., to hand out to those who know how to use the system and take advantage of all services that are offered in our community. Can you imagine how many families could have been helped year after year with all the money that the TV station raised in the past? What is more important, free gifts, a few pieces of clothing, a bag or two of groceries, or helping a struggling family with children stay in a home environment and off the streets? It is not difficult for me to realize which would be more effective.

Two weeks after the TV station held the 1996 marathon, it reported that the shelves of the Council of Christmas Cheer were almost empty, showing the shelves on TV. Our local paper also had a report saying that they were in need of more donations. What happened to the $300,000? The following quote applies. "So much to do; so little done."

A few years ago there was an article in the Santa Barbara News-Press saying that the former director and a deputy of the Alliance for Community Development (the poverty aid program) stole $157,000 over a four year period by padding their salaries. The city gave this group $49,484 over a two year period. Over the years, other charities the city has given money to have also embezzled.

I realize that most social programs start out with good intentions, and some good is still accomplished today, but at what expense! They are not solving our problems, and many are only a band-aid; the expense of running them is no longer efficient because of all the bureaucracy involved.

The money is not reaching those most in need, but going for administrative costs, etc., and we, the people, can no longer isolate ourselves from that TRUTH! When we are exposed to a wrong that needs to be righted, we must act to correct it. Each one of us must use our power within to help, and to speak out even if it is not a popular thing to do or is offensive to other people. If we don't, then we are guilty, and must share part of the blame for the mess that we have in the world today which will only continue to get worse.

Perhaps you can now understand why I feel anger when I read in the papers or hear on the news about the growing problems of homeless families in America. Another problem is that we have too damn many charities. Santa Barbara has close to 100,000 people. We have dozens of social services and charities that are scattered throughout the city, and they all have their own building or space on which they pay rent or mortgage payments. It is very inefficient and a waste of money. We would have plenty of money to help the homeless in our community if they all joined and worked together under one roof so there would not be duplications of rent, phones, utilities, insurance, etc.

It would also make it easier for the people to go to one place for all services, and the people who know how to work the system and take advantage of it would be easier to eliminate. If this could be done in all communities the size of Santa Barbara, across America, we could make a big dent in helping the less fortunate. Even in the larger cities, all services could be combined and utilized in several locations instead of dozens scattered throughout a city.

Shortly after we closed our rummage center, I checked to see how much money the city donated in 1992-1993 to social services and local charities. It was over $1,000,000. Our local citizens also donated hundreds of thousands of dollars. Many of the social services and charities are as shrewd in taking advantage of the people and Government services as the people that take advantage of their services.

John P. Sears, a political analyst, wrote an article for the Los Angeles Times, August 4, 1996, "Politics Aside, Credit Clinton for Welfare Act." I quote from the article: "The treatment of poor people became a business, the profits of which could be measured by one vital statistic. By all reckoning, less than 50 cents of every dollar spent by the federal, state and local governments on the poor actually reached the impoverished. More than 50 cents of every dollar went to those who were 'looking after' them." It's a bureaucratic mess! All the more reason why we should be helping families on a personal basis.

What I have shared with you about my experience, I took from an article that I wrote in January, 1994, and I sent it to the Santa Barbara News-Press. It was not published. I also sent copies to President Clinton, Governor Wilson, (Calif.), our mayor at the time, all city council members, and to our local TV station which yearly sponsors the marathon for the Council of Christmas Cheer. I received a letter from President Clinton and a phone call from the Santa Barbara News-Press explaining to me that they understood why I wrote the article, but that they would not be able to publish it. The local TV station also phoned, telling me that they agreed with me, etc. However, several weeks later I received a letter of attack from the vice-president and general manager of the TV station (the person who sent the letter is no longer employed there) which I happily responded to. No one from our city or state government responded. Everything in the article that I wrote was my true experience in our community. That alone speaks volumes for the bureaucratic mess in our city and state government. They obviously don't like to tune into the truth.

Mrs. Dole's comment that she wants to encourage the people to give to charity, as charity stands today, is the wrong message for America! She is not suggesting that we take a long, hard look as to why the less fortunate in America are suffering more every day in spite of the millions of dollars that are donated to help them. What she is suggesting is the status quo! That's politics and the wrong direction to help the less fortunate.

In 1995 the news media reported that non-profit organizations in California that hired professional fund raisers in 1994 only received one out of every three dollars they raised and that some non-profits ended up owing the fund raisers money because they had no money left after paying high salaries and expenses. One example is Toys for Tots. The fund raisers they hired raised close to 11 million dollars in 1994 and Toys for Tots did not receive any money from them. In 1994 professional fund raisers pocketed about 100 million dollars in California. It is a rip-off of the American people, and we have the power to stop it by getting more involved and by making sure that the money we donate to help the less fortunate is reaching them.

The news media reported in December 1996 that more than 600 million dollars had been given by the top philanthropists that year to universities, medical research centers, and cultural institutions. But not to organizations to help the poor. L.A. Times staff writer Al Martinez wrote in the latter part of 1996 that roughly 3.5 million Americans are millionaires. Another 36 million live below the poverty level, and the gap between them has steadily widened by almost 13% from 1989 to 1994.

With more than 36 million living below the poverty level and, according to the news media, that figure will continue to grow. It is very disturbing that these top philanthropists are not giving to the poor! Perhaps it is because they are aware of the high salaries paid to the top CEO's of non-profits, and all the waste and abuse of non-profit charities. But they don't have to hand money over to them. With all of their money, they can set up their own organization and make sure those who need help will receive it.

I read an article in 1992 by Mike Feinsilber, Associated Press, that said a survey was made by the Chronicle of Philanthropy, a biweekly newspaper, after the scandal of William Armony, who resigned as president of United Way of America in a controversy over his $463,000 yearly salary plus generous benefits and high style travel. The article said that two of the nation's best known human service agencies, The American Red Cross and Planned Parenthood Federation of America paid the head people in their organization $200,000 a year. The Muscular Dystrophy director was paid $248,808. The Heart Association paid $246,000. The American Cancer Society paid $208,231. Save the Children Federation paid their top CEO $204,593, plus $52,587 in other compensation, and there were others. That was back in 1992. God only knows what any of the above CEO's receive today.

On 12-3-96, Maureen Dowd, a staff writer for the New York Times, had an article published in our local paper, "When giving is actually receiving." She questions why the top philanthropists must slap their names on their good deeds. She quotes Michael Kinsley, the editor of Slate, Microsoft's magazine in Cyberspace, "Anonymous giving is the loveliest kind of giving, which has gone out of fashion in an era when charity to a social climber is what a rope is to a mountain climber."

In 1991, President Bush promoted his "1,000 Points of Lights" campaign to encourage volunteerism in America in order to help those less fortunate. Four years later, Marva N. Collins, founder of the Westside Preparatory School for inner-city children in the Chicago area and an original Points of Light director, was quoted in the media. "It's a facade. I think that is all it perhaps was ever intended to be."

The "1,000 Points of Light" was supposed to be a small organization, but according to an article in the L.A. Times, January 1995, it has steadily grown and has become more dependent on federal funds than when it started. The article reported that the starting salary for the president of the foundation was $185,000 a year and the top 13 employees averaged $80,000 a year. According to the article, the foundation spent close to $400,000 in 1991 and '92 to buy new furniture and equipment and more than $22 million was spent on glitzy promotions, consultants, salaries, travel and conferences. Only 11% of the budget has provided direct assistance to volunteer efforts across America.

According to the National Charities Information Bureau in New York, in 1996 there were about 500,000 charitable organizations in America, and their numbers are growing at a rate of 30,000 a year. Is the growing trend of non-profit organizations used for true charity or for self-interest? Elias Beadle wrote, "Half the work that is done in the world is to make things appear what they are not."

Now that I have dropped out of charity work, I continue to help by following the guidelines that our group Anonymous Givers used. Anyone can do that. You also can contact your local charities and ask for profiles of families that are in need of a helping hand and are trying to help themselves. You can pay a month's rent for them or give them a gift certificate for food. You can do this openly or anonymously. Just don't give your money over to someone else to do the job because you are giving your power away. You have no guarantee that the money will be used for the purpose you want it to be used. If your finances are tight, gather your neighbors together and have garage sales or small parties. What our group did was a lot of fun, and it gave us tremendous joy knowing that we were helping another person in their time of need. That is the only reason we are all here. People who help people and expect nothing in return are sincere and effective. They are in touch with God because they are living the religion of the heart.

Unfortunately there are too many citizens that have an agenda because they feel it is important to be important. It is the only reason that they get involved in charity. They love the limelight and have a great need to shine and be recognized. They expose their phoniness as they try to fill their large egos. From my experience, they usually are difficult to work with because they are so controlling.

Then there are the power people who are in a position to really make a difference in this world, but they use their position as a vehicle for their own social ambitions instead of having concern for the whole.

If everyone in the world could tune into the purpose of life, which is to love and care for each other, not expecting anything in return, all people's basic needs, which are shelter and food, could easily be satisfied. But that will not happen until people stop worrying about prestige, power, recognition, and/or personal gain; and they tune into God's way which is love, sharing, compassion, charity and kindness to all.

There is an old saying that you can give without loving, but you can't love without giving. When you choose to have a partnership with God, you are love-centered and not self-centered; and when you give of yourself to others, it is without expecting anything in return.

Myrtle Reed, an American author, who wrote Lavender and Old Lace in 1902 and who passed in 1911 at the age of 37, was ahead of her time when she wrote the following. "Put joy in the world and it will come back to you with compound interest, but you can't check out either money or happiness when you have made no deposits." The giving of your love and time to those you meet daily will lift your spirit and keep you filled with joy.

FOURTEEN

THE PATH

If we could but see the pathway ahead,
And the power to change should we choose,
And gamble the worth of the final gain,
Or fret over all we might lose.

Our pathway has crossed and crossed over again,
And each crossing seemed to answer a need.
Yet neither had noted the cause or effect
As to where and to how it might lead.

If one of us altered the course of his way,
And had given his path a new twist,
Just might have passed as ships in the night,
And a beautiful experience missed.

How nice it is that the path remained true,
For in this part of life the crossings now end,
And await for sometime in the sweet by and by
When I come to the arms of a friend.

Reverend Edmund L. Foard

A few years back I was having lunch with some friends. We talked about the mess the world is in today, and we all had our own opinion as to some of the reasons why. One friend felt that the decline of America all started in the 1960's with the hippie generation. She thought the youth back then didn't see much hope for their future because they would be unable to have all the material things that their parents had, so they rebelled and called society greedy. Another friend said that we were very lacking in spirituality, and another said that parents no longer are good role models like they were in her youth. She also said it started with the hippie generation. I felt it was because we gave our power to everyone else instead of using it ourselves, and of course, I was referring to organized religion and to our government. If the above opinions are compiled, we get a pretty clear picture of what is wrong in America today.

When I came to California in 1964, the elderly man who got on the bus in Minneapolis and who sat next to me said he was repulsed by so many hippies on the bus. There may have been seven or eight. He could hardly take his eyes off of the hippies several rows ahead of us. He turned to me and said, shaking his head, "Look at them. They look shabby and lost. If they think we live the wrong way and the world is going to hell, one day they will be able to look back and take some credit for it." Back then I didn't know what to think. I only knew that to look at them bothered me. I couldn't understand why they would choose such a life style.

The elderly man asked me what I thought. I said, "I don't know. They bother me some." I asked him what he thought they stood for.

He gave me the strangest look and said, "Nothing. What they do is an excuse for free sex and drug taking. Can you imagine what America will be like when they raise their kids? This country is going to hell."

Today, we do live in a fast-paced world and a society where moral and spiritual guidance is lacking; where the average person gets kicked around and where money, respect, and recognition is flowered on those with high visibility regardless of their morals or qualifications.

Daily on the news we see innocent people whose lives have been shattered by the negativeness of our society. Their raw wounds are visible for all the world to see. This is because children have not been taught God's laws, and they are being raised in homes where there is a lack of parental love, guidance, acceptance, emotional stability, patience, and/or understanding. They end up being a problem for society because they are uncaring, unfeeling, and unloving. They have not been raised to accept responsibility or have respect for anything, not even for themselves. Parents do not make them a top priority, and then they wonder why their child does not fit into society and ends up in prison or worse.

These kids are not ignorant. They have nothing to hold on to. They are starved for love and direction that will give them some meaning for life. How can we expect them to fit into society and succeed in life when they have not been given the necessary tools to do so? How can they possibly give what they have not received? Everyone loses: society, parents, and the children who will, without a doubt, have a rough journey ahead of them. And all because we have lost touch with God and His laws. It is up to the parents to teach their children about God and His laws because children are born innocent and ignorant. They do not know the difference between right and wrong. If somewhere along life's path they do not learn, they will be shut out from ever finding heaven within, and the parents must accept the blame.

Often my husband would come home from teaching and tell me stories of what some of the kids did in school, and it would give me sick stomach feelings. I am talking about some kids, not all kids. John Locke, an English philosopher, wrote, "Parents wonder why the streams are bitter, when they themselves have poisoned the fountain." Lydia Sigourney wrote, "Sins of the parents may be visited upon their children, but it is that the sting may strike back into the parents hearts."

Back in the mid-eighties I read an article in the Los Angeles Times written by Al Baldernama, a retired detective. He said in his 27 years as a detective and working with troubled children, school drop outs, he asked them the same question, "Why did you do it?" The response was almost always the same, "My parents don't care or love me. They let me do whatever I want." Parents who fail to do their job are usually eager to pass the blame on to others when their children fail, get into trouble, etc. But the responsibility goes to the parents! When children are not taught by their parents that all their actions, good or bad, have moral and spiritual consequences, who else can teach them? The only other adult person that they spend hours with is the teacher, who is already overworked and underpaid. But I honestly don't think we have any other choice. I recently read in the paper that The American Association of School Administration feels that a course in Ethics should be an integral part of the school curriculum; also courses in Respect and Responsibility should be taught.

If children are taught by the parents as soon as they can understand that when they do something wrong they only hurt themselves because it is a negative action, and it will come back to them, just as a positive action will come back to them, you can bet they will take notice and listen. And as soon as they enter pre-school, when their minds are still like sponges and they can absorb all they are learning easily, the consequences of right and wrong should be reinforced. They will tune in, and it will make a real impact on their young minds, and it will stay with them through their lives. It should continue to be taught in all grades because there will always be parents who are not there for their children; and that will be one way we will be able to reach them and help them fit into our society.

The news and entertainment medias must also do their part and stop giving attention to those in our society who have nothing positive to offer to our children because it gives the wrong message.

Many parents who are not there for their children usually had parents who were not there for them, and they are passing on exactly what they received. It's like a ball that just keeps on rolling, and it must be stopped now! When we plant a garden of vegetables, or flowers or a tree, unless we take good care of it, the garden will not sprout, the flowers will not bloom, and the tree will not grow. Well, our children live in the garden of life, and we need to make sure that God is also in their garden and that parents make them a top priority in order for them to bloom and flourish. For years I looked for and wanted God in my garden of life. I wanted Him to be a special part of my life, and I now know that it is not difficult to bring Him into our lives. It is very easy because He is within us. Once people realize that, all it will take to have a wonderful spiritual journey in life is the desire to know God and live His laws of love and He will do the rest. But parents must know the above in order to teach it to their children so that they can live a true spiritual life as God guides them with His divine love and wisdom in all that they do as they walk the earth plane.

Reverend Foard told me in one of our conversations that if this is all there is, then why should any of us worry as to how we live our lives. What difference would it make if we lived a selfish, uncaring, unloving, greedy life. What difference would it make if we did whatever we wanted and went after everything we wanted, no matter how we got it.

But, he said, "This is not all there is. That is why most people try to be the very best they can be, because they understand there is something after this life, but they have no idea what." He went on to say that once souls reach the other side, whatever Karma they created while here will certainly be there waiting for them, good or bad. We have been kept in the dark because we have been taught to follow instead of leading ourselves by learning to use that little voice within. If people were taught to use that little voice within, they would not have accepted all that has been thrown at them from all directions of life.

In many of the books that I read, I felt a handful of them were an insult to one's intelligence. I could hardly believe that someone would actually publish them. The ones that were written by organized religion were a total turn off because of all the control. Ah!! But the joy I felt in having found books by many wonderful authors who just believed in God and had no particular religious affiliation. Their books were very enlightening and uplifting.

Jean Bruyere wrote, "When a book raises your spirit, and inspires you with noble and manly thoughts, seek for no other test of its excellence. It is good, and made by a good workman." In one book there was a quote by Walt Whitman: "Whatever satisfies the Soul is truth." To me that meant that if what I was reading felt right to me, then it was right for me. In having reached this awareness, I got very excited because I felt something was happening within me. I was not exactly sure what it was at first, because it was happening slowly, but it gave me the joyous feeling that I was right on track in finding the answers that I was looking for. I just knew it! No matter what I was doing, driving the kids to school, gardening, housework, whatever; my mind would fill up with thoughts that I knew were coming from God because they felt right to me.

One morning after dropping the children off at school, I was anxious to get home to do some gardening. I turned off the freeway, started up the hill where I lived, when I suddenly got this tremendous urge to go to the beach. It was a strange, fast urge, and in the 14 years I had been married, I had never gone to the beach by myself, but always with Mel and the children. I didn't even think twice about not going, that is how strong the feeling was. I drove to the beach, took my shoes off, got out of the car, and hurried down to the ocean. I walked in and out of the water for several hours. It was one of those beautiful, Santa Barbara winter days just before a storm is to arrive, a slice of heaven.

As I was walking back to my car, I heard someone call my name. I turned around, and over on a small grassy area was a lady that obviously knew me. I walked over to see who it was as I did not recognize her from a distance. Even as I got up close and said hello, it took me a few seconds to realize that I had worked with her at my very first job shortly after I moved to Santa Barbara. She stood up; we exchanged a few words, and then she asked me if I would like to join her for a cup of coffee at the small cafe there on the beach. At first I was going to say no, but she looked so sad I said sure.

After we sat down, I asked if she was okay. She asked me why I asked her that. I told her she had such a sad look on her face. Her eyes filled with tears as she raised her hands up to hold her head. I asked if there was something I could do.

She said, "Not really, it's a personal problem."

I said, "I am a good listener." But she didn't respond to my remark and instead asked me about my life. I told her about my children and husband, etc.

She hadn't changed much from when I first met her. I thought to myself, "She must be around 55 now." When I asked her about her life, she poured her heart and soul out to me. Towards the end of what she was telling me, she said, "I am so empty inside. There is no joy or love in my life." She said she had prayed and prayed to God to bring both back into her marriage.

Well, after hearing her story, I couldn't fathom how that would happen. I suggested that perhaps she was asking God for the wrong things. Maybe she should pray and ask Him for guidance and direction because I didn't believe that God wanted anyone to stay in a loveless and joyless marriage.

She said, "I can't divorce because my family wouldn't accept it."

I asked her if her religion was Catholic and she said yes. I then told her the story about my sister Rose. I didn't get very much response from her, and I felt maybe I had overstepped my bounds. I got up from the table shortly thereafter because I had to leave to pick up my children from school. We had talked for close to two hours, and I was surprised when she asked me if I could meet her again the next morning for a cup of coffee at the same place.

I said, "Sure, if talking more might be of some help." I gave her a hug before I left, and she did respond warmly, and that surprised me because she was not an overly warm person.

The following morning, after having coffee, we decided to walk along the ocean. Once again it was a beautiful, stormy day. She told me about her life growing up and what it was like being raised in the Catholic religion, how strict her parents were with her since she was an only child, etc. She said that her father was so religious that at Easter and Christmas, he went to church twice a day. She said that after I had told her about my sister going against the Catholic Religion in spite of all that the priest had said, a light went on within her and that is why she wanted to talk some more. She said she never ever thought that she would be able to go against her religion, but after our conversation the day before, it became more of a possibility in her mind.

I was surprised when she told me that I had been in her dream the night before, because she was also in mine. After we shared our dreams, I think we both knew what she was going to do. She left the beach that day, I know, with a plan. We kept in touch from time to time. Six months later she got a divorce, and less than a year after that, she phoned to tell me she was getting married and moving to another state. The following Christmas, I received a card from her signed love and joy, with the words "love" and "joy" underlined.

Back then, I just thought I was helping a distant friend by listening. But after our second beach visit, for several days her story kept going through my mind. I then realized that I am the person I am today because of my childhood experiences. It was shortly after that, the resentment I felt towards my parents left me. I realized that I was responsible for my life. Today, there is no question in my mind that God sent me to the beach that day because my distant friend needed someone to talk to, and we both would be helped. That was why my intuition was so strong. I have gone back over those two days so many times, and I always say thank you God, not only for that experience, but for giving it to me on such beautiful winter days. I love stormy weather.

Regarding the article that I wrote, "Feed Catholic Spiritual Hunger," out of the 54 calls that I received, two were from ladies that were very unhappy about the article because they were Catholic and didn't agree with me. Both of them asked why I didn't read the Bible instead of all those other books. I replied that the Bible was changed by man, and I found it confusing, and it was not easy reading. I asked both of them if they knew which version was the correct one, since there is more than one Bible as well as all the rules and regulations for different religions. They were not able to answer.

One lady asked me, after I asked her which Bible was correct, how much education I had. I asked her what difference it made and how did that question fit into this conversation.

She responded, "I just wanted to know."

I then asked her if she knew who was responsible for writing the Catholic Bible. Her response floored me. She angrily said, "Jesus wrote the Bible."

I said, "According to the books I read on His life, Jesus did not know how to write, so He could not have written any Bible. The apostles wrote the Bible for Him. In fact, many of the words that Jesus spoke, which appear to be authentic, according to the books I read, are not found in the Bible, and research about His life shows that Jesus never said a book should be written with opinions and beliefs. Man did that."

Her anger really increased as she said, "You obviously believe everything you read, and I do not care to have any more conversation with you," and she hung up.

In 1995 I read that there are about fifteen hundred different religions in the world today. The dictionary defines religion as: "recognition of man's relation to a divine or superhuman power to whom obedience and reverence are due; faith in and allegiance to God or Gods. Efforts of man to obtain the goodness of God. Beliefs, attitudes, emotions, behavior or man's relationship with the powers and principles of the Universe."

I wrote in the first part of chapter twelve about religion of the heart that Jesus taught when He walked the earth. Obviously from the books that I read about His life, the world's Christian religions do not follow what Jesus said; if they did we would not have many of the problems in the world that we have today.

I believe that one day people will return to the simple teachings of Jesus and that goodness will replace organized religion. Then we will be able to live the religion of the heart that Jesus promoted while on the earth, and we will not give our power away to anyone. The principle of our existence is love. I visualize a chain of love that is created by each person reaching out in his or her own neighborhood, city, or town, and that chain goes on and on all around the world.

Impossible? I don't think so! We all have to get involved in order for that to happen. People often complicate ideas, yet I have found that simplicity is the best clarity in everything that I do. A chain of love would be a simple way of reaching out to others in their time of need, and the love would reach to all corners of the world. Love is God, and most people love each other and want to reach out and get involved in caring for others, to be a part of something that touches another person's life that would help to make a difference. Our thoughts would be positive and uplifting because love links all people together and by reaching out to others with love, your whole being is filled with joy. Love can heal the world. Thoughts can heal the world. If you put the two together, as a chain from person to person, you have an unbeatable combination. The whole world would have a new level of awareness. It would be a very simple process if we all participated and it came from the heart.

It would certainly help to wipe out all the so called non-profit, charitable organizations as well as those that do direct mailings and use 80% of the money they raise for salaries and administrative expenses, and it would also wipe out the fund-raisers that they hire that also rip the people off. Some non-profit organizations have CEO's that are paid hundreds of thousands of dollars each year, and on top of that, some still rip money off the top because it is so easy to do. United Way has been in the paper several times with such a scandal as well as other organizations. The news media reported in March, 1996, that Frank Williams, former executive director of Staten Island-based American Parkinson's Disease Association, pleaded guilty to stealing more than $1,000,000 intended for research to combat degenerative brain disorder.

The Santa Barbara News-Press had an article on 12-23-96 about the March of Dimes and Michael L. Curtis who served as one of the Trustees for the charity. Mr. Curtis owes the March of Dimes 2.7 million dollars that he collected from the Candy and Gum Ball machines from 1991 and 1995. The President of the March of Dimes, Birth Defects

116

Foundation, allowed Mr. Curtis to keep 1.7 million of the money he collected from 1991 as a loan because he was having financial problems and because he promised to pay it back. Several years later a plan was set up for repayment of the money over a 20 year period. To date Mr. Curtis has paid only $100,000 of it back. The March of Dimes reported on their tax returns that the money was a contribution from Mr. Curtis, not a loan. He also failed to turn in $800,000 that he collected in 1995. The March of Dimes is now concerned about getting the money back from Mr. Curtis.

I read in the Los Angeles Times in 1996 where direct mailings have become a good business for people because they only have to give a very small portion of what they collect to the cause, and they can pocket the rest, which adds up in some cases to millions of dollars. It is easy money and a rip-off of the people, and it obviously is happening all across America. It is legal for these solicitors to pocket millions of dollars and there is no law in effect that can stop them.

The report also said that they target the retired senior citizens, because they are the most vulnerable, by sending out scare letters, telling them that they will fight for this or that cause and especially a cause that could affect them directly. They promise to lobby legislators and fight issues for them; they also sell your name to other direct mailings and make good money from that.

Prime Time had a segment in the early part of 1996 on Telemarketing in America. They reported that the only goal of those who are involved in this rip-off business of the American people is to make as much money as they can without a cause. They reported that one in three Americans are approached by phone and that one in six send money which adds up to 40 billion dollars a year. They exposed people on their program without them knowing so that the viewer could see how easy it is for them and how convincing they are with their continuous and suave flow of words over the phone that convince the people they call that they are legitimate. The saddest part of all this is that once again it is the elderly that are hit the hardest and ripped-off the most. Telemarketing professionals buy and trade lists with each other as well. It is big business. And the people are the ones that have made it a big business. Just say NO! when they call and hang up!

Politicians are just as bad as the Telemarketers. They send out direct mailings (non-profit) to help them pay off their debts, but they don't tell you that. They always have a cause for your donation, and they also pass your name on to other politicians when they retire.

Hazel, a dear family friend of 28 years, passed in 1995. The last years of her life I helped care for her. I recall the first time I sat down with her to help her pay her bills. She also had a pile of letters from non-profit charities and politicians. When I looked the letters over, I thought to myself, "Does she give to all these people? This is a rip-off." When I asked her, she said yes.

I asked, "How do you choose who to give to?"

"Well," she said, "I don't like having to make decisions anymore. It's hard, so we can just send to all of them."

I said, "Hazel, this (as I picked up all the envelopes and held them in one hand to show her) is a rip-off. Now that I am helping you, I am just going to throw these in the trash."

She said, "But some of them look like good causes to me."

I said, "Sweetie, this is only a gimmick, and I am throwing them all away. If you want to donate money, we will find a good, local cause or family to help. That way you will know where your money is going. You have no guarantee your money is being used for the cause you want. Most of these requests are from rip-off artists."

Hazel, who was 91 years old at the time, said, "Well, if you say so." She was receiving dozens of requests not only from politicians, but every non-profit group imaginable. Some I hadn't even heard of. At first I threw them away, then one day I decided to keep them to see how many she received in a month.

When Hazel passed to spirit, I had two and half years of non-profit direct mail that was sent to her. The charity pile was 16 inches high, and another pile from politicians was 14 inches high.

I would like to share some of the letters that I saved. They all disturbed me, but the following, especially the ones from the politicians, were the most disturbing because they are supposed to protect and help the people, not rip them off. Here is a small sample of what Hazel received.

Several requests came from Senator Bob Dole. One was a fancy-looking certificate, very professional. In his letter to Hazel, he told her he hoped that she would join him as a full partner (that really impressed Hazel). He told her he really needed her help to keep America strong, free, and proud. Hazel was always very patriotic. She wanted to send him $100.00. She told me he had been in politics for a long time. He wouldn't take advantage of the people.

She received eight requests from Dan Lungren, Attorney General of California. He sent her a very impressive membership card with a number on it. A little box was checked that said voluntary dues $20.00. I had no intentions of sending him any of her money, but I asked her, as I did with all of the requests, how much she would have sent. She pointed to the little box, after looking it over, and said, "I owe $20.00."

I said, "Sweetie, you don't owe $20.00, that is voluntary."

She took the letter back from me and looked at it again, and said, "Oh, I thought I owed that."

U.S. Senator Phil Gramm sent an important-looking survey document thanking Hazel for her help and to please return the necessary information within 18 days. She received several requests from him, of course, expecting a donation for that important document that she must return back to him within 18 days.

She received several scare letters from the Republican National Committee (she was Republican) asking her for money so that they could protect her. The Annual Fund Campaign Committee gave her a deadline to return her money donation. Dick Cheney, former Secretary of Defense, and at the time an ACU advisor, had these words in the donation area, "I am enclosing my ballot, and I understand that to cover the cost of printing, distributing, tabulating, and circulation of results I should enclose a contribution. I understand you will mail me the ballot results when you release them to the media." This was to defeat Clinton's Health Care Plan. When I read the above to Hazel I was laughing so hard, and I said, "Hazel, how stupid do they think people are. We'll wait to read the results in the paper."

Hazel looked at me and said, "You know, you're right. I would have sent money to Dick Cheney."

Charles Colson, who was sent to prison due to his involvement in the Watergate mess, wanted to send Hazel a free book, the title was written on the envelope, just because he wanted her to have it. The letter pulled at her heart strings because she liked Billy Graham, and his name was somewhere in the material sent to her. Colson blessed her, hoped she could send a donation very soon to help the lost souls in prison.

Matt Fong, California State Treasurer, wanted his good friend, Hazel, to send a donation just because he believed in the American dream and in order for him to be elected he needed to count on his friend, Hazel.

Sgt. Stacy Koon, who was in prison due to the Rodney King beating, told Hazel he was in prison, behind bars, and if she believed he was innocent and in justice, to please send a donation. He blessed her and also had a special piece of stationary attached for Hazel to write a personal note to his wife. He also told Hazel that his wife was a fine Christian lady and the mother of his children.

Newt Gingrich wanted to protect and extend the New Republican Congressional Majority. He asked her to please rush her ballot which was enclosed and to send at least $15.00 today.

Ollie North sent four different letters. The first one asked Hazel (he used her name) if she would do him an honor of serving on his U.S. Advisory Board. It would be helpful to him if she would because then he could list her name as an advisor. He sent a family picture. In the second letter Mr. North didn't mention about his advisory board. He sent a beautiful color proof photo of his family to remind Hazel that they both had strong family values. He said if she sent a donation, she could select the family photo and that he would enlarge it to an 8 X 10 for her, or another photo of himself in his marine uniform. He thanked her in advance for making such a generous sacrifice on behalf of our country and children. He didn't forget to remind her to be sure to select the photo she wanted. In other words, make sure you send your donation. In the third letter, Mr. North addressed it to "friend" this time, not to Hazel, as the first two were. Again he was asking her to serve on his advisory board, another family photo was included. In the fourth letter Mr. North glued two pennies to the top of the first page, telling Hazel that he enclosed his two cents, since he would like her two cents worth of thoughts, of course.

I could go on and on, but I am sure you get the picture. Elderly people are taken in much more by the slickness of words in all direct mailings because many of them get easily confused, are lonely and without family near them; and it makes them feel important when their first names are used, and they are referred to as friend, and partner; and it impresses them when the sender of the letter tells about their family and some personal thoughts.

The amount of money sent through the mail to all the non-profits adds up to billions of dollars. If that money was channeled directly to the less fortunate by making sure that their basic needs of life were met, we would make a real difference in the world.

I read a report in 1996 that said we have 1.2 million tax-exempt groups in operation today. We, the people, are the ones, as I wrote earlier, that keep them in business. The only way our government will do anything about this rip-off is if we voice our opinion very loud and clear. The reason that these non-profits thrive is because we don't speak out. It's not okay to know there is a problem and not do anything about it. When we become aware of a wrong we have to help correct it. I know that I am repeating, but it is so important. We must all get involved by taking a stand and stop sending all non-profits money through the mail!

Most non-profits also use the money sent in by the people to keep making more money by sending out more requests. Their goal is not to help the cause that they tell you about. It's a profitable cycle for them that just goes on and on, and we no longer can ignore it. They have fenced us in for years with this rip-off.

Many people spend their whole lives waiting for someone else to get the job done. Well, we all are that someone else, and if we all do our part, we can slowly but surely clean the mess up.

The rip-off of our senior citizens in this country is so sad! I find it difficult to believe that the elderly who are the most vulnerable cannot be protected by writing laws that are strongly enforced to stop these rip-off artists. It is disgusting! It is a rip-off of the American people from those without any conscience. It is greed in capital letters and self-serving.

I have a friend whose elderly mother lives in another state, and a few years back she lost two thousand dollars. She sent the money thinking that she had won a trip. When I asked my friend how she was so easily fenced in, she said, "My mother lives in fear of someone attacking her, and she is afraid to go outside of her house even during the day because of all the crime she sees on TV. My mother does not have an exciting life, and she won't come to live with me. I have a hard time keeping tabs on her. When I asked her why she sent the money, she told me because it was exciting to think that she had won a trip."

Her story tells us that not only the young but also many older people live in fear and have nothing to hold on to today. However my heart tells me that it is the young people that we need to worry about the most. They look around and see the mess in the world and all the severe problems that we have created in our society, the high rate of divorce, the dysfunctional families, drug abuse and teenage suicide; and it only adds fear and confusion to their young minds because if we can't clean it up they have to wonder how can they. They don't know what lies ahead, and it creates hopelessness and feelings of despair for them.

The moral sense of right and wrong is powerful in each person; however, if parents are not there for their children, their children are not going to care about what is right and wrong, and they will do whatever they want to do. If parents do not bond with their children, their children might bond with someone else who may not be a positive influence in their life.

It doesn't matter how much attention and concern our children receive from our society as a whole or from the community they live in. There is absolutely no substitute for parents and their unconditional love. It is so very important for all parents to realize that and to know that they are also responsible for creating and maintaining a happy home environment for their children. Unconditional love and a happy home for our children should be the number one priority in all parents' lives. Children that come from happy homes, knowing that they are loved, will bond with their parents, and will feel comfortable in discussing openly all the negative aspects of life that they see daily such as drugs, sex, alcohol, etc. Children that bond with their parents will share their inner feelings, even anger, without worrying about their parents judging them.

So that today's young people and future generations have meaning and quality in their lives we must now turn to the parents, and they must get their act together! Parents have a tremendous responsibility to their children and they need to make their children a top priority in their lives. Parents need to teach their children about God and His laws. Parents need to give their children love, attention, and guidance, and it must come from the heart. Parents that let their children know by their actions that they are special and important and put their children ahead of friends and material things will help their children all through their school years. Children who have loving, hands-on parents will develop a good sense of self-worth, and they eventually will find a good direction in life that will enable them to flourish and evolve to their full potential. But most important, children will feel loved! Parents who are good role models will set an example for their children; their children most likely will pass it on to their children, and it goes on and on. Our children will then not live in fear as so many of our youths do today. Life will have meaning for them and they will love themselves. This will give parents peace of mind and their children something to hold on to, like a security blanket for life that will last even when the parents pass to spirit.

If we start now it would perhaps take only two decades to reverse what we have created in this world by the lack of good parenting, and by not having God in our lives. The English philosopher, Francis Bacon, wrote: "Parents who wish to train up their children in the way they should go, must go in the way in which they would have their children go."

If some children fall through the cracks in spite of receiving all the love and guidance possible, the parents will be able to be guilt free. Sadness will hit them, but not guilt!

When fear invades our minds, no matter at what age, confusion takes over, and we are unable to find God's light within or the answers to anything in life, and that is when people turn to drugs, alcohol, and cults. (It's all so sad that I hate to even write about it.) Emerson wrote: "Fear springs from ignorance." We live in a controlling society and world, and many people follow without ever questioning all that goes on around them. They go around living like robots because they have been kept in the dark, as Reverend Foard said, for hundreds of years and it has corroded their inner power.

Two Los Angeles teenage girls, one 14 and the other 15, tied their wrists together and jumped off of a cliff overlooking the ocean to their deaths. Friends that gathered at the cliff were shocked that they had done this. One friend told a news reporter, "You know life sucks so much as it is now; a lot of (teenagers) don't know if it's going to get better or not, I guess, this is their only way out. They feel they can't talk to the parents or anybody." Another friend said, "I think the blame should be put on society and this world because it's like something drove them to do it." Another friend said, "It's not normal for someone our age to do something like that. It's kind of sad."

The above is a prime example of young kids being lost without any direction in their lives. Many young kids who have been in trouble with the law have said in interviews held by the news media that they turn to violence and crime because it makes them stand out in a crowd, and they feel important among their peers. Obviously these young kids have been raised in moral poverty by their parents, and it is sick to realize what they are capable of doing. Society cannot just toss them aside, we must try to reach them in order to help them. God obviously has not been a part of their lives because they are unaware of His laws and the meaning of Karma. Parents who are too busy to listen to and spend time with their children build no foundation for their children to stand on, and then they wonder why their children commit suicide, take drugs, etc.

There are two ways that our children can receive help outside of the home:

1. The educational system should bring back vocational schools. They never should have been deleted to begin with because many children who graduated from high school over the years were sent out into the world without any special skills at all. In 1991 statistics showed that 70% of all high school graduates did not go to college. What percent of the 70% have become problems to our society over the last 6 years because they were sent out into the world without any skills? If they were raised in homes where the parents were not there for them, and then they graduate from high school without any skills, they already have two strikes against them because they have been given no opportunity to realize their potential or talents that could help them fit into our society. College is not for everyone. It is time to bring back <u>vocational schools</u> so that children who do not plan to go to college, for whatever reasons, are given the opportunity to learn a trade that will help them fit into our society; then they will know that they have something to offer.

2. The movie and entertainment industry as well as the news media must stop profiling all the wrong people who have nothing positive to offer to our youth of today. The negativity in the movie and entertainment industry is disgusting!

The educational system, the entertainment industry and the news media are not blameless. They have helped to create the mess that we now have in our world today. It's time that they do their part to help clean it up.

125

God is good, and He has a plan for each one of us. The only way we will find the plan that He has for us in this lifetime and be guided by Him is if we tune into Him (not organized religion) and we are made aware of His laws and live by them and practice good parenting. It also is the only way we can save the world and help our children, as well as ourselves, to find the truth; and it will give all of us something to hold on to.

Starting when children are old enough to understand, they should be taught by their parents that God is within them, and that is their power. They should be taught that the religion of the heart is the only religion that they should ever follow. They should be taught that God will always take care of them, that God created the world and all the people in it, that God is never absent from our lives, and that He loves all people equally no matter where we live in the world or what the color of our skin is. They should be taught that God's protected light shines on everyone, good and bad, and that we have that same light within us that will lead and guide us through our journey in life in everything that we do. They should be taught that the negative aspect of our society is caused by ignorance of all the above and that God gives us all free choice, and free will. As we grow on our path in life it is up to us to gather the knowledge that is necessary to find the answers to take us on a positive journey through life. Plato wrote, "Better to be unborn than untaught, for ignorance is the root of misfortune."

Children should be taught that God's plan is that we should all live in harmony and unity with one another; that their thoughts will create reality because thoughts have power; that all their actions, good and bad, have consequences; and that the soul has no color and lives on in spirit. They should be told that the most important thing you leave behind and also take with you to spirit is the love and kindness you have given to others in life here on earth; and that all negativity will keep their souls from soaring here and in the spirit world.

And I have to repeat this again: It is so important. Children should be taught to never, never, follow an organized religion or give their power to anyone because it will only blind them to the truth.

If you have the desire to know God and want to find Him on your own, talk to Him and tell Him all your thoughts and remember that He is within. It's not difficult to find Him. Meditation will help you, and it will help you to stay tuned in to Him. Your mind will slowly open up like a parachute with all of God's love and guidance as all fear leaves you. Your family and friends will see a positive change in you, and you will be so filled with joy that you will be anxious to share with others what you are experiencing.

Be patient and learn to take one day at a time, and expect to be guided along the way. Keep the faith and know that He will put everything you need to help you in your path, as He guides you. If unusual things (that are positive) happen and can't be explained, just flow with it. It is confirmation that you're going in the right direction.

Most important, stay tuned to your feelings within and don't let anyone else tell you that you're going in the wrong direction. Several people were very vocal in telling me that I was turning away from God in my search and tried to pull me in to their beliefs. I blessed them and continued on because I knew I was on the right track.

Once you find God within you and you apply the religion of the heart, it will be easy for you to use your intuition because it will give you clear feelings to know what is right and wrong in everything that you do.

If you want to find what it is that you are supposed to be doing in this lifetime, stay tuned to the God within you, and He will eventually reveal it to you. If you have dreams and plans for what you want to do in your future, and it feels right to you, that is God giving you the message to go for it.

When you become aware of your power within you, it guides you in everything that you do, and you will be a free spirit because you will be able to think for yourself. The challenges that you encounter in life along your journey you will overcome, knowing that you and God are in charge and that everything that happens to you is for a reason and are only learning lessons to help you grow along your path.

I share the following with you because I believe that it applies to life. I brought it with me when I moved to Santa Barbara 33 years ago. I have no idea who gave it to me.

There's a Reason

For ev'ry pain, that we must bear,
    For ev'ry burden, ev'ry care,
        There's a reason.

For ev'ry grief, that bows the head,
    For ev'ry tear-drop that is shed,
        There's a reason.

For ev'ry hurt, for ev'ry plight,
    For ev'ry lonely, pain racked night,
        There's a reason.

But if we trust God, as we should,
    It all will work out for our god,
        He knows the Reason.

Life is meant to be enjoyed. It is what God wants for all of us. Reverend Foard told me: "God is not a bellhop running around trying to give you everything you need; we must do our part and God will do his."

From my experience, when you bring God into your life, you don't have to second guess where He is because you will feel His presence at all times; and you are then in touch with the Creator of Life and the Universe, God.

FIFTEEN

No Turning Back

I went to a church with a friend of mine.

I was searching with an open mind.

I didn't expect to find what I did.

And as I walked out, I was like a joyful kid.

I knew I had discovered something new.

I was so happy to have found some more clues.

There is no turning back: I have found a new path.

Thank you, Lord, and Reverend Foard.

Charlene Abundis
October, 1987

Justus Baron Von Liebig wrote, "Receiving a new truth is adding a new sense." In the Fall of 1987, my friend Carmen called and asked if I would like to go with her to a meditation class that was being held at a small Spiritualist church in town, The Church of The Comforter. I was unable to go that evening. She then asked if I would like to go to an All Message service with her the following Wednesday. I asked her what an all message service was. She said that a teacher at school that she worked with told her about the church and that Reverend Foard, the church minister, gave you messages from your family in spirit. I thought about it a moment and then said, "Why not. Sounds like it would be an unusual evening."

We arrived at the Church of The Comforter at 6:30 Wednesday evening. As we entered the front door of the church, there was a lady sitting right inside of the door. She asked if either of us had ever been to a message service at the church before. When we said no, she said, "Write your question on this," as she handed us a 3 by 5 piece of paper. "When he calls your number out," which she wrote on the top corner of the paper, "say good evening, and then he will give you a message."

I asked her, "Is that all you have to do?"

She replied, "Yes, he goes by your voice."

I asked, "Can we ask any question we want?"

She replied, "Yes, it doesn't matter what you ask."

We paid $3.00 each. Carmen was number five, and I was number six.

We visited as we sat in the church waiting about 15 minutes when an older gentleman walked out from a back room which was behind the altar. He looked our way and smiled at both of us, and we smiled back.

Carmen said, "He sure gives off a lot of love, doesn't he?"

I said, "Yes, his smile alone shows his love."

The message service started with Reverend Foard. The first lady to receive a reading seemed to believe what he was telling her because she was quickly writing it all down as he spoke.

Before I go on, I would like to mention that during my search for God, I had read a little about mediums; I learned that they can transfer thought messages from the spirit world to the earth plane. I never gave it any importance, nor did I ever have any desire to pursue one.

When Reverend Foard said number 5, Carmen said hello. He asked her if she had ever been in a Spiritualist Church before, and she said that neither of us had. With that warm loving smile of his, he said, "My, but you are brave ones." He then gave Carmen a message. I could tell by watching her that she could relate to the information because of her response back to him. I didn't know anything about Carmen's family and who had passed, so I sat there waiting anxiously for my turn.

When he called out number 6, I said, "Hello, Reverend Foard."

He said, "So this is your first time, too?"

I said, "Yes, it is."

The following is my exact reading: "I have a lady here who has not been in the spirit world too long. It could be your grandmother." I thought to myself, they have both been dead for more that 40 years, it couldn't be them.

I said, "My mother died early this year."

He said, "Yes, she says she is your mother. She says to tell you how happy she is that you are here tonight. You make her very happy; you are the first she has been in touch with here on the earth plane. She said she is so happy to be out of the body, that the treatment was worse than the disease." Then he said, "She had cancer."

I said, "Yes, she did."

"She wants you to know she is very happy and well, so happy to be out of the body, that two days before she died, her mother came to her and told her to let go. She says you were not back there when she passed and did not go to the funeral. She is happy for that because it was not pleasant."

By this time I was crying; I could not believe what I was hearing. He went on to say, she says there are many of you and many names. I can't get them all. Charles, your brother."

I thought, "My God, I have a brother Charles."

131

"She wants you to thank them all and tell them she loves them all very much. Tell them she is OK. She says she wants to thank the person who has been lighting a candle every day for her." (I found out later that was my Uncle David.)

The tears were really flowing down my face. He went on to say that my mother had given me a large tablecloth and 12 napkins. The first thing that came to my mind was guilt. Did she know I gave them away? I dropped that thought quickly as he was telling me more, and I didn't want to miss any of it.

He said, "Your mom thanks you. She says you made a difference in the spots where there was so much hurt. You made it easier for her. She has someone with her that was buried on a cold, snowy day. I did not get his name."

I knew it was my dad as I was there for his funeral and it was a cold, snowy day.

RF told me again how relieved she was to be out of her body, that I should thank them all for their love and prayers, that there were many.

A few thoughts in regards to my message. I knew without a doubt that he was in touch with my mother's spirit. When my mother gave me the tablecloth and napkins, I told her I didn't want them, that they were too fancy for me. She said she couldn't give them to anyone back home without hurting someone's feelings, so she asked me to please take them and tell no one. I was the only one who had moved away from home, and that is the only secret my mother and I ever had. But she mentioned the table cloth so that I would know that it really was her who was in contact with Reverend Foard. When the readings were finished, I asked Reverend Foard if I might give him a hug because I knew that I had found another truth to help me on my journey in life.

He said, "Yes, of course you can."

I gave him a hug, and I told him I wished that I had found him years ago.

He said with his great smile, "It doesn't matter; you have found us now, but I don't know what took you so long. This is better than a B-grade movie."

He had a great sense of humor. We noticed that with the first reading he gave that evening. He then told Carmen and me about a meditation class they had at the church on Friday nights and about the 11 o'clock church services on Sunday. I told him in no way was he going to get rid of me now.

When I walked out of the church with my friend, I knew I had found fact and not just belief. Once outside, I turned to Carmen and said, "Look at me. I am just shaking so bad I can't stop. My teeth are actually chattering; I cannot believe this. I am so excited." I was anxious to get home to tell Mel and the children about my reading.

When I walked into the house I was on an emotional high. I wished I could have put Reverend Foard in my pocket and taken him home with me for my family to meet. I couldn't let go of the feeling that I had found something special, and there was absolutely no question about it. There was no turning back for me now.

I excitedly told my family, and the first thing Mel asked me was, "What did you fill out? What questions did you answer? What did you tell him before?"

I said, "Nothing, honey. I just wrote a question on a piece of paper. When he called my number out, I said, 'Hello,' and that is when he gave me the reading."

Catana said, "Mom, I believe you. Remember after Cottonbell (our cat) died, I told you that she comes to me every night. Well, she still does."

I asked her in what form Cottonbell came to her; and she said she could hear her purring every night.

When she had first told me about Cottonbell, I thought it was just because she missed her so much, and that it was her way of dealing with the loss. More about Cottonbell later.

I told Mel I wanted to phone my family in Minneapolis and tell them the news. I phoned my sister Annie because I knew she had a phone line that three people can be on at once. She got my sister Rose; my sister Darlene had the flu, so her husband Ed got on the line.

After I shared my reading, Ed said, "Char, how did he know all that?"

I said, "Ed, he is a damn good medium. Never in a million years did I ever think I would be sitting in front of a medium, but I have read about them, and he obviously is good." They were anxious to know more, and I told them as I got more information I would share it with them.

When I hung up, Mel still wanted to talk about it, so we tucked the children in bed. Armando was not at all interested in hearing any of this. Mel got us each a glass of wine and I again went over the whole experience.

He said, "Honey, if this is true, what a revelation this is."

I said, "Honey, I know it's hard to believe, if someone told me what I just told you, I would have to go for myself to check it out. Also, if someone had handed me a Spiritualist brochure in the past, I would have thought these people were crazy and would have thrown it in the trash."

When I went to bed that night I couldn't sleep, I felt such energy. I kept thinking, "I can't believe this. He was in touch with my mother's spirit." As I lay there I just knew it was so, and even though it seemed so far out from anything I could ever imagine, I knew this was for real. God had opened another door for me in my search. I wanted to know more about Spiritualism and Reverend Foard, who introduced me to a whole new world.

The next morning I was still on a natural high, and I thanked God for sending me in this new direction. I decided to clean house. Even though I hate to do housework, I do love a clean house. I started in the master bedroom. It was raining outside, and I love listening to the rain. I opened the sliding door so I could hear the rain drops as they hit the deck. I felt so happy with such high energy. After I finished dusting the bedroom, I went into Catana's room and started to dust, then I realized that it had stopped raining. I left Catana's room to get a rain tape to play while I continued cleaning. Then our dog, Honeybear, came over to me, and I realized that I had not fed him yet.

I went into the kitchen, fed Honeybear, and by the time I got back to Catana's room, it had started to rain again. I forgot about the rain tape. I went back to dusting; and a few minutes later, just as I was about to leave her room and go into Armando's room to dust, I heard a clicking sound. I stopped and thought, "What is that noise?" I walked over to look out of Catana's bedroom window, and all of a sudden the rain tape started to play. I looked at Catana's bed and sitting on the floor next to her bed was her small tape recorder which was playing my rain tape. Catana often listened to the tape while doing her homework, and she obviously had taken it out of my room the night before.

I then realized that the clicking sound was the tape being rewound. I tensed up. What was happening here? And then I said out loud, "Wait a minute. You have read about this sort of thing happening in several of the books you read." I got so excited. I left the tape on. My friend Linda was coming to the house for lunch that day, and when I told her about my reading with Reverend Foard the night before and about the rain tape playing, she said, "Char, do you think it was your mother?"

I said, "I don't know if it was my mother or not, Linda, but I do know that it is a sign from God letting me know that I am on the correct path because it all feels so right to me."

The following Monday morning I had another strange experience after breakfast. Each morning as I am preparing breakfast, I turn the radio on which I always have tuned to the same local station. After breakfast the family left to get dressed. I cleaned up the kitchen and hurried to also get dressed because I had to drive Armando to school. After I got dressed, I was about to go into the kitchen to turn the radio off when Catana and Mel said they were leaving. I walked them outside, came back into the house, and went into the kitchen, and Armando was sitting at the table intently listening to the radio. I said, "Come on, honey, time to go."

He said, "Wait, mom, I want to hear the rest of the lady's story."

I asked him if he had changed the station, and he said no. I walked over to the radio, saw that the station had been changed; I stood and listened for a minute. Then I also wanted to hear the end of her story.

A lady was telling a story about truth. I obviously missed most of her story, but what she was now saying really had my attention.

She said, "The moral of this story is when you find truth, you must share it with others and not hide it. Without truth we are blind and cannot see. Truth is like light that travels in a straight line and is connected to God."

I grabbed a pen and paper so I could quickly write down what she said. I turned the radio off and looked at Armando, and said, "Come on, sweetie, we're running late."

When I returned home, I phoned Reverend Foard and told him about my two experiences. I told him I had read about things like this happening, and asked him what he thought about it. He said that the spirits were just reassuring me that they were in touch, that it happened all the time to people that have an open mind, also to remember that spirit helps us, but it actually is God's hand.

The following Wednesday, Mel, Catana, and four friends went along with me to Reverend Foard's message service. Armando wanted no part of it. I was the first to get a reading from our group, and the first thing Reverend Foard said was that he had somebody by the name of Alice here who said she was so happy and well, and to tell all that she likes it where she is. "She is telling me that she could not tell people what she was thinking or feeling when she was here (on the earth plane) because people did not understand her." Then Reverend Foard replied in a very deep, low voice, "Well, I love you, too."

My cousin Alice had just passed a few days before. When Reverend Foard had replied in such a low voice, "Well, I love you, too," no one but I would have understood. My cousin had a very deep voice and she always greeted me by saying, "I love you."

Mel's reading was very good, but he felt that Reverend Foard was just a very good mind reader and that he had a talent. Mel could not accept the fact that he was communicating with spirits. Catana and my friends all had good readings. My friends still talk about it today.

The following day, Kate, one of the friends who was with us the night before, called. She said, "Char, he is so good and so special. I understand what you mean about him throwing off love." I had told my friends before they went with me that they would feel Reverend Foard's love the moment they set eyes on him.

I continued to go weekly to the message services as well as having a private reading, which lasted about an hour. I would like to share a few readings with you, but before I do I would like to tell you more about Reverend Foard, a very special person who had come into my life.

SIXTEEN

LET THIS BE MY SONG

Hark, oh, my Soul! There's a messenger near.
Hold back the doubts; let the message flow clear.
Break not the silence that brings forth the tide
For the Angel of light to come and abide.
Let His peace and His love light flow the night long
With love from the future -- let this be my song.

Rejoice then, my Soul! Thou has caught the refrain
From the halls of tomorrow, free of hate's guilty stain
With rapture and love that binds Soul to Soul
With all creatures brothers, our godhead is whole.
The past holds thee bound with fetters so strong
Oh, reason thee free -- let this be my song.

Sing, oh, my Soul! The sweet ballad of light
Revealing the cruel and barbaric night.
Oh, turn thee away, and look back no more.
The daylight of logic reveals a new door.
Thy slumber is fretful, for the night is so long.
The dark age is over -- let this be my song.

Love, oh, my Soul! Awake from thy dream.
The ages malign thee, but the future is clean.
Thy slumber must end, righteous tyranny past.
The new age of love is dawning at last.
Break with the creeds of ignorance and wrong.
Love all life together -- let this be my song.

Reverend Edmund L. Foard
August 1956

138

Lois Cook, a good friend and medium who is now in spirit, and whom I met through Reverend Foard, told me that her family shortened Reverend Foard to RF. Since this chapter is about Reverend Foard, and his name is used often, I will use RF.

When RF was kind enough to accept a dinner invitation with our family at our home the Saturday before Christmas, I told him that I wanted to tape our conversation during the evening because I had so many questions I wanted to ask him, and I would like to get his answers on tape to review from time to time. He suggested that I purchase two tapes. I should have purchased three tapes because the evening lasted longer than either of us thought it would, and I ended up taking notes as well. He shared how he got started as a medium and other wonderful stories. The following is the conversation we had that evening, plus a few thoughts of my own.

RF told us he was born February 6, 1910, in Lake Charles, Louisiana. But he grew up in the foothills of the Ozark Mountains. He attended Wesleyan Methodist College in Marion, Indiana and shortly after World War II broke out, he enlisted in the United States Coast Guard. He said he was 44 when he actually started working as a medium but was aware of his abilities before that time.

I asked RF how he got into Spiritualism and this was his reply. He said that his mother and grandmother were both mediums, but they did not charge for readings. As a child there were always spirits around his house, so it was a very natural occurrence for him. When he was about 4 years old, he looked at a rocker in the room and saw a man standing next to it. He turned to his mom and she told him that was his Uncle Tom. Then, when he looked back at the rocker, he was gone. He said that he was introduced to spirit at a very young age.

He went on to say that when he was 24 years old he worked in a hotel in Miami, Florida, as a desk clerk. A "cute gal" checked in from Washington, D.C. Her name was Pat. When she later came down to the desk, he could tell she was getting ready to go somewhere, so he asked her where she was going; she said to church.

He said, "This time of the day?"

She said it was a Spiritualist Church.

He told her he was through for the day, and if she would like to wait a minute, he would go with her. "Of course, you know," he said, "I had to go along with her so that I could protect that pretty little thing from all of the vultures."

He added, "I was going to go and blow all those spiritualists to pieces, but that night I realized there was nothing I could put my finger on, so I had to go back with her again. She then joined a development class; I had to join too, of course, you know, to protect her. There were 12 or 13 people in the class who would say that they saw this and that, but when the teacher asked, 'Mr. Foard, did you see anything?' I would reply, 'I didn't see a damn thing.'

"The teacher said, 'Well, you will.'

"Pat decided to go back to Washington, D.C., and I stopped going to class then. One night I woke up, and beside my bed stood a great, big Indian. I was almost paralyzed. I reached to pull the light on and he disappeared.

"The next day I went looking for another room. I found one on a corner that had windows where the street lights shined in. I called the teacher and told her I would not be back. When she asked why, I just said, 'I won't be back.'

"Then she asked, 'Oh. you saw something?'

"I said, 'Yes, and I didn't like it one bit.'

"Then three or four weeks later, when I was working a split shift, I got home late one night. Some kids had shot out the street light with a BB gun. I went upstairs and went to bed. About three in the morning, I woke up and over in the corner of the room was this same Indian. He knew he had frightened me the last time, so he stood a distance away. I went back to sleep.

"World War II broke out, and I enlisted in the United States Coast Guard. It was always a secret where we were going, and one night a crew member asked, 'Foard, do you know where we are going?' And I blurted something out, and I will be damned if that wasn't where we ended up."

He said he would often blurt out of his mouth where they were going, and the skipper was very concerned about the leak.

"When I was headmaster, we had a bad storm one night and everything got wet, so we pulled into port to air and dry everything out. The navigator came over to me and said, 'Foard, we have to be out to sea in half-an-hour.'

"I said, 'No way can we do that.'

"The Skipper said, 'I will help get everything secured down.'

"When we were through, I said, 'Well that's about the last of it. I guess it will do until we get to Hudson Bay.'

"He looked at me and asked, 'Where did you get that information?'

"I replied, 'What information?'

"He said, 'Hudson Bay.'

"I replied, 'I don't know.'

"The Skipper said, 'Only the navigator, decoding officer, and I knew that. There is a leak here, and we are going to find it. Foard, after we get under way, come to my state room.'

"I thought, boy, I am in trouble now. I later went down to the state room, and I decided to tell him that I have an Indian that tells.

"He said, 'You have an Indian that tells you?'

"I said, 'Well, not really; he just blurts it out of my mouth, and I don't know what he is going to say.'

"He looked at me like I was crazy, and I told him about the Indian.

"He said, 'Well, Foard, I believe you and your story about the Indian, but for God's sake, don't tell anyone else about it. They'll lock us both up.'

"During another bad storm one night, and it was rough, I was on deck at the helm, and I saw something dash by me real fast on the right. I looked and saw nothing. Then it dashed by me real fast on the left. Again I saw nothing. Then it came and looked me right in the face. It was the same Indian that I had seen in my room.

"I asked, 'What the hell are you doing here?'

"He said, 'Me watch over the ship.'

141

"I said, 'Do you think you can get it back to port?'

"He said, 'Me think so.'

"I said, 'You do that, and I will be working with you guys when this is all over.'

"When I got out, I went to Chicago, got a job and a place to live, and joined the Spiritualist Church."

Catana asked RF how he sees things, and he said, "When you shut your eyes and picture someone you love, well, that is how I see them." He told Catana that spirits have to be within three feet of him so that he can pick up their messages.

She then asked, "When the spirits say that they are going to help you, how do they help you?"

He replied, "Through your dreams or your daily decisions, and sometimes something will hit you that is not at all like you. That, also, is their help."

He then told her, "But you must ask for help. They cannot help you unless you ask for their help, and it's very important to thank them every time." He told Catana that the best time to ask for help with a problem or decision is just before going to bed. That is when the power is the strongest and the most powerful.

Another question Catana asked was whether you could choose what you wanted to look like in the spirit world. He said that you usually look like you did around your peak which is 26 or so in your prime. But when the spirits appear to him, they look like they did when they actually passed over because that is how they are to be remembered by those left behind. He said our bodies are actually perfect in the spirit world.

She asked if the spirits took a long time to travel from one place to another, and he said, "No, that all they have to do is have a thought and they are there."

He said, "Just a thought and everything is at your finger tips; there is no distance or time in the spirit world."

I asked RF if the spirits' minds are clearer in the spirit world than when they were here on earth, and he said, "Oh, yes, they see very clearly up there. All the confusion and clutter that they might have had here is all cleared up.

When you get messages from your mother and father, guides, and teachers, it is all very clear."

I asked if they could see way into the future, and he said that some could with experience, others not so far; but when they give you messages regarding your future, they are seeing what lies ahead for you, and by telling you, it helps you in your daily decisions and life. He said we have so many limitations here on earth that we do not have in the spirit world.

When he said that, I recalled one evening while I was waiting for the message service to start. I began talking to a gentleman who I had seen there many times before. I asked him how long he had been coming to see RF; he said about 11 years. He also said that he got all his answers from RF and that if I were to check with anyone who was a regular, that they would all tell me the same thing. He helps you to go in the direction that is best for you; and that he is always right on. He added that it has always worked for him.

When I asked RF about what the gentleman told me, he said he did not approve of people coming to him for all their answers.

He said, "They use me as a crutch, and that is not good. They are here to find their own answers, and it is OK to get some help, but since they pay their three dollars, I have no choice."

During our Christmas evening, RF said that those who are very materialistic here on earth will find the mind will have great difficulty letting go of it when they reach the spirit world. He said it can take souls years and years to let go of the material and to realize that they must change their attitude in order to grow in the spirit world.

One Sunday there was a visiting medium at the church. She said, "It can take people up to 100 years or more to change their minds in the spirit world if they were very materialistic on the earth plane. Those who are materialistic here will end up below the 3rd sphere."

She added, "We should not be denied a comfortable life on the earth plane; we all need food, clothes, a roof over our head, and a car. But how many roofs, how many cars do we need? We should know how important it is to reach out and help others, to give love whenever we can. Our purpose here is to reach out and help; that is what it is all about. If we do not do it right here, we will have to start all over in the spirit world, and it is a lot harder up there."

She continued, "If we give about ten percent of our time in helping others and reaching out on the earth plane, we will find ourselves way ahead of others when we reach the spirit world and might find ourselves on the 3rd sphere. Anything below the 3rd sphere is not desirable."

I asked RF if he agreed with her.

He replied, "Oh, yes, she is right, if people could just know what it is all about; that how they choose to live their lives on the earth plane will determine where they go in the spirit world."

He said that by reaching out and helping others on the earth plane, you will be advanced when you reach the spirit world. All the good you do here is all recorded somewhere and is never forgotten.

He said, "It is important to know that what we do here is what counts on the other side. Material things should not be important on the earth plane. They will only hold you back when you reach the spirit world."

Mel asked, "Who goes below the 3rd sphere?"

He said, "That is the lower element. People who harm others, greedy people. Wealth is OK to have if you get it by not being greedy. People who are successful here on the earth plane through hard work and helping others, by being loving and caring as they go along, will have the same wealth in the spirit world and continue to be successful."

I asked why some people can see the spirits and others cannot.

He said, "We all can see the spirits. We need to train our eye. Babies can see the spirits, but as they grow older they are brainwashed to believe that they do not." He said that cats and dogs see spirits.

Then Armando asked if dogs have spirits that come to them, and he said, "Yes, your dog has a puppy that comes to play with him. I saw it earlier this evening."

I asked RF if he recalled when another visiting medium at the church had said that spirits travel faster than light, and that light travels 186,000 miles a second.

He said, "Yes, take for instance a propeller of an airplane. You can see it when the motor starts, and it goes so fast that the propeller disappears because of the speed, and you can look right through it. Well, spirit is like that. With such a high rate of vibration, it disappears. Everything in the spirit world is very much like the earth plane. It's just a higher rate of vibration and therefore it becomes invisible. A good example is if you take sugar and put it in a glass of water; it will disappear, but you can taste it; it's still there."

He said, "We don't lose a thing when we die. We are the same one minute before we pass to spirit as we are one minute after we pass. It's so simple. It is like the ebbing of the tide, a receding wave, very peaceful, and we just continue on but with no restrictions in the spirit world, and we eventually go to the sphere we feel comfortable in." When you dream at night you leave your body. That is why our dreams are so weird because of the lack of restrictions. I mentioned my dream book earlier in this book. I asked RF if he, too, believed that we are actually getting messages and learning in our dreams.

He said, "Oh, yes, that is the purpose, but most people don't realize that. They don't understand their dreams and don't know how to apply them to help them in their daily lives."

Armando asked if spirits pick up your thoughts, and RF said, "Yes, that is how they communicate with you."

I asked RF to explain his view about throwing out a positive and a negative thought to the universe.

He said that if you throw a bad thought out to the universe, it will have a negative effect, and if you throw out a positive one, it will have a positive effect, that negativity draws negative and positive draws positive.

I asked him if we throw a negative thought out, could we not then throw a positive one after it and catch it.

He said, "Charlene, my father always said, the bad will come back to you much faster than the good. I suppose you can throw a positive after a negative and try and catch it, but I can't promise that you will."

I asked him if he remembered when, at one of his message services, I asked my mother about reincarnation and what she knew about it. He said that when he gives messages he does not always remember them later.

My mother's answer back to me was that no one there, that she knew, had seen any evidence of it. You could move up the scale, and you could come back and help answer questions, such as she is now doing for me. My father also came through in that reading; and he said that in the 15 years he had been in spirit it had not been offered to him, and that where he is they also know nothing about it.

During that same reading RF told me that when my dad gave him that message to give to me that he asked my dad if he would like to come back to the earth. My dad said, "No, thank you, I will stay right where I am."

RF said he had asked hundreds of spirits if they would like to come back to the earth plane, and they all very happily said no, thank you.

When I asked RF if he believed in reincarnation, he said he used to teach it, but no longer does; that his guide, Scottie, who went over in the early 1700's, said there is no proof of it.

I asked him, "How do you explain when people are hypnotized and regressed back to other lives?"

He replied, "When you are hypnotized, you leave your body, and perhaps other spirits around you step in and take you back to their lives."

RF went on to say that Mae Taylor, who was his last teacher in Hollywood and who now is in the spirit world, told him after she was there, that she went to every plane, that there are seven spheres, and that each sphere has seven planes.

She said that she could go as far as the 6th sphere and no further. If she did go to the 7th sphere, she could not come back. It would be like shedding your body when you left the earth plane.

He said, "One of the things she told me about is the plane where the murderers are. They all had the identity of everyone they killed in their aura. Wherever they went in the spirit world, all of the other spirits could see what they had done, so they all stayed together on the same plane by choice." RF said they could work on moving up by helping others. For example, like your mother and father help you, it helps them to move up to a higher sphere much faster; otherwise, they have to work in the spirit world, and it is much slower. He added, "We might as well work very hard on the earth plane to get it right because it's much harder to do it up there."

When I asked RF if you could go to any plane you wanted, even if you were a criminal here on earth, I found his answer very interesting.

He said, "Yes, but as I said, they won't stay very long because they will feel so uncomfortable that they are anxious to leave. Everybody knows what they have done. Spiritualism does not believe in punishment; evil comes from ignorance of God's law, and all actions do have direct results.

"When they arrive in the spirit world, they go to the sphere that they feel comfortable in, and then it is up to them to work in the spirit world by offsetting the injurious acts they did while on the earth plane. They do that by helping others, by sacrificing, doing good deeds, having positive thoughts that will help them also move up; but as I said, you may as well get it right while on the earth plane because it is much harder and takes much longer in spirit."

I told RF that my mother, in many of her messages, kept thanking me for opening a door for her and for other spirits she had been able to bring back to me that also gave me messages through the readings he gave me.

I asked if she is thanking me for helping her to achieve a higher sphere, as well as helping the others. He said, "Yes, she might be on a higher sphere than some of those spirits she brings back to you, and she obviously has chosen to be very active in the spirit world because she has brought many spirits here to also give you messages. When she thanks you for opening a door for her, it is because you are helping her to climb higher by being open to receive her messages of help. By her bringing other spirits to the message service to also give you messages, it also helps them.

Charlene, it helps them all to climb to a higher level. But it looks like your mother is anxious to help the others climb by bringing them to you, and her benefits on the other side will certainly be rewarded."

I told RF that I was surprised that more spirits did not come through for me on my first reading. He said that the spirits are also learning in the spirit world, that they are not always sure how to go about it.

He said, "Remember, when they die, nothing changes, they just live on. If they were not aware of Spiritualism on the earth, they take that ignorance with them to spirit. Your mom is a fast learner and your dad has now joined her. The more messages they can get to you through meditation, dreaming, or through a good medium, the more they will get used to it, and they will be stronger each time they get through to help you. You will feel more energy from them also."

I told RF that on the way home from a message service my friend Kate said, "Char, I am sure the spirits are waiting up there for someone down here to knock on their door or to ring the phone to wake them up."

RF said, "She's got that just about right."

I recall the third reading I had from RF. My cousin Alice came through again, with my mom, and they said that they were so excited because they were finally waking up down here. "Here" meaning the people on the earth plane.

I asked RF if there is a purgatory in the spirit world.

He said, "Yes, but it is not for punishment. It is just for an adjustment period. After 49 days you must leave and then go to the sphere you feel comfortable with. You can leave anytime before the 49 days are up."

When I asked him about his guides, he told me that he has several, but the one that is with him most of the time is Scottie, who is always there for him.

I asked him how we get our guides.

He said, "Like attracts like, and, of course, you will have your family, friends, and relatives up there who are eager to help as well. If anyone wishing to join the group is not congenial, he or she is not allowed in."

I asked RF if he knew when spirit enters the body, and he said with the first breath.

I asked him if babies grow in the spirit world.

He said, "Yes, they will grow in the spirit world just as they would here on the earth plane." I told him that we had lost a baby almost full term. "Well," he said, "then it will please you to know that babies and children are raised as angels."

I read many years ago that we are born with 30% of our personality and the remaining 70% is developed. I asked RF if he agreed with that.

He said, "That is just about right. Yes, it is very close to that."

Catana asked if people who are married on the earth plane stay married in the spirit world or come together again.

He said, "Not always. They can come together if they like, but some of them don't. It's up to you."

In one of my readings I asked my mom if she and dad were on the same level, and she said no, that they were both on different levels. She said that they do meet and come together, but before she got there, daddy, who had been there for 15 years, had done nothing. When he saw that he could no longer dominate her, he decided to join her in school.

The one thing that came through loud and clear during our discussion this Christmas evening was that Spiritualism is so simple. I expected to find out that it was very complicated. RF said that many people try to complicate it, but it is simple. Spiritualism simplifies everything.

RF turned to Catana and told her that she was a walking piece of art, that she was very talented and it showed in everything she did.

Catana loves drama and has been in school plays since kindergarten. She told us from the time she was 5 or 6 years old that she was going to be an actress, and by the time she reached seventh grade she said she was an actress. She now is an actress.

Then RF said, "Armando, I see two inventions over your head."

I said, "Really, RF, Armando has always told us that he was going to be an inventor someday."

RF said, "Armando, you have an inventor from the spirit world working with you." Then he looked at me, "That is why he wants to be an inventor." Armando was so happy to hear that.

RF said to Armando, "Thomas Edison was a spiritualist. When he was a boy he came home from school one day with a note from the teacher saying to keep him home because he was too dumb to learn. It made his mother furious so she started to teach him herself." He added that Thomas Edison had 1093 patents, and they all came from the spirit world.

RF turned to me and asked, "How come you never told me Armando wanted to be an inventor?"

I said, "Because he didn't want to go to you for a reading, and I would not force him to do something he was so opposed to, so this is really exciting."

Armando said, "YEAH!"

Catana then told RF something that I had completely forgotten. She told him that when she was 6 or 7, I put her down for an afternoon nap; and she woke up with all of the covers pulled off her, and three men stood by her bed. One was a doctor, and the other two had suits on. She said she didn't know how the covers got off her, but she was scared so she pulled them up over her head.

RF said, "Well, Catana, those were some of your teachers and guides letting you know they were working with you from the spirit world."

I then remembered when she came out from her nap and told me the story. I thought it was her great imagination working overtime, but not anymore.

RF looked at Mel and said, "You have written something that you are now revising. What is it, Mel?"

The look on Mel's face revealed he was shocked by that question. Remember, he believed that RF was just a good mind reader. Mel replied, "Yes, I'm revising a screenplay."

RF said, "You will also be writing a historical story."

Mel had already completed a historical screenplay, and he planned to write several more. RF knew that Mel was skeptical. He told me, "Mel will tune in when it is his time."

HB (Honeybear, our dog) decided he needed some attention so he started acting up to entertain us for awhile. When he decided to take a rest, RF told us about his sister Laura's poodle, Gigi. He said that his sister who had no children absolutely loved her dog. He often thought that if anything happened to the dog that his sister would die. Well, one afternoon he decided to take a nap on the sofa because he knew he was going to church that evening, and it would be a long night. He lay with his face turned to the back of the sofa, and then he felt two little pushes on his back. He said, "I turned around, and there was Gigi. I immediately tried to call my sister, but there was no answer, so I called my other sister who lived 20 miles away from her. She said she didn't know if the dog was OK or not, but if anything happened to the dog it would kill Laura, and she assured me that she would continue to try and contact Laura and get back to me."

On Monday morning Laura called and asked, "How did you know we had to put Gigi to sleep?"

RF said, "I didn't. I just knew she no longer was in this world anymore."

His sister said she took her to the vet and that she was full of cancer, so they decided to put her to sleep.

When I asked RF if he was the oldest in the family he said, with his great sense of humor and smile, yes, both of his sisters were younger than he, but he was the best looking.

We had picked RF up at 5:00 p.m., and five hours later we took him home; I was almost sure we had drained him. I asked him if we had, he assured us that we had not, and that he had a most enjoyable evening. I told him that it was a very special Christmas evening for us, as well, and that he had no idea how special it was to have had him with us.

The children and I decided to ride along with Mel to take RF home. When Mel picked him up, he invited Mel in to see his antique musical machines, and when we arrived at his home, he wanted to know if I and the children would also like to see them. Yes!

As he explained to us how each machine worked his face was like a joyful kid. It was obvious to me that this was the highlight of his evening. He told us that very few people had been invited into his home to see "his toys." He said, "I am sort of private, you know," as he wrinkled up his nose.

I said, "RF, you throw off happiness in every direction with all your charm and personality." He replied, "Well, I don't know about that, but I can tell you that I now have everything I have ever wanted in life. I have it all right here in Santa Barbara, and I have never been so happy."

His surroundings were very simple and uncomplicated, just like he was. I knew he played the organ beautifully during the church services, but I had no idea how much he loved music. As we were saying our thank yous and good nights, walking out the door, we each had a turn playing with his musical doorbell.

We no sooner got into the car than Armando said, "Mom, I just love RF. Why didn't you force me to go along for a reading before?"

I said, "Sweetheart, you are 13 years old. You know I wouldn't force you to do something that you didn't want to do, unless it was necessary."

He said, "Well, you should have. I want to go from now on." Throughout that evening Armando had not said much, but I could tell he had taken it all in.

I can visualize as I write this. Mel was sitting in the chair next to the fireplace, and Armando was sitting on the floor, about three feet away from him leaning back against the ledge of the fireplace with Honeybear laying across his legs. RF, Catana, and I were sitting opposite them. Whenever I would look at Armando, his eyes were wide open, and he was in awe of all that RF was saying and not missing a word. It was a beautiful picture seeing Mel, Armando and the dog, with the fireplace glowing in the background. At the time I thought I should get up and get the camera and take a picture, but I didn't want to interrupt the flow of RF's talking. That scene will always stay in my mind.

When we arrived back home, Catana and I plugged in the Christmas tree lights again, and Mel lit the fireplace for us before going off to his office. Armando went into his room to read, and Catana and I made some hot chocolate and talked for several hours. It was one of those evenings that you just don't want to end. RF energized all of us.

Catana said, "Mom, if the spirits are there to help us with our thoughts, why do we pray to God for things?"

I said, "Honey, God is everywhere; everything is God. It's just good to know that we also have our guides and family in spirit to help us. I guess you can call them God's helpers. Before I did any of my search, I often prayed for help; and even though I didn't know how to find God, I now realize that I always had my prayers answered. When we ask for something and it is right for us, God puts the wheels in motion."

RF told me that there are many mysteries, that he certainly doesn't have all the answers, but just to keep an open mind. One thing for sure he said is that we live on and that a good medium can put us in touch with our family, friends, and guides in spirit. "But remember that crutch," he said. "Don't over use it."

SEVENTEEN

THE BIG FLOW

There's a river that flows like a mass on the move
Testing the shores, yet follows its groove.
Who knows whence it rises, this ocean of calm
Flowing over my feet, giving healing and balm?
Is the path always gentle from yon snow covered height?
Has the rhythm and song now changed into might?

There's a channel of thought flowing free without bind.
A gift to the senses from the infinite mind.
Whence sprang ye to be, and what is the goal?
Was it here before man; was it born with the Soul?
Has its pathway been easy in a slow gentle course
Winding its way outward from the Infinite Source?

There's a great tide of love flowing ever so free
Unmindful of law, but for all that may be.
Whence grew thee so lovely, out of mischief and mire?
Ah! No, little seeker, it is born of desire.
Did it grow from a seedling? Was it ever that small?
Ah! No, it is life and given to all.

There's a phenomenon to life in a mysterious flow
Baffling the sages and they that should know.
They flounder and guess and weil round the bier.
And plant in each bosom superstition and fear.
Free us from the Ignorant; hold reason supreme.
Send all teachings back till they're coming out clean.

Reverend Edmund L. Foard

My first reading from RF was in the middle of October, 1987. I would like to share a few more readings with you that "blew my socks off." I will add my thoughts after I explain the reading. Keep in mind that in order to get a message you do not have to ask a question. RF, as well as other visiting mediums that he invited to the church, go by your voice vibration. RF said no two voices are alike; we are all unique and different. At the end of each Sunday service, a few messages are given to some of the people, and they are usually short.

At the end of the first Sunday service I attended, RF asked for my voice. I said hello; and he said, "I have your mother, Ida, here. She apologizes for an odor. She is not telling me any more about the odor, so you will have to figure that one out." He added, "She is very happy and says to tell them all I love them." He went on to say, "She is holding a maple leaf in her hand and to tell you that she has been sitting under this tree on your deck. A man with her sends love, and she thanks you for opening a door for her after her passing."

This was only the third time I had been to RF's church. The first time was with my friend, Carmen; the second time was the following Friday evening to attend his meditation class, and the Sunday service was the third time. RF did not know my mother's name, so I was surprised when he said Ida.

This is how her "odor" message applied to my life. My mother was a smoker. Whenever she would come to visit, she would have to go outside to the deck, or if it was raining, go into the garage and open the door and smoke. We do no allow smoking in our home. For the most part, she would smoke on the deck. When we landscaped the house, we planted a maple tree between two connecting decks which had a large opening. That maple tree is the one that my mother would sit under and smoke; she always commented as to how beautiful the tree was. She said it was one of her favorite trees because the leaves turned such a beautiful color in the fall.

One evening after dinner, when we were watching the news on TV, she went out for a cigarette. She never had only one, sometimes two or three, so she spent a great deal of time smoking on our deck. When she came back in this particular evening, Armando was sitting on the sofa, and she went over and sat next to him. She then grabbed him for a hug, and he plugged his nose and pulled back. He was about seven years old at the time. I knew it tore at her heart because she was a very sensitive person. I felt so bad. I said, "Mom, I'm sorry, but you smell of smoke, and the kids don't like it."

I later explained to Armando that grandma is very loving and sensitive, and by pulling back he hurt her feelings. I told him that I understood why he pulled back, but next time she hugged him just to go along with it because she loved him very much.

At a Wednesday evening reading, RF said, "I have so many spirits here for you tonight. Boy, you came from a fun-loving, partying family, didn't you?"

I said, "Yes, I did."

He said, "Well, they are having a party in the spirit world. They are dancing and singing. They send you beautiful vibrations and a lot of love. They are getting a kick out of watching you down here. They said that you should slow down and take all at a slower pace. Your dad is here. He said that they were waiting for your mother to come over, and they threw a big ball for her."

Well, as I mentioned in the first part of the book, they were a real partying family.

The following is from Catana's reading: "A beautiful spirit comes to you from your mother's side. It is your grandma. I see you swaying to music." Then he asked her if she like music and she said yes. He added, "They tell me you are very dramatic and good at pantomime. You will feel all kinds of new things coming to you. Your grandma is a beautiful person. She has her father here with her."

Catana asked, "Is my grandma taking care of our cat, Cottonbell?"

RF had his eyes closed and said, "Well, she said she doesn't really like the critter that much. It was around here a while ago." Then he opened his eyes and looked at Catana and said, "But don't you know, she comes to you every night?"

Catana said, "Yes."

"Your grandma said that she will take care of it if you want her to, but she is not crazy about the idea."

Catana was 15 years old when she received the above reading from RF. She was taking piano lessons and had been for six years. She had just finished a school play and recently had participated in pantomime skits in her theater class at school. But the most important part of her message, as far as Catana was concerned, regarded Cottonbell. Until this reading, she kept asking for another cat, even though we had a dog, but Mel and I said no, with our busy schedule, one house pet was enough.

On the way home from the reading, she said, "Mom, I told you Cottonbell comes to me every night. I am so happy."

That same evening I received the following message. RF said, "I have a gentleman here by the name of George. I think it is your father. I missed part of the name. Anyway, he says he is your father. He sends you love and beautiful vibrations. I also have a Henry or a Harry. I am not sure of the name."

When he asked me if I could place that name, I said no.

He said, "Well, it is a small name. Anyway he sends you a lot of love and vibrations." And then said, "How about Tiny?"

At first it didn't register with me; then all of a sudden it hit me, and I said, "Yes, my Uncle Herman. That's it."

"Yes, he said it is Herman. Your mother Ida is here and some other friends. I cannot get all the names. They all send you beautiful vibrations. They all love you so much, and send love to all."

I did not ask a question that night.

My dad's full name was Simon George. My Uncle Herman was nicknamed Tiny because he was so big. I always called him Uncle Herman. His brothers, sisters, and friends would often call him Tiny. More about my Uncle Herman in a few chapters.

My friend Kate was with me this evening, and before I give part of her reading, with her permission, I must tell you a story that she shared with me about a cat she had before I met her.

When she and her husband Dave and daughter Mia moved to our street, they brought with them two beautiful cats. One was a female Siamese who enjoyed the outdoors for hunting; this cat had been beaten up numerous times by another cat who lived next door and had required surgery several times.

One day her cat disappeared so they put an ad in the local paper. Another family in the neighborhood by the name of Jensen responded to the ad; and sure enough it turned out to be their Siamese. Kate and her family were overjoyed to have the cat back. After a short stay the cat returned to the Jensen's house. Kate said, "Char, we all loved that cat so much, especially Mia; but it was always down at the Jensens." So they told the Jensens they could have the cat, and they bought Mia another.

I didn't know Kate or her family at the time this all happened, but I did know the Jensen family.

Whenever I would visit them, they were so excited about this beautiful cat that had adopted them and told me how much they loved it. Mr. Jensen passed on to spirit a few years later, and the cat stayed with Mrs. Jensen.

Now, back to the reading; when RF called Kate's number, he went into her message. At the very end of her message, he jerked and said, "Yes," then looked at Kate and added, "I just got a jolt from a spirit." He asked her, "Do you know someone in the spirit world by the name of Jensen?"

Kate and I looked at each other, and she answered that we both did.

He went on to say, "Well, he is here and, yes, he knows you both; but he writes thank you over your head. He thanks you twice."

That evening when I got home, I called Mrs. Jensen but she was out, so I left a message asking her to call. She phoned the next morning. I asked her if I could come over for a few minutes, that I had something to tell her, and I didn't want to tell her over the phone. I knew how much she loved that cat. I also knew how very much she missed her husband, and it was still hard for her to accept that he had passed on.

When I explained Kate's reading to her, she said, "Oh, Charlene, he must know what a comfort that cat is to me. I have her sleeping in my room each night and just hearing her gives me such comfort."

I asked her if she would like me to ask any questions of RF for her when I returned the following week.

She said, "If only I knew he was happy and busy. You know how active and happy he was here."

"Yes." I told her I would ask.

The following week I asked RF her question. He said, "I do not have him here, but someone here will speak for him."

I asked if he was busy and happy.

RF said, "He is very busy working on an invention with an inventor in the spirit world. He is very happy."

When I told Mrs. Jensen the next day, she said, "Oh Charlene, five years before he passed, his best friend, who was an inventor, died; and it hit him so hard. Now you tell me that. It is so interesting." She also said she didn't think she could go to RF for a reading right now, and she never did. But I do know it helped her very much to have received the answer she did.

EIGHTEEN

A RAINBOW

Look up, little fledgling,
Away from sad trow.
For the heavens are bright
Neath a lovely rainbow.

How can such beauty
Appear from nowhere?
Life's laughter and tears
Have willed it be there.

We hide now the source
Of your rancor and bale.
So cling fast to love
'Til she's lifted the veil.

The cycle is ending.
A chapter will close.
Look up to your heaven
Full of beautiful bows.

Reverend Edmund L. Foard

The late part of October, 1987, I was feeling stressed knowing that November and December were going to be very busy and hectic. Our Anonymous group was having a fundraiser at my home, and Catana would be rehearsing for a school play, which meant that we would be going back and forth to school three times a day for several weeks. Armando had a birthday coming up, and birthdays for the children are always a big deal in our family. My aunt, who was in her 70's, and had to be on oxygen 24 hours a day, was also coming out on a visit. Along with my regular schedule and Thanksgiving, Christmas, etc., I knew it would keep me running.

At the end of a Sunday service, RF gave me the following message. "I have your mother here and her mother, and they said the next two months all will be coming very fast for you, and they said now don't go and get dizzy on us." In chapter 10, I explained about my dizziness caused by stress. That day, when I arrived home from church I immediately started preparing lunch for the family. Mel was downstairs working, and when he heard me in the kitchen, he was up those stairs in seconds, wanting to know if I had a reading that day. I said that I had, and then I told Mel the message that RF gave me.

He said, "How does he do it? He is so talented."

I said, "Mel, why can't you just accept that RF communicates with the spirits. I don't understand you!"

Mel was still having a hard time believing that RF was able to communicate and get messages from the spirit world. On the other hand, he could hardly wait to hear my messages, which indicated to me that he knew RF wasn't just a mind reader. I knew in time he would open his mind, instead of just waiting for RF to mess up somehow and then saying "see." Well RF didn't mess up.

My Aunt Helen arrived the last week of November and spent part of the Christmas Holidays with us. When I shared with her about RF, she said she would like to go with me the next time I went because she has always felt spirits around her.

Since she had to have oxygen 24 hours a day, it was difficult for her to get around because she had to pull a small machine with her all the time, but I took her to meet RF at the next message service. I would like to share her reading with you, but I need to respect her privacy. She did, however, have a very good reading. She was amazed about all that RF knew. Her husband Eddy had come through. She said to me, "I now know how you feel. It is exciting."

I said, "Auntie, if you want to go for a private reading I will be happy to take you. He charges so little."

She said, "No, I don't need to go anymore. As I told you before, this is not new to me. I have always felt my parents around me."

For my reading that evening, my mother told me that she came to me in a dream last night (remember, we are out of our bodies when we dream and are visiting the other side), so she wanted to know if I remembered the dream.

I said, "Yes, I did, but I only remembered that she was in my dream, and married to a strange man. Tell her I am sorry. I have been working on remembering complete dreams, but I lose some of them."

RF then said, "Your mother said it's OK. She will do the talking. Just be aware that she is there helping you and will always be with you." RF added, "Your father is here. He doesn't have much to say. He sends love, and then someone here said we are all ready to go for broke."

My Aunt Helen was sitting to my right, and she jerked around and looked at me, when RF said "we are all ready to go for broke." I thought she was going to fall off her chair with excitement.

After my reading she leaned towards me and said, "That was Eddy (her husband) who said that; he always said that." She was so excited.

I said, "Auntie, you had your reading just before mine. He just decided to add his two cents worth because you were here."

My mom, dad, Aunt Helen, and Eddy were friends for as long as I can remember. My aunt loved the evening with RF, and I felt that once she returned home, it would be one of the highlights of her trip because she talked about it daily.

Six days before my aunt was to leave, she asked me if I would be going to RF's Wednesday night message service. I told her no, because that day was Mel's birthday. She said, "Well, the next time you go, I want to go with you."

I told her that she was scheduled to fly out on Tuesday of next week, and that RF's message service was on Wednesday. I asked her what caused her to change her mind and want to go back for another reading.

She said, "Something is telling me to go back."

I said, "Well, let me check with Mel. I am sure he won't mind if we go on his birthday."

When I asked Mel, he said, "Oh, honey, it's no big deal. Take her and go."

We celebrated Mel's birthday during dinner; afterwards, Helen and I left for the service. She was again so excited with her reading; her family's name came through, and much more. She had a special question, and she received an answer that lifted her spirits. On the way home she said, "I had a question answered that has always bothered me, and the answer is exactly as I thought it would be, and all these years I stressed wanting an answer to that question, and I knew the answer all along. This has been very good for me. I know when I get back to Minneapolis, I will wish I could come back."

My reading that night went as follows: "I have your mother here. She sends love to the person next to you. Your mother says she sees your house unfolding with Christmas, that she has been here with you over the Christmas season, and it was always so beautiful. It will always be with her. She said you have so much love and happiness in your home and family. Another family member elsewhere has a lot of unhappiness; one person especially, is very unhappy. You have so much. Please share it with them. One is in need of a lot of understanding and needs to be understood. She sends love to all. That is Ida, and she says she did not know about the church when she visited you, you never took her. Your grandma and grandpa are here. I have an Al and a Hilda here also."

Well, I never took my mother to the church because I didn't know about RF then. The Al that came through was my mother's brother, my favorite uncle on her side of the

163

family. Hilda was my cousin, and I have some very special memories of her when I was small.

When we arrived home that evening, I was anxious to call my family back in Minneapolis because of the message that someone was in need of understanding, but I decided to wait until the next day so we could spend the rest of the evening celebrating a little more birthday cheer with Mel.

The following day I called my sister Annie, and told her the message mom gave me through RF.

She said, "Mom sure got it right," and explained to me why my one sister was depressed.

I then phoned my sister who was depressed, and we had a long, phone conversation. Mom's message was right on.

My mother came through for me in most of the readings; she also brought in other relatives who had messages for me, as well. And the messages always applied to my life!

In another reading, my grandfather, my mother's father, came through and said that he was always with my "Precious Ones" and was looking after them.

Anyone who personally knows our family, knows that I have always referred to Catana and Armando, even before they were born, as "Precious Ones." All cards I send out are signed, Mel, Charlene and "Precious Ones." I loved that message from my grandfather. He passed when I was about five years old, but I do remember him.

Several weeks after my Aunt Helen left, I received a reading from RF that I must say "blew my socks off" again. RF said, "I have a gentleman here. Boy is he tall, over 6 feet and slender as a toothpick. His name is Walt. He said he is your uncle. He said that you were cheated out of an inheritance from him and your aunt, and he feels bad about that." My Uncle Walt was very tall and very slender.

Three weeks later I received another reading that related to the above message, but before I share that with you, let me explain about the inheritance.

When I moved to California in 1964, I kept in touch with my Aunt Lena and Uncle Walt. (I wrote about them in chapter three and what bright lights they were in my life growing up.) Aunt Lena was my mother's sister, and they had a rift that separated the two families for several years.

My dad told my brothers, sisters, and me when the rift started, that he did not want us to have anything to do with Aunt Lena and Uncle Walt. He wanted us to take my mother's side or her feelings would be hurt. Well, I was around 19 then, and I told my dad, "You cannot expect us to avoid them. They have been a great part of all of our lives since we were born. We are like their children, dad. They don't have anyone else."

They did not have children of their own. For years they lived on a farm and moved to the city when the farm was too much for them to keep up.

My dad got angry with me and said, "What the hell is the matter with you? Why are you taking your aunt's side?"

I said, "Dad, I am not taking her side. Why do I have to choose? I love you all. They have given me some of the happiest memories of my life on the farm."

He got angry with me and called me a few choice names, so I left the room. I went outside and sat on a small grassy hill for a very long time trying to sort this all out. I knew in my heart I could not turn away from them; it just went against my grain.

As I sat there, I vividly recalled our many times at the farm; my sister Barbara and I would be sent out to the pastures to bring the cows in for feeding and milking. We would jump over the creeks and then call the cows, "Bossey, bossey," then the head cow would come in; and once she came the rest would follow. We often had to chase a cow that decided to run the other way, and we loved it. We played in the hay and wheat barns, collected eggs from the chickens, fed the pigs and other animals.

In the evening, when all the chores were done, Aunt Lena or Uncle Walt would go into the small town of Swanville, which was a few miles from the farm, and bring back gallons of homemade ice cream for all of us. When it wasn't ice cream, Aunt Lena would whip up fresh cream from the day's milking, and add sugar, and we would pile the cream inches high on homemade bread.

As I sat there recalling those special memories and the memories after they moved to their home in the city (I was tuned in enough at 19 to know those were special times for me), I knew I had no choice. I was going to go against my dad's wishes. My Aunt Lena and Uncle Walt were both getting up in years, and not in the best of health, and I loved them. I also told my aunt and uncle that I didn't want to be in the middle of their rift because I loved them all.

My aunt said, "Honey, we don't want you to be in the middle. Your uncle and I are thankful that you come and visit us so often."

When I left for California, my aunt and uncle told me that they had a will, and that I was in it. I told them that I was not interested in their money, and my aunt said, "We just want you to know how special you are to your uncle and me and how much we love you." We promised to write each other and to always keep in close touch.

My Uncle Walt passed several years later, and the one good thing that came from his passing is that it brought my mother and aunt back together.

My aunt and I continued to write, and she began phoning me at least once a week. She was lonely without Uncle Walt.

I got married in 1967, and she said she would come out and visit us as soon as her health got better. We stayed in close touch, but her loneliness was pulling her down, and her calls were now twice a week and around 1 A.M.! She worked nights, and when she got home, she could not sleep and would get depressed. She would always apologize for calling so late, but I told her not to worry, that it was always good to talk to her anytime.

She always complained about her brother Herman (executor of her will) and his son. She said they caused her many problems, and she didn't know how much more she could take from them. Her last call to me was on a Friday morning, and she told me that she had contacted an attorney, that she was changing her will, that Herman and his son would not be happy with the change, and that she could not take any more from them. She said she had an appointment to see the attorney the middle of the following week. My

Aunt Lena did see the attorney and was supposed to return in several days to sign the new will, but she never made it as she had a major heart attack and passed on.

My mom called. She asked me if I knew anything about the will, and I said no. I didn't want anyone to know what she had shared with me because those were her wishes.

Several days later my sister Rose called and told me that I was in the will and had better get back there as everything was in limbo because Aunt Lena had voided the old will, and since she never made it back to the attorney to sign the new will, Uncle Herman was going to do what he wanted; and told me, "I don't think you will get anything."

This was in 1968, and my aunt's estate was worth a lot of money. I don't think anyone ever really knew the final figure or what was actually in the new will because Uncle Herman kept everything to himself.

To ease his guilt, he gave the few that were mentioned in the will each $500.00. My sister said I was foolish not to come home and fight for it. I told her I didn't think Aunt Lena and Uncle Walt would want that. Uncle Herman would one day pay for his greed.

After the reading where my Uncle Walt said I was cheated out of an inheritance, three weeks later I received the following message: RF said, "I have an uncle here, your mother's side of the family. He says his name is Herman (Tiny), and he said he is having a hard time resting in the spirit world because he cheated you out of something."

My Uncle Herman passed about five years after my Aunt Lena. I think the year was 1972. I received the above message in 1988. Sixteen years later he was still paying for his greed and having a hard time resting in peace in the spirit world. On the way home that evening after the reading, I said, "Uncle Herman, I forgive you, but I am afraid you have to work on the others that you also cheated."

Another message I received from RF: "I have your mother and father here, and WOW! is your mother ever dressed up." He had his eyes closed and a smile on his face. You could tell he was enjoying what he was seeing, and he asked my mom out loud what she was wearing. He then looked at me and said, "Anniversary time, HUH?"

My dad had passed over 15 years ago, and as the years went by, I honestly had forgotten the date. I thought for a moment, then said, "Oh yeah, their anniversary was sometime in March." I wasn't sure of the day.

RF said, "Your mother said you forgot?"

I replied, "Yes, I am afraid I did."

There was more to my reading, but it was the above message from my mom and dad that was very exciting.

As soon as I got home I phoned my sister Annie; and she said, "Yes, it was this month. I am not sure of the date though. Let me get Rose on." Remember she had the phone line where you could get three people on at a time. When Rose got on the phone, she said yes, that March 23 was their anniversary date.

After I hung up I told Mel about the reading. He just looked at me, staring. Catana was in the room and said, "Well, dad, what do you have to say about that?"

He said, "Honey, there is no way he could have known that. I've been hit over the head."

I said, "Exactly, Mel, it's about time you're hit over the head. I had completely forgotten the date myself and that is why I had to call my sisters to verify it."

My mother had come to RF during his private meditations, and she always had a message for him to give me. So I decided the following morning to call RF and asked him if he could recall what my mother was wearing. I knew he didn't remember all the messages that he gave to people, but I thought he might remember what she had on because, in the six months I had gone to him for readings, I had never seen such delight on his face as when he asked my mother what she was wearing.

He said, "Well, as you know, I have gotten to know your mother pretty well from coming into my meditation. She always had a house dress on with a low neck, I knew she didn't wear high collars.

I said, "You're right RF, she was a very simple dresser and hated high necks." I asked him if he recalled what she had on.

He said, "I usually don't pay any attention, but I remember that dress she had on. It was a long, white dress,

168

with long sleeves that had ruffles around the wrist and a high neck with large ruffles like they used to wear in the olden days. It was all glittered with rhinestones, and she looked beautiful. Your father was all dressed up also with a shirt that had a wing collar."

I said, "I thought you would remember, because you looked so taken back."

He said, "Charlene, it's not very often that I remember anything when I give messages. But the picture of them standing there was a sight to see. I have never seen a dress like that ever. It was obvious that they wanted to make a real impression on me, and they certainly did."

I told him I phoned my sister and they had confirmed the date.

He said, "Well, that is good to know."

I told him what Mel said, and he replied, "Well, now that he is open to spirit communication, he will start to feel them much stronger."

NINETEEN

DREAMLAND

My dream book each night
is by my side.

So the spirits can use
the symbols as a guide.

Each morning I wake
anxious to see what
lessons I've learned in
dreamland you see.

I have found a new tool
to help me along.
It gives me a lesson
and helps me sing my new song.

As the day ends, and
my song has been sung,
I am tired but happy
knowing another one
will come.......

Charlene Abundis

I would like to explain more about the dream book and the messages that I was receiving from my dreams. When I told RF about Betty Bethards' Dream Book Symbols for Self-Understanding, that I was getting messages from my dreams that applied to my life, that I was actually being guided by my dreams, and that the symbols from the book were what really helped, RF said, "When you dream you are out of your body, and that will give you an idea as to what it is like in the spirit world. The only difference is that we have the silver cord, so we come back into the body. Dreams are often strange because there are no restrictions in the spirit world. But if people learn to work with dreams, as you are doing, they can ask any questions and get answers because dreams give us messages to help us in our daily life, and many people also have visions in dreams. It's important to stick to just one dream book and keep it near your bed. The spirits will use the symbols in the book to give you messages in your dreams."

In this chapter I will share the following dreams, and in a later chapter I will share a few more. I had a dream that I had won the state lottery. Since I was not a lottery player, but Mel was from time to time, I got excited. In the dream I was with a group of movie stars; the only name that I could remember was Jack Klugman. I had filled out some numbers on a lottery card, as did everyone else in the dream. We were all sitting around, visiting with each other, and a lady said, "Charlene, you won."

I turned around and said, "I did?"

She said, "Yes, a million and half dollars."

I walked over, looked at the numbers and saw them very clearly. I was elated. I then turned away from the numbers and started talking to someone, and then I said to myself, in the dream, "Hey, you're dreaming. Wake up and write those numbers down."

I did wake up, but by the time I focused, I could only remember three of the numbers, 17, 18 and 42. I tried so hard to bring the others back, but I could not. I lay there for a long time trying to see them, some numbers were the top half of the 20's and 30's. At breakfast that morning (Friday) I told Mel and the kids about my dream.

That evening at meditation class I also told RF. He asked if I remembered the numbers. I told him only three, but that there was a pattern in the dream, and I had to try and figure it out.

He said, "Well, once you figure it out, continue to play those numbers until they come up."

Saturday came, lottery day, and it was a very busy day.

Mel said, "Honey, I am going to play the lottery. Did you analyze the pattern?"

I said, "No, I haven't had time." But I wrote down the three numbers 17, 18, and 42, plus I chose 24 because I knew it was in the top half of the 20's, and I chose 33 because of the same reason, and another at random.

That evening we had a commitment, and when we arrived home I phoned to see what lottery numbers came up. The three that I remembered came up, and I was off by one or two numbers on the others that I chose.

If I had only taken the time to figure out the pattern and played more tickets, I might have won.

I was still very excited because spirit gave me the numbers. I asked RF if the spirit world knows what lottery numbers will come up. He said that someone in my band in the spirit world, someone I knew, wanted to give it a try and that, yes, sometimes they can see them. He said he knew one person, who was a spiritualist, who had won the lottery after getting the numbers in their dream.

A week later, Mel had a dream that gave him lottery numbers, but he could only remember two when he awoke. He played the two and four others at random. The following morning he told me that the two numbers came up and if he had analyzed his dream, he also would have won.

In both of our dreams, the lottery cards were not like the cards actually are. I know now that we both will analyze carefully any other lottery dreams.

The following is another dream. My mother and I were sitting and visiting. My sister Darlene, and all of her family were in the room, as well as Mel, Catana, and Armando. We had all decided to go out for dinner. Then mom said she didn't want to go, after all. Before we left the

172

room, there were balloons filled with helium that covered the ceiling; attached to each balloon was a string with a key dangling from it. You couldn't walk around the room without being hit by the keys. My mom stayed in her chair and the rest of us left the room. I was the last to walk out.

I closed the door, then said, "Oh wait a minute, I forgot the key to lock the door." I went back in, took a key off a balloon, then went back to join everyone in the hall. I closed the door, took the key, and locked it. End of dream.

That evening I went to the message service, and received the following reading from RF. He said, "I have your mother and dad here and some other friends are with them. Your mother said that there is a new door in front of you, and you can use any key you want to open the lock. It's going to unlock very easily. You will have all kinds of keys that will unlock it, and when you do, you will have good things waiting for you."

I have had many dreams that I was able to tie in to the readings that RF gave me. Before I was introduced to Spiritualism, one Saturday morning I woke up at 6:30, and I knew I had to phone my sisters to tell them about that night's dream because it was also meant for them. I was already using Betty Bethards' dream book, and I knew that my dreams were giving me messages.

Before I called my sisters, I told Mel my dream. He agreed that I should share it with them. I phoned Annie, and she got Rose on the line. Minnesota is two hours ahead of us, so it would be 8:30 there, and I knew they would be up. I will not share the dream here, but I will share what response my sister Annie had. When I finished telling her and Rose the dream, I said, "Annie, do you understand the dream?"

She said, "No."

I asked Rose if she did.

She said, "Yes." She then explained the dream to Annie.

Annie said, "I don't believe this. Explain this to me, Charlene. Two weeks ago I dreamed that you would call us early in the morning to tell us about a dream you had, that applied to us, and I would not understand it, but Rose would. How can you explain that?"

173

Annie asked me that question because of the many phone conversations we had had while I was searching, and she also knew that I was working with my dreams as a guide.

I said, "Annie, I really can't explain it but, in the many books that I have read, they talk about the power of communication with someone thousands of miles away. God knows that I have shared with you what I have found in my searching, and I think it is just His way of giving us confirmation that we're on track. He works in many ways, Annie. He knows we are connected."

Annie and I had other dreams that we called each other about, and there was no question that we had met in the dream world on the same night because the dreams were so similar.

I also knew that God was giving me these experiences with Annie so that I could help her. She was searching. She phoned me to tell me that she had gone to a medium who gave her information that really piqued her interest. "But," she said, "I can tell you this lady medium is nothing like RF." Annie would give me a question to ask RF, and he was always able to get an answer from spirit for her. I will have more about my sister Annie and dreams in a later chapter.

One Friday afternoon I couldn't find my car keys. I looked for them for fifteen minutes, and I was irritated because I had to pick the children up from school. I knew they were in the house somewhere because I drove them to school that morning. I phoned the school office and asked them to please tell my children I would be a little late. I ended up asking a neighbor to drive me to school to pick them up.

That evening, Mel and the children helped me look for the keys, but we couldn't find them. For two days I looked for those keys. On Sunday evening I went to bed. I woke up in the middle of the night because someone had told me in a dream that my keys were in my blue jacket, which was in the car. I immediately got up, checked the jacket and, sure enough, there they were. Then it all came back to me. I had arrived home after taking the children to school, instead of going directly into the house, I decided to sweep the driveway because the winds had been so strong during the night that it was filled with leaves, etc. I had my blue jacket in the car, and without even thinking, I put my keys in the jacket pocket and left it in the car.

After that experience, whenever I gave a friend a gift, it was always <u>The Dream Book</u> by Betty Bethards. A quote: "If you have knowledge let others light their candle by it."

TWENTY

TURNING TO THE LIGHT

There's an urge in the Soul
Calling out in the night,
Cursing the darkness,
And praying for light.

For night brings a gloom
So bleak and so stark.
Nothing so hopeless
As a soul in the dark.

'Tis then that sweet Nature
Lifts the curtain of night
So gently and slowly,
Lest blinded by light.

Then turns the lost Soul
As dawn lifts the fear.
Full courage restored,
And the path is now clear.

That Soul now a winner,
Has suffered and won,
And now, like the sunflower,
Always turns to the sun.

                              Reverend Edmund L. Foard

RF said, "Spiritualism proves that life is not a mystery, and allows us to know what is beyond the grave."

I would like to go back to when my dad had his first heart attack and his out of body experience. Several years later I decided to do some research. I never came across the word "Spiritualism" in my research. And yet Spiritualism, in my opinion, clears up all the mystery that these books throw at you. It explains it all so clearly and makes it easy to understand. We live on. It gives no victory to the grave.

RF told me that Spiritualism has been judged by all religions, but Spiritualism does not judge any religion and respects all the good in other religions. He also said that if the news media would give us coverage equal to that of other religions, it would not be such a secret. It would allow people to know the truth rather than think of us as a negative force.

RF said Spiritualism does not believe in hell, as some other religions do, and is a science and philosophy, as well as a religion. Through demonstration of mediumship, it proves the continuity of life by communicating with entities in the spirit world who have experienced the change called death.

He said in Spiritualism nothing dies; it just changes. There is no death, our loved ones are waiting for us on the other side. "If more people knew that," he said, "their grief would not last long, and they would feel joy, knowing that they will see their family and friends again." He said all they need to do is think of those they love, and they are here with us; we just can't see them.

Omar Khayyam wrote:

> Strange is it not? That of the
> myriads who
>
> Before us passed the door of
> Darkness through,
>
> Not one returns to tell us of the
> Road,

Which to discover we must
travel too.

Spiritualism certainly blows that poem out of the water. As I researched Spiritualism and compared the many notes that I had taken about out-of-body experiences, it was amazing to me that they were explaining exactly what Spiritualism is. But because they were out of their bodies for such a short period, it was a very limited view.

Two excellent books about out-of-body experiences are <u>Life After Life</u> and <u>Reflections on Life after Life</u>, both by Raymond A. Moody, Jr., M.D.

Neither of the above books mention anything about Spiritualism, and yet they explain exactly what RF had told me about Spiritualism. Listed below are a few of the experiences that I read in the above books about people who died then came back into their bodies. My comments follow.

1. That it is a place of knowledge. All knowledge is available to you right then and there. You absorb it quickly.

Comment:

There is school in the spirit world. My mom and dad verified that for me in readings that I received from RF. There is opportunity to grow and to better yourself so that you may climb to a higher sphere, but you have to obtain the knowledge. No one can do it for you.

2. That your mind is very clear. You have great perception and see things very clearly.

Comment:

RF said in the spirit world you see very clearly. All of the confusion and blind spots which you might have had on the earth plane are gone.

3. That love is what it is all about. We must help and do things to help others on the earth.

Comment:

Exactly as Spiritualism says.

4. That there are beautiful bright lights, happy music, wonderful feelings. Everything is so beautiful, everyone seems so happy.

Comment:

I believe that has to be one of the higher spheres.

5. I knew all the answers. There is not a question that I did not have an answer to.

Comment:

You find all of the answers up there. There is nothing but knowledge to help you grow and better yourself.

6. I did not go where my family was. I was in a terrible place. I saw all the harm and mistakes I made on the earth plane. It all came before me.

Comment:

I believe that must have been a lower sphere.

7. People were very sad and depressed looking. They looked like they had no direction in their life, just walking around looking down.

Comment:

I believe that also had to be one of the lower spheres.

8. A person who had tried suicide said he would never do it again. If you gave away the gift of life that God gave you, you would have to do it all over again in the spirit world.

• • •

RF said that if one chooses not to grow in the spirit world and just do nothing, they will always stay in the same state. He also said that many people who have out of body experiences quite often visit the different spheres and planes that I explained in Chapter 16.

I asked RF if they were getting a brief look as to what they had in store for them, and he said yes. Those who didn't like what they experienced out of the body should consider themselves lucky because they were given a preview of where they would be if they hadn't returned to their bodies. They now know that they must change their ways on the earth plane in order to be in a better place when they pass over. In practically all of the out-of-body experiences that I have read about, the people who have returned to their bodies have said that their lives have taken on a positive change and a good direction.

I met RF in October, 1987. During the year I knew him, I took 30 to 35 people to him for readings. His message service was packed each week, and every week many were turned away.

Besides being such a good medium, RF was a very humble man. He never really knew how many lives he had touched. His love came across to everyone in capital letters. Our family felt nothing but love from him. I asked him if spirits gave him negative messages for people. He said, "Oh, yes, but I never give a negative message. I always turn it into a positive, so that it would help rather than hurt the person."

I asked him why he didn't charge $5 a reading instead of $3. He said, "Oh, no, Charlene, I couldn't do that. The only reason I charge $3 is because I have to keep the church doors open; if I charged $5, many people would not be able to pay. You can't be a medium and do it for money. It is a gift from God to help others, and if you charge large amounts of money, you will lose the gift."

There are mediums in this town who charge anywhere from $125.00 to $150.00 for a reading. When I asked RF what he thought of that, he said it was greed, and their gift would not be pure or last.

Whenever I had a high number for a reading, I would end up staying late at church. One evening a friend and I decided to wait until RF was through with his last reading. When he finished, he stood up and asked a lady sitting in the back of the small church if she would like a reading.

She said, "I don't have a number."

He said, "Well, you come sit here in front of me, and I'll give you a reading."

She then said, "I don't have any money either."

He said, "That doesn't matter." He did that so often. He was such a special man.

Our family was very lucky because, in the year we knew him, he spent, besides that Christmas evening, Easter with us, and he often joined us at our home for dinner and many other occasions.

My sister Annie and RF never did meet in person, but I shared everything with her. She called me every other week asking if I could ask RF a question for her. He was always able to give me an answer that really helped her.

One question she asked me to ask him was, "Why do we have so much pain in our lives?" He told me to tell her that each person creates their own reality with their own thoughts. We are free to make our own choices, and when things don't go right for us, we have no one else to blame but ourselves, and usually there is a good lesson for us to learn from the experience.

RF knew Annie pretty well through me because he said, as he wrinkled his nose, "She might not like to hear that one." He was right! He said, "Tell Annie that love is all there is. It's the most important thing in the world," and then he said, "She does a pretty good job of giving her love to others." He was right again. He said, "Tell her if we make a mistake, we should learn from it, then throw it over our

181

shoulders without looking back because God does not look back. Tell her we are all one mind, (then pointing to his chest) and God is right in here." He gave me an analogy for her. He said, "If we take an empty cup down to the ocean and fill it up with the ocean water, and step back holding the full cup of water, it is still the ocean, but separate." He added, "I read that somewhere and it will make it easier for her to understand that we are all one."

He said to tell her that just to know there is God is not enough. You must have daily contact with Him through meditation and quiet time because you cannot get messages with all the static and noise around you every day. You need to listen and be quiet to hear.

When I told Annie the information that you just read, she said, "Char, why don't you guys bring Reverend Foard home with you on your next trip, I would love to meet him in person."

I said, "Annie, he has a busy life. Why don't you come out for a visit; then you can meet him. He will give you a private reading. I know just your plane fare would be worth a reading from him. He said he also would like to meet you one day."

She said, "Tell him that if he will come to Minneapolis, I will pay for his complete trip."

As much as my sister wanted to meet RF and get a private reading, she knew that she would never come out for a visit. But she was willing to pay for him to take a trip back to Minneapolis because she knew he was a special man. When I told RF what Annie said and that she would pay for his trip, he said, "Can't do. I have my hands full right here."

One Saturday morning I convinced Mel into leaving all the house and yard chores so that we could go out for breakfast and then take a ride through the countryside near Solvang, which is north of Santa Barbara. It was such a beautiful day, and as we left the house I felt such a peace within, knowing we were getting away from the normal rat race of life. Half-way through our eating breakfast, I got this terrible feeling that something was wrong. It hit me so fast. I couldn't understand why. I said, "Honey, let's forget Solvang, I've changed my mind."

182

He said, "Talk about being fickle."

I said, "I just don't feel right. I feel like something is wrong." We went home.

There was a message on our answering machine from my friend Lois Cook, "RF is not doing well, would you please call Dr. Wyatt to see if I can take him in today. Please call as soon as possible. It's very important." I called, and she said, "Oh good, you got my signals."

I asked, "What signals?"

She said, "When I phoned your home and you were not there, I asked spirit to get a message to you that RF was not doing well. I see you got it!"

I said, "Boy did I ever get it!" That was a first for me, and it has happened several times since.

RF was experiencing a lot of pain, and would tell no one why. We found out later that he had cancer in his hip area which caused the pain. He would not go to the hospital, and said the only doctor he would see was Dr. Wyatt, a good friend of mine, whom he met when giving him a reading.

Several days later when I was visiting RF, he asked me how Annie was.

I said, "She is fine. I talked to her a few days ago, and she asked me how you were doing."

I asked him if they had something going that I didn't know about, and with that famous smile of his, he leaned forward, wrinkled his nose, and said, "Well, she is pretty special, you know."

I said, "Yes, I do know that."

One week later I received a phone call at 4 A.M. from Lois. She asked if I would contact Dr. Wyatt and ask him if he would meet them at the hospital. She and her husband Jim were rushing RF to emergency. I phoned Dr. Wyatt, and then I also went to St. Francis Hospital. I arrived before anyone else and thought perhaps, in my haste, I got the wrong hospital. I inquired at the desk and the nurse said, "Oh no, not Reverend Foard from the Church of the Comforter?"

I said, "Yes."

She said, "I have had readings from him, and I was going to phone him again this week."

Just then Lois and Jim arrived with RF and Dr. Wyatt right behind them.

Several hours later, when we were leaving the hospital, the same nurse called me over and asked if we could give her a number that people could call. She said that the last time RF was in the hospital, several years earlier, the switchboard was going crazy, and they were unable to handle all of his incoming calls because they didn't have enough help at the hospital.

When RF came home from the hospital, my friend Lois, who would be looking after him, phoned and asked if I could relieve her in the mornings or afternoons. I said yes.

The first morning I arrived, RF's front porch was loaded with flowers, homemade goodies, and cards. He had only been home two days and wanted no visitors. He needed his energy to deal with his pain because he would not take pain pills.

I asked him why he didn't want to take pain pills, and he said, "Because when I get to the other side, I want to be free of any drugs. Drugs will hold me back."

One morning he said that he didn't expect to last more than a few weeks, but that he was happy to be at home.

I said, "RF, I am not happy that you're leaving so soon. I have so much more to learn from you, and our family is going to miss you."

He said, "You have learned everything you needed to learn, and your path is set. Much will come your way. You have poppies and flowers on both sides of your road."

Several days before he passed he said, "You know, Charlene, that little church means a lot to me."

I said, "I know it does, RF. I don't want to upset you; but you'll know anyway, I don't think the church is right for me. I became a Spiritualist and attended church because you were there. You opened a very exciting door for me."

He said, "You don't need the church. You'll find your way."

I felt so bad, I said, "Well, I'll give it a try. I promise."

Three months after RF passed, I couldn't stand it any longer. I left the church; it was all wrong for me for many reasons. I decided to take my new knowledge and apply it to my life, knowing now that God has been and always will be my guiding light.

RF made his transition to the other side on Friday, September 2, 1988. He was 78 years old and had been a certified medium for 26 years. He was well known from coast to coast. He had been on television and radio programs and appeared in the National Spiritualist of Churches "World Beyond Series."

People came from all over California for his Wednesday night readings. One Wednesday when I arrived at the church at 5:00 P.M., a lady was hurrying down the street. When she got to the church steps, she asked, out of breath, "Am I early enough?"

I smiled and said, "Yes."

"Oh good," she said, "I heard he is wonderful, and I planned a week's vacation here in Santa Barbara just so I could get a reading from him."

RF is missed by many people. Even after nine years I think of him all the time.

Within a month of meeting RF, I told him that I thought I would write a book about what I had found through his opening the door to a new world for me that was so exciting. I told him that the few experiences that I had had, I shared with some friends, and they were as awed as I was. He said, "Well, during the day, I'm pretty much free. Call me and I can give you so much information."

I said, "I can be a pest when I am looking for answers to anything."

He said, "You won't bother me."

Two months later, and after our Christmas evening with RF, I started to write the book. I felt that I had enough information to write my story. But questions continued to pop up in my mind, and I was phoning RF five days out of the week, Monday through Friday, sometimes twice a day. He never was short with me, but after a month or so I was feeling a little guilty, phoning him so often.

One day during our phone conversation I said, "I have decided to call you three times a week. I will save my questions instead of phoning you every day."

He said, "Charlene, you're not bothering me. You can call me every day if you want."

The following day I didn't call him. About 5:30 that evening, he phoned me, and said, "Well, if you're not going to call me, then I am going to have to call you."

I said, "RF, I just feel like a pest, you know how much I love our conversations."

He said, "Well, don't feel that way. Now I am not going to tell you again. Do you have any questions for me?"

I said, "As a matter of fact I do, but we were just getting ready to go out. Can I phone you in the morning?"

He said, "Yes, make it after nine."

I was so excited to have this very special man who was so wise and loving in my life. After our conversations, I made a point to type all of the wisdom he gave me. He often said to me when I asked him a question, "Well, I don't have all the answers, but let me give you what I have."

RF knew he was going to spirit several months before he told anyone. One day he called and said he wanted me to come by because he wanted to give me something for Armando, Catana, Mel and myself to always remember him by. I said, we don't need anything to remember you by, you are so special, we will never forget you. What's the hurry anyway? He said, "It's just that I want to give them to you now."

He gave Catana a beautiful, small, clear bowl from the 1940's. He gave Armando a watch, one that he had worn for years. He said that he didn't want to embarrass Mel, but did I think Mel would like one of his sport coats. I asked him to show me which ones he no longer wore, and I selected a light purple coat because purple was RF's favorite color. Mel has it in a protective cover in his closet. He said he had books for me and gave me a stack. I told him I would return them after reading them. He said, "No, these are for you to keep. I want you to have them."

I knew then that RF was telling me his time was short here on the earth. I thanked him and was so happy to receive his gifts, but I felt a sadness, too, because we had known him for less than a year and loved him so much.

It wasn't until after RF passed to spirit that I was able to read all the books he gave me. I knew that he had selected these books because they had a wealth of information to help me relate to all that he taught me while he was here. And as I read each book, I felt that he was talking to me through them.

I told RF that I felt he must have been an angel that was sent down from heaven because of all the light and love he gave to others. He threw his head back and really laughed. "I don't want to disappoint you, Charlene, but an angel I am not. I have had my times in life." He had no ego, and he never judged others. His only goal was to give love to all he met.

The following thoughts that I have listed below in numerical order stem from the many conversations I had with RF. When I asked him if his guides and teachers were responsible for all the knowledge and wisdom that he gave out so lovingly to others, he said, "Yes, I cannot take all the credit. Of course I read a lot, and most of it jives with what I get from my guides, which is confirmation."

In all of the books that I read, after the dream that I had that sent me to the library, if something that I read felt right to me, I made a point to take notes on it. I had pages of notes that I asked RF to read several months after I met him. I told him that I would like his views on what felt right to me. It amazed me, after he read them and said they were right on. The 56 points listed below we both agreed on. You will find some repetition, and I apologize for that; but I did not want to leave out any of what I found in my research that RF agreed with or any of the wisdom that he gave me in his own words.

Wisdom and thoughts from RF

1. The law of Cause and Effect applies to everyone when they reach the spirit world the same as it does on the earth plane.

187

2. We take our personality, thoughts, feelings, and memories in our soul to spirit; but the most important thing of all that we take with us and leave behind is the love, kindness, and charity that we gave to others while here.

3. We just walk through a door when we pass. We have our natural body, or as Betty Bethards says, our earth suits, on this side and the spiritual body in the spirit world. We move from one place of consciousness to another, and God's laws apply to both the earth plane and the spirit world.

4. The next world is all around us in the very air we breathe.

5. When the body dies and the spirit leaves, we will be exactly as we were on the earth plane with one exception. We gradually go to the sphere that we feel comfortable with, which has to do with the Karma we created on the earth plane.

6. Usually greedy or self-serving people will end up in poverty on the other side because they have built up no treasures over there.

7. All the good deeds people do here will take them to a higher sphere when they pass over.

8. Many souls are shocked when they arrive in the spirit world because they realize that they are not dead. They feel new joy and wonder how they were kept in such ignorance and blindness about living on.

9. In the spirit world everyone speaks from his thoughts.

10. Everyone has good and evil spirits with them. Good spirits have a direct line to God (heaven), and when they pass over they will end up on a higher sphere. Evil spirits have a direct line to negativity (hell) and will end up below the 3rd sphere when they pass over. God cast no one into negativity (hell). People do this by living opposite of His laws because they turn themselves away from God.

11. God can protect no one that does not acknowledge Him and His laws.

12. It is up to us to find the path that we desire to walk on the earth plane that will help us attain our goals and be fulfilling.

13. Because we have free choice and free will, we decide if we want to follow God's law and live the good life (heaven) or an evil life (hell).

14. In the spirit world, good spirits shine in the light of God and evil spirits appear dark and live in darkness and are very unpleasant to look at.

15. Heaven (higher sphere) and hell (below the third sphere) have their own societies and every spirit belongs to some society.

16. Heaven (higher sphere) or hell (below the third sphere) is not the same for everyone. We receive heaven on the other side in accordance to the quality of heaven that we have within us on this side. The same applies to hell. It is a mirror. You will receive exactly what you have here. Heaven is love of God and hell is evil and love of self.

17. People get messages from the spirit world in their dreams. Often a thought will hit you during the day that comes from out of nowhere; that also is spirit's help.

18. The more we strive to live God's love through our thoughts, words, and deeds on the earth plane, the more His light will shine on us and the world.

19. There are good and bad mediums. It is up to you to select a good medium, just as you must select a good doctor or a lawyer.

20. RF said, as a medium, he received messages from spirit by thought and often a name was written out for him, but he had to be quick to catch it because it disappeared so fast! Sometimes pictures would appear with the thoughts.

21. Small children up until the age of seven or so, often have spirit playmates; but as they get older they are brainwashed to believe logically; and logic says that they do not have spirit playmates. That is one way that logic screws us all up.

22. Usually earthbound spirits are spirits that died, and they do not realize it, or they cannot find the light on the other side. They remain in limbo, and they must raise their vibration in order for someone to help them. Often they were very materialistic on the earth plane and have a hard time letting go of that, and they don't want to leave their things. Spirits can be earthbound for hundreds of years. Sometimes they stay in limbo because they have committed an injustice towards someone and desperately want to make amends and they can't, which is another reason they remain earthbound.

23. You attract what you are. Positive attracts positive, negative, negative.

24. It is up to you to create what you want in life.

25. You are what you think because thoughts become reality.

26. You must cultivate the mind and keep it open in order for it to grow. When someone comes to a conclusion, his or her mind stops growing. It takes an intelligent person to keep an open mind.

27. It is important to always keep an open mind because just when you think you have found the answer, something will come along to change your mind, and you will realize how little you really know.

28. There are many mysteries in life, and so much for all of us to learn here, and even after we pass to spirit.

29. People who do not believe in God or a higher intelligence are spiritually void.

30. Many who call themselves Christians live in blind ignorance of the spirit world.

31. The sun that shines in the spirit world is the light of God and stands for truth. It is not like the sun that shines on the earth plane.

32. Animals are born with knowledge that is suited to their nature, but man is not. That is why man needs to be taught about God and His laws. If he is not taught, he is unable to think spiritual thoughts or live a spiritual life.

33. If people do not acknowledge God and His laws while here and live life in such a way that they have no regard for anyone else and believe that by getting the last rites on their death bed that they will automatically go to heaven, they are only fooling themselves and will have a rude awakening when they arrive in the spirit world.

34. The Soul is not punished on the other side if it has not acknowledged God's laws on the earth plane. It just continues on as it did on the earth plane, and will end up on a low sphere because it has turned itself away from God.

35. God's love is unconditional. He does not punish us for negative actions. We punish ourselves by our negative actions, just as right actions have their own reward.

36. Charity and good deeds towards others allows God's light to continually shine on the givers, but it must come from the heart and not from the ego or be self-serving.

37. The ego does not allow people to see the real problems of the world because it leads them away from common sense and gives them a false sense of power.

38. Many people follow the laws of our society not because they feel it is right, but because they fear the loss of their reputation. They have no foundation to stand on, and when they pass to spirit, they will have a rude awakening because you cannot do good out of fear or for glory. You must do good because it is the right thing to do and God's Law.

39. Good deeds directed towards others send warm, loving feelings out to the world. Self-serving deeds send cold feelings out to the world.

40. Those in love with worldly things and themselves live exactly opposite of God's laws. While they are here, they might feel they have heaven on earth but will be very distressed when they find themselves on a lower sphere once they arrive in the spirit world. (RF said a good example of how to live your life is the TV show, "Little House on the Prairie.")

41. Hypocrites are those who do good for the sake of self and only for the appearance of looking good.

42. Don't think that having all the money you want, becoming famous, or reaching a position in life that puts you in the limelight will bring lasting happiness. For a short period it will lift you, but it is not lasting like God's love is. If you don't have God in your life, you will be forever searching for happiness because it does not come from worldly things.

43. Happiness lies within you. Don't look for it outside of yourself. It is not in other people or material items.

44. Each person has their own unique talent that God gave them, and no two people have the same voice vibration or fingerprints. We are all different just like each snowflake is different.

45. Meditation sharpens your intuition.

46. With so much noise and static around us everyday, it is important to find a quiet place to meditate in order to hear that little voice within. Nature is God's gift to the world, and if you meditate there, you will never be more peaceful.

47. We have all the answers right within us. But we must learn to trust our higher self, our God spark; both are the same as intuition.

48. Intuition is knowing that you know, without knowing why you know, and you automatically know to follow it.

49. We should never have fear in sharing the truth.

50. People that are walking the same spiritual path are usually anxious to share their experiences with others, and that helps take them to a higher level of awareness.

51. When someone does you harm and you become aware of it, you don't have to hate that person. Forgive them. You can hate the sin that has been cast upon you, knowing it is wrong; but if you hate that person you will only be harming yourself because it will come back to you. Turn it all over to God and ask Him to fill your mind with love; and by doing so, you release your negative emotions under His law of love.

52. We must never sit in judgment of another because if we knew the whole story, we would understand and not judge.

53. Some religions teach that if babies or children die before being baptized they will not be able to enter into heaven. THAT IS WRONG!

54. You do not have to go to church to be a Christian. The Bible says that a Christian person is one who lives the teachings of Jesus: love, peace, compassion, kindness, forgiveness, patience and charity to all.

55. We all have teachers and guides in the spirit world who are always with us. Some of them are very old souls, and they have a lot of knowledge, and some are not so old.

56. Love is the power that holds the Universe together.

57. God is the only One who knows where you've been, where you are are, and where you are going.

58. Energy is God and love is God's energy that flows through us.

59. By tuning into God's energy within you, His love and light will guide you to do all things the right way and at the right time.

60. God is our intuition; and He gives us our visions.

•   •   •

RF gave me the following stories about John Quincy Adams, the 6th President of the United States, and James Garfield, the 20th President of the United States.

On his eightieth birthday, John Quincy Adams was met by a contemporary on the street of Boston and was asked, "How is my friend, John Quincy Adams?" He answered in words that have since become classic: "John Quincy Adams, himself, is very well, thank you; but the house he lives in is sadly dilapidated. It is tottering on its foundation. The walls are badly shattered, and the roof is worn. The building trembles in every wind, and I think John Quincy Adams will have to move before long. But he, himself, is very well."

RF told Catana and Armando about Karma and taking the high road of life. He told them that they should never follow anyone but to turn within for their guidance. I told him that I have a saying on my refrigerator, "If you want to be someone, be yourself." I know that is why he gave me the following quote from James Garfield:

"I do not care what others say and think about me. But there is one man's opinion which I very much value, and that is the opinion of James Garfield. Others I need not think about. I can get away from them but I have to be with him all the time. He is with me when I rise up and when I lie down; when I eat and talk; when I go out and come in. It makes a great difference whether he thinks well of me or not."

I have one last thought before ending this chapter. When we were driving RF home after our special Christmas evening with him, I told him that I was very excited that he had come into our lives. He said, "I feel the same. Most people who are exposed to a new truth feel that way. But I must warn you again about that crutch. We must find our own answers that come from within. It's OK to get help from time to time."

I responded, "I don't like the message you're giving me. There is so much more I want to learn from you."

He said, "Well, it's not a message to upset you. It is to make you realize how important it is for you to find your own answers in order for you to grow on your path. Good mediums can help someone get on the right path when it comes to Spiritualism, but then, it's that crutch, that crutch that I worry about because it stops people from growing, and they become stagnant. But you're not ready to let go yet. There is more that you can learn from me. However, don't follow anyone who is anxious to tell you that they can lead you because you can easily be led astray. God is the only one that can lead you because He knows what is right for you and He is within."

That advice is exactly what I had found in my own research, and I know that this special man, RF, was truly in touch with God. He said, "We will not find what we refuse to see, and we will not do what we refuse to dare." He did not know who the author was of the quote.

TWENTY ONE

THE CORDS ARE BROKEN

The cords have all broken
And set thee apart
As the giver of life
Draws thee close to her heart

Close, close to the source
In its infinite ways
Now guides and protects thee
And never betrays.

A mother once cradled thee
Close with her kiss,
And thee knew in a moment
No stranger was this.

The same arms, the same loved ones
Are lingering nie
To welcome thee home
To that sweet by and by.

Reverend Edmund L. Foard

My Uncle Dave, whom you read about in the first part of this book, passed to spirit in May, 1992. He lived in Minneapolis, close to my brothers and sisters. When my sister Annie phoned and asked me if I would be coming home for the funeral, I told her no. I said that I would not be coming home for any more funerals, but to please include me in the flowers, and I would send my share of the money.

I said, "Annie, if I should pass on to spirit before any member of my family in Minneapolis, I do not want any flowers sent, and no one should come to Santa Barbara because there will be no funeral or service. I will be cremated."

She got very upset, as she often did, and said, "Char, you did the same thing to the family when you got married."

I said, "Annie, we have had this conversation too many times. You know Mel and I didn't want a big wedding, that is why we went to Las Vegas to get married."

My sister was easily upset, and in the past, when she got upset in a phone conversation with me, she would say, 'I have to go," and she would hang up on me. Well, our present conversation came to a quick end, as she did just that. I decided to meditate, and 10 minutes later there was a soft knock on the door of the room I was in.

It was Mel, he said, "Honey, I am sorry to bother you, but Annie is on the phone again."

I picked up the phone receiver and she said, in a very loud voice, "Well, what the hell do you want us to do for you, anyway?"

I laughed and said, "Annie, don't worry about it. I have no plans to check out for a long time."

In that same conversation, we agreed that if I was to pass to spirit before she did, no flowers would be sent. If anyone wanted to do something, they should get a gift certificate for groceries and give it to a less fortunate family.

If she passed to spirit before I did, she wanted me to come home for her funeral, and at the service I could explain what we had found out through RF about life continuing on in the spirit world.

She said, "You know, Char, if I should die before you, the people in the church will think we are crazy."

I said, "Annie, the difference between you and me is that I don't care what people think. I was 47 and you were 51 when we found out, without any doubt in our minds, that we live on. It's given us both a peace within. Many people are kept in the dark, just like we were, who are looking for answers to life, and what happens after we die. If the people in the church think we're crazy, that will be their problem, not ours."

She chuckled, and said, "Well, I won't be here, anyway, to worry about it if I die first."

Annie often phoned, asking me to interpret dreams that she had. I had sent her Betty Bethards' dream book, but she never used it. Several months after mom passed, she phoned and said that both mom and dad were in a dream she had, and that she felt a lot of love from them. She had that dream several times.

About a year later in one of our conversations, Annie said, "Char, last night I was lying in bed unable to sleep, when all of a sudden a bright light appeared across the room; I looked and dad was standing there. How could that be?"

I said, "Are you sure you weren't dreaming?"

She responded, "I was awake."

I asked her if he said anything to her, and she said, "No, I just felt a lot of love coming from him. It is the same type of love that I have felt from both him and mom when they were in my dreams."

I said, "Mom and dad know the path that we have found through RF, and the love that you feel coming from them is because they now know how hard your life has been. It also is God's way of reinforcing all that we have learned from RF."

My dad appeared to Annie once more after that, but he never talked to her. She just felt a lot of love.

The first part of May, 1994, I was in the kitchen preparing breakfast when Catana came in. She said, "Mom, I had a dream last night that was sad. I don't know if I should tell you or not." Catana by that time had been working with her dreams for at least six years using Betty Bethards' dream book. She knew that her dreams were giving her messages and guidance.

I stopped what I was doing and said, "Tell me the dream."

She said, "Auntie Annie died, and you had to go home for the funeral."

I said, "Honey, death in a dream also means the old is dying, to make way for the new to come in."

She said, "No, mom," as she slowly shook her head and finger back and forth. "This was different."

I said, "I'll phone her a little later, honey, and see if she is feeling OK." Annie phoned me before I could call her. I asked her if she was feeling OK. She said, "I've had a few severe headaches, and I am going to make a doctor appointment tomorrow." I said, "Make sure you do, Annie, and don't put it off. Call me and let me know what the doctor says." She said OK.

Several days later I phoned her because she did not call me back, and I wanted to know what the doctor had to say. She said she still had not gone, that she was helping an elderly friend. I was furious with her. I said, "Annie, get your act together and put yourself first for once, will you!" She said, "I promise I will call tomorrow." She then asked me to order some vitamins for her. I always ordered her vitamins and arranged to have them sent directly to her because I knew she would never follow through and order them herself.

I phoned Annie three or four times in the next week and a half, and she still had not gone, in spite of still having the severe headaches and promising me each time that I talked to her that she would. She told me she was still busy helping a friend. My sister had always put off taking care of herself, but she always gave her time and energy to others even if she did not feel well.

Early Friday morning two days after my last phone call to her, my brother John called and said they had rushed Annie to the emergency, and he said, "You might want to come home. It doesn't look good."

Catana had her dream three weeks before, and when my brother called, I knew that Annie would be going to her next life.

I told my brother that I would not be coming home right away, but I would phone in a few hours to see how she was doing.

I phoned the hospital three times that day, and Annie had not improved. When I meditated that evening I asked God for Annie's highest good. I awoke early the next morning with the following dream:

I was walking down the street I live on to the house of a friend, who is a doctor. I walked up his steps, past my mother (remember she is in spirit), who was talking to the doctor, and into his house. The house was completely empty. The carpet had just been cleaned and the walls were newly painted. I walked to a window, pulled the drapes back and thought to myself, as I looked out the window, "Mom sure did a good job painting." I walked over to the wall and with my index finger I touched it; the paint was still wet. Then I walked out to the porch, where my mom and friend were still talking, and she turned to me and said, "We are preparing for Annie to come over and planning a big party for her. How many people will you be inviting?"

I said, "Thirty."

She said, "Well, she will be joining us." Then I woke up.

In Betty Bethards' Dream Book, the number 3 in a dream means that the dream has a spiritual message. I knew that my mother was giving me the message that Annie would be starting her new life in the spirit world.

In spite of telephoning my family six times in a two day period, I did not tell them about Catana's or my dream. Annie was not conscious, and I didn't want to upset them. On the third day (Sunday), when I spoke with my sister Darlene, she said that she did not want Annie to die, but according to the doctors, if she lived she would be paralyzed. She said, "I know that Annie would not want to live like that."

It was a very emotional conversation because everyone loved Annie, especially her family, and she was only 57 years old.

I decided to tell my sister about Catana's and my dream, but I told her not to tell the rest of the family yet. I felt they might not believe the dreams were giving us a message, and they would think that I was being negative. I don't even know if my sister believed me, but she agreed not to tell the rest of the family.

I knew it would be just a matter of days before Annie passed. I didn't want to go back and wait at the hospital for that to happen; instead I continued to call my family at the hospital three times a day, morning, noon, and in the evening for the next four days.

Thursday evening when I phoned the hospital, my sister Darlene told me that they had just met with all of Annie's doctors, and they advised that the family should discuss pulling the support system because Annie's body had deteriorated so bad that there was no hope.

I said, "Dar, Annie has left her body. She is in her next life already. It's the right decision."

She said that my sister Rose and brother John wanted to give her every chance. I asked her to put Rose on the phone. She said, "Char, I don't think you should tell her."

I said, "Annie is not coming back, Darlene, she has started her new life in spirit. Put Rose on the phone."

When Rose came to the phone I told her about Catana's and my dream. We both were very emotional. I told her that I would ask mom to come into my dreams during the night and let me know if that would be the right decision.

I knew it was the right decision. I said, "I'll phone you in the morning if she gives me an answer." I knew if mom came into my dream and gave me the answer, it would make it much easier for my family to pull the support system. I also knew that Rose would not question it because of the prior dream that applied to her.

That evening in my meditation, and also before I went to bed, I asked mom to please come into my dreams and give me a very simple, clear answer. Yes or no.

I had the following dream: I was back in Minneapolis on a theater stage. I and my brothers and sisters were standing in a half-moon circle. My mom was standing next to a large piano, and with her index finger she motioned for me to come to the piano then pointed for me to sit on the bench in front of it. I looked to my left, where my three sisters and two brothers were standing. Annie was not in line.

I walked over to mom; she said, "Now sit down and play the piano."

I said, "Mom, I can't play the piano."

She said very loudly, "Yes, you can." The "yes" was very loud and the "you can" soft. There was my answer!

I phoned my sister very early that morning to tell her the dream.

She said, "Well, Char, I guess God just kept Annie here long enough in order for us to accept the fact that she was leaving us."

I told her I would make the arrangements to fly home that evening. My suitcase was already packed.

Early that afternoon, Darlene's husband, Ed, phoned and said, "Char, we are going to wait until Monday to pull the support. Last night, after Dar talked to you, she went in and held Annie's hand, and it twitched; and Dar thought maybe it was a sign from Annie not to pull the support, and Dar is really having a hard time with this. The nurse told her it was just a nerve reaction, but we are going to wait."

I said, "I understand, Ed. I will fly home, then, on Monday. I do not want to sit at the hospital."

That same evening in my meditation, I asked Annie to please come into my dreams and let me know how she was doing on the other side.

That night I dreamed that I was standing in a very large empty room, the walls were bare. I turned in a complete circle as I looked at each bare wall. I then stopped, facing a wall, and Annie walked through the wall, then a door appeared behind her. I was so excited in my dream because I was aware that I was dreaming and that I was getting my answer from Annie. I said with great excitement, "Annie, how are you doing?"

She responded, "I'm doing great, Char." Then music came on and she said, "Come on, let's Lindy." And we danced all around the empty room. Annie had taught me to Lindy when I was a teenager. It was our favorite dance.

She looked great in the dream, appeared to be in her 20's, and she was very happy. When I awoke I was very emotional because as I wrote earlier, my sister had a difficult life. It was joyous to see her so free and happy.

Early Monday morning, as I was packing my personal items, Mel said, "Honey, are you sure that you don't want to wait until the family calls and tells you that they pulled the support system. You don't know how long Annie will last."

I said, "No, her body will not be alive by the time I get there."

He said, "You don't know that!"

I said, "I know it, honey, I just know it."

After I had the dream where my mother told me that Annie would be joining her in spirit, whenever a special thought of Annie came to my mind, I would type it out. I ended up with 18 double spaced pages. On the plane I sorted out the thoughts that I wanted to read at Annie's service. I timed myself to see how long it would take to read them: eight minutes. I decided that when I got to Minneapolis, and before the funeral, I would try and shorten it to five minutes.

When my family met me at the airport Monday evening, they said that Annie had passed that afternoon. It was ten days after she was rushed to the hospital. As we were walking over to get my luggage, Darlene told me that the priest from the church wanted to see me before the funeral. I asked her why. She said, "He wants to know what you're going to read at the service." I kept my cool, but my adrenaline shot up. It would be none of his concern what I wanted to read at my sister's service. I thought to myself that the church I walked out of many years ago is still all about control.

The day before my sister's funeral, I, along with other family members, went to see the priest. I told him about RF and explained in detail what Annie and I had learned from him and what Annie wanted me to read at her service. I asked him if once I had the exact thoughts written out if he would like to read them at her service or if he would prefer that I read them.

He said, "No, I would not like to read it, and what you have there, you cannot read either."

After my past experience with the Catholic Church, how could I possibly be surprised at his control!

I asked the priest if he believed we lived on. At first he hesitated in answering me, but then he said yes, but that he didn't believe in spirit communication or spirit guides helping us.

I then asked him if he believed in angels. It took him longer than I thought it should for him to answer that question, but he did say yes. I asked him what the difference was.

He responded, "I don't believe we can communicate with spirit."

My cousin Liz, said, "Char, why don't you read it after the services when the guests are eating downstairs."

I said, "No, Liz, I would not do that to the father. This is his church. If I can't read it at the service, I won't read it at all."

I had not thought for one minute that as a family member I would not be able to read what Annie and I agreed on. If I had known it, I would not have gone home for her funeral. I do not believe in all the rituals, and I do not like the display of public emotions because we do not die. We live on. However I did not get upset with the priest because I have learned that everything that happens to us in our life is for a reason.

I was staying at my sister Rose's home, and she decided to go to the early evening mass the Saturday after the funeral. I went along with her because she lived 40 miles out of the city, and we had plans to meet the family after the mass. I had no car.

As we were walking out of the church, the same priest stood by the exit of the church to greet the people as they left. When I got up to him, we exchanged a few pleasantries, and just as I was to move on, he said out of the blue that I should go home and change my clothes and start wearing lighter colors.

I said, "Father, I am not wearing dark colors because Annie has passed on to her next life. I happen to love dark colors. I never wear light colors." That day I had on a dark, cobalt-blue outfit, and for the funeral I wore black. As I walked away from him, I could not believe the audacity of that man, and to think he has fenced in a church-full of people to follow him.

The cost of my sister's funeral was somewhere between $8,000 and $10,000. The family also decided to put in a stained glass window in the church as a memorial not only to Annie, but also to my mom and dad. I did not approve of this because I felt such things are for show, and it does not mean a thing to family or anyone in spirit.

Annie wanted a funeral, and the family in Minneapolis made sure it was the best she could have. I went with family members to select the coffin. We really had some good laughs as we walked around the coffin room trying to decide which one would be best for Annie's body. They were priced from $1,700 up. I suggested that since Annie was in spirit now, she knew how foolish it was to spend all this money, so we should just get a simple, pine box, as it was only her earthly wrappings that went into it.

My sister Rose said, "We can't put her in a pine box."

I said, "You won't be putting her in a pine box. She is standing right here next to me, and she is telling me not to spend a lot of money."

My cousin Liz was checking out the back room area that no one was supposed to enter, and had found something even cheaper than a pine box. Liz and I laughed so hard, and I told the funeral director who was with us that I thought an expensive casket, or any casket, is a total waste of money; and that when a soul arrives in the spirit world they realize there is no benefit in spending so much money for a funeral because it does not lift mankind or love in the heart. I said that the cost of Annie's funeral would go a long way in helping several less fortunate families.

He said, "I absolutely agree with you, Charlene, and I understand how you feel; however, we have to do what the people want in order to make them happy." Then he added, "Come with me. Let me show you something." He took me over to some very small boxes. Some were ornate. He said, "This is my choice. Total cost, around $500.00, depending what box you chose." He, of course, was talking about being cremated.

Death has become as commercialized as Christmas. People are spending enormous amounts of money, which does not mean that we love the soul of our loved one who has passed on to spirit any more. We live in a world where people follow rules, behaviors, and thoughts that society throws at us; and that fences us in with all that it dictates to us, just like organized religion and politics do.

In the latter part of 1996, I read an article in the paper that said thieves are plundering the cemeteries, taking valuable decor such as angels, statues, benches, anything of value that is placed on the grave site. The stolen items end up in antique stores and flea markets where they bring high prices as garden decorations.

Not only are the people being ripped-off by the high expense of a funeral but also by the thieves who are stealing the decorations from the grave sites.

The soul is infinite energy that lives on forever; it cannot die because it is energy and energy cannot be destroyed. We don't die! So why are people going into debt to put on an elaborate funeral or even a simple funeral for their loved ones when we live on? I have friends who were financially struggling to raise their families and went into debt for a simple funeral. Why? Because our society makes you feel guilty if you don't spend a lot of money. It is so sad because most people feel they do not have any other choice. But they do! All they have to do is learn to tune into their spiritual intuition, the divine gift that God gives to everyone to guide them on their journey in life. When a person learns to use their intuition and then follow it, they no longer will be fenced in by what our society dictates to them or worry about what anyone else might think.

TWENTY TWO

GOD, I HAVE FOUND YOU!

Heavenly Father, I have looked for
You for a long, long time. Now that
I have found You within me, I will
always stay tuned in to You.

Without You there was no purpose, and
with You I find all my answers and the
reason for living.

You light up my life every day and in
every way. You are always on my mind in
everything I say and do. You are the light
that I need as I travel my journey in life.
You fill my heart with joy.

I trust in You and I will live each day in
love. I know that You will laugh with me
and that You will cry with me, and guide me to
new horizons.

Thank you for opening the door to You   .
through my dreams. I am grateful that no
one can take You away from me because
You are my silent partner in life.

Charlene Abundis
July 6, 1996
Santa Barbara, California

The following article was published in the Santa Barbara News-Press in the editorial section on 12-16-95.

We are all capable of healing ourselves

Once again the Catholic Church does a great disservice to humanity. Pope John Paul has canonized 274 people as saints in his 17 years as Pope. The latest one is a noble-born Frenchman, Eugene de Mazenod, born in 1782. He obviously was a good man who helped the poor, started a mission in 1816 which is still active today, and he eventually became Bishop of Marseilles.

The reason the Catholic Church has made him a saint is because two people prayed to him and they were cured.

What is the Catholic Church telling us? That only certain people have healing powers? That's hogwash! God is in each one of us and has given each one of us our own divine, inner healing powers.

Neither the Catholic Church nor any other religion has a patent on miracles. We are all capable of healing ourselves. It only takes faith and believing you will be healed. If praying to someone else helps, fine, but the healing is your faith in God and your own healing power.

The second President of the United States, John Adams, wrote a letter to Jefferson, the third President, in 1815 and in it he said: "The question before the human race is whether the God of nature shall govern the world by his own law, or whether priests and kings (Popes) shall rule it by fictitious miracles."

I have read the life of Jesus several times, and He believed in religion; but it was religion of the heart, and when He walked the Earth He felt all other religions were a control of power over the people, and He despised religion that did not come from the heart. He said the kingdom of God is the religion of the heart because it was a pure and good religion without forms, temples, and without priests.

Deepak Chopra says that the heart is not just an organ; it is intelligence and wisdom.

The truth is very simple! We all have divine healing powers because God is in each of us, and He made it so!

Charlene Abundis
Santa Barbara

The following article was published by the Santa
Barbara News-Press on 4-15-96:

VATICAN CITY
Cardinal critical of 'saint factory'

An elderly Italian cardinal, in rare open criticism of the pontiff by a
prelate, says Pope John Paul II is elevating too many people toward
sainthood.

The Vatican "has become a saint factory," said 85-year-old Cardinal
Silvio Oddi in recently published memoirs, according to excerpts in
several Italian newspapers Sunday.

John Paul has elevated more people toward sainthood than all of his
20th century predecessors._La Stampa_ newspaper estimated nearly
1,000 have been canonized or beatified, the next to last step before
becoming a saint.

I received seven phone calls from the community in
regard to "We are all capable of healing ourselves." One lady
said she absolutely agreed that we all have our own healing
powers and that she had healed herself many times. Six
other ladies phoned. They said that they also believed we are
capable of healing ourselves, and in their own way asked me,
"Do you heal yourself? How do you go about it?" I responded
that I do heal myself all the time, and that the answer of
"how" is in the published letter. It only takes faith and the
belief in our own inner healing powers that God gives to
everyone.

Eighteen years ago I pulled my sciatic nerve, and in
spite of the pain which was excruciating, and my husband
and some friends telling me to go to the doctor, I refused to
go, and said it will go away. For four days and nights I
hardly slept; the pain never left me. I also had two little ones
at home to look after. On the fourth day, when my husband
came home from work and found me crying, he insisted I go
to the doctor. I said, "I hate going to the doctors. If it's not
any better tomorrow, I will go."

That night as the prior nights I was up and down
trying to deal with the pain. I never take any medication,

but that night I took two aspirins. I also used a hot water bottle and a heating pad but nothing helped. I laid on the floor for as long as I could and then went back to bed with tears rolling down my face. I said, "Oh, God, please take this pain away. I don't want to go to the doctor." I then fell asleep.

I got up in the morning to prepare Mel's breakfast, and he asked, "How do you feel?"

I said, "Great! The pain is gone."

We were both surprised, but we didn't question it. The last thing I remember was asking God to take the pain away before I fell asleep.

Shortly after my mom passed to spirit I started part-time work in a small office; I was the only other person in the office besides my boss. Several weeks after I started, I woke up on a Monday morning with the same dizziness and nausea that occurred in Minneapolis when we had gone back to visit my mom. But this time it was worse; I could hardly get out of bed. Mel took the day off work, took the children to school, and then came back to take me to the doctor, as much as I hated the thought.

My usual doctor was not in, so I had to see another. The doctor said the dizziness would come and go, that there was nothing to worry about, and no medication would help. She said just to take it easy, and it would go away in about a week.

I had to go in to work the following day because my boss was leaving on a business trip. I told him I would come in and answer phones and do whatever light work I could. I was anxious for the week to end and with it the dizziness. One week went by, two weeks, and into the third week, with no relief. I called my regular doctor, who said that it can last up to six weeks and just to take it easy.

I thought, God, not six weeks of this. It stressed me even more. All of my movements were in very slow motion. That was the only way I could keep it somewhat under control. I never knew when the dizziness would hit me. I couldn't bend over at all; I was afraid to turn my head to look left or right without turning my whole body because those actions sometimes brought the dizziness on very strong. I was walking around like a straight rigid robot. I was barely able to function at home or at work. Fortunately my boss was very understanding. In spite of the dizziness and nausea, I kept on with my routine, hoping it would get better. I even did an exercise that the first doctor said would help. She said whatever action brought the dizziness on, I should repeat that same action several times, and it eventually would get better. When I repeated the action it made my dizziness and nausea even worse. I did not get better.

At the end of the fourth week, I started to slowly turn in bed and it hit me like a brick. I stopped turning and I said out loud, "Oh, God! I can't take this anymore. Please help me, take the dizziness away."

I laid, waiting for the dizziness to lighten up, and then I heard someone say, "OK, CHARLENE."

I capitalize "OK, CHARLENE" because the voice was so loud. I opened my eyes, and I thought, "Who said that?" I looked at Mel, but he was sound asleep. I realized I was sitting up, and at first I felt scared. Was someone in the room? It took me a few moments to realize that the dizziness and the nausea were completely gone. I got out of bed, bent forward, up and down and sideways. I turned around, I did all this several times, it was gone! My dizziness was gone! I felt great.

The next day at work, my mind kept going back to that voice. I then recalled that in one of the books that I had read, it said that when you ask God for something, He is always there for you. I thought, "Was that God talking to me?" I had never experienced anything like that before.

Soon after that experience, I took Armando to the library so he could do some research on a school project. I went to the spiritual section. I found a book that looked good, so I sat at the table with Armando to read it. A half-hour later Armando was finished, and I decided to check the book out.

That night, after dinner and the chores were done, I sat down in my favorite bedroom chair to read it. I soon came to a part that said, "When you ask God for help, He is there for you. He will help if you believe, and don't be surprised if He talks to you out loud." I started to cry. I knew I had heard the voice of God, and I felt so happy. Catana walked into the room just then and asked me why I was crying. I told her and she said, "Mom, you shouldn't be crying. You should be happy."

I said, "Honey, I am happy; that is why I am crying. My heart just feels joy. I've experienced what this writer wrote in the book."

After my daughter left the room, my mind kept going back to the voice. I then remembered that the last thing I said before hearing it was, "God I can't take this anymore. Please help me, take the dizziness away." I realized then that with my sciatic nerve, many years earlier, the last thing I remember before falling off to sleep was asking God to take the pain away. I thought about both incidents, and I knew that this was not a coincidence, that God had healed me both times. Then I remembered something that I had read in the book The Life of Jesus, "Have faith and believe, and you will be healed." I knew that my being healed again was a message for me and that another truth had been revealed to me. My dizziness has never come back.

Before I started my search to find God, I recall watching a program on TV about drugs and teenagers. A young girl said she had beat the drug problem and was now helping others. When asked how she was able to overcome her drug problem, she said, "I was healed by God, and I heard his voice." I remember at the time her comments frustrated me because I wondered what she had experienced, and I wanted to know how she found God. I now know. I decided to go to the library and check out books just on healing. I had read about healing but not in detail, and since I was searching for God, I never gave it a lot of thought. Once at the library, I selected three books on healing. As I was walking over to check them out, something within told me I didn't have the right books, or I wouldn't find the answers I was looking for. I really didn't know why I felt that way, so I glanced through the books before checking them out. When I finished, I closed my eyes and was trying to understand why I felt the way I did. Nothing came to my mind, so I checked them out.

That evening, after dinner and the chores were done, I went in to my bedroom to meditate, and I asked for guidance as to why I had those feelings. Nothing came to me during the meditation. After my meditation, I began to read one of the books, but could not get into it, so I set it aside and picked up another one and again, same thing, and with the third book, too, and I set it aside.

When I went to bed that night, I still had the feeling within that something was not right. I asked my spirit guides to give me the answer in my dream as to why I felt that way. I dreamed I was sitting in a class with other people, and the teacher said that we could ask any question, and he would give us the answer. He said he was a medium. I was about to ask a question when someone came into our room and said that I was wanted in another room. I went in to the next room, and my husband was standing there holding a candle. The room was dark and all I could see was his face and the candle. I walked over to him and asked what he was doing here. He said, "I want to show you the light." I was confused because I didn't understand what he meant. Then the room lit up, and we were in a huge gym with only a few other people, the teacher, myself, Mel and three or four others. The teacher pointed to his chest and said, "The light is in here," and then he told me to go over and practice my healing. I got up, still confused, and walked over to a lady. I didn't know what was wrong with her, but I touched her head, and she was healed and very happy. Then someone came running towards me, for what reason, I don't know, because I woke up.

The next morning I looked up the dream in Betty Bethards' dream book. The symbols told me that I had inner healing power. I thought to myself, "If I have inner healing power, then everyone else does too." That evening I sat down to read one of the healing books that I brought home from the library. Now I was able to tune into the book. Two weeks later I returned the three books, and didn't check out any more. I found insight in the ones I read, but what became crystal clear to me is that I didn't even have to read the books because my spiritual intuition told me that God gave me the answer in my dream. Another truth had been revealed.

When you learn to work with your intuition, you will find it guides you; and your answers will come fast as to what is or is not right for you. The process in getting answers quickly depends on how sharp your awareness is of your intuition. William MacMillan, who wrote the book The Reluctant Healer, wrote, "One minute you know nothing and the very next minute you know it." It's that simple! And you will learn not to question the guidance, but to follow it.

We all have the power within us to heal ourselves. I have read that people can heal by the laying on of hands, or a healing can come about from others praying for you. Some people can be healed immediately, and that is considered a miracle. Other healings can take a week or even months, and the change can be gradual and the effects cumulative. One book said that healing works only when you let go of fear and remain positive, that all fear is from negative thoughts that stop the healing process, that health is the positive and the illness is the negative. Your mind must visualize a healthy body because health absorbs the illness. Whatever works, all healing is God's divine law that operates through you with your faith and believing. It is not in a crystal, a stone or a cross, church or a temple. It is activated through your faith and believing.

Once I realized that I had the healing power within me, I never doubted, when I asked for a healing, that I would not be healed. I have used God's healing power over and over again. In addition to the prior healing experiences I told you about, I have on several occasions strained my back lifting heavy items while doing charity work. I would go to bed, and have a talk with God, and ask him to heal my back or whatever else needed healing. I would thank Him, and go to sleep. The next morning I would be healed. I never question that I won't be, because I know I will be. It is clear to me that if you have a positive mind with faith and believing, healing is a simple process. You ask, you let go, and you let God.

One book that I read during my research said that all you have to do is to ask God just once, whether it is for a healing, or something positive that you want to happen in your life or for someone else. If you asked more than once

214

then you don't believe or have faith. You only need to ask one time, and then you can thank God as often as you want, a hundred times a day or more. Faith, believing, and positive thoughts are the key to healing. It is the key to everything good that you want in your life. It works! I have always told my children, "You do your part and God will do His." Once again very simple!

Twenty nine years ago, after my first pap smear test, the doctor told me it was not normal. He said not to worry, but that it was important for me to have a pap smear every year. I did so faithfully until the age of 44. Family life and my daily rat race were overflowing my plate. Each week I would say, next week I will make the appointment. My intuition was telling me to go, but I kept saying next week. Two years went into three when I had a dream that gave me a very clear message. I was actually inside my uterus, being shown that I had a problem.

I woke up from the dream, and I was scared. That morning I phoned the doctor's office, telling the receptionist that it was urgent, and she was able to get me in. That same morning my friend Lois Cook, the wonderful medium whom I met through RF, and who now is in spirit, phoned me. She never gave readings to people for money, but if she received a message from spirit for any of her friends or family, she would always make sure to call and give it to them.

She asked me when I had my last pap smear test. I knew that besides my dream message, her guides gave her a message for me also. I did not tell her about my dream until after she gave me the message. She said she didn't want to scare me, but her guide told her that I had put off having a pap smear too long, and I no longer could wait. She said, "You will be OK, but you must have it now." I then told her about my dream.

My pap smear showed that I had pre-cancerous cells, and I needed to have surgery. Several days after my surgery I had to return to the doctor to be checked. He asked me if I had ever been a heavy smoker in my life.

I replied, "I have never smoked. Why?"

He said, "What you had we usually see in women who are heavy smokers."

I said, "I grew up in a house that was always full of smoke because both of my parents were heavy smokers and my sister and brothers smoked when they got older and still lived at home." I asked if that could have caused my pre-cancerous cells.

He said, "Yes, that could have been the cause."

Before I was married, my friend Pat and I moved to Padaro Lane in Carpinteria, 10 miles south of Santa Barbara. We rented a place on the beach. Next door lived a married couple. They had been teachers and now were retired. They were the sweetest and kindest people I have ever met. I just loved them. When I would come home from work, I had to walk near their side door, which entered into their kitchen, to get to my apartment. She would often call out my name and ask me to wait a minute in order to give me some homemade sweets, or she would invite me in for a cup of coffee and a treat, and without fail, she would always give me a smile as I passed by. One day I realized I had not seen her for some time.

I decided to go down and see if she was OK. Her husband came to the door when I knocked, and he looked so sad. I asked him if his wife was OK and he said, "She just died here at home." I was shocked! I asked him if she had a heart attack, and he said no, then gave me a complicated answer and I said, "Oh, I am so sorry, couldn't the doctors help her?" He said, "We don't believe in doctors. We are Christian Scientist." It shocked me when he said that. I told him I would miss her and gave him a hug. He looked so lost and alone. I wanted to do something, but I had no idea how to raise his spirits.

I rarely saw him after that. The few times I did, we would chat, but the bright light that I had seen coming from within him before his wife passed was out. He told me he might move because his life didn't have much meaning now. He said, "I didn't expect my wife to die so soon."

I moved from the beach a few months later, and the day that I was packing my car he came out and wanted to know if he could help me. I thanked him and said that I was fine. I told him that I would miss him. He asked me where I was moving to. I said back to Santa Barbara. I asked him if he had made a decision yet as to whether he would move or stay. He said he might move to an active retirement center where some friends were living. I gave him a hug, and I told him I would stop by in a few weeks to visit. He said he would like that.

I stopped a few weeks later and took him a small box of candy. He told me he had started to golf again and was just leaving to meet his friend. The next time I stopped by, I was on my way to Los Angeles with a friend, and I just wanted to say hello and give him a hug. No one was home. I got married shortly after that, and life goes on.

But I'll never forget the day that he and his wife invited me to join them on their front porch overlooking the ocean. They were so positive and loving with great joy in their hearts as they talked about the house being such a good deal and that their dream was to always live on the shores of the ocean. They talked about their grandchildren and how much they enjoyed the ocean when they visited them and all their future plans with their family.

What hit me hardest in meeting these dear people is how fast our lives can change from happiness to sadness. After she passed, he came across as a cold, unfeeling man, but he wasn't cold and unfeeling; he was just very sad. He had no sign of joy or happiness in his soul or heart anymore. Today I realize that he and his wife gave their power away, and because of it, they were fenced in; and the future dreams they told me about never came to be. I wondered if they were Christian Scientist for most of their lives. If so, it must have worked for them, and perhaps it was just her time to pass on. Deep down I wanted to know if he blamed God or his religion, but I couldn't bring myself to ask him. Only God knows.

I have a dear friend whose religion is Christian Science. However, she is guided by her intuition as to when to go to the doctor.

I recall reading an article years ago about a doctor who said that when patients came to him thinking they had a problem, and he couldn't find anything wrong with them, he would give them a sample of aspirin and tell them that the pill would take care of it. They would leave the office thinking they now had the drug that would heal them, and he wouldn't see them until they had another problem. He said that proved to him how very powerful the mind is. It can heal you or make you sick. Benjamin Franklin wrote, "God heals and the doctor takes the fee."

Positive thinking, power of the mind, faith, and believing in our own inner healing powers all work because it all comes from God. Good doctors are healers that God also provides us with. He also gives us free choice to choose what we want to believe as we travel our road in life.

I have always been a high-energy person and sometimes I go at such a fast pace that I throw myself out of balance, and I will end up with a flu or a cold. It doesn't happen often, but when it does, I know that I am to blame.

My friend Lois Cook, phoned me early one morning just as I was about to dash out the door and said, "I got a message that if you don't slow down, they're going to slow you down."

I had so many things going on at the same time, and I knew I was getting out of balance. I told her by the end of the week I would be able to slow down and take time for myself. Two days later, in a rush, I was carrying a box of material to a neighbor, and as I stepped off the curb, I twisted and sprained my ankle. I thought I had broken a bone because it immediately swelled up and got black and blue. That evening Lois phoned and said, "Well, I told you they were going to slow you down."

I asked her what message she got this time, and she said, "I saw you twisting your ankle."

I said, "Well, you're right."

She said, "I told you, the warning was strong!"

In 1994, I stopped at a friend's house to drop something off; as I drove into the driveway, she was out in the yard, and I was surprised to see her daughter Heather with her. Heather was attending college in another city, so I asked her if she had a few days off. She said no, that she came home because she didn't feel well. My friend then insisted that I stay and have lunch with the family. Heather was sitting at the table but not eating, and I asked her why. She said she had a migraine and couldn't keep anything down. My heart went out to her, you could see the pain on her face.

I asked her if she would like to go with me to a temple which is located in the hills behind Santa Barbara, and I would lead her through a simple meditation that could take the pain away. She agreed to go. We were there in half an hour.

I often go to this temple to meditate because it is so simple and beautiful and sits high in the hills with glorious views of the ocean and is surrounded by the golden sounds of nature. I had no clue what would happen to Heather. I just knew that I had healed myself, and if I could, anyone could. I asked Heather to write in her own words about that day. She sent me the following:

Heather Hoffacker:1.21.1996
"For the majority of my life the word "migraine" has been a bad word. To me, there is nothing more painful or distracting because the center of pain is in your head. You can't sleep, eat, think, concentrate or hold any food down.

By the time I had made it to high school and college, I was experiencing the nightmare of the migraine at least twice a month, sometimes more but never less. With these migraines, I would experience vomiting and diarrhea, and I could not attend school or work. They were completely disabling.

I had been to several doctors, been on special restrictive diets, tried dozens of different medications to no avail. Still suffering, I was willing to try anything. It is at this point, where I could stand it no longer, that I let go and put the pain into Charlene's hands.

I will never forget the day that she came over to my parents' house and saw me suffering. She told me that I could take away the pain if I let her show me how. We drove up to the temple, a very secluded and quiet property that is surrounded by the beauty of nature. She told me that I had the power to heal myself if I opened myself up to praying for the positive and closed myself off from the negative. After we had been there awhile, my headache had subsided and then vanished.

219

From that day, I only suffer with migraines when I let myself accumulate stress and focus all of my energy on the negative tasks of life. Anyone can heal themselves. It is a mind over body situation and I know that it works."

•　　　•　　　•

On our way to the temple, I guided Heather through a simple meditation. I told her that once we got there, the meditation would last no more than a half-hour, and I would let her know when it was time to close down. I also told her that she was in charge of what happened to her.

Just before the end of the meditation, I felt tremendous heat coming from my hands. I had never experienced that before, and that little voice within told me to go over and lightly place my hands around her head. As I did this, Heather opened her eyes. I said, "Honey, just relax; I want to try something." I had my hands on her head for maybe three minutes. I then told her we would close down. I asked her how she felt. She had a glow that lit her whole face up.

She smiled and said, "It is gone!"

I said, "Honey, I knew it would be. I heal myself all the time." We walked out of the temple, and, as we stood there on the steps for a few minutes, we inhaled the glorious beauty of nature all around us. I am sure she felt the same wonder of that moment as I did. It's a feeling that makes you one with nature. It filled my soul that day as it always does.

I then suggested that we go to the little gift shop on the property. While there, my little voice within said to buy a certain small box with an elephant on the top with its trunk pointed up. I put a small bead that I had in my purse in the box.

Heather was standing in the middle of the room as I was paying for it and I turned and said, "Honey, I want you to have this," and handed her the box.

She took it and said, "Oh, I love elephants," and her eyes got teary.

I said, 'Well, I thought you would. Whenever you have a migraine, I want you to take this little box out, and that will remind you of the power you have within you." I explained about the bead and I gave her a hug.

I said, "Honey, you have God within you, and you used your inner, positive, healing power because you had faith and believed. That's all it takes." We turned and walked out of the door and were about to walk down some stairs when we heard a loud bang from inside the shop. We stopped, looked at each other, and went back in. By now the sales lady had come around from behind the check out desk and there, on the floor, about five feet from where Heather and I had been standing, a cast-iron Buddha which was about two feet high, had fallen off its stand which was still on a shelf and was about a foot high. It was now lying on the floor.

The lady looked at both of us and said, "What happened?"

Heather said, "We didn't do that."

She said, "Oh, I know you didn't."

The three of us stood there for a few seconds wondering how it could have happened. There was only one other person in the shop but far from this area. Just then that voice within told me that God did that to validate exactly what I had just told Heather. I said, "I know what happened. God did that, Heather, just to let you know that you are in charge and now in touch."

The next morning, I phoned Heather to see how she was feeling, and she said that she woke up in the middle of the night with the worst headache she had ever had in her life. "It hurt so bad," she said. "I meditated, and it went away."

I said, "God gave you that headache honey. He knew that you would meditate and it would go away. It is just confirmation of your inner healing powers that you used yesterday. God wanted you to know that it was no accident."

I told Mel about the Buddha, and I convinced him to go out to the temple with me the following day to see how heavy that Buddha was. We entered the gift shop, and I showed Mel the Buddha. He tried to lift it, and so did I. Mel said, "This is heavy. Are you sure it fell over?" The cashier that was there yesterday was not in the shop that day, so I just looked at Mel with a ready to punch you look. He said, "I believe you." Being a doubting Thomas, he knew I didn't appreciate his questioning what Heather and I experienced.

What Heather accomplished in meditation, anyone can. Since then, I have other friends who have also healed themselves through meditation. Again, I must repeat, with faith and believing and a positive mind, you can place all your health problems, stress, fears, and worries on God's altar of love, and then let go of it. If you choose to live in the negative, then you can't possibly have faith and believe; and sickness, fear, and stress will surely be there waiting for you. Emerson wrote, "No one owns the day who allows it to be invaded with worry, fear and anxiety."

Less than a year later, another good friend told me during a phone conversation that she just got over a migraine and was tired of having them. She knew Heather and she was aware of Heather's healing experience, so I asked her if she would like to learn the simple meditation that would put her in charge. She said, "Yes, the next time I get a migraine I'll call you right away." Two weeks later she phoned. We arranged to meet at the temple, since it was located between our homes. Before we went into the temple, I went over the simple directions of the meditation with her. The following is her experience as she wrote it:

Rosanne Van Wingerden

"My first experience with meditation was introduced to me by my wonderful friend, Charlene. I have experienced migraines for about 20 years, and Char said meditation had helped Heather and would also help me. The day we met at the temple I was having a migraine. She gave me a brief introduction into the world of meditation. We removed our shoes and entered the temple.

"I opened my mind to meditation and healing and soon I was experiencing a tingly feeling from the base of my neck to the front of my head. My grandmother, whom I have had many encounters with in my dreams, appeared first; and she was smiling at me and whispering loving phrases to me in Italian. A number of friends and family members were standing, smiling at me. I could feel my eyes tearing, and I felt an incredible sense of warmth and love. I saw a white light and an open gate, and Jesus was standing before me with his arms outstretched. A friend, whose little daughter had passed a few years earlier appeared, and she spoke to me and asked me to remember her mother on the anniversary of her death which would soon be upon us.

"I felt Charlene touch me, and we closed down. We then went outside and sat on the steps of the temple. I could not speak. I was crying and literally shaking, my whole body was; but I felt an intense happiness. My migraine was gone.

"Since that experience, I meditate often. It has such a calming effect on me. When I have a migraine, I remind myself that I am in God's hands, and that with His help and guidance I am in charge of my life. I ask for a healing, and incredibly it works for me.

"I must also tell you that I have had numerous experiences in my meditations usually involving my grandmother. Sometimes other friends or relatives, and even people that I hardly knew, come to me and give me a message which I sometimes have to decipher; but usually the message is quite clear, asking me to call a loved one. I always follow through, and it never ceases to amaze me that the one I am to give the message to needs some help or encouragement; and I always end up knowing my calling has been a help and a comfort to them. Sometimes I will just hear a gentle voice telling me not to worry, that all is OK."

●　　　●　　　●

Rosanne, as well as Heather, had been to several doctors, and given different medications that worked for a short while, and then another and another. They both had concern about taking so many medications and what it might be doing to their bodies with no lasting results. They are in charge now through such a simple process of faith and believing in their own inner healing powers. God will do the rest!

Rosanne stopped by my home one morning to drop something off, and she said she could not stay, that she had a migraine and was anxious to get home so that she could meditate.

I asked her if she would like me to try and give her a healing.

She said, "If you don't mind."

She sat on a stool and I stood behind her, placed my hands on her head and prayed for a healing.

Fifteen minutes later, I said, "OK, I am through. How do you feel?"

She said, "It's gone."

I was surprised, and I knew God did this, not me. I asked her what she felt.

She said, "I felt intense heat on my head," and I told her that I felt intense heat coming from her head.

She said, "My head started to spin, then you ended the healing and my headache was gone."

I said, "Rosanne, this is all in God's plan." It amazes me what faith and believing can do.

Rosanne had another experience several months later. She said she had a bad headache and decided to meditate lying down. She said she raised out of her body, and there were many people all around her; but she could not see the faces, and then she said her head started to spin, like it did last time at my house only much, much faster; and then she realized she was back in her body and her headache was gone.

Here is another friend's story in her words:

"The evening brought me to Charlene's door with total absence of joy in me, and in its place, an anguish I had felt lifelong on some level. But now it had escalated to beyond any ability to cope. I have known extreme pain in the physical sense, and this was far worse; in essence this pain, too, was experienced on a very physical level. But no name is found for it in the English language. I tried to explain my "pain" to Char by telling her that it felt like the fear you have before the dentist drills, or some equivalent, only magnified a hundred thousand times, or to a volume that fills you so completely that you cannot hold any more, abject fear, the kind you feel in your body and must escape. But even with logic and reason there was <u>no</u> escape.

"When I stopped at Char's house it was on impulse. I had experienced migraines for about 25 years, intense and debilitating, becoming worse as I grew older. New medical information revealed that some migraine sufferers develop a cycle of headaches because of the medication they take. The cure becomes the cause. I had tried everything that I knew to try and stop them. Under medical supervision, I controlled my diet, avoiding any foods that are known triggers, modified my sleep patterns, was treated by chiropractors, faith healers, physic healers, lymphatic massage, allergists, neurologists. I practiced positive thinking and tried countless medications.

"Every avenue which I knew, I tried and exhausted over those 25 years. Char has from time to time offered to work with me because of my headaches. I knew that she was sincere and had had success with other mutual friends of ours; healings were taking place. I wanted to let her try to heal me, and that was always my plan until the pain would start, then even calling her seemed out of the question. I could not fathom moving to a sitting position, and the prospect of riding in a car to the temple was more than overwhelming.

"I decided to take my chances with the headache rebound theory of medication, causing recurring head-aches. The medical information explained that the only way to break the cycle is to stop all medication. This exercise generally causes a migraine to be triggered and lasts up to three weeks. This was a hard task, but I saw it through to the end and was rewarded with no more migraines. I can never have pain medication. Even Tylenol will start the cycle again.

"The migraines were gone, but my body seemed to go into some kind of shock. I did not sleep at all for what seemed like weeks at a time. My nerves were frayed. I got progressively worse and worse during a four month period until the absolute breaking point which landed me at Charlene's home. I was there because I knew in my heart that she was a dear friend who would care that I was in trouble. And she did. She opened her arms and heart and her home to me, and I was so anguished that I let her know everything that I was experiencing. I asked Char if she could give me a healing. She had me sit on a stool facing the beautiful view from her home.

"I had my eyes closed while Char worked on me. She told me to imagine a healthy body for myself, and the image came without effort. She said to reject any negative that came and accept only positive. I had fear that this, too, would not work for me, and the moment I thought of fear, an image came into my mind that the word f-e-a-r was painted on 4 golf balls, each one holding one letter. I imagined stepping up and hitting each letter very hard with a golf club until each one disappeared from view. Then the golf balls reappeared with the word "love" on them.

"I felt better immediately after the healing. I once again felt the fear start to come back, and I used the golf ball image to keep the fear away. We then sat and talked while we had a cup of tea. I felt miraculously better. I definitely did not feel as I had prior to the healing. The change in my whole mind and body was incredible, remarkable, absolutely total. I had experienced a miracle from God.

"I awakened the following morning and felt better than I ever remember feeling. I can understand for the first time why people treasure their life experiences so much. This was all new to me, and I thank God and the heart of a friend for this miracle."

•　　•　　•

I have not used my friend's name because of her family's high visibility in Santa Barbara. Also, what she wrote was very private, and I know she would never share it with anyone else. She did tell me, that if I felt it was necessary, I should use her name because she said, "We must let others know the powers of God that we all have within us."

When my friend came to the door, I was surprised to see her. I instinctively knew something was wrong. She would never barge in on anyone without calling first.

She said, "Char I am sorry to bother you. My car just brought me here. Do you have a shoulder I can lean on."

I said, "Sure, come on in."

We sat down in the living room, and she explained to me what she wrote in her own words. I had never seen my friend like this before and I have known her for 16 years, so I knew this was not easy for her.

I had no sooner thought to myself, "Could I give her a healing? No, this is beyond anything I can do," when she asked me if I could give her a healing. I immediately said yes, and added, "Let me get a stool for you to sit on."

I couldn't believe I said yes. When I left the room to get the stool, I felt so much pressure, and thought, "Oh God, I can't heal her. You have to. I'll do my part; but, please, please heal her. She is such a special person and in so much pain."

I prayed so hard in the short time it took me to get the stool, and when I got back to the living room, I told her about thinking positive over negative, that I had read that in a healing book, and I knew it worked.

She sat on the stool, and I used the same procedure I did with Rosanne; I put my hands lightly on her head, and I cannot tell you how hard I was still praying; and all of a sudden, I felt this tickling all over my face, and I was reminded that I had a lot of help. Whenever I meditate, or often just through the day, I feel the same tickling, and I know that spirit is with me.

Twenty minutes later I moved in front of her and said, "Sweetie I am done. How do you feel?"

She opened her eyes, and she had that same glow on her face that Heather did. Her whole face had changed from a look of pain to light.

She said, "Char......I feel great. Thank you! You healed me."

I said, "I did?" I was surprised, and I added, "I didn't heal you. This is so exciting and awesome. God healed you."

She said, "I know, Char."

My friend and I are in touch all the time, and she is just doing great.

•　　•　　•

When Catana was four, our pediatrician suggested that I take her in for a hearing test. She never had any problems, but since he suggested it, I made the appointment.

She was given the test as I sat with her in a small room. When we finished we were asked to wait, and then we were called into the doctor's office. I was told she should be brought back in six months because her test indicated she was unable to hear certain sounds. I left the office without making an appointment because I honestly knew she didn't need any more tests or anything! I just knew it.

Several months later a mother whose son attended the same pre-school that Catana did, phoned and asked me if I could work her shift at the pre-school the following week because she had to take her son to the ear doctor. I said yes. I asked her if her son was having ear problems, and she said no, that the last time she took him in for a general check-up, they said that he didn't hear certain sounds and that she should make sure he was checked in six months again. I asked her the name of the doctor, and it was the same doctor that I took my daughter to. I told her that I was given the same information but that I chose not to go back. She said, "You didn't?" with great concern in her voice. I said no, that I could not believe that my daughter could not hear certain sounds because I was in the room sitting next to her when she was being tested, and the test went quickly and smoothly, and my feelings told me not to go back.

I was surprised when she asked me a few weeks later if I had changed my mind and might still go back.

I said, "No, I have no intentions of going back."

She said that they told her to schedule another appointment for her son in six months.

I said, "Well, you have to do whatever feels right to you. It just does not feel right to me."

When Catana was in high school, this boy attended the same school. His mother came up to me, introduced herself, and asked me if I remembered her.

I said, "Yes, how are your son's ears?" reminding her of the conversation we had many years before.

She said, "After three times I never took him back. It was just so expensive."

I again asked her if his ears were OK now.

She said, "Absolutely, he has never had problems."

I said, "Neither has my daughter."

She then added, "I might have continued to go back because you put your faith in a doctor, and when they keep telling you to come back, you worry that something is really wrong. When you said it didn't feel right to you, I decided, after the third time, that it didn't feel right to me either."

The following article was published in the Santa Barbara News-Press on 3-25-96.

Apparent vitamin E benefit called surprising by doctors

By DANIEL Q. HANEY
Associated Press

ORLANDO, Fla. -- Doctors are astonished by a British study's conclusion that a dime's worth of vitamin E seems to reduce heart attacks by 75 percent when taken daily by people with bad hearts.

"I'm puzzled. Most of my colleagues are puzzled," said Dr. Thomas Ryan of Boston University.

After all, vitamins are sold in health food stores and supermarkets. If one of them really works so well, Ryan asked, why hasn't someone noticed before?

"It's pretty amazing. Unbelievable, really," said Dr. W. Douglas Weaver of the University of Washington.

In fact, even the researchers themselves seem taken aback by their discovery.

The researchers, led by Dr. Nigel G. Brown of Northwick Park Hospital in suburban London, published their findings in Saturday's issue of the journal Lancet and presented them to the world's heart specialists Monday at the annual meeting of the American College of Cardiology.

"We were surprised by the magnitude of the result, but it does seem to be true," Brown said.

Vitamin E is one of a group of nutrients known as anti-oxidants. Heart disease often results from the accumulation of lumps of fat in the walls of blood vessels.

However, this fat in the blood may be harmless unless it is oxidized - the same process that turns iron brown and makes food spoil. Oxidation is one of the steps that put fat and cholesterol into a form that is deposited in the arteries.

Differences in the amounts of antioxidants in the diet might, for instance, help explain why people who live in Mediterranean countries have less heart disease than Americans and Northern Europeans.

Dark green leafy vegetables, whole grains, wheat germ, nuts, seeds and legumes are high in vitamin E, and it can be found in higher concentrations in vegetable oils such as safflower and corn oil. It would be difficult to consume enough of these each day to match the same amounts examined in the study, however.

In recent years, doctors have noticed that folks who consume lots of vitamin E supplements seem to lower their risk of heart attacks. But until now, no one has conducted a large experiment to see if vitamin E pills actually do this.

The British team enrolled 2,002 people with serious heart disease and randomly assigned them to take either dummy pills or pills containing either 400 or 800 international units of vitamin E a day. (The U.S. recommended daily allowance is just 15 units for men and 12 for women.)

After 17 months of follow-up, 50 people had died of heart disease and 55 had suffered nonfatal heart attacks. Fourteen of the nonfatal heart attacks were in the vitamin takers, 41 in the placebo group.

That did not translate into longer life, however. The deaths from all kinds of heart disease were evenly split between the two groups. The researchers say there are possible explanations for this, including the high rate of congestive heart failure, which vitamin E does not help.

The researchers said they believe the health message is clear - up to a point.

Dr. Morris J. Brown of Cambridge University said he is recommending 800 milligrams of vitamin E daily for his patients with angina pain. He cautioned, however, against urging the vitamin on people who have no outward signs of heart trouble, since they were not included in the study.

Vitamin E pills typically cost about 10 cents apiece when bought by the bottle in a supermarket.

In 1968, my mother, at the age of 50, had a heart attack. Over the years, prior to the attack, she had had numerous fainting spells but never went to the doctor. It was her choice not to. At the time of her attack, I was married and living in Santa Barbara. I called and told her that I had been doing research on vitamins, and I read that vitamin E was good for the heart, and I would send her a couple of bottles.

She said, "You better wait until I check with my doctor." The following week she phoned and told me that her doctor said vitamin E was only good for your sex life and that with heart problems, she certainly didn't need to increase her sex life.

I said, "Mom, he is out to lunch. You need to take all vitamins and especially vitamin E," but she said no.

Less than two years later my mom and dad came out for a two month visit. She told me her doctor said the fainting spells were caused by her heart problems, that her heart was badly damaged, and if she had another heart attack, she might not survive it.

I put both my parents on vitamins while they were here with us. But first I took them to have their blood pressure checked, because if they had high blood pressure, I would start them on a small dosage of E then gradually increase it up to the amount I felt would be best for them; otherwise they could get severe headaches.

My mom's blood pressure was up, my dad's was OK. Just to be safe I started both of them on 100 IU of vitamin E and 6,000 MG of vitamin C - 2,000 in the morning, 2,000 at noon, and 2,000 in the evening, plus a good one-a-day vitamin. By the time they left Santa Barbara to return home, they were taking 800 IU of vitamin E along with the above C and the one-a-day vitamin. They told me that they felt good, so much better than when they arrived. I sent them home with two months supply of the above vitamins for each of them.

My mother faithfully took her vitamins for the rest of her life; my dad stopped shortly after returning home. The doctor who told my mother that vitamin E was only good for her sex life checked her after she returned home from Santa

Barbara and said that her blood pressure was good and her heart seemed stronger than ever. He said continue on with whatever it is you are doing. She received the same positive report on all her future checkups for the heart. The doctor even said that he was surprised she was doing so well.

Ten years later, she had a breast removed for cancer. The day before she went in for surgery, I phoned my sister Rose and told her to make sure that mom was allowed to take all her vitamins into the hospital with her, and I told her to increase her vitamin A, C, and E, and gave her the amounts to increase them to.

My sister called back to tell me that the doctor said mom could take all of the vitamins into the hospital with her except the vitamin A. I told my sister to tell the doctor that this was our mother and that we knew what was best for her and that vitamin A was a very important vitamin for her to have in case of an infection and for her healing. I also phoned the doctor's office, but he was not in, so I left the message that my mother must be allowed to take A into the hospital with her, and if he would not allow her to do that, I wanted a phone call back because we knew what we were doing, and we were going to fight for this. The following day my sister Rose phoned and said that the doctor said OK.

My mother had her surgery on a Thursday. I called and talked with her on Friday and Saturday, and she was doing great. When I phoned her on Sunday evening she told me she would be going home in a day or two, in spite of telling us before she went in that it would be a two week hospital stay.

She said that earlier in the day her doctor asked her if it was OK to bring 6 to 8 physicians in to interview her. They asked her if she smoked, drank alcohol, or coffee. They wanted to know her eating habits and her exercise schedule. They told her they had never seen such a fast healing after a mastectomy, that this was a first for them.

My mother did not have good eating habits; she was a heavy smoker and coffee drinker; and had no special exercise program other than her normal routine of housework. She continued to smoke heavily and during the next ten years had more surgeries for cancer. The doctors told her if she stopped smoking she could live 15 more years, especially since she recovered rapidly from her surgeries. She chose not to stop. Twenty years after her heart attack, she passed at the age of 70 from lung cancer. Her heart was as strong as ever; too bad she didn't heed the advice to stop smoking.

My sister Darlene phoned me the night before my mom passed to tell me that the oxygen, which mom had been on for several months, was no longer helping her and that they rushed her to the hospital. She phoned again in the morning and said that mom passed during the night and said, "I will never, as long as I live, forget mom squirming on the hospital bed like a worm, trying to get her last breath. It was the worst thing I have ever experienced."

My sister Rose and I agree that if mom had not been taking vitamins she would not have lived past the age of 55 because of her heart problems. But she lived to be 70 because of all the vitamins she took and her faith, knowing they were helping her.

•   •   •

In 1990 Uncle Dave, my dad's brother who was a diabetic, phoned me. He was very emotional and soon crying. He had just come from seeing his doctor, who told him it looked like they would have to amputate his foot. He had broken his ankle a few months earlier and the ankle would not heal. He said, "I can't live without a foot."

I said, "Uncle, listen to all that fear that is coming out of your mouth. You're not going to heal anything with such negative thinking." He said, "I'm telling you what the doctors told me." I said, "I will check with Steve at Kaysers Health Foods. (Steve had helped him before and is very knowledgeable.) I will call you back. When you hang up, take a few minutes to be silent and ask God to help you use your own inner healing powers, and thank Him immediately for your healing."

I phoned Steve. Yes! There was something that would help. I immediately went to Kaysers, picked it up and mailed it overnight delivery so my uncle would have it the next day. As soon as I arrived home I phoned my uncle, who was still very upset, and I asked him if he had a talk with God, yet. He said, "Yes, and I already thanked him."

I said, "Great, you only have to ask Him once, but you can thank Him a million times a day if you choose." He said, "OK." I told him that I had sent the package of what Steve recommended, that he would receive it in the morning, that he should start taking it immediately, and that there was a note in the package with Steve's directions as to how many he should take, etc. I also told him to increase his vitamin A, C, E, the vitamins that I already had him taking. Five days later my uncle phoned me and was ecstatic. What Steve had recommended was working. The skin was already healing. I sent him two more months supply per Steve's recommendation, and within several weeks the ankle was totally covered with new skin, and he was doing great.

He said, "The doctor was surprised. It's like a miracle, honey."

I asked him if he thought it was a miracle.

He said, "Well, yes, the doctors weren't able to give me anything to heal it. They were going to cut my foot off, but thanks to you, Steve, and God, they didn't."

I said, "Uncle, you better thank yourself also. It was your faith and believing, along with your inner healing powers that God gives to all of us, that helped this miracle."

My Uncle Dave was a very special man. He was loved by all of his family and his many friends. But he also was a very hardheaded person, and he didn't like to take advice from others. I honestly think I baffled him at times, but he always took the advice that I gave him.

I recall the first time he visited Mel and me. It was in 1973. The first breakfast I fixed him, I put a small container of vitamins near his plate.

He picked up the small container and asked, "What's this?"

I said, "Vitamins for you."

He said, "This many?"

"Uncle Dave," I said, "you know how they help mom."

He said, "OK." Three or four days later he said, "You know, I think I feel better. Could it be the vitamins?"

My uncle spent two weeks with us and before he left, I took him to Kaysers, and he bought a three months supply of vitamins to take back to Minneapolis with him. He often phoned to ask me if it was OK to add garlic pills or a mineral to his diet. He was also doing his own research. He told me that when he asked the doctors about taking vitamins, they said it was fine with them, but my uncle said he knew with their attitude that they thought it was a waste of money. "However," he said, "I know they are good for me because I have never felt so good."

My Aunt Helen, who I wrote about earlier, came out with my mother to visit us in Santa Barbara. She told me she had read all the information I had sent her about the vitamins, and she would like to start taking only vitamin E and C. Two months after she returned to Minneapolis, she telephoned asking which vitamin would cause her hair to turn dark in front. She was 62 at the time, had been gray for years, and now her hair at the front of her head was coming back in its original color.

Why are the doctors who were quoted in the article written by Daniel Q. Hanely (page 229) so surprised about the benefits of vitamin E? Where were they when Canadian Doctor Wilfrid Shute published his research in the 1960's about the benefits of E for the heart? Why have they not tuned into his research or read the book he wrote in 1969 Vitamin E for Ailing and Healthy Hearts? In the book he gives detailed information about his research and the benefits of vitamin E! If they weren't practicing physicians at that time, why haven't they learned of his research in medical school? It was public information in the 1960's.

I did my research on vitamin E at the library. Mel and I also read about the benefits of E in the newspaper as well as Prevention Magazine that we later subscribed to.

After the doctor told my mother in 1968 that vitamin E was only good for your sex life, I sent all the information that I found in my research to my mother so she could give it to her doctor. I told her to tell her doctor I would like a response back from him. He never did respond back to me, but he told my mother that it was all rubbish. After my parents returned home from their two months visit with us, and after her doctor had given her such a good report on her check-up for her heart, etc., she feared telling him that she was taking vitamin E and all the other vitamins because she didn't want a negative response from him. He was, in her opinion, a nice doctor but too closed-minded and would never accept that vitamins were beneficial.

Our family has been taking vitamins for almost 30 years. My husband and I take 1200 units of vitamin E daily and 10,000 mg and more of vitamin C throughout the day, as well as other vitamins. Our children also take vitamins. We started giving them small amounts when they were a week old and each year we increased it. Now as adults they take the same dosage that we do. We also have eaten only natural and organic food for 30 years in our home. We have had family and friends who have come to us asking for help when they are having problems and the doctors are not able to help them. They have never been disappointed with the benefits received from taking vitamins.

When the doctor told me at the age of 25 that my pap smear test was not normal, I didn't think it was a big deal. I assumed that other ladies my age had the same problem. Up until I had my surgery 25 years later, I still didn't think it was a big deal. I never discussed my pap smear test with anyone other than my husband, and the doctors never seemed to be overly concerned that they were not normal. I don't want to sound negative, but I can't help but wonder if I would be here today if I hadn't taken vitamins and minerals and had a good diet over the last 30 years. I now know that having an abnormal pap smear test is not normal. I should have been concerned.

Whenever I would hear on the news or read in the paper about the medical profession, a doctor or the FDA putting down vitamins and health food stores, I would fume inside! I always took the time to write them letters with my views. I only received one response back over the years and that was from the FDA, and they sent me a large packet of bureaucratic crap that someone put together, and it made absolutely no sense to me.

If you want to take charge of your health and not be fenced in, use your healing powers and get acquainted with the health food stores in your area. Talk to the employees about your health concerns. They also have dozens of wonderful books that will help you educate yourself on the benefits that the body receives from taking vitamins and minerals. Then, when your doctor tells you something that does not feel right to you, or they can't help you, you will have another direction to go in.

Kaysers in Santa Barbara has been a Godsend to our family and friends. I have sent dozens of people to them over the years when their doctors were not able to help, and they have been delighted with the end results of the help they received from Terry, Steve, Sandy, as well as other employees. Steve is like a walking encyclopedia, absolutely amazing! Kaysers, and, I am sure, most health food stores, keep up on all the recent research of vitamins and minerals to help the body. What Steve recommended for my Uncle Dave to take, I hadn't even heard of. I have thanked Kaysers' employees many times for their help, but I would like to say it again in this book, "THANK YOU!"

Vitamin E and C are considered the miracle vitamins because they do so much for the body and work well with all other vitamins. Do your own research and find out what vitamins do for the body. My purpose of sharing all these stories is not to put doctors down, but to show you how not to get fenced in and to take charge of your own health. I thank God I followed my intuition and was able to help my mother and uncle. Had they not then trusted their intuition, the outcome would not have turned out to be positive for them.

•   •   •

I have had the following article for 10 or 12 years. I have no idea who published it:

EASY WAY TO CUT PAIN OF ARTHRITIS IN HALF

By BOB KALL

You can slash arthritis pain in half - and dramatically reduce stiffness in joints - just by following a special vitamin-mineral plan, say medical experts.

The amazing plan promotes healing of arthritic joints while cutting inflammation, says arthritis expert Dr. Charles Brusch.

"You'll allow yourself more flexibility and freedom in your movement," he enthused.

"This vitamin-mineral approach also can help your body be at its strongest so that (arthritis) drugs will have the most effect - and so your body will be able to cope best with the arthritis."

The plan is good for people with both osteoarthritis and rheumatoid arthritis, says nutrition expert Dr. Wilber Currier.

Here is the plan, with daily dosages suggested by Dr. Brusch, Dr. Currier, and veteran arthritis specialist Dr. Robert Bingham:

- Vitamin C - Take 2,000 milligrams (mg) a day, divided into two or four equal doses.
- Vitamin B Complex - Take two high potency tablets a day.
- Vitamins A and D - 10,000 international units (IU) of A and 400 IU of vitamin D daily, or take one tablespoon of cod-liver oil on an empty stomach.
- Vitamin E - Take 800 IU daily.
- Calcium - Drink two to three glasses of milk a day, or take 1 to 1.5 grams (1,000 to 1,500 mg) of calcium. Buy the form that's "chelated" - specially processed so it's more easily absorbed.
- Magnesium - Take half the daily dosage you take of calcium. For example, if you take 1,000 mg of calcium, take 500 mg of chelated magnesium.

Dr. Bingham, medical director of the National Arthritis Medical Clinic in Desert Hot Springs, Calif., revealed: "Of the 500 patients we see each year, 60 to 70 percent have vitamin and mineral deficiencies which contribute to their arthritis problems.

"And we've found that by improving their diets and supplementing the diets with vitamins and minerals, patients can cut their pain by 50 percent - and relieve the stiffness and soreness in the joints.

"The supplement program also strengthens the patients so they can live fuller lives. Golfers who had to quit, start playing again. Patients who had to stop driving cars can actually ride bicycles.

"It's amazing how it can just turn their lives around!"

Extra amounts of these vitamins and minerals are badly needed by arthritics because common treatments for the disease - including aspirin and steroid drugs like cortisone - can have harmful side effects, the experts pointed out.

The doctors agreed the recommended dosages are safe, but say you should inform your doctor if you decide to go on this program.

The reason I included the above article in this book is because I have passed it on to others and they have thanked me because it helped them so much.

TWENTY THREE

President Lincoln said,

Let us have faith that right

makes might, and in that faith

let us to the end dare to do

our duty, as we understand it.

As I explained in an earlier chapter, I was following my inner knowing without realizing it by just following what felt right and wrong to me. However, once I realized that this feeling was God within, guiding me, I used it all the time. Occasionally when I let my emotions reign, I soon realize that I make mistakes. When you stand for truth and follow what feels right to you, your intuition, inner knowing (it's all the same), you will always win. But this chapter is not about winning. This is about trusting your inner guidance, which enables you to make the right decisions all the time. The experiences that I share with you in this chapter, Mel and I have encountered in our married life, and before I found God within me. I have selected the following experiences because I believe they could easily happen to anyone.

I also hope that by sharing them with you, it might help you, the reader, not to be fenced in by anyone, whether it is family, friends, neighbors, or someone who is considered to be an expert, or in an authoritative position. I am sure that you will see how easily Mel and I and our children could have been fenced in, in a losing position, if we hadn't used that inner knowing to guide us.

I have never been able to "go by the book" or "follow the cows" in my life. I am sure I have broken most of society's rules just because they didn't feel right to me.

Before Mel and I had children, we would hike on weekends in the nearby Santa Barbara mountains. We'd leave about five in the morning so we could inhale the beautiful sunrises, and arrive home by mid-afternoon. Mel had a whistle game call that he always took on the hikes, and when we would stop and rest, he would blow it. Seeing the different animals that would respond to the whistle was always fun and exciting.

I recall one hiking trip when we were resting below a cliff which was about 30 feet straight up and 30 feet in front of us. Mel blew his whistle and a cow appeared, at the very edge of the cliff. Mel continued to blow and another cow appeared next to it, and another, and another. We were cracking up. There obviously was a cow pasture above us, and the cows just kept coming. There must have been 20 cows, all lined up in perfect formation, looking down at us. It was so precious to watch them come one at a time as Mel blew the game call. I said to Mel, "I now understand the saying, 'Don't follow the cows.' " It was a very vivid and unforgettable experience.

A year after Mel and I were married, we bought our first home. Four years later, a local contractor was building a custom home down the street from us for a couple. One Sunday afternoon, after coming home from a ride in the countryside near Solvang, there was an open house sign on our street. We curiously followed the arrow and were surprised to see that it was the custom built home. We went in and I asked the agent why the couple was not going to occupy it. She said, "Well, they changed their mind and the contractor put it on the market."

After we arrived home Mel telephoned a real estate broker friend who later that day came over with the key to the house for sale. We checked out the house and the surrounding property.

We made an offer and it was accepted! No sooner had a sold sign been put on our property when a neighbor friend stopped by to visit. She said she was surprised that someone had bought the new house down the street. I asked her why she was surprised. (We had told no one we were buying the house.) She said, "Because blacks are buying the home next door to it, and that was why the people who had it built backed out."

She went on to say that she really felt sorry for the family that would be living directly across from the black family because, when they built their home several years earlier, they put a lot of money into it; and they didn't deserve to have a black family move in across the street from them. I felt my blood pressure go right through my head. I kept my cool, though, and said, "I don't know what difference it makes what the color of our skin is. Why does that disturb you so much?"

She said, "Blacks moving into an area of expensive homes is not good."

I cannot tell you how furious I was with this friend. I said, "Well, it might surprise you that Mel and I bought that home."

She looked at me and said, "You're kidding!"

I said, in an irritating tone, "No, I am not, and I cannot understand people like you who are prejudiced. We are all a part of God's wondrous whole, and His light shines on each one of us, regardless of the color of our skin."

I could not believe what came out of my mouth because then I didn't even know how to find God; I always wondered how others did.

When I said that my neighbor's face dropped and she asked, "Did you know that blacks were going to be living next door?"

I said, "Yes, we certainly did. In fact we have met and talked with them, and they are lovely people."

I know she was embarrassed and did not know how to respond to what I had just told her. Once she spread the word around the neighborhood that we were buying the house, several other neighbors approached us, and they were as surprised as the first neighbor. I couldn't believe it! They thought that they were better than black people. It gave me such a sad feeling, I honestly felt sorry for them.

My husband had a friend who was the vice-president of a local bank, and he phoned Mel after he found out through a mutual friend of ours that we were moving and told Mel that we were making a big mistake moving next door to a black family and if we could, we should get out of the deal to buy the house because we would lose money; our property value would go down. Again we were shocked! This was the vice-president of a local bank!

Once our old home was sold, we only had to add another $12,000 to buy our new home, which we are still living in. We didn't have a yard in our old home. Our new home gave us a huge yard for the children to play in, and we did not have to leave our neighborhood. In every way our move was such a positive experience with hardly any stress because of our realtor friend's help which was beyond the call of duty. Not to mention that our home today is worth double the value of the home we sold. A great investment!

We didn't care if our next door neighbors were black, brown, yellow or white. All we wanted was to have nice people living next door, and they were the best. I believe they felt the same way about us. Years later when they moved, we were sorry to see them go.

When I had a neighborhood birthday party for my children, their precious children came to it, and when they had a neighborhood birthday party, our precious children went to it.

I believe the prejudice in the world is brought on by only a small minority of people who obviously are not aware that the soul has no color. And that the color of our skin does not make one different from anyone else. We are all people and part of the human race. Anyone that holds prejudice in their hearts is on the losing end of life.

Several years later a for sale sign had been put in front of the newly built home directly across the street from ours. One afternoon, while I was out gardening in front of our home, an open house was held, and people were coming and going most of the afternoon. Several families came over and asked me about the area, the schools, etc. One family who looked at the house was black. Afterwards they went back to their car, but the driver, a lady, walked over to me and asked general questions about the area. I said, "Well, I don't know if you're prejudiced or not, we only have one black family that lives in the neighborhood."

She cracked up laughing, and her laugh made me laugh.

She said, "No, I am not prejudiced. Are you?"

I said, "No, but unfortunately we have some white families that are."

We started talking about life in general and were laughing a lot. About five minutes later, another lady who had been sitting in the car, got out, came over, and asked us what we were laughing about.

We told her and she laughed as well, and said, "Gee, the real estate lady who told us about this property asked if we were prejudiced because it was a white neighborhood."

I said, "I have to ask you, is your real estate lady black or white?"

The second lady said, "She is white; that's why I am laughing."

I said, "Well, you're nice people. I hope you buy the house."

The first lady said, "As much as we like the house, we won't make an offer. Mother, who is sitting in the car, would be living with us, and there are stairs, and she has great difficulty walking up and down stairs with her arthritis."

In spite of our new home being a great investment today, when Mel and I moved in, it was during a heavy rainy season. Our roof leaked in four of the rooms. When the first leak started, we phoned the general contractor. He said it was not unusual for a new roof to leak. Yeah, right! He arranged for the roofing company that he sub-contracted to come out and fix the leak.

The roofing contractor came out 6 to 8 times the first year. We were very concerned, realizing that the roof had major defects. After our first few conversations with the general contractor, Mel and I knew we were going to have a fight on our hands. What we didn't know is that it would last for four years.

Not only did we have a leaky roof, we had no electricity in three of the rooms. Outlets were in the walls, but they didn't work. We had sliding windows we could not open. The windows were supposed to lift out easily so they could be washed, but we couldn't get them out. When the contractor sent someone out, they had to force the windows out, and then we saw that the screens didn't fit properly because there were gapping spaces on the sides. The problems went on and on. All of this shoddy workmanship was not visible to the eye.

This same contractor built in our area 8 to 10 other homes over the next few years, and they all were having many of the same problems we were having, plus other problems. One lady, whose disabled husband was in a wheel chair, not only had a leaky roof and window problems, but she also had hot water coming out of her cold water faucets and vice versa.

A few years later our dishwasher stopped working, and a week later our stove no longer worked. When we checked the warranty package for the appliances, we discovered no warranties for either the dishwasher or the stove.

When I telephoned the contractor's office and said I was not able to find any warranties in the package left with us, I was told he was not in, but I should call a local retailer who sells the brand, and that they would come out. When I did, they said that without a warranty they could not come out without charging us, and that they needed to have permission from the manufacturer.

I could tell once more that we had another uphill fight on our hands. I phoned another local retailer who sold the same brand and explained the problems. He was very kind and asked me what the model numbers were. When I checked the numbers and gave them to him, he told me that those models had been discontinued several years prior because of so many problems. I then phoned the contractor back and gave them the information that I had. They told me that there was nothing they could do and suggested that I phone the manufacturer.

I phoned the manufacturer, who said that all they could do for us was give us a 20% discount if we chose to buy new appliances from them. I told them that giving us a discount was unacceptable, and I asked them why they sold defective merchandise to a sleazy contractor to begin with.

I said, "According to one of your dealers here in town, the appliances were taken off the market because of so many problems."

He said, "All we can do is give you a discount." I told him that I would settle for nothing less than new appliances.

I fought so hard! I finally was able to get the name of a top executive. I phoned him four or five times within a week, and his secretary always said he was not available, and in spite of leaving my name and phone number, he never returned my calls. The last time I called, the secretary said that he was not available, I told her that this was a personal and urgent call. She put me right through. That's how busy he was.

I told him the whole story, and he had no choice but to listen. I said that I would take my story to the news media if I had to because their company knowingly sold defective merchandise to a sleazy contractor who knew it, and that no warranty would be given with the appliances he put in the homes he built. I was angry and he knew it.

He said that he would take care of the problem, and he took my name, address, and phone number. Two hours later we received a phone call from the first retailer that I had phoned. He said we were to come in and select new appliances, and there would be no charge.

I thanked him, but said that I would be going to one of his competitors because they were kind enough to check the serial numbers and told me the appliances that I had were taken off the market because of so many problems.

I immediately hung up and called the top official back and once again his secretary said he was on another line. I said, "Please give him this message." I gave her the name of the retailer I wanted to go to, and also gave her the number so her boss could phone them. I received a call back within a half hour from the retailer. We got new appliances, and there was no charge! We never heard from the CEO again to see if we were happy or not, but this time we got warranties with the appliances.

Back to the roof problems: When the rainy season started the second year, we not only had all the old leaks back, we also had new leaks. The roofing contractor was constantly coming out. The third year the same thing, all the old leaks back as well as new leaks. After what we had gone through the last few years with the contractor and sub-contractor, we decided to contact the city inspector's office and explained why we wanted them to come out. A city inspector came out, and we had a ladder all set up for him to climb up on the roof. He climbed to the top step of the ladder, looked the roof over, but did not get on the roof. I was standing there, waiting for him to go up. He came down the ladder and without saying anything, he started to write up a report. I asked him if he was going to go up on the roof.

He said, "I don't want to break your red tiles."

I said, "How in God's name can you tell what is wrong with the roof by standing on a ladder and looking at it?"

He said, "We usually know what is wrong with red tile roofs that leak."

I asked, "Well what's wrong with it?"

He said, "I want to discuss this with my supervisor first. I'll get back to you."

I asked him who inspected the work during and after construction. He said that his office did. I said, "Well, then why do we have a roof that leaks in all of the rooms if you guys did your job?"

He said, "I don't know, ma'am," in an arrogant manner.

I said, "Well, you know what, I do know why we have a roof that is faulty, and that's because the city inspector who checked this roofing job and who is responsible for making sure the public is protected from shoddy workmanship obviously did not do his job properly. I am going to contact the State Contractors Board and get an attorney if I have to."

He didn't seem worried with that threat.

I said, "This house is only a few years old, and we not only have a roof that has dozens of leaks, but we have had to be on the contractor's case because of faulty work that was done throughout the whole house as well. How can you say that the city inspector did his job?"

He was very nonchalant, and, as he finished writing up his report and handing me a copy, said, "I will send you a written report with my findings."

I said, "Your findings! The report will be very interesting to read."

This city inspector was as arrogant as anyone could be; I could not believe it. I didn't get upset with him until I realized he had no intentions of trying to discover the main cause of so many leaks. He came out with no intentions of getting on the roof, and he was patronizing me.

When we got his report, it said that since the contractor is willing to repair the leaks, there was nothing they could do. So we telephoned and told the general contractor and roofing contractor that we wanted a new roof put on, but they said it wasn't necessary, that they would repair all leaks.

I then phoned and spoke with the top administrator in the city inspector's office. He told me there was nothing they could do if the contractor was willing to work with us. I knew that something was not kosher here, and I decided to put my energies into another direction because I was getting nowhere. I phoned another neighbor who was also having problems, and we made an appointment with a well-known local attorney. He told us that he couldn't promise we would win the case, and that his fees might cost us more than it would cost to put on a new roof.

My neighbor and I went to all the homes built by this contractor in our neighborhood and asked the owners if they would like to join us in a class action lawsuit. Since we were all having problems, we could go after the contractor, have everything repaired that needed to be repaired, and we could share the expense.

In spite of the problems they were all having, none of them wanted to get involved. I felt that they looked at my neighbor and me as trouble makers. They didn't say it, but their actions did. My neighbor then decided, since no one wanted to join us, to drop out because she didn't want to spend the money to try and win.

Mel and I knew we were going to fight this and win, even if we had to represent ourselves in court. And that is exactly what we ended up doing. For a full year, every day after teaching, Mel went to the law library and studied the laws and what an attorney had to do to represent someone in court.

We phoned a local roofing company, explained our problems, and asked if they would send someone out to inspect the roof and give us a written report. We would pay for their time and the report because we needed it to bring a lawsuit against a contractor. They said they'd phone me back in a short while, that they were busy. When they did, they said they were too busy to come out, that we should try another contractor. I told the man that I talked to that we would be patient, that we wanted his roofing company because it was the largest and most well known in Santa Barbara.

He said, "I am sorry, but we don't want to get involved with another roofer's problems and a lawsuit."

I then phoned the other roofing companies. I was honest and told them everything, and they all said no. They didn't want to get involved for the same reason.

I phoned the first roofing company again, telling them that the other roofing companies did not want to get involved either. I asked if they would please come out. I needed to know what was wrong with our roof. He again said they were too busy. I again said that we would be patient.

He said, "Ma'am, we don't want to get involved."

I said, "I can't believe that no one will come out. All we are asking for you to do is to tell us what is wrong with our roof. We will pay you, and you won't be that involved other than the report you write."

He said, "Sorry, we just can't help you."

Thankfully I kept my cool, even though my anger was deep, and I said, "Then you leave me no choice but to report you to the Better Business Bureau because you are not being ethical, and I am going to take my story to the news media." I hung up. Five minutes later he called back and said they'd be right out.

Their man spent a lot of time on our roof, and when he finally came down, said, "It looks to me like you need major work done." He wrote up a report, and when we asked what he thought it might cost, he said, "I'm not going to bid on it. We don't get involved with another contractor's headaches."

Into the fourth year we were still fighting, and once the rains started, we had 35 leaks throughout the house. I had already written to the State Contractor's Board to report the general contractor and the roofing company, as well as the City Inspector's office for failure to help us find out why we had so many leaks.

Forms were sent to us that we immediately filled out and returned. I made xerox copies for us. Several weeks later I phoned and asked when they would be coming out, and I was told that it would take four to six weeks because they were busy. Two months later no one had contacted us.

I phoned and was told that they didn't have a file on us. I explained to the lady that I had made xerox copies and that I would send copies of those to her. She said OK. I couldn't believe their inefficiency.

Two weeks later, the State Contractor's Board acknowledged that they were in receipt of the xerox copies. But that they needed the originals. When I had sent the copies, I explained in my letter why they were copies and gave the name of the lady who had told me to send them in.

I then phoned the State Contractor's Board. I was furious. I talked to the same lady, but she said she didn't remember me and asked what happened to the originals.

I said, "How the hell do I know what happened to them. You guys were the ones that lost them, not me."

She said that she would have someone contact me who would make arrangements to come out, but they couldn't contact the contractor until the State Contractor's Board checked out the roof.

Arrangements were finally made for the inspector to come out and check our roof. Mel was not going to be home because he had to work. Before he left, he set up the ladder for access to the roof.

When the inspector arrived, he went up the ladder, stood two steps down from the top, stretched his neck, and looked the roof over for maybe two minutes. When he came down, I asked him if he was going to climb up on the roof. He said, "I already have your roofer's report," and he started to write up another report.

I asked, "How can you possibly write up a report when you didn't check anything out?"

He said, "I do this all the time, this is my job. You will receive my written report in a week or so."

I asked him where he got our roofer's report. He said, "From the City Inspector's office." That comment turned a light on in my head because I had not sent the report to the City Inspector's office, I had only sent a copy of it to the general contractor and to the roofing company who had put on the roof.

I asked him if the City Inspector's office had sent him his copy? He said, "No, I stopped and picked it up before I came here."

Now I became very angry because, again, I knew something was not kosher. I said, "We've waited months for you guys to come out and check the roof because of all the leaks. We obviously do not have a quality roof in spite of the fact the house was brand new when we moved in. I am a tax payer, and your not getting up on the roof and checking it out is unacceptable to me. Something here is not right, and I suggest you check the roof out instead of standing on the ladder just looking at it, even if you have our roofer's report. Your office told me our roof has to be checked out by the State Contractor's Board before they can contact the contractor."

The man stood there and just looked at me, and did not respond to what I had just said. Thirty seconds later he said, "I'll be stopping at the City Inspector's office before I leave Santa Barbara, and I will send you a report."

I asked, "Is there any source higher than you that I can contact because I don't like the fact that we have waited all this time for you to come out, and you won't go up and check our roof out."

He replied, "You can call my boss."

I asked for his name, so he wrote it down for me on a piece of paper.

For several weeks I called many times trying to reach his boss; he was never in but I left my name and number each time, for him to return my call. I finally played my little game, and when I called, said it was personal and urgent, and I used a different name. I was put right through. I told him that I had been trying to reach him for several weeks, etc. He said he was on vacation. I didn't believe him. But I explained the reason I called him, and he said that he would check into it and would see that someone got back to me. I told him I would like to hear from him personally, that I was tired of being pushed around by his office. He said he would get back to me. Two days later I received the report from the man who had come out. It said that there was no visible repair work needed, that a copy had been sent to the contractor and city inspector's office.

I could not believe this was happening. I called his boss, and I was again told he was on vacation. I said, "I just spoke with him two days ago, and he told me the reason he had not returned my prior phone calls was because he was on vacation." She asked me to hold, I did for about a minute or so, and then I was disconnected. I immediately phoned back. She said, "Ma'am, all I can do is give him his messages." I then told her that I wanted to speak to the man who was sent out by the State Contractor's Board. She said he was not in. I told her this call was in regard to a report that was sent to me, and it was very urgent that he return my call. He did so the next morning, and I told him I was furious about his report because he didn't even get up on the roof to check it.

He said, "I got up on your roof."

I could not believe what I was hearing. I told him off and said, "I am contacting our local congressman, and the governor to expose you for failure to do your job." I asked him if he and his boss, and the city attorney's office, were paid off by the contractor because I could not believe this nightmare we were in, and that as a tax payer our rights were being violated.

It was a very heated conversation. He said, "The contractor that you're going after already has 22 lawsuits filed against him."

I replied, "I bet he does, and they were probably all filed after the State Contractor's Board and the City Inspector's office failed to do what they are supposed to do, and that is to protect the people."

He said, "I just thought I would let you know that you will have to stand in line and probably never collect."

I said, "You're not gonna scare us off like you obviously have others. We're fighters, and we're going to win, and we will collect."

He said, "Good luck," in a patronizing tone. I hung up.

I wrote a detailed letter to the State Contractor's Board and sent copies to our local congressman, to the

253

mayor's office, and to the governor's office. I asked them all to please respond to my concerns. I received no response back from any of them.

Somehow a lady in the community heard about our fight with the contractor, and she phoned and said, "I would love to come aboard to help you in any way I can. I've had to deal with this contractor, and he has absolutely no ethics at all." Her help was appreciated.

It is my opinion that when people do not fight for their rights in any situation, they can't possibly have peace within themselves. If Mel and I had not fought for the roof and everything else that was wrong with our house, neither of us today would have peace within.

Some of the home owners who didn't want to get involved in a class action lawsuit are still having problems today. The saddest part is that some of the homes have been sold and resold and the families now living in them have to deal with these problems.

The original owners were fenced in because of their lack of knowing the power within them and their rights. They obviously had fear of not winning and didn't want to come across as trouble makers.

Twenty-two years ago, some laws favored business more than the consumer. I also feel that the reason the personnel at the State Contractor's Board and the City Inspector's office were so arrogant is because many people are just like our neighbors. They don't fight for their rights and are scared off by all the rhetoric officials throw at them. That's also why sleazy contractors are able to stay in business at all. We are often our own worst enemies because, unless we stand up and fight when we know we are in the right and realize that God will always be on our side when we stand for truth, the ineptness in our government will never be exposed or stopped. Also, those people who don't stand up and fight when they should, make it much more difficult for those of us who do and who chose to use our power within.

Mel and I went through a lot of stress, but we never gave up. We won and we collected our money. In the court system, Mel represented our side, and he was up against two

254

well-known, local attorneys. After the judge made the decision in our favor, they both came over and shook Mel's hand and said he did a great job. One even said, "I hope we don't have to come up against you again."

The attorneys were lying through their teeth, and I stood up four times in anger and said, "Your Honor, they are outright lying." After the fourth time I stood up, they asked the judge to send me out of the room.

The judge said, "Mrs. Abundis, I must ask you to sit down and be quiet."

I said, "Your Honor, this is very difficult for me. We are here for the truth, and they are lying through their teeth."

He said, "Please, sit down. One more outburst and I will ask you to leave the room."

Well, I stood up two more times, refusing to listen to the garbage and lies that were coming out of their mouths, but the judge never asked me to leave the room or to be quiet again.

Two days after the judge ruled in our favor, we received a letter in the mail from him telling us that had we asked for water damage to our home, he would have given us that also. He thanked us for fighting and standing up for our rights.

No one will ever convince me that the City Inspector's office and the State Contractor's Board were not all working together to help the contractor. I have no proof of anyone receiving a payback, but it would not surprise me one bit. There is no other explanation for what we had to go through.

I sent a copy of the judge's ruling to the City Inspector's office and to the State Contractor's Board and told them I felt they were the most unethical and unprofessional people I have ever had to deal with, that their job was to protect the people, not sleazy contractors. I wrote, "I don't know how those of you who were involved in helping this contractor can sleep at night. Karma will catch up to you!"

Our local paper reported in 1996 that the contractor we fought some 22 years ago is having financial problems and that some of the prime properties that he owns in Santa Barbara are going up for auction because he owes millions of dollars to a bank, and he can't pay it. It looks like Karma caught up to him on this side. The poet, George Herbert, wrote, "God's mill grinds slow, but sure."

•   •   •

When my daughter Catana was 3 1/2 years old, Mel and I thought it would be good for her to go to a pre-school three mornings a week so she could have interaction with other children. Our son Armando was 1 1/2 at the time, and we lived in a neighborhood with no little girls her age, only a few boys.

One afternoon I took Catana and Armando to visit several pre-schools in our area. I liked the one down the hill from our home, so I made an appointment to go back in order to make the arrangements for Catana to attend.

It was the middle of the school year. I met with the owner of the pre-school, who was also one of the two teachers who worked there. I told her I liked the school; I asked if I could send a natural snack with Catana each morning. She said that was not necessary because the school made arrangements with the mothers to help out several times a month and that they took turns supplying the snacks for all the children.

I said, "We eat only natural foods with no preservatives, and the other day, when we were visiting, during the snack time, the children were eating fritos, and cookies, and drinking punch. I don't want that for Catana. If it is a problem, we can find another school for her."

The lady said, "Oh, no, that's no problem. You can send a snack with her each day." I made arrangements for Catana to attend the school.

When we got back to the car I explained the arrangements to Catana, and she understood.

The first day Catana was at the school, I did not stay with her. When I went to pick her up, I asked the teacher how she did. She said fine, but Catana did not want to join the others in the room during snack time, so I let her sit outside and have her snack. She said she felt that Catana would join the other children after a few days at school. I told her that Catana was very, very strong-willed, that I would stay the next time to make sure she joined the others during their snack.

When we got to the car that day, I asked Catana why she didn't join the rest of the kids during the snack time.

She said, "I wanted to stay out and play."

I said, "Honey, the pre-school has certain rules that all the children must follow, and I am going to stay next time, and you have to go in. Do you understand?" She said yes. I stayed with her the next time even though she didn't want me to, and when time came for snacks, she didn't want to go in, so I took her to the side, and said, "I told you in the car about the rules, Catana."

She said, "I didn't have to go in last time."

I said, "The teacher should have forced you. Now you get in that room and, whether I am here or not, you eat your snack in that room. Do you understand?"

She was not happy but said yes and went into the room.

The third week of school, when I went to pick Catana up, the teacher asked me to stay a few minutes. She took me to the side and told me that Catana had refused to go in for snack time the prior week. "I feel she refused to go in because she doesn't want to be different than the other children and wants to eat what they eat."

I calmly said, "When I asked her if she went in, she told me that she did. I will deal with Catana. But what you are telling me is not the reason she won't go in. She wants to stay out and play. Catana has a very strong spirit and a strong mind. She is testing you. You have my permission next time to be very firm, and don't give her a choice. I will also have another talk with her."

Once in the car, I said, "Young lady, why did you lie to me?"

She immediately knew what I was talking about and said, "I want to stay outside and play."

I said, "If you lie to me again, you will be punished. Do you understand me?"

She asked, "How will you punish me?"

I said, "Just don't you lie to me again, because you will not like the punishment. From now on you are to go into the snack room. Do you hear me?"

She said yes. "And," I added, "I am not going to tell you again. Do you understand that?" She said yes.

The following week I worked one day at school, and she reluctantly went in. But two days later, when I went to pick her up, the teacher said, "She wouldn't go in. I really think it has to do with her not wanting to be different, and she wants to eat what the other kids eat, and I don't want to force her."

I said, "Look, I am sorry this is not working out! I will find another school for her. I do not want her eating junk food."

She quickly responded, "Oh, no, we will work with her."

I said, "Well, then, you're going to have to be strong with her. If you are strong with her, she will listen to you. I know my daughter. She is testing you, and she knows when to push, and she will push and push. What you are telling me is not the reason."

She suggested that before we talk to her together, that I talk to her myself one more time.

As I walked over that day to get Catana from the playground area, another mother stopped me and asked if I had a few minutes. I said yes, and I instinctively knew this was about Catana and snack time. I asked, "Is this in regard to my daughter?"

She said, "Yes. The mothers here feel that you are doing your daughter harm because you won't let her have the same snacks the rest of the kids have, that is why she will not come into the room to eat her snack. She doesn't want to be different than the other children."

I kept my cool, and that was hard for me, and I said, "Look, I don't care what you or the other mothers think. I have already discussed this with the teacher. Does she know that you 'mothers' planned to talk to me?"

She looked at me for a few seconds, then said that I was out of touch because I insisted that my daughter eat something different than the rest.

I looked directly at the mother, I stayed calm, and said, "Don't tell me that I am out of touch, or what you think is best for my daughter. If you want your kid to eat cookies, fritos, and drink punch, full of preservatives and chemicals, that's fine with me. My daughter is not going to be fed junk food."

I got Catana and left. I no sooner got to the car and started it when another mother came hurrying over to the car, with a little baby in her arms.

She said, "May I talk with you?" I let her talk for a minute or so and said, "Thank you for your concern, I have already been approached about this matter, and I no longer want to talk about it with you or anyone else," and I drove away.

When we got home that day, I sat her down and told her very firmly that I had had it with her and that I was tired of her not going into the snack room to eat her snack with the other children. I said, "Young lady, you are treading on thin ice. If you do not go in when the other children do, I am going to take you out of the school, and Catana, I mean it! Do you understand me very clearly?"

She started to cry, and a few seconds later she said, "I'll go in, but what does treading on thin ice mean?" I had to turn around because I started to laugh. I pulled myself together and explained to her that I would punish her by taking her out of the pre-school. It was a great pre-school, Catana loved all the activities, especially the arts and crafts; however, if she did not go in the next time, I was going to take her out for sure.

Two days later, it was a cold, rainy morning. I walked Catana in and waited until the teacher pinned her name tag on her jacket. Then I went back to the car with Armando and was strapping him in his car seat, when a mother came running out of the school yard carrying a baby and hollered, "Mrs. Abundis." Because it was lightly drizzling I got into the car and rolled my window partly down so I could talk to her.

She came to the window, stood there without an umbrella holding this little baby that maybe was 15 months old, and in a very authoritative tone said, "I would like to talk to you."

It wasn't hard to guess what it was about. I stayed calm even though my adrenaline shot up. She stood there holding this little baby that only had a diaper and a light kimono on, no shoes, nothing to cover the little one's arms or legs, the baby's nose was running into its mouth. The mother, however, was properly dressed for a cold, rainy day.

She said, "We mothers are very concerned about your daughter, and we don't want to upset you, but we feel you are causing her psychological damage because you will not allow her to be like the other kids and eat the same snacks they do."

I looked at her for a few seconds, then said, "Are you through?" She said yes.

Then I lost it. I said, "First of all, how dare you tell me that I am causing psychological damage to my daughter when you are standing there in this cold rain with your child's nose running. And it's going into his mouth. You don't even have the baby properly dressed for this weather. Go back and tell the owner and all the mothers that if one more person approaches me, I am taking my daughter out of this school."

She toned her manner way down and said, "I didn't mean to upset you."

I started the car and said, "Just take proper care of your own child and don't worry about my daughter." Before I pulled out of the parking lot and onto the street, I looked through my rear view mirror, and she was still standing in the rain looking at the direction of my car. All I could think of is that her poor little baby must be cold.

I was angry at these mothers, Catana, and the teacher; and I was tempted to take Catana out of school whether she went in that day or not. Later when I went to pick her up, I sensed some mothers looking in my direction.

I got Catana and left. I asked her if she went in and she said yes. But I knew my daughter, and if she thought I was going to take her out of school, she would have said yes, even if she didn't go in.

When we got home, I decided to telephone a mother who the second week of school had approached me and said that she supported my natural snack idea and she wished she had the nerve to send them for her little boy, too. I told her that we all have choices to make, that the owner agreed to my bringing a natural snack before I enrolled Catana; otherwise I would not have chosen this school.

When I asked her if she was working at school that day, she said no. I told her why I wanted to know; and she said that her friend worked that day and that she would call her and get back to me. She phoned back in a few minutes and said, "Yes, she went in."

Only one other mother had let me know that she supported me; she also told me it was only a handful of mothers who were concerned. I told her that I was sure that 'handful' were the three who approached me. The first mother that approached me apologized several weeks later, telling me they obviously were wrong to interfere because Catana did settle in and was very happy.

That same year the children were taken on a field trip to the Museum of Natural History. When it was snack time, the children went outside to eat their snacks on the grass. Later that day when I picked Catana up, a mother came over to me, and she was laughing. She said, "Your daughter had all of us running around when it came time for snacks. When we realized that she left her snack at school and she refused to eat what the other children were eating, the mothers were running around like crazy trying to find a snack for her. Finally, one mother remembered that she had small boxes of raisins in her car, and she got a box for Catana. We also gave her water to drink."

I decided to attend the school's next board meeting, and I spoke of my concern about serving junk food snacks to the children. Another mother, who obviously didn't like the fact that I was new to the school and speaking out, stood up and contradicted me, saying the snacks are not junk food.

I stood up again and I told the board members that when it was my turn to bring snacks, I brought cheese, vegetables, and fruit, and the children happily ate the food. I said that I also felt a disservice was being done to the children, who would eat anything that was put in front of them, even junk food.

The following September, when the school information was sent out to the parents, I was happy to see that they were now listing what snacks should be brought for the children to eat. No junk food! Most of the mothers in the new school year were delighted that there would be no more junk food served.

When Armando was 3 1/2, he also attended the same pre-school. After a week or so, he asked if he could also take his own snack, like Catana did, because he didn't like what they gave him to eat. In fact, when they tried to encourage him to eat one day, he said, "No, I don't eat junk food." By then it was not junk food. It was different from what he was used to eating, but not junk food, so I packed him a natural snack each day to take to school.

I know that the teacher and the mothers who tried to fence me in with their beliefs meant well, but I resented them trying to tell me that they knew my daughter better than I did.

What surprised me was that the mothers who brought the junk food had no idea that this food had no nutritional value. They didn't know what junk food consisted of or anything about preservatives and chemicals that are put into our food. That was 20 years ago. Thank goodness things have changed. The consumer is now more aware of preservatives and the nutritional values of food because the laws have changed. Manufacturers have been forced to label all foods so we know what we are buying.

• • •

As I look back, during the first four years of grade school for Catana, and also for Armando, I had to do double duty, volunteering my time, supervising their lunch period and playground time after lunch. My children stood out because of our natural eating habits. I told them it was alright to be different. They understood, but it was not always easy for them. The following story is one example of what they and I went through in the private Catholic school that they attended.

When Armando started the first grade, the first week the kids started to harass him during the lunch period because he had alfalfa sprouts in his sandwiches. They told him he was eating weeds and grass, and one kid told him he was eating poison. We found out very fast who the biggest bully was in the first grade; he took Armando's sandwich and threw it on the ground, telling him he was sick to eat that stuff. The mother who was supervising the lunch period that day sent the kid to the office and gave Armando the kid's lunch. When I picked the children up from school that day, Armando told me what happened and said that he didn't eat the sandwich because it was only jelly. Armando had an egg salad sandwich that day.

I knew I better volunteer to help supervise as an extra for the next few lunch days; and I called and told the school office why. I felt this bully would try to get back at Armando. Sure enough, the next day, as Armando walked out of his classroom with a friend, lunch in hand, the bully, who had two other kids with him, walked over and tried to stop Armando and his friend from going to the lunch tables. I immediately got over there, and asked if there was a problem. Armando was surprised to see me as I did not tell him I would be there. The bully kid said, "No, I want Armando to sit next to me at lunch." Smart Kid!

Armando, however, chose not to sit next to him. But before lunch was over, I went to the first, second and third grade tables and told the children that I was now in charge of punishing any kid that harasses any other kid during lunch and on the playground after lunch. I told them the punishment would not be pleasant and that none of them would like it.

When I picked my children up from school that day, Catana, who was in the third grade, asked me if I was in charge of punishing the kids. I said, "Yes, whenever I work the lunch and playground I have permission from the office," which I did not have. But I know it gave them a feeling of security, knowing that Mom had some power at school to protect them. Whether my telling them that was right or wrong, I didn't care because it helped their young minds to know I would be there for them. The lunch time harassment stopped.

Several other mothers also did double duty supervising the lunch period and playground area because of their concern for their children. The bullies were in every class from 1st through the 8th grade, girls, as well as boys. These bullies were obviously lacking attention at home; but I must admit that I wanted to shake the devil out of them.

The school was very lacking in discipline, and complaints to the principal would only get a few days action. It really bothered me and the mothers who were doing double duty when the word got out that the principal thought that we were over-protecting our children. I wrote a very strong letter to the principal and all I got back was a very patronizing response.

• • •

I hope I am not boring you with the school stories, but I have one more I would like to share because of what happened to Armando in this same school. It could happen to any child in grade school, that is why I want to share it.

Prior to Armando entering the third grade, learning was a positive experience for him; he was happy with his teachers and his grades were good; he liked school. Three months into the school year in the third grade, Mel and I noticed that Armando was nervous, and his usual positive attitude was lacking in everything he did. He wasn't negative; he just existed. Not much joy in his usually bubbly personality.

I was at school a lot, but I never noticed anything unusual, so I asked Armando if everything was OK at school, or if there were problems with other kids. He said no, that everything was OK. I met with his teacher, told her our concern, and asked her if she was aware of his nervousness or of anything that might be causing it. She said no, but that she did have to push him to get his work done.

We told her he had always been eager to do his school work and he had good grades, and that his home life was very positive. We felt something was very wrong.

She said she didn't know what it could be, and that she had no answers for us. But she would observe him more closely.

Since Mel and I could not put our finger on what was bothering him, we closely observed him in everything he did at home and whenever we had a family outing, without him knowing.

A group of us school mothers had signed up to work on the Christmas boutique. A mother that I had met and had only spoken with once, phoned me and asked if I would do her a favor and phone the mother that was in charge of the boutique the prior year because she needed some information from her. She explained that she and the mother had had some problems in the past. I said yes, and I phoned this mother whom I had never spoken to before.

When we finished our conversation regarding the Christmas boutique, she said, "Charlene, are you aware that daily the teacher calls Armando names, such as stupid, and picks on him?"

I asked her how she got that information, as my blood pressure went through the ceiling.

She said, "My daughter tells me. She is in his class, and she said that today the teacher almost had Armando crying. She also said that the teacher constantly picks on him and is always hitting his desk with a stick when he is doing his work, and it scares him so much that he jumps in his seat."

I got a sick feeling in my stomach, and I was furious! I asked her if the teacher was doing this only to Armando or to the other children as well. She left the phone, and when she returned, she said, "My daughter said she only does it to Armando." I thanked her and I immediately phoned several other mothers who had children in the same class. I found out that they were well aware of the abuse, and that two of the mothers were also concerned about their children having upset stomachs and not wanting to go to school. One mother took her child out of school instead of helping solve the problem by getting the teacher removed from the classroom. I couldn't believe she wouldn't stay and help us fight in order to help all of the children who, we found out later, were affected by this teacher abusing them. She never even told the school the reason why she took her child out.

One mother told me this teacher had a dislike for boys, and she already had gone to the principal's office about it and nothing was done.

I said, "My God, why wasn't this brought out into the open so that all the parents were made aware of what was happening?"

That same night Mel and I went into Armando's room. He was doing his homework at his desk. I asked him if what I was told was true, and he said yes.

I said, "Sweetheart, why didn't you tell us when we asked you if everything was OK at school?"

He said, "She doesn't only do it to me."

I said, "Honey, there is something wrong with that teacher. Just because she abuses the other children in school does not mean it is right. I am going in tomorrow morning early before school starts and have a talk with her."

The next morning we arrived at school a half-hour early. When I walked into the teacher's room, she was sitting at her desk, and she sensed my rage. She asked if everything was OK. I had Armando and Catana stay out on the playground, which was right outside her door, and I said, "No, it isn't. What the hell do you think you are doing to my son and the children in this classroom by calling them names such as stupid and dummy, and hitting their desk with a stick?" I told her I found out what she was doing to the children last night after talking to several mothers.

She said very calmly, "Your son doesn't do his homework. He sits and looks out the window when he is supposed to be working."

I walked right to the door and called Armando in from the playground. I calmed down and I asked him, "Honey, do you turn your homework in every day?"

He started to cry. My heart fell! I hugged him and said, "It's OK, sweetheart. You can tell me."

266

He said, "She makes me very nervous. If I don't get it out of my folder fast, she hits my desk hard with a stick, and I can't find it then."

I asked him what he did with his homework.

He said, "It's in my desk folder."

I checked his folder, and in the very back, he had four or five homework assignments that had not been turned in.

I said, "Honey tell me what else she does to you."

He said, "When I'm doing my work she hits my desk hard with a stick and tells me to hurry."

I walked him over to the playground and said, "It won't happen any more, honey. Go play. I need to talk to her some more."

I went back into the room, and I wanted to pull every hair out of her head. I said, "I was just in here 2 weeks ago and asked you if there was anything you noticed that could be causing Armando's nervousness. You never told me about him not turning in his homework."

She replied, "You never asked."

I said, "Lady, you have no idea with whom you are dealing." I was almost crying I was so furious. I said, "You have been abusing my son, and other children in the classroom, and I am going to the principal."

She calmly said, "Go to the principal."

I left the classroom, went over to Armando and told him that his teacher and I had had a talk and that everything was going to be OK. I knew he was worried. I started walking to the office when a friend, who worked at the school and had walked by my son's classroom and heard me hollering, asked me what happened. After I told her just the bare facts, she said, "It is not the first time. Go to the principal and be firm."

I went to the principal, and in spite of telling me she would get right on it, she did absolutely nothing. Two days later, my husband phoned her and said that he was going to spend the whole day in this teacher's classroom.

The principal said, "You can't do that without notice because I am busy, and I have to arrange to be there also, and the teacher needs to prepare."

267

Mel said, "You have had two days to get back to us. I will be there at eight tomorrow morning."

This teacher, we later found out, only picked on the sensitive 7 and 8 year old boys. She never harassed the bully kid (the one that threw Armando's sandwich on the ground) or other aggressive boys in the class.

Armando was a sensitive boy back then, and he still is today. It has always been his nature. Catana also had aggressive kids in her class, so Mel and I decided to have both the children take karate lessons through grade school. The damage that this teacher could have done to Armando as well as the other children that were being affected by her abuse scares me. It could have been irreversible had we not found out and stepped in to stop it. I plead with all parents to tune into your children and get as involved as you possibly can with their school and all of their classes. Longfellow wrote, "A torn jacket is soon mended, but hard words bruise the heart of a child."

We wanted to put Armando in another school because we had great concern that the teacher would be even harder on him, but he was very upset with the idea, and he didn't want to leave his friends. So we monitored this teacher for the rest of the school year.

I made sure that all the mothers were made aware of the problems with this teacher whom the school did not remove that year. However, she did not return the following year, and the principal, who did nothing to help, ended up leaving also because the parents got involved, and she was exposed as well as other inefficient teachers who were asked to leave within the next two years.

Throughout our children's schooling we have always been involved and have had to stand up many times for them. I even fought for a few of my children's friends because their parents worked and were not aware of what was going on. An interesting aspect of the situation is that, whenever I offered to help in Armando's classroom, this teacher would tell me, as well as a few other mothers, that she didn't need any help in class. Of course, I found out why.

Mel and I were so very concerned about Armando's nervousness, and we knew that we would not stop searching until we found out what was causing it. I would never have phoned this particular mother that told me about Armando being abused if I had not been asked to. I know the mother would never have called me either. The circumstances that brought the whole situation to my attention began in such an innocent way. All this tells me is that God works in very strange ways sometimes, and we will always get an answer if we don't ever give up and keep the faith, believing that we will find the answer.

TWENTY FOUR

THE SPARROW

When you've worked hard to master the game,
And have given some time there to serve
Then you bolted the fort of security,
To view life beyond yonder curve.

Know, you dear Soul, that wherever you are,
That you splash in great oceans of light.
Not one sparrow falls in this kingdom of love,
For protectors watch over their flight.

It all becomes clear when you start looking back,
And the logics make sense to the end.
If only you trust and believe in the force,
This control then is surely your friend.

As daylight is failing, a brighter light shines
And reveals best the false and the true,
And shows the great will in its infinite love
Watching over the sparrow and you.

Reverend Edmund L. Foard

This last chapter is "The Hodge Podge Chapter" because of the mixture of thoughts, experiences, etc. that I want to share with you.

The following article that was written by Bob Barber, a local free lance writer in Santa Barbara, really piqued my interest because I have used dreams for the last 12 years as guidance in my every day life.

I phoned Bob Barber and asked him if I could use the article in a book I was writing. I explained what the book was about, and he said, "You sure can, and when Father returns to Santa Barbara in a few years, I think you should meet him. He is the nicest man I have ever met." I told Bob that I would love to meet him, and I would look forward to his return. I thanked him for letting me use the article, but once again, I would like to say to this very nice man, "Thanks, Mr. Barber!"

profiles in faith   Santa Barbara News-Press 1-27-96

PRIEST RETURNS TO INDIA WITH OPEN MIND

BOB BARBER

A Catholic priest from India has concluded a 2-year visit to Santa Barbara and returned home where he plans to start an ashram (house of prayer) which will emphasize spirituality as a way of being in the world.

The Rev. Joseph Purappanthanam, 49, an expert on world religions who specializes in dream work, came here in August 1993, to earn a master of arts degree in counseling psychology at Pacifica Graduate Institute, Carpinteria.

He chose to attend the institute, he said, because it emphasizes his principal interest - dream work in psycho-therapy. He now is a pre-licensed therapist, an intern in marriage, family and child counseling.

He said dream work is divine communication. "God speaks to us through dreams, which are like X-rays of our souls. Looking at dream images is looking at the soul. The dreamer is the final authority on the meaning of his or her dreams."

On the biblical attitude toward dreams, the priest quotes Joel 2:28: "I will pour out my spirit on all mankind; your sons and daughters shall prophesy, your old men shall dream dreams, and your young men shall see visions."

Also, Numbers 12:6: "Hear my words: If there is a prophet among you, I, the Lord, will make myself known to him in a vision. I speak with him in a dream."

Purappanthanam observes, according to St. Luke in the Acts of the Apostles, dreams and visions occurred frequently and at important moments in the life of the early Christian community.

He also quotes a Jewish saying: "A dream unexamined is like a letter unopened."

He says studies indicate, in general, introverts are more inclined to remember their dreams and extroverts are more likely to forget them.

The soft-spoken priest says he is vitally interested in creating a non-violent human society and quotes the psychiatrist Carl Jung as saying all violence is repression and projection. He believes dream work is the most effective way to combat the two negatives.

"Even when we deny our repressions and projections, our dreams bring them up again and again until they are dealt with. They won't leave us at peace until they are confronted," he says.

"The ashram will be a house of prayer meant for all religions, all cultures, all nations. Through working with dreams, both individually and in groups, I hope to promote peace and nonviolence among all humans and peace and cordiality between the warring religions.

"Another specialty of the ashram will be the practice of the Yoga of dream work to promote personal, interpersonal, inter-religious and international fellowship and a spirituality based on the model of partnership.

"Our understanding of gods and goddesses, to be humanly complete, has to become inter-religious. Spirituality of the future will have to become more and more intercultural, and spiritual guides and masters must be more multi-culturally experienced and, obviously, multi-lingual."

He adds the ashram will be a place for a psychotherapy adapted to Indian culture and spirituality to promote personal, social and ecological healing.

The Catholic Church has given him support and a few acres of land in Indore in Madhya Pradesh (central India), with some small buildings to house the ashram and dialogue projects.

Purappanthanam said he plans to return to the United States in approximately two years, to conduct additional dream workshops and retreats.

A professor of Indian religions and philosophies for the past 16 years, he is a member of the Society of the Divine Word, an international missionary congregation, which was founded in Holland in 1875 and now has about 4,200 priests and 800 brothers serving in 60 countries.

It is believed his ancestors were present when St. Thomas the Apostle came to India in the year 52 A.D. Purappanthanam's family attends Syro-Maliabar Church. He was born in Palai, in Kerala State, a member of St. Thomas Christian Church, and he "grew up imbibing the church's great respect for other religions."

The oldest son in a family of five boys and two girls, he said, "On my mother's side of the family, there has been a long tradition of priests. My mother, who originally wanted to be a nun, loved to read about the saints and I grew up hearing all about their lives.

"At one point, I rebelled against religion, but I met a Benedictine monk who made me at peace with Christianity and gave me a deep liking for Christian tradition."

He felt drawn to the priesthood, and had a strong sense of being called. "It is the only way of life that makes sense to me," he said with a serene smile.

After studying at Athaneum in Poona, he was ordained in 1977 in his home parish in Kerala State. Purappanthanam earned a master's degree in Indian philosophy from the University of Poona in 1983, then went to the Society of the Divine Word's seminary in Mysore, where he spent 10 years, teaching Hinduism and Buddhism.

He says that the mystical traditions of Hinduism and Buddhism gave him a synthesis of the two religions with the Christian faith. He still practices Hindu and Buddhist meditation techniques, and teaches Yoga.

The priest speaks his mother tongue, Malayalam, plus Hindu and English. He knows two more Indian languages and reads and understands German and Latin. He enjoys reading poetry in his spare time and said he favors the works of Longfellow and Emily Dickinson.

He has guided more than 200 retreats and dream workshops in India for Christians, Hindus, Buddhists, and those with no religious affiliations. While here, he conducted dream retreats in Santa Barbara, Seattle, Chicago and Spencer, Mass. As part of his internship, he held workshops on the spirituality of aging.

In 1994, he offered a program in Santa Barbara on "Symbiosis of East and West - a Meditation on Mary, the Mother of Jesus." He taught a general introduction to Hinduism and Buddhism in Santa Barbara, and held a retreat on "Symbiosis of East and West."

Also he moderated a course titled "Unity in Diversity: Multi-cultural Spirituality." In addition to his other activities, Purappanthanam has celebrated Mass once a month at the St. Anthony's Seminary Chapel, where he attracted a full-house crowd at his final Mass the Sunday before he left.

The priest, who has resided at the Santa Barbara Mission while in the U.S., deplores "the exaggerated extent to which individualism and consumerism has affected some of humanity, the ever-increasing violence and use of drugs, and the breakdown of the family system."

He said what struck him most profoundly in this country was "the great diversity of the geographical, ethnic and cultural backgrounds. The rich variety is both a great blessing and a big challenge."

He adds that "Santa Barbara is the best city I have seen in the United States. It is one of the very good cities in this country. It is peaceful, beautiful, and socially harmonious."

Bob Barber is a Santa Barbara free-lance writer.

•   •   •

I vividly remember as our high school class practiced walking down the aisle for graduation how depressed I felt. I knew that once I graduated I would be on my own, and I would have to find my way in life the same as my older brother and sisters had. I knew my sister Annie would always be there for me, but she was now in her early twenties working full-time, and she had her own life to lead. Even though we were still close, I felt so vulnerable and more alone than ever. After the graduation ceremony, as I was walking down the hall to exit the school with my sister Barbara and my mom and dad, I started to cry. My mom put her arm around my shoulder and said, "I thought you would be happy to graduate." I wasn't crying because I was leaving school. I had a lost feeling within me, and as I walked down the hall, without any guidance or direction in my life, I had no idea where I was going or what would happen to me. Today when I look back, it was a very sad period of my life. I remember thinking back then, "Now what do I do?" I felt totally alone and lost.

When Catana was four years old and Armando two, we rode along with Mel the day after school was let out for the summer so he could turn his keys in, etc. While we waited in the car for Mel to return, several high school kids walked by, and I wanted to cry. All the feelings that I experienced when I graduated came back to me, and my insides ached because I couldn't help but wonder how many kids who graduated that year might be experiencing and feeling what I did when I graduated. The following two years we also rode along with Mel to turn his keys in. The feelings pulled me down so much that I told Mel that in the future he should just take the children and go without me.

• • •

My sister Barbara, who is a year and three months older than I, was born with a very rare bone disease which causes her bones to break very easily and because of her disease she was held back in the first grade. In spite of her disease, and always having to be very careful all through grade school, she always protected me from other kids who would try to hurt or tease me. She wasn't mean at all; she just had a power that emanated from her that would scare the other kids away.

By the time she was 21, she had broken more bones than her age, and today she is in a wheelchair. But what an inspiration she is to all the people around her. She keeps on like the little train in the story that is going uphill and keeps saying, "I know I can; I know I can." She has also developed a strong faith in God, which, she told me, helps her to keep positive on a daily basis.

In my teens, it was my sister Annie that always looked out for me, and over the years we had many conversations about life. I remember one summer night; it was hot and muggy outside, and we were unable to sleep, so we went outside and sat on the front steps of the house.

When I told her that I wanted to marry a farmer and live on a farm, she said she didn't think I would be happy living on a farm. I said, "Oh yes, I would, Annie. All I have to do is think of the memories that Barbara and I had on the farm with Aunt Lena and Uncle Walt, and the many times we ran through the creeks, fields and pastures and played hide-and-seek. I loved it, and I felt so free and happy; just thinking of those times I feel happy." She said that she never had those kinds of memories. I remember feeling sad for her and wishing I could give her some of mine. When I was 15 years old, she wrote on the back of a picture that she gave me that she didn't know what she would do if she didn't have me to tell her problems to.

A week or so before I left Minneapolis for Santa Barbara, she told me with great sadness that she was really going to miss me. I said, "Annie I don't know what I am going to do without you either, but I have to go because it feels right. If I stay you can come out to live with me." She said that she might do that, but down deep inside I knew she would never come. She told me to be sure to take care of myself because she would not be there to protect me. When she told me that, I wanted to protect her, and I felt bad that I would not be around for her to talk to. She told me to be careful who I got involved with because I hadn't lived away from home, and I was naive about life.

It wasn't until I moved to Santa Barbara that I realized the fact that trees and sidewalks were not always there, that someone had to put the sidewalk in and that a seed needed to be planted in order for a tree to grow. Many other realities hit me as well. I was 22 years old, and I had lived my life up to that point just existing, doing only what I had to do in order to keep on; I was mechanical and not using my mind or tuning into the reality of life at all.

Shortly after moving to Santa Barbara, it seemed as if the world opened its doors for me for the first time. I was finally waking up and tuning in to everything around me. The idea of how to protect myself came to me out of the blue one day, and when I thought about it, I got excited because I knew it would work. After I got married, had my children, and they entered school, I had to add more protection to my idea, and that I will explain later in this short story, but the following is the first idea that I used.

I created a tree of life in my mind. I allowed all the people I knew on the tree: my family, friends, neighbors, and co-workers. Whenever someone who was on my tree did or said something that was unkind to me or to anyone that I felt didn't deserve it and I saw it, I would take a pair of mental scissors and cut that person off my tree. Unkind acts, no matter who was at the receiving end, have always given me a sick stomach feeling. My tree worked for me because no one knew what I was doing. Only I knew, and it gave me a strong feeling of power to protect myself. Whenever I cut someone off my tree, I would mentally send them good wishes. Years later I told my friend Rosanne about my tree. She said the type of people I cut off my tree were the type of people that were usually toxic to her also. So, to borrow her phrase, toxic people to me are people who are unkind.

I have never been unkind to anyone that I have cut off my tree. I avoid them if I can, and if I can't, I treat them with kindness, keeping as much distance as I possibly can between us. This visualization was a very easy way for me to protect myself, and I have never ever had any regrets about any of the people I cut off my tree. Early on I realized that there were other benefits having my tree of life to protect me. I don't carry or drag people around with me who are not good for me; I never felt weighted down in having to deal with them, and I always had room to add someone on to my tree that I knew was good for me.

My tree also helped when meeting new people. When I would meet someone and my feelings told me that I didn't like this person very much, or something bothered me about that person, I knew it was a warning to stay on guard and not allow them to get near me. The few times over the years that I let my emotions take control over my inner knowing, and allowed such a person near my tree, I learned a good lesson; and I was always sorry. I would end up cutting them off. It also taught me more and more to trust my intuition.

Years later, while my children were in school, during the day I had time to do volunteer work at their school as well as in the community. It was during that period of my life that I became aware of people who use other people for their own benefit. They take your time and energy, and if you let them, they would suck you dry. I also became aware during that period of people with egos. This bothered me very much because they seem to have a tremendous need to be recognized and feel important, for no other reason than they thought it was important to be important.

It was during this time that I added extra protection for myself by putting a mental fence five feet high and five feet away from and around my mental tree of life. Within minutes of meeting people who were takers and/or with big egos (once you're tuned in they are not hard to spot), I kept them outside of my fence, and I could still have a conversation with them if necessary or even work with them because I felt protected.

If at this point I had to cut someone off my tree, and that didn't happen very often, I wouldn't just cut them off. I would mentally pick them up and set them outside of my fence. That way I had no clutter around my tree, and when I visualized my tree of life, I had only green grass all around it which was neat and clean.

When I built my fence, I also sent love to all those outside of the fence as well as good wishes.

I added the love because of an experience that I had while standing in the grocery store check-out line one evening. This experience was before I added my mental fence for extra protection. Mel and I, along with the children, were going to play a game one evening, and they wanted me to make popcorn. I was out of popcorn, so I told them to set the game up, and I would dash down to the store and buy some. As I stood in line I was rather impatient because there were four or five people with carts ahead of me, and there was only one other check out counter that was open and in that line were as many people waiting to be checked out. Years ago I formed the habit of humming whenever I felt impatient while standing in line. Without realizing it, I was humming a song as I stood waiting.

The lady directly behind me asked, "Are you humming 'Love Is A Many Splendored Thing'?"

I thought for a second and said, "Yes, I have several songs that I automatically hum when I have to stand in line, that is just one of them. It helps me to deal with my impatience."

She asked, "What are the other songs?"

I said, "My favorite is 'Zippy Dee Do Da,' 'I Believe,' 'The Best Things in Life Are Free' and 'Don't Fence Me In.' "

She said, "All oldies, just like me."

She looked like she was in her mid-seventies. She was a very sweet lady, and I asked her what she did when she got impatient.

She responded, "I send love to whoever or whatever irritates me because it is the most important thing in the world."

I asked her how she sent love, and she said, "I just think of the word love, and I feel it surrounding me, and all people and things near me." She went on to say that love is the only path in life to take in order to be happy and have joy in your heart. She said, "When you send out love, it comes back to you." I have never forgotten that conversation, so when I added my fence, I decided to send love as well as good wishes to all those that I kept outside of my fence. Swami Muktananda (Indian Guru) wrote a small book of thoughts, and I saved the following: "Love is the sole reason for living and the sole purpose of life."

One of my high school teachers told our class the following story: "Some Indian tribes would draw a line around their village and no one with hatred in their hearts could cross that line. The few that did met with disaster." She said she had actually visited such a village, and said it was very obvious to her that the line helped them to live peacefully among each other because they felt protected. She also said she felt that living close to nature as they did played a big part in their peaceful ways. We all have the power to draw a line or to put a fence around us and our homes if we feel it is necessary to protect ourselves or to keep out any negative energy from those whom we feel we need protection from for whatever reason. I have cut friends, neighbors, and even family off my tree of life. I put them outside of my fence in order to protect myself.

The type of people that I find toxic might not be toxic to you, but once you are aware of what type of people are toxic to you, find a way to protect yourself because it is so very important. If sending love, having a tree and/or fence work for you, that's great. Just be sure to protect yourself from those who are toxic to you because if you don't, they will add stress to your life, and you will never find peace within or even be able to love yourself because you'll always be out of balance.

RF said that we must all learn to protect ourselves from people that we know are not good for us because if we don't we will be the losers. He also said it was OK to get angry at another person if they have wronged you because it forces you to look at the action that hurt you, and then you'll know what you need to do to protect yourself. However, he said you must always send them love because what you send out you get back. In other words, you can hate the sin, but not the sinner. When someone has wronged you, bless him/her by sending love, not because it is deserved but because you deserve it.

•   •   •

Throughout our home I have many plants, and about seven years ago, Catana and I were discussing an idea that I had. I was sitting on the sofa, Catana was sitting in the lounge chair opposite me, and in between us was a coffee table with a large Boston Fern on it. When I asked her if she thought my idea was good, she said yes. The top part of the fern swayed back and forth as if someone was vigorously fanning it. Catana looked at me and said, "Mom!" I said, "I know, it has to be spirit telling us to go for it." That has happened several times.

Shortly after the above experience with the swaying fern, we had the following: our kitchen door opens into the garage and when coming in from the garage, the kitchen, dining room and den can be seen. It is all very open with high beam ceilings; over the dining table is a large chandelier. I was sitting at the counter that divides the kitchen and dining area, talking on the telephone with a friend, and Catana was in the den. When I told my friend that I was thinking about going away on a retreat for only a few days by myself, the chandelier started to sway back and forth as if a monkey was swinging on it. I said to my friend, "My God, we're having an earthquake."

She also lives in Santa Barbara and said, "We're not having an earthquake."

I said, "Yes we are. The chandelier is swinging back and forth like crazy."

Catana said, "Mom, none of your hanging plants are swinging."

Then Catana and I looked at each other and we knew that spirit was giving me the message to go on the retreat. Just about then Mel walked into the kitchen from the garage, and the chandelier was still swinging.

He said, "We're having an earthquake."

I said, "No it's not an earthquake."

He said, in an anxious tone, "Yes, it is. Look at the chandelier."

Catana said, "Dad, it's just spirit confirming mom's plans. Look at all the hanging plants. They're not moving."

Mel looked! When we told him about spirit moving the Boston Fern, he had no other explanation as to why the top of the plant swayed back and forth. It was winter time and all the doors and windows were closed. We told him it was confirmation from spirit, but he just didn't believe us. Now with the chandelier swinging like it was, Catana said, "Dad, take a good look at the plants again. They're not moving. It is spirit." Mel looked at the hanging plants again. I know he didn't want to believe what we said. The look on his face told us that he didn't have to say a word.

• • •

One evening when RF joined our family at our home for dinner, I was telling him some plans that we had for the family, and just as I was about through telling him, my whole body got chilled and I said, "My God, I just got the chills, look at the goose bumps on my arms."

He said, "That is just the God within you confirming what you just told me is right on."

I said, "Really, RF that happens to me all the time."

He said, "Well, now you know. It's confirmation that whatever you're talking about is right on. Always follow it. It's another way of receiving help from within."

•   •   •

In the summer of 1995, we bought new carpeting for our home. A week before the carpet was to be installed, I cleaned out all the closets, every dresser drawer, and storage area in the house. I came across two boxes filled with written notes of my memories going back over 35 years. I thought I would always want to keep them. It took me one complete morning to read the notes in just one of the boxes, and I ended up throwing many of them away. They were exciting when I wrote them, but in re-reading them they weren't that exciting now. I saved the notes I wanted to include in this book. I also took all of my quotes out of both boxes. I didn't take the time to read all the notes in the second box. I searched through the box and took out the notes that I knew I wanted to use in this book.

I put the second box on a shelf in the garage, and a few weeks after the carpet was in, Mel decided to clean out the garage. He came in with the box of notes and asked me if I still wanted to keep them. "Just leave them by the door," I said. "I'll quickly look through them." Later that day, I looked through the box and decided it was in a mess, and no longer organized. Feeling that I had taken what I wanted out, I took the box to the trash. I walked back into the garage, and that little voice within told me to go through the box one more time. So I retrieved it from the trash and put it back on the garage shelf, telling myself I would go through it when I had more time.

Almost a year later, when I was about to start the last chapter of this book, Mel was putting some new shelves up in the garage. He came into the house and asked me to come out and check out what he was going to throw away or donate to a charity in case I might want to keep some of the items. I took the box of notes back in the house so I could go through them. I ended up keeping a shoe-size box full of memories, which includes the following experience. I threw the rest of the notes away.

Re-reading the experience seemed like it happened to me only a few years back and not 32 years ago. It is a real treasure to me now because I have found God, and I now know how He works in my life. When I think that in my haste I almost threw it away, I just take a deep sigh!

In Chapter Twenty Two, the healing chapter, I told you of my dizziness and of my hearing a very loud voice say, "OK, CHARLENE," which I later realized was God's voice. I explained I had never experienced anything like that before. Well, I did experience God's voice some 32 years ago, but since I was not tuned into God back then, and I didn't know how to find him, the experience I had meant nothing to me. If I had not rescued the box, I never would have remembered the experience. Even in my notes, I wrote that the voice must have been my imagination because there was no other explanation as to why I would hear a voice.

One Saturday morning in 1965 when I lived on the beach in Carpinteria, a friend and I made the following plans. I would leave the beach area where I lived and walk along the beach towards Santa Barbara, and she would leave Santa Barbara and walk towards Carpinteria. Once we met, we would walk back to Santa Barbara, then she and her husband would give me a ride home. To travel the distance by car is about 10 miles.

When I began my journey, the tide in front of my apartment was high. The homes were set back a good distance from the ocean with a wide sandy beach in front of them. I was naive about the dangers of high tides, and did not realize that there might not be as wide a beach along the ocean strip I would be walking as there was in front of the homes on Padaro Lane, so I took off. After an hour I saw that the tide was getting higher. It scared me a little. I was glad I had wrapped my purse in a thick plastic bag that I tied with a thin rope around my shoulders and carried it over my back to prevent it from getting wet.

When I got to an area where there were railroad tracks above a slanting cliff, I was not able to walk past because of a slanting wall that went down into the ocean. With the tide being so high, I was unable to see how far out the wall went into the ocean, so I was afraid to try and walk around it. I instead climbed the cliff with my bare feet, and when I got to the top, I walked the tracks to the other side of the wall, and then I worked my way back down to the beach. Further on I came upon a group of apartments, and with the tide still rising, I thought maybe I should try to get to the road and walk the rest of the way to Santa Barbara. But I thought, no, my friend coming from the other direction would wonder what happened to me. I expected to see her anytime soon.

I continued walking, and when I came to a high cliff, I walked as close to the cliff as I could. How I wished I had worn some tennis shoes. I only had a pair of thongs in my purse to wear once I got to Santa Barbara. I was walking on nothing but rocks near the cliff, and my feet were already sore from stepping on rocks that I was unable to see due to the high tide. My toes were also sore from stubbing them as I walked. Each time a strong wave hit me I fell and I got up as quickly as I could, working hard to keep my balance on the rocks before the next wave would hit me. I knew that I had cut my knee on a rock from one of the falls, but all I could think of was getting past the cliff area, hoping there would be a wider beach ahead of me.

I realized I had gotten myself into a very dangerous situation. I thought maybe I should go back to the apartments, but as I looked back I no longer could see them. Then a huge wave knocked me down again, this time when I managed to get up, I thought, "I am not going to make it. I am going to drown." Fear took over my whole body, and that is when I felt someone was with me. Then I heard a voice say, that I now know was God, "One day you will write about this experience and your life." All the fear left me. I knew that I would make it to Santa Barbara and that I would be OK. The voice was not as loud as when I heard, "OK CHARLENE," but it was a strong voice. I made it to Santa Barbara, but I never met my friend along the way.

When I got to Santa Barbara, I went to the hotel across the street from the beach and phoned my friend. I couldn't understand how we could have missed each other. In fact, thinking back to that experience, I didn't see another person on the beach that day. I never thought that my friend would have turned back because when I tell someone I am going to do something, I just barrel ahead and do it. When she answered the phone and I said hello, she immediately asked, "Where are you?" I said, "At the hotel across from the beach." I asked her why she didn't meet me as we planned. She said that the waves were so high when she started, she immediately turned back, went home, and phoned me, but of course there was no answer. She asked if I walked the road. I told her I'd walked the beach. She responded, "How could you walk the beach with such a high tide and strong waves?" I said, "I did." She said, "We'll be there in a few minutes to pick you up."

When she and her husband arrived to picked me up she asked again how I possibly could have walked the beach the whole way. Her husband said, "Well, just look at her. She's soaking wet." Not only was I soaking wet, I had sand in my clothes, my hair, and my under garments. I had a big gash on my knee; I had cuts and blisters on my feet, my hands were even scratched from falling. On Monday, when I went to work, my feet were so blistered and sore I had to wear soft sandals for several days. My experience is a perfect example to me that God interferes in our life even if we are not aware of Him or know how to find Him.

• • •

One Friday around lunch time, I went to pick up Armando from pre-school. Several mothers approached me and asked if Armando and I would like to join them and their children at Taco Bell for lunch. I had to decline because our family was leaving that afternoon, as soon as Mel came home from teaching, on a weekend trip. Armando said, "Oh, mom, please can we go, I have never been to Taco Bell before." I knew he was more excited about possibly going to Taco Bell than being with his friends. I said, "Honey, next time we'll go. I have so much to do at home, and you still have to pack your suitcase, remember?" We had just bought him and Catana their own little suitcases to pack for the trip, and they were both so excited about that. But now it seemed going to Taco Bell was more exciting than packing a suitcase. He was very disappointed, and I said, "Armando, I promise when we get back from our trip, one day I will take you to Taco Bell for lunch, and next time we are invited to join your friends we will go, OK. Is that a deal?" He looked sad, but said OK.

Several weeks later, on a no-school day, I was driving past a Taco Bell on my way home from grocery shopping. Armando said, "Mom, can we stop at Taco Bell now?" I said, "Honey, I don't think I have enough money, but let me check." I pulled over to the curb, checked my purse, and found that I only had a small amount of loose change. Armando said, "You can write a check." I said, "Sweetheart, I didn't bring my checkbook, I only brought one check for the groceries, but I think I have enough change for one taco." His face lit up. I went around the block, and we pulled into the lot at Taco Bell. It was shortly after 11 A.M., and there were no customers in the place. I ordered a taco, and as the girl reached behind her and took one off the shelf and wrapped it, I was getting my change out. I was embarrassed to realize I was a dime short. I had not been to Taco Bell for years because we didn't eat fast foods, and when I went in, I didn't even check what the price was for a taco. I said to the lady, "I am sorry, I didn't plan this. I will have to come back."

But before I left the counter, I thoroughly checked my purse to see if I had anymore loose change at the bottom. I didn't. I looked down at my precious four year old son whose face once again looked sad. I said, "Sweetheart, I am sorry. We will have to come back. I am a dime short." I took his little hand and my heart felt his disappointment. We walked to the door, I opened it to exit when right in front of me there was something shining very bright with the sun hitting it. I reached down to pick it up, still holding the door with my body, and it was a brand new, 1978 dime. I was stunned. I stood for a moment, and I knew without even thinking about it that God put that dime there for us. I said, "Armando, God just put this brand new, shiny dime here for us so you could have your taco." His little face lit up again, and I went back in and bought him the taco. I was still searching for God then, but I knew He put that dime there. I just knew it! That is another experience I had knowing that God has interceded with His awesome power that always amazes me.

• • •

One evening we had some special friends over for dinner, Tony and Bonnie Zaharias, and I shared the above story with them. Tony said, "I have a story to tell you." With his permission, I share his story as he told it to Mel and me that evening in his own words.

"When I was much younger, I was staying with a Greek family up in New York state. I was new in this country, so I was kind of hesitant to go and ask for extra things, especially money. But that particular morning, I knew that I didn't have any money for my bus fare, which was exactly 17 cents, to take the bus across town, and then from there to meet the truck which would take a group of us to the painting factory to work. I knew if I missed that bus I would not make the connection, and I would lose my job. And I was kind of shaky that morning. What would I do? When I left and was exiting the house from the main door, I looked up in the sky, and I said, 'If You are really up there, and if You really take care of us, well, You know what I need. I need 17 cents.' And to my amazement, which until this day I really find hard to believe, I didn't even go three yards further and there it was, a dime, a nickel, and 2 cents on the ground. Why couldn't it be a quarter or maybe 20 cents? Ever since then, that story has stayed alive in my mind. It kind of reminds me of the basic thought that there is really something up there."

• • •

The following story is another example of the awesome power of God. When RF came home from the hospital and before he passed to spirit, his sister, Laura, who was in her seventies, and a nephew, came from out of state to be with RF and also to help Lois and me out. One day, when I arrived at RF's house, Laura was very frustrated and she said, "Oh, Charlene, I am so happy to see you. I was trying to put new elastic in Edmund's pajama bottoms. Since he has lost some weight, they won't stay up, and I am having trouble with the machine. This gadget fell out." She held out her hand and showed it to me. "And I don't know how to put it back in."

I said, "Gee, Laura, I'm not very good either at things like that; I'll see if I can get it in, though." I took the gadget from her hand, sat on the chair and put it under the needle area. Before I could even try to figure it out, it was as if someone took it from my hand and pushed it into place in the machine. I did absolutely nothing; it automatically went in place. I turned to Laura and said, "Laura, it went in by itself." She said, "Oh, that was so quick. Thank you." I said, "I didn't put it in, Laura; it just pushed up and went in by itself." I knew spirit did it. She said, "I have been trying to put that back in place for a half an hour. What did you do?" I said, "I just told you; it went in by itself; probably one of RF's spirit guides put it in." She looked at me in a very strange way and said, "I don't believe in that." My friend Lois, the medium whom I wrote about earlier in the book, told me that RF told her that he always embarrassed his family when he would visit them. He said, "They love me, but they don't understand what I do." So I understood why she said what she said.

• • •

At night we leave a small night light on in the hallway which shines into our bedroom. One night I awoke to the sound of a faucet running, full force. I sat up in bed thinking, "Who is running the water so hard?" I got up, and standing still for a moment, I realized that the noise was in my head. I thought I must have an ear problem, so I went into the kitchen and got a garlic pill, squeezing some into each ear. I previously had read that garlic is a good remedy for ear problems. I went back to bed still with the noise in my head, and I no sooner lay down when suddenly I was standing by the door where the night light shines in. And I was looking at myself lying in bed. It must have taken me 30 seconds to realize what was happening, and it scared me, and then I was back in my body in bed. The noise was gone.

If we didn't have the night light shining into our room, I don't think I would have seen myself lying on the bed. I would never had known I had a very short out-of-the-body experience.

The next day I asked RF about it. He said, "Just another experience to let you know that your body and your soul are separate. If it happens again, don't be afraid; you can program yourself to travel anywhere you want in the world." It has never happened again. But I wanted to share it in case something like that happens to you; don't be afraid. Had I known that I could travel anywhere, I wouldn't have been so scared; but I didn't understand what was happening to me at the time.

•   •   •

MY POEMS

I can't explain this path I walk.
It seems so right for me.
It gives a tilted view of life
Unlike what others see.
The cruel deeds I've witnessed
That life can ill afford,
Looks different worn on others
Tho it strikes a tender cord.
Seeing pathos mixed with laughter,
Or the pain of friendships torn.
I just call 'em as I saw 'em
In these little balls of corn.

Revered Edmund L. Foard

RF told me the above poem was his favorite of all those he had written.

•   •   •

I must share this one last memory with you. In the summer of 1981 our family made plans to go back to Minneapolis for a summer vacation. I went shopping for some last minute items that I needed. I stopped half-way through my shopping at a small coffee shop. I sat next to an older gentleman at the counter. I ordered my coffee. The man asked if I had children. I said, "Yes, two."

He asked, "Do they have musical talent?"

I replied, "Well, they will be starting piano lessons in the fall."

He reached into his pocket and gave me a card that had the name Irma Starr written on it. He said, phone her, and tell her I gave you her name and number; she is the best.

When I got home I phoned her. She said she had no openings, but when I returned from my trip, to call her and that somehow she would get my children in.

When they did start lessons with her, she was 85 years old. My reason for including her in this book is that this very special lady lived the religion of the heart. The following story, just one of many I could share with you, shows the soft, graceful kindness that she held in her heart not only for our family, but for everyone that she touched. Ms. Starr was a golden treasure to all the people that knew her on the earth.

One hot, muggy Monday I picked the kids up from school. I forgot that they had piano lessons that day so when they asked, "Mom, can we go down to the beach? It is so hot," I said yes.

When we arrived home, Ms. Starr had left a gentle message on our answering machine. "Charlene, I hope that everything is alright. You didn't make it to piano lessons today." I immediately phoned and apologized, and told her I forgot and took the children to the beach.

She said, "Well, if you would like to come Wednesday at 4:30, after my last lesson, I will be happy to give Catana and Armando their lessons."

I said, "We will be there, Ms. Starr, thank you for understanding."

Again on Wednesday I forgot. It was another scorching day, and I took the kids swimming over at a friend's home. When I arrived home after five, she had left another message. I could not believe that I had again forgotten. I immediately phoned her and apologized, once again explaining that it was so hot that the kids wanted to go swimming, and the heat must be getting to my head since I had forgotten again. Again we made arrangements for a lesson, this time on Friday at 4:30. I forgot again! When I arrived home, I heard her soft message on the machine, "Charlene, I am going to close down for the day. I hope that everything is alright. You didn't make it to the lesson. We will just start again on Monday."

I didn't phone her back but I immediately went down and bought her a dozen red roses. She loved flowers and all of nature. When I arrived at her home, she opened the door, and I put my hands over my eyes and handed her the roses.

She said, "My dear, you didn't have to do this."

I said, "Yes, I did, I can't believe that I again forgot; it's the least I can do."

She said, "These roses cost more than your lessons would have."

I said, "I guess it must have been the heat, or maybe I am just out to lunch, Ms. Starr."

She smiled, she never got upset, and said, "Well don't fret about it, and thank you for these lovely roses. We'll try to get back on track next week."

That dear lady only charged $5 a lesson when everyone else that I checked with was charging $12 and $15. I asked her why she charged so little. She said, "I don't do it for the money. I just want to pass on what God has given to me and help others who want to learn how to play the piano." She also told me not to get angry with the children if they didn't practice every day. She said, "Children are like candles. You must be very careful not to blow out their light

291

because it might not come back." I think the following letter that my daughter wrote and was published in the Santa Barbara News-Press gives a very good description of this gentle giant who lived to be a few months shy of 100 years old.

Piano teacher shines

Ms. Starr, my piano teacher for 14 years, who also taught my brother Armando for 10 years, passed to spirit last week. This unbelievable lady would have been 100 years old in a few months. Up until January of 1996, I as well as other lucky people were able to receive the benefit of her classes and talent.

My mother always told my brother and me that Ms. Starr was LOVE in capital letters, and that she was almost sure that she was an angel sent from heaven to share her love and kindness with so many people.

My reason for writing this letter is because she would never allow our family or anyone to give her any type of recognition or celebration in any way. All she ever wanted to do was to give to other people.

I would just like to say now that she can't stop me, our family thanks you for all your love, for all your light, and for all the joy that you gave to us and so many others while you were on Earth. You truly are the greatest and brightest star in the universe and I know that I speak for many other people when I say that.

Catana Abundis
Santa Barbara

• • •

The following prayer for a loved one I absolutely love. I have no idea who the author is, or who gave it to me. I find great comfort in reading it on a daily basis. It is a powerful prayer.

Prayer for a Loved One

Dear Heart,

I will not worry, fret or be unhappy over you.
I will not be anxious concerning you. I will not
be afraid for you. I will not give up on you. I will not blame
you, criticize or condemn you. I will remember first, last and
always that you are God's child. I know you have His Spirit
in you. I trust this Spirit to take care of you, to be a Light to
your path, to provide for all your needs.

I think of you as always being surrounded by God's loving
Presence, as being enfolded in His protecting care, kept safe
and sure in all things. I have confidence in you. I stand by
you in faith and bless you in my prayers, knowing that you
are growing and finding the help you seek.

I see the love you desire filling your heart and enriching your
world. I now behold the complete wholing-healing of you -
physically, mentally, emotionally and spiritually. I know all
your financial needs are right now being fully met.

I have only good feelings in my heart about you, for I share
with you the freedom to live your life as you feel guided by
your Indwelling Christ. Your way may not be my way, but I
trust the Spirit of God in you to show you the way to your
highest Good. God love you. I love you, and all is well.

I believe in you and I behold the living Christ radiating
through all that you are! For so it is!

•　　•　　•

Here is another prayer that I have had with me since I was 17 years old. Again I have no idea where I got it, I have sent it to many people when I needed to let them know I loved them and wished them happiness. It was not titled when I received it, so I gave it the title of "Happiness."

"Happiness"

I said a prayer for you today
I know God must have heard,
I felt the answer in my heart
Although He spoke no word.

I didn't ask for wealth or fame
I knew you wouldn't mind.
I asked Him to send treasures
Of a far more lasting kind.

I asked that He be near you
At the start of each new day.
To grant you health and blessings
And friends to share your way.

I asked for happiness for you
In all things great and small.
But it was for His loving care
I prayed for most of all.

Author unknown

•   •   •

Another prayer that I am sure you will enjoy as much as I do:

Life is Eternal

I am standing upon the seashore
A ship at my side spreads
her white sails to the morning
breeze and starts for the blue
ocean. She is an object of
beauty and strength and I
stand and watch her until
at length she hangs
like a speck of white cloud
just where the sea and sky
come down to mingle with
each other. Then some one
at my side says; "There!
She's gone."
Gone where? Gone from
my sight - that is all. She
is just as large in mast
and hull and spar as she
was when she left my side,
and just as able to bear her
load of living freight to the
place of destination. Her
diminished size is in me,
not in her; and just at the
moment when some one at
my side says, "There! She's
gone," there are other eyes
watching her coming, and
other voices ready to take
up the glad shout, "There
she comes!"

Author unknown

· · ·

Anyone who loves God's art of Nature and has experienced the four season's of the year, the changing clouds in the skies, and has stood on a lake shore and viewed the mirrored reflections of trees and mountains in the water, or experienced the changing colorful skies during the glorious sunrises and sunsets, cannot help but to be awe-struck by the magnificent and spectacular wonder of its beauty. Beautiful Nature is a priceless treasure, God's invaluable gift to the world. There have been times that I have cried tears of joy as I viewed Nature; and it filled my soul so completely, overwhelming me to the point that I didn't think my eyes could absorb all the beauty I was viewing. Nature is a very spiritual experience for me, and it makes me feel that it is all mine; and yet I know it belongs to everyone.

Mother Earth is our home, and the crimes that people have committed, and still are committing, against her makes me very sad and very angry!! Our oceans, lakes, rivers and streams are polluted. The air we breathe is polluted. Our forests are being cut down. So many precious animals are being harmed and are dying due to the abuse of the earth and the use of pesticides.

We are out of harmony with the earth, and we must unite now in order to save it for future generations. Our earth has the ability to heal itself, but it can't do it alone. We must all do our part by getting involved and speaking out against those who have no conscience or could care less about our beautiful planet.

The following letter was published in the editorial section of the Santa Barbara News-Press. I cried when I read it. I phoned Mr. Baboolal and asked him if I could use his letter in the last chapter of this book. He said yes, adding that others also called him to express the same sad emotions I had. Thank you Mr. Baboolal!

Earth needs immediate, prolonged attention

I do not know who my mother or father is for I have been separated from them for millions of years. Where did I come from and why am I here are the questions that I ask myself time and time again. As I search for my roots traveling in the universe from west to east day after day, I feel somewhat weak and strained and tired.

I came here long before you, your forefathers or any living thing. Your ancestors have walked on me, hunted and grew food on my back, fished in my streams and have survived for millions of years with the bountiful resources I have provided them.

But now, I feel I have been trampled on.

You have carved me up, polluted my waters and killed my fishes. You have polluted my air and are destroying my forests. I have been crying out for help but only few are listening. I cannot support life for as many years in the future as I have done in the past.

Parts of me have already died. Other parts of me are paralyzed and still others are too weak to continue. I feel frail and am limping along like a hurt and destitute man without shelter. I am heating up faster than I would like too, because you have polluted my air too much and I am gasping for clean air.

Today, I could hardly keep my cool. Acid rain is aching my bones and strip mining has cut into my flesh. Clear-cutting my forest have exposed me to the harsh elements of nature.

I am bleeding to death.

I need immediate and prolonged attention.

I need care in order to regain my health so that I can again provide for you and future generations for a million more years.

Sona Baboolal
Goleta

•   •   •

The one thing that could unite all the people of the world like one big family is LOVE! It is universal; it does not discriminate; it is non-denominational; it costs nothing, so

297

you can't buy it. It can be given away every second, minute, and hour of every day, day in and day out to another person just by lending a helping hand, giving a smile, by sharing, and by being kind.

Love is the only thing that you can constantly give away and as much as you want and still have tons left and at the same time never feel depleted because the more you give away the more comes back to you many fold.

When you live in love, you will always be filled with joy, and your whole being will emanate with happiness. You will create your own paradise on earth, as well as a rainbow that will connect with all the other rainbows of people who live love. Most important you will know that you have found the purpose of life and are in touch with God because God is love and love is God. That is all there is.

People who are unkind, controlling, self-centered or with egos will wonder what it is that has given you such happiness. The simple answer is LOVE.

As I mentioned earlier in the book, for hundreds of years we have been fenced in by what society has dictated to us by telling us how to think, what to do, how to act, and what is right or wrong for us.

The English author, Robert Southey, wrote, "All animals live and follow by instinct and obey the laws of nature, but man in willful neglect of the laws of God loses sight of the end of his."

You must learn not to follow others, but to listen to and trust that little voice within, your own intuition, your God power that God gives to everyone, regardless of the color of our skin, and you must apply the religion of the heart, because it is the only game that matters as you travel your journey in life; and unless you do so, you will never make your own paradise on earth or create your own rainbow in this lifetime.

You are, as Betty Bethards says, the writer, director, and creator of your life. But you do not have to find the pieces to your puzzle of life alone because you do not travel your journey alone as you learn and grow from all the lessons that are put in front of you in this big school of life. God is your silent partner, and He is never absent from you. Tune into Him, and He will help you to create your heaven within on earth. Shakespeare wrote, "Heaven, the treasury of everlasting joy." A quote: "Heaven must be in me before I can be in heaven." It's very simple if you tune into the God within you. DON'T GIVE YOUR POWER AWAY, AND LET YOUR LIGHT SHINE FROM WITHIN.

LOVE

Addendum: I have had two profound experiences that I have not included in this book because they are lengthy. One of the experiences I have written into a screenplay. The other has to do with healing, and in time, I will be able to tie it into a beautiful story and share it with you.